Marks in a Lifetime

DIANE GREENWOOD MUIR

Cover Design Photography: Maxim M. Muir

ISBN-13: 978-1544855066
ISBN-10: 1544855060

Don't miss anything from Diane.
More information at nammynools.com.

Bellingwood Series
All Roads Lead Home – Bellingwood #1
A Big Life in a Small Town – Bellingwood #2
Treasure Uncovered – Bellingwood #3
Secrets and Revelations – Bellingwood #4
Life Between the Lines – Bellingwood #5
Room at the Inn – Bellingwood #5.5
A Season of Change – Bellingwood #6
Tomorrow's Promises – Bellingwood #7
Through the Storm – Bellingwood #8
A Perfect Honeymoon – Bellingwood #8.5
Pages of the Past – Bellingwood #9
The River Rolls On – Bellingwood #10
Look Always Forward – Bellingwood #11
Out of the Shadows – Bellingwood #12
Home for the Holidays – Bellingwood #12.5
Unexpected Riches – Bellingwood #13
Reflecting Love's Charms – Bellingwood #14
Capture the Moments – Bellingwood #15
Memories for Tomorrow – Bellingwood #16
All I Want for Christmas – Bellingwood #16.5
Marks in a Lifetime – Bellingwood #17
Bellingwood #18 – Coming June 25

Journals
Find Joy – A Gratitude Journal
Books are Life – A Reading Journal
Capture Your Memories – A Journal

Re-told Bible Stories *(Kindle only)*
Abiding Love - the story of Ruth
Abiding Grace - the story of the Prodigal Son (Coming Soon)

CONTENTS

ACKNOWLEDGMENTS

Gratitude is a large part of my life. The thing is, it's something you learn. It's something you practice. It's something you do. Many of my earliest memories of holidays are not only filled with fun and play, but with those moments around the dining room table when Mom insisted we write thank you notes for gifts we had received.

But I learned to be grateful and for that … I'm incredibly thankful.

I'm thankful for Max and his photography. I can't imagine these books now without his gorgeous photographs.

I'm thankful for Rebecca Bauman who reads the raw, unedited chapters as they are completed – never criticizing, just encouraging. And when I constructing the cover, I rely on her enormous talent for design, to help me finish the cover. She's always right.

I'm thankful for those who help me edit these manuscripts. They pick up details and help me make the books so much better. Thank you to: Carol Greenwood, Alice Stewart, Fran Neff, Max Muir, Linda Baker, Linda Watson, and Nancy Quist. And to Judy Tew who has an astonishing eye for detail.

One name I'm missing this time is Edna Fleming. This dear, wonderful woman taught me so much about editing, about joy, about living. She died the week after I finished writing this book and it hurt to not send the manuscript to her. I miss Edna.

I'm thankful for the extraordinary people who make up the Bellingwood community on Facebook. Unique, interesting and wonderful folks who remind me of the truth of Bellingwood – amazing people fill this world. We find them everywhere. Spend time with us at facebook.com/pollygiller.

CHAPTER ONE

"Polly, where are you?" The frustration in Rebecca's voice told Polly the girl had yelled those words more than a few times before coming up the steps.

"In the front bedroom," Polly yelled back. When they lived at Sycamore House, there had been a strict no-yelling policy, but until the intercoms were hooked up in this big old house, sometimes yelling was the only way to find each other.

Rebecca ran into the room where Polly was cleaning plaster off the floor; her face flushed from exertion. "I tried texting and you didn't answer. Why didn't you answer?"

Polly pointed to the other end of the room where her phone sat atop an upside-down five-gallon bucket. "Sorry. What's up?"

"Just a minute." Rebecca bent over, put her hands on her knees and breathed loudly, looking at Polly to see if she had elicited a reaction. When none came, the girl stood back up. "I looked everywhere. Your truck was in the driveway, but I couldn't find you."

"Guess you didn't look here." Polly dropped another chunk of plaster into the wheelbarrow. "Is there a crisis?"

"No."

"Then walk with me and tell me why you're chasing through the house, yelling my name."

"If you'd answered my text, I wouldn't have had to run. This is a big house. Is it okay if I spend the night with Kayla?"

"What's going on?" Polly chose to ignore the passive aggressive tone of her rather dramatic daughter. She was putting it all down to adolescence ... for now, at least.

Rebecca shrugged. "Nothing. We just thought it would be fun."

"Your cats will miss you." Polly only had to go out the door, then to the end of the hallway. Henry had parked a dumpster in front of the house and built a ramp for Polly to push the wheelbarrow up to the window. She managed to get most of the plaster into the dumpster, but it often landed in the yard. He scooped it up later with the bobcat.

"That's not fair." Rebecca put her hand on the handle of the wheelbarrow. "They'll sleep with the boys."

They pushed the wheelbarrow up the ramp together. Polly slid the wide window open, tipped the wheelbarrow up, and with a jerk sent most of the plaster floating to the ground.

"Whoops," she said with a laugh.

"You really do have terrible aim. So can I go?"

Polly shrugged and pulled the window shut again. It was cold outside. "I guess. Just make sure the cats are taken care of before you leave."

Rebecca flung her arms around Polly. "Thank you. I'll be home tomorrow morning before it's time for my art lesson." She ran back down the hallway.

"Wait," Polly yelled. "What time are you going over there? Isn't Stephanie working tonight?"

Her daughter had already turned the corner and didn't respond. Polly set her jaw. What were those girls up to? "Rebecca?" she called out.

Rebecca slowly came back around the corner. "What?"

"Isn't Stephanie working tonight?"

"Yes."

"And what time were you planning to go over to their apartment?"

"We just wanted to have some girl time by ourselves," Rebecca whined. "We never get to do anything alone. There's always …" She spread her arms out to encompass the entirety of the Bell House. "… so much family around. I'm nearly fourteen."

Polly laughed out loud. "You are four months away from being fourteen, but I guess at your age that's close enough. What's the big deal about tonight?"

"Nothing." Rebecca looked at the floor. "We just wanted to be alone. Maybe we'll cook dinner by ourselves and watch television and paint our nails. You know. Girl-stuff. No parents, no brothers, no sister. Just us."

"Is that true?" Polly put her hand on Rebecca's shoulder. "That's really all you want?"

"I swear." Rebecca looked up with hopeful eyes. "I really, really swear."

"Does Stephanie know about this?"

Rebecca's eyes lowered again. "Not yet."

"Oh honey. You have to be smarter than this. When were you going to tell her?"

"When she got home and I was there."

"Then I think the sleepover is off for tonight."

"Come on," Rebecca whined. "You were okay with it a second ago."

"I was okay with it when you were planning to be honest. But I'm not okay with you lying to either me or Stephanie. At all."

Rebecca spun and headed for the other end of the hallway. When she wasn't stomping, she was sloughing her way across the wooden floor. Polly waited until she crossed into the other end of the house and held her breath; waiting for the inevitable door slam.

Bang.

Yep. There it was. Tonight was going to be so much fun.

Polly took the wheelbarrow back into the bedroom and picked up her phone. This was the first upstairs room they'd worked on.

Heath and Hayden had pulled plaster and lath off the walls and ceiling, then moved into the back corner room. She was directly above what would become the living room and the back corner was above the library. They were removing the wall between the two rooms in order to build two bathrooms on this end of the house. The immense front room would be turned into two smaller bedrooms.

Polly hoped that these would be the most difficult rooms to renovate, but that was just wishful thinking. The bathroom in the central part of the second floor was a disaster. Everything needed to be replaced. Once they started in there, more renovations would happen. Henry insisted that taking it down to the frame made it that much easier to rebuild things. She wanted to believe him.

The old servant's quarters above the kitchen weren't in much better shape. When they finished this house, Polly only hoped that she would still be young enough to enjoy it.

Then she realized that if Rebecca was here, that meant everyone was home.

Noah and Elijah were doing their best to fit into their new school, but it wasn't easy. Bigotry, bullying, and ugliness were always going to be part of their lives, and it hadn't taken long to rear its ugly head in the elementary school. The thing was, it was only a few kids, but they were loud, mean, and relentless. She and Henry had already been to a meeting with one of the children's parents, but left knowing there would be no resolution. The boys hadn't made many friends yet. School had been back in session for a little over a month and Polly knew better than to expect things to be easy, but she'd hoped for a small bit of grace.

Bellingwood Elementary was growing. The town's population was growing. There were quite a few Hispanic families in town, but diversity wasn't something familiar to the community. It was funny, in a sad sort of way. If people talked about blacks in Bellingwood, they spoke of Camille at Sweet Beans. Some people knew that Nate and Joss had adopted two little black children. And then there was that one black man who had lived in town fifteen years ago. Nobody knew where he went and for the most part, they really couldn't even remember his name. He'd come in to work at the plant, but hadn't lasted very long. They thought maybe he'd moved to Ames. You know, because more of his kind lived there.

The thing with a growing community, though, was that diversity came as a natural part of that growth.

Billy and Rachel had moved out of the apartment over Polly's garage at Sycamore House and into the new apartment building on the south side of town. Their neighbors across the hall were a couple who worked in Boone and Ames. The young man's parents still lived in India and his wife was Chinese. Polly met them once at Davey's when she picked up dinner after a long day of construction. They'd been out with Billy, Rachel, Doug and Anita.

After living in Boston for so many years, it was difficult for Polly to realize that these people stuck out because there were so very few in town who looked different from everybody else. Change came slowly to small Midwestern towns.

She opened the big central doors and stepped onto the landing in the foyer. This room had completely transformed since the beautiful Christmas and New Year's Eve parties they'd held. It looked like a warehouse now, with boxes and furniture stacked all around the room. Polly pulled the doors shut and headed down the south stairway. The worst of it was that the garage at Sycamore House was still filled with boxes and furniture. They'd only finished emptying the apartment last weekend.

Henry was the one who insisted they completely clear out of the apartment. He'd gotten tired of bits and pieces of their lives dribbling into the new house. Especially when it meant that someone, usually Polly, complained about needing something and not being able to find it. She wasn't sure if this was much better, but at least he could point to the foyer when she whined about a missing colander.

Everything had come in all at once and Polly's next task was to sort through the stacks and piles, giving them at least some order.

She opened the door to the kitchen and stood silently while listening to the chatter at the table.

"You have to divide here," Rebecca said. "Try it again."

The huff of frustration had to be Elijah. Noah was more patient and had a good grasp of math skills.

Andrew walked across the room to the pantry and caught Polly's eye. "Hi, Polly," he said.

She walked into the room as if she hadn't been spying on them. "I didn't expect to find you working on homework on a Friday night. It's the weekend."

"If I do it now, I won't have to do it on Sunday." Elijah hopped down from his chair and ran over to give her a hug.

Polly held him tightly and whispered, "I love you," before releasing him.

Elijah was the most affectionate boy she'd ever known. When they'd visited last summer, he'd been willing to hug and be loved, but now that he was settled in her home, he made sure to get close to her before he left for school in the morning and every day after school. He hugged her tight before going to bed, and whenever Henry, Hayden or Heath came home, he ran to get a hug from them as well.

Noah was more reticent, but Polly and Henry both made sure that he got as many hugs as they could give him.

She had worried about the boys, knowing the stress that Elijah had been under when they came to visit last summer. The boys only slept when they were surrounded by the walls of the sofas in the living room. The first few nights at the Bell House, they'd begged to have Obiwan sleep with them, but now the only night that held any stress was Sunday night before school started for the week.

Polly took Elijah's hand and walked with him to the kitchen table. "How was school for you today, Noah?" she asked, bending over to snuggle his shoulders. She kissed his forehead and sat down beside him.

"It was okay."

"Did you learn anything fun?"

He shrugged. "I suppose."

"Who did you sit with at lunch?"

He looked at her. "Sam."

"Sam who?"

"Sam Johnson. He's kinda new too."

"Elva's oldest son?" Polly glanced at Elijah. "Were you there?"

He looked at her as if she had lost her mind. "Yes. I always eat with Noah."

"That's what I thought. Do you like Sam?"

"He's okay," Elijah said. "He said that he gets to ride the horses."

Polly nodded. "He probably does."

Rebecca laughed.

"What's so funny?" Elijah asked.

"Those horses belong to Polly. You can ride them any time you want to," Andrew said.

Both little boys turned toward Polly. "Those are *your* horses?" Noah asked. "Can we really ride them?"

Polly frowned. "You rode them last summer. I seem to recall that you, Mister Noah, were afraid until you got on the horse with Jason."

He looked away. "I was just a little boy then. I'm bigger now."

"You are definitely bigger," she agreed. "I'll see about finding a good time for you to ride. Maybe Samuel could ride with you. It would be fun."

Elijah shook his head. "He'd laugh at us because we don't know how. He says that he's really good."

"Nobody is going to laugh at you. Samuel had to learn how to ride, just like you will."

"He'll still laugh," Elijah protested.

Noah pushed at his brother's arm. "No he won't. Sam's nice. It's okay if he is better at horses than us." He turned to Polly. "Sam has to eat his own food. He has dia ... dia ... something."

"Diabetes." She pointed at the plate of brownies that had been decimated. "His body doesn't produce insulin to help him manage sugar like that. He has to be careful."

Elijah snagged the last brownie from the plate. "He can't eat brownies?"

"I'm sure he can. But not very many and not very often," Polly said. "You should invite Sam to come here after school with you." She stood up so Elijah could sit back down beside his brother.

"He'd probably have to bring his sisters," Noah said. "And his little brother. They all walk to the barn together unless someone picks them up. Is that man their dad?"

"No. That's Eliseo," Polly said. "Remember? Their uncle. He's the one who helped you get on the horses."

"Oh. He's got that bad face."

"He was burned," Andrew said. "In a war."

Polly realized that in the month since they'd moved to Bellingwood, the boys hadn't been exposed to much of her life. There had just been so much going on. Between getting them into their new school and helping them settle in with the family, not to mention the chaos of moving and construction, she'd lost control of things again. When everyone was home together, Polly liked being able to huddle up and enjoy family time. They'd had several raucous game evenings on weekends.

"I tell you what," she said. "One of these days we'll go over to the barn. You can see the horses again and talk to Eliseo. Maybe we'll ask him about having Sam visit after school."

"Without his sisters," Elijah said. "Gabriela is in my grade. She's always picking on me."

"That's 'cause she likes you," Noah taunted. "You've got a girlfriend. You've got a girlfriend."

Elijah swatted at his brother. "No I don't. And especially not her."

Polly wasn't getting involved in that one. She beckoned to Rebecca and Kayla and led them into the adjoining dining room. She still hadn't done anything more in this room. The table that had been built in here was still in the same place, but now was filled with boxes of dishes and other items from the kitchen.

She pushed the door closed behind them. "Do you want to tell me what the real plan was for tonight?"

Kayla looked at Rebecca. Rebecca's return look was an attempt to shut her friend down.

"I'll call Stephanie," Polly said. "I don't like it when you lie to me."

"I didn't lie," Rebecca said.

Polly glared at her. "You wanna try that again?"

"It wasn't a lie. I just didn't tell you that Stephanie didn't know."

"So you were planning to lie to Stephanie?"

The girls looked at the floor.

"Kayla?"

"She wouldn't care."

"If you weren't planning to do something wrong, you wouldn't have felt the need to lie at all. Tell me everything. Right now."

Rebecca bit her lip and looked at Kayla, who had yet to look up.

"We just wanted to make our own supper and do our own thing without any adults looking over our shoulders," Rebecca said.

"So if I had come over to the apartment about eight thirty, what would you have been doing?"

Kayla snapped her head up and looked at Rebecca, who rolled her eyes as she shook her head. "Nothing," Rebecca said with as much defiance as she could muster. "We would have been watching television."

"Is that true, Kayla?" Polly asked.

Kayla looked to the side and muttered, "Yes."

"I see. You two stay here." Polly opened the door and walked into the kitchen. "Andrew, what are your plans for this evening?"

He looked at her in surprise. "I. Uh. I." In desperation, he looked behind her for Rebecca.

"No. She can't help you. What were your plans? I want an answer."

Noah and Elijah watched the interaction with wide eyes.

Andrew slumped in his seat. "Nothing. I wasn't going to do anything tonight."

"Not watch television or read a book or write one of your stories?" Polly asked.

"I guess. Maybe. I don't know."

"You weren't planning to meet up with Kayla and Rebecca and maybe a couple of other friends downtown?"

"How did ..." Andrew stopped himself, but he knew it was too late.

"She didn't," Rebecca said, coming out of the dining room. "You just told her. It was no big deal, Polly. We were just going to Pizzazz. A bunch of friends wanted to hang out."

That still didn't ring true with Polly, especially when Andrew and Kayla's faces showed surprise at her words.

"You wouldn't have had to lie to me about going to Pizzazz," Polly said. "I'm disappointed in all three of you. Since I still don't have the truth, I'm going to have a conversation with Stephanie and Sylvie. We'll figure out what's going on."

"Fine," Rebecca spat. She slapped her hand against the wall. "We were going over to the Alehouse to listen to a band. Are you happy now?" She pushed past Polly and ran down the hall.

When her door slammed shut, Polly turned to the others in the room. "The answer is no. I'm not happy now. I'm disappointed." She put her hands on Noah and Elijah's shoulders. "Boys, why don't you go to the family room and watch television."

The two little boys took off as if a firecracker had been lit underneath their feet.

Polly rubbed her forehead. "I don't even know what to say to you three. This was so unnecessary." She turned and headed down the hallway to her own room. Right now she didn't care what Andrew and Kayla thought or even did. All she knew was that she needed a quiet minute to decide what *she* was going to do next.

CHAPTER TWO

A light tap on Polly's bedroom door got her attention and she looked up from her desk.

"I called Stephanie," Kayla said. "She said that whatever Rebecca has to do as punishment, I have to help."

Polly wanted to laugh. Her friends had all heard about Rebecca's bathroom cleaning punishments. Most of them wished they'd thought of it when their kids were young. Instead of laughing at Kayla's words, though, Polly nodded.

"I'm sorry," Kayla said.

"Thank you."

Kayla stood in the doorway staring until Polly grew uncomfortable. "Go on back to the kitchen," Polly said. "I need to speak with Rebecca."

Kayla turned and left.

They really were good kids and when Polly thought about it, she wanted them to try to break rules every once in a while. The last thing she wanted was to raise a timid rule-follower. It was the lying that infuriated and disappointed her. Now to make Rebecca understand that.

Polly got up, rubbed Obiwan's head as she passed him and stepped into the hallway, then rapped on Rebecca's door. "Rebecca, I'm coming in."

"Fine."

Oh joy.

She opened the door and pushed clothing out of the way as she crossed to Rebecca's bed. The girl was face down in her pillow, her arms flung over her head.

"Are you ready to talk about this?"

"No reason to. You're just going to tell me what I did wrong and then punish me. We don't have to waste time talking. You're the boss. You're always the boss."

"What do you think made me the angriest?"

Rebecca turned toward the wall, away from Polly, but that didn't stop her from using her sassiest tone of voice. "Because I chose to do something without asking you first. But you would have said no and I wanted to do it. I never get to do anything I want. I always have to do what you say."

Oh, Polly loved this child.

"You might be right. I might have said no. But we'll never actually know for sure, will we? You didn't give me a chance."

"You would have said no. I'm sure of it. You never let me do anything that I want to do."

"Is that truly a conversation you want to have with me right now?" Polly asked.

"Well you don't."

Yep. Adolescence was going to kill Polly. She wondered how her father ever allowed her to live through it.

"Do you think that being aggressive and trying to start a fight with me is going to make this conversation end up in a better place?" Polly asked.

"Like it matters."

"I guess that's your answer. Well, here's what we're going to start with. By tomorrow morning when you leave for Beryl's house, you will have written down on this notepad here ..." Polly picked a pad of paper up off the floor. "... every single thing

12

you've wanted to do and couldn't because I said no. Then on a second page, I want you to write down each thing that I've either let you do, encouraged you to do, or helped you to do since school started last fall."

Rebecca turned over. "How am I supposed to remember all of that?"

"You have all night long to come up with the list. Or, if you decide to stop because the second list is so out of control long and the first list has exactly three items on it, that's fine too. You just have to bring those lists to me and tell me that you're sorry for saying that."

"That's all I have to do?"

"Oh no." Polly shook her head. "That's just for your smart-mouthed remarks. We're only getting started. Kayla just came to apologize to me for her part in this. She actually told Stephanie the truth and accepted Stephanie's punishment." Polly emphasized the word truth, hoping Rebecca would catch on.

"What was Stephanie's punishment?"

"That she had to help with whatever I handed out to you."

"Great. That just means it's going to get worse."

"Maybe. We'll see how things go. I'm waiting to find out if Andrew tells his mother what happened."

"I don't see why you're making such a big deal out of this. It isn't like we were going down to Boone or something. We just wanted to hear a band play."

"So you think that's what this is all about?"

"What else is there? I wanted to do something you didn't want me to do."

Polly turned to leave the room. "I thought you were the smartest kid in the class. You can stay in here until you figure out what the real problem was this afternoon. I'm going to hang out with the boys in the family room."

"Wait," Rebecca called out.

Polly put her hand on the door sill and turned back. "What?"

"It's because I lied."

Touching her nose with her index finger, Polly smiled. "You

got it. You didn't lie just once, but you kept making up new lies you thought I would accept. One after another, you dug that hole deeper and deeper and then got mad because you were caught. Honey, that was no one's fault but your own. I can take a lot from you, but I will not accept lies. Especially when you do it right to my face." She pointed at the pad of paper that she'd dropped on Rebecca's bed. "Start with the list of things I won't let you do. The first one on there should be that I wouldn't let you go hear a band at the Alehouse tonight, even though you never really asked me."

Polly stepped into the hallway and pulled Rebecca's door shut. Just as she arrived at the doorway to the family room, Andrew came toward her.

"I'm sorry," he said.

"For what?"

"For not telling you what we were doing."

"Have you talked to your mother?"

He looked at her in shock. "No. She'll kill me."

"Imagine that," Polly said with a laugh. "Either you tell her or I do. Your choice."

"That's not a choice. That's death."

"Death when she hears it from me will be much worse than if you tell her yourself."

He put both hands on his head and groaned.

"Choices and consequences, Andrew. Always remember that those two go hand in hand."

"It's not fair."

Polly smiled at him. "That's life. Talk to your mother." She went on into the family room and found Noah and Elijah huddled together at one end of a sofa. "Hey, boys."

They looked up at her with wide eyes.

"Is Rebecca in trouble?" Noah asked.

Polly nodded. "Yes she is."

"You're really mad at her?"

Polly lifted a shoulder. "I'm disappointed. I was mad for a few minutes, but I'm over that."

"So you aren't going to hit her?"

Polly lifted her eyebrows. "Hit her? No. I'm not hitting her. She'll have some punishment, but no hitting."

"You didn't yell either," Elijah said. "That usually comes before hitting."

"There will be times that I yell," Polly said. "When I get really mad, I might make a lot of noise. But that doesn't mean that I'm going to hit anyone."

"I told you," Elijah said to his brother.

She realized that they'd been so busy this last month, things had actually been fairly calm around the house. This was the first real altercation she'd had with Rebecca in a while. Heath and Hayden were too busy to get in trouble and any arguments she had with Henry were handled behind the closed doors of their bedroom. But even those were few and far between.

The boys had been on their best behavior since they arrived, which was surprising now that she thought about it. They'd done anything she asked of them, made sure they were ready to go to school every day, dressed in their best clothes. They did their homework, usually with the help of Rebecca and Andrew, and didn't ask for anything out of the ordinary.

It hit Polly that this wasn't normal behavior for little boys.

"Do you remember when the milk spilled last summer?" Polly asked. She sat down on the other end of the sofa. Obiwan had followed her and climbed up between her and the boys.

Elijah slowly nodded as he put his hand on Obiwan's neck and rubbed back and forth.

"You thought I was going to be angry about that, but I wasn't, was I?" she asked.

Noah sat forward. "I thought you were going to kill him."

"No you didn't," she said with a small laugh. "But I understand that you experienced different behavior before you came to our house. Making mistakes is okay. I won't be mad at you for mistakes."

They nodded in unison.

"But here's the thing. If I get mad at you, what does that mean?"

Their faces sagged as they looked at each other and back to her.

"It means that I'm mad at you for doing something. But it doesn't mean that I don't love you. I will always love you and you can't do anything bad enough to change that."

"She's right."

Everyone turned to look at Heath who stood in the doorway.

"She told me the same thing," he said, coming into the room. "Polly promised me that I couldn't do anything bad enough to make her stop loving me. And I tried a couple of things, but she is always there even if she's mad at what I did."

"Do you still love Rebecca?" Elijah asked.

Polly smiled. "I love her so much. In fact, I need to just go tell her that." She stood, walked past Heath and gave him a quick hug, then went back to Rebecca's room and rapped on the door. "I'm coming in again." Polly opened the door.

Rebecca was curled into a ball on her bed with her face buried in the pillow.

"I love you, Rebecca. The boys just reminded me that I needed to say that to you. Even though I'm angry and disappointed, it doesn't change how much I love you."

"I'm sorry," Rebecca choked out, her voice cracking. She turned, allowing Polly to see how red her eyes were from crying. "How come I always do stupid things?"

"Because you're thirteen and independent. It kinda comes with the territory. How are you doing on that list?"

Rebecca pushed the notepad toward Polly. Sure enough there were three items on the first list. She couldn't go hear the band. She hadn't been able to spend the night with Kayla, and Polly hadn't let her go to a dance last fall. That dance had landed on the same evening that they celebrated Marie and Bill Sturtz's forty-first wedding anniversary.

Polly flipped to the next page and smiled as she read through the much longer list of things Rebecca had gotten to experience.

"I forgot about these things until you told me to remember," Rebecca said. "I'm sorry."

"Thank you. Now why don't you go into my bathroom and

wash your face. We still need to decide what the three of you kids are going to do for punishment."

"It isn't fair that Andrew and Kayla get punished. This was all my idea. They just said yes. I'll do all the work. Mine and theirs."

This was the Rebecca that Polly enjoyed parenting. She was really quite selfless.

"I believe that the two of them made their own decisions," Polly said. "If nothing else, they should have told you no."

"They did," Rebecca replied, slumping back against the pillow. "I made them."

"Then maybe the next conversation I have with them is that you aren't always right and when they know that, they need to stand up to you. They can take responsibility for their part in this." Polly sat on the bed beside Rebecca. "I had a really difficult conversation with my dad when I was about your age."

"Did you get in trouble a lot?"

Polly chuckled. "More than I want to admit. But Dad told me that I was the kind of person other people liked to be with and I had a choice. I could either be a good influence or a bad influence. People recognize what kind of person you are. Parents would know whether I was a good or bad influence. If they thought I wasn't safe for their kids to be around, they'd make it difficult for me to have good friends. I got one of my friends in bad trouble once. Her mom decided she didn't like me because of it, so I never played with Annie again. All because I did something stupid. I want Sylvie and Stephanie to trust that you won't ask their kids to do bad things. Don't you?"

"I never thought about that," Rebecca said. "I want them to trust me."

"I know you do. Go wash your face."

Polly and Rebecca left the room. Rebecca headed one way and Polly toward the kitchen. Heath had dropped into the couch with Noah and Elijah in the family room and the little boys had taken positions on either side of him.

Kayla and Andrew looked up from the table when she walked in.

"I called Mom," Andrew said dejectedly.

"And?"

"She said that I'm cleaning all of the bathrooms at home. Do you know how many that is?"

Polly laughed out loud.

"And then she said that I had to do whatever you told me to do to make it right with you. And if Stephanie wants me to do something, I have to do that too."

Rebecca walked into the kitchen and flopped into a chair.

"Here's the deal," Polly said. "The three of you are in trouble not because you wanted to go to a concert, but because you lied to me. I don't know how I would have handled a request to go hear that band. If it had been important, I might have found a way to make it happen, but now, not so much." She leaned on the table. "Andrew and Kayla, Rebecca tells me that all of this was her idea and you tried to tell her no."

The two kids nodded in agreement, hope returning to their eyes.

"But you let her bully you anyway. That makes you accomplices and you get to take some responsibility for that."

The hope that had begun to burn brightly dropped away.

"What do we have to clean?" Andrew asked.

"Funny you should mention cleaning," Polly said.

Rebecca groaned. "Oh no. How bad is this going to be?"

"The apartment at Sycamore House needs to be cleaned."

"The whole place?" Rebecca gasped. As soon as the words were out, she slammed her hand over her mouth. "Sorry. We'll do whatever."

"Tomorrow afternoon, the four of us are going over to Sycamore House. I will help. My goal is to wipe down the bookshelves, dust, and mop the floors in the bedrooms and living room. If we can get one side of the apartment cleaned out tomorrow, that will be enough." She shrugged. "If I wait long enough, the three of you will do something that gets the kitchen side of the apartment cleaned too."

"But there are two bathrooms on that side," Andrew whined.

18

"Yes there are," Polly replied. "You're going to get a lot of practice. Maybe you'll think twice before you let Rebecca push you into doing something you know isn't right."

Kayla pushed at Andrew's arm. "I think we're getting off easy."

"But you don't have to do this *and* clean bathrooms at your own house," he said.

"I always clean the bathroom. That's part of our deal. Stephanie washes the laundry and does the kitchen. I do the bathroom, the living room, and fold the laundry. We each keep our own rooms clean."

"I'm sorry, guys," Rebecca said. "This is all my fault. I tried to tell Polly that you didn't have to help with my punishment. I'm really sorry."

The back door opened and everybody turned as Hayden came in and shivered. "It's cold out there today." He kicked his shoes off and left them on the porch. "What's going on in here and where are the boys? I have something for them." He held up a bag then put it down while he took his coat off.

"You didn't bring anything for me?" Rebecca asked.

Hayden strode across the room and mussed her hair. "I have that for you. It's enough, right?"

Pounding feet down the hallway accompanied Noah and Elijah's approach. "Hayden!" Elijah yelled and ran right at the young man. Hayden lifted him into a hug and returned him to the floor before doing the same for Noah, who just beamed at the attention.

"There's a bag on the back porch with something in it for the two of you," Hayden said.

The two ran for the porch.

He grinned at his brother. "You'll remember this. We had so much fun."

"What did you get?"

"You'll see."

Noah carried the bag back into the kitchen, while trying to fend off his brother's hands as they pawed at the purchases.

"Let's take that into the foyer," Hayden said. "There's room to play."

Everybody followed Noah into the foyer. He didn't get too far in before dumping the contents of the bag onto the floor.

"Hot Wheels," Heath said. "This is so cool. I remember playing with these all the time. You bought tracks and everything."

"It's okay?" Hayden asked Polly.

"It's fabulous," she said.

"There's so much space in the foyer to set it up. I bought a bunch of track."

"Look at this car." Elijah brought a package over for Polly to look at. "I'll bet it goes fast."

"There's a truck like Henry's," Noah yelled. He ripped the package apart and sent the truck rolling across the floor. "That's so cool."

"Where's my family?" Henry called out from the back door. "I brought presents."

The kids all looked at each other in surprise, then at Polly.

"I don't know," she said. "He didn't tell me."

Noah looked with yearning at the race tracks, then at Polly again.

"Go on. All of you. We have all weekend."

"Come on, everyone," Hayden said. "Let's see what Henry brought home." He herded the kids back through the door and into the kitchen.

Polly walked across the floor and picked up the little truck, then tossed it back and forth in her hands. Having a family was exhausting and exhilarating all at the same time.

CHAPTER THREE

"What's all this?" Polly asked.

Henry put a large box on a chair at the table and pulled out piece after piece of hand-made wooden items. "Doug Schaffer has been practicing new skills and I told him that I'd buy some of the items he created."

Heath gave Henry a skeptical look. "He's using your wood, your tools, is working on your time, and you paid him?"

"It's his talent that's worth the money," Henry said. "He's doing great work and most of this is done after hours."

Hayden glared at his brother. "It's none of your business what Henry does with his employees." He picked up a multi-colored wooden bowl. "Did Doug turn this on the lathe?"

Henry nodded. "Isn't that nice? Glued up a bunch of scrap and then made this. All of it's from scrap." He handed Polly a rectangular piece and reached in for two smaller square pieces. "These are for you."

"What are they?" she asked, taking one in her hand. "They'd be great trivets on the table."

"Exactly." Henry reached back in. "I have candlesticks and two more bowls." He grinned and took out two small step stools that had been painted a smoky blue. Noah's name was stenciled on the top of one and Elijah's on the top of the other. "These are for you boys. Until you're tall enough to reach everything, you can use them."

"Thank you!" Elijah cried. He put his stool on the floor, stood on it, then tapped Heath on the shoulder. "I'm almost as tall as you are now."

Heath laughed and rubbed Elijah's head. "Yes you are." Whatever tension that had built because of his outburst regarding Doug Shaffer was gone.

"Andrew and Kayla, please take something you'd like to have," Henry said. "I knew you'd be here so I picked up a few extra items."

"Could I take a candlestick?" Kayla asked. "I should give it to Stephanie to say sorry."

Henry glanced at Polly, who just shook her head and smiled. "Of course. You can take two that match."

Andrew reached in and put his hand on one of the turned bowls, then looked at Rebecca. "What do you want?"

She shrugged. "I don't know."

"You should take the other candlesticks. They'd be pretty in your room."

"Polly won't let me have candles."

He looked at Polly, then back at Rebecca. "Maybe one of those flameless candles."

She smiled and bumped against his shoulder, then reached in and took another set of matching candlesticks. "Thank you, Henry. This is really nice."

"Thanks, Henry," Andrew said. "I'll give Mom one of the flat bowls. She'd like it over the kitchen sink for her jewelry."

Henry took out a third set of candlesticks and another pair of bowls. "Heath, which would you like?"

"I'm sorry I said anything," Heath replied.

"No big deal. Which?"

Heath pointed at the candlesticks. "I like those. Thank you."

Polly bent over to Noah, who had sat down on his personalized stool and whispered in his ear. "Tell him thank you."

"Thank you, Henry," Noah said softly.

"Thank you!" Elijah said. "This is a great day. We got cars and a stool."

"Cars?" Henry asked.

Hayden stepped toward the foyer door. "I brought home race tracks and cars for the boys."

"You didn't." Henry grinned. "In there?"

"Yeah."

"Boys, we need to take a trip to my old house this weekend," Henry said. "I have boxes of track and cars in the basement from when I was a kid. We'll set this up all over the foyer. On top of boxes. Up and down the stairs. It will be awesome."

Noah and Elijah's eyes grew bigger with every word Henry said. "Really?"

"Really," Henry replied. "Let's go see what Hayden got to start you out with."

Polly put the truck she'd been holding in Henry's hand. "You're a nut. I had no idea."

"I'm a boy," he protested. "I had race cars. Dad and I even built a big table for them one year. That's all been torn down." Henry put his hand on Heath's shoulder. "Let's see what damage we can do to the foyer."

"Boys, put your stools in your bedroom first," Polly said. "Then you can play in the foyer as long as you want tonight."

Henry kissed her. "I was going to work in the office this weekend, but now my plans have changed. We're playing with cars."

"Of course you are." Polly put her hand out, stopping him from leaving with the others. "Come with me to our room."

He waggled his eyes at Rebecca, Andrew and Kayla.

"Ewww, gross," Rebecca said. Then she realized what Polly was doing and slumped her shoulders. "Don't be too mad at me."

Henry gave her a confused look and took Polly's hand as they walked down the hallways. "What's up?"

"In here." Polly closed the door to their bedroom. "I had some trouble this afternoon with the older kids. Rebecca, Kayla, and Andrew tried to go to the Alehouse to hear a band this evening and the two girls lied to me about their plans. Rebecca fabricated a big story about wanting to do adult things with Kayla at the apartment: make dinner, watch television without supervision, girl stuff. It sounded strange, so I pushed and they just kept lying until she finally got it out."

"Damn it," he said.

"Oh, the drama was quite …" Polly searched for the word without success. "… dramatic."

"What band is playing at the Alehouse?"

She chuckled. "That's your question?"

He gave his head a quick shake. "No. Sorry. So what happened?"

Polly was still laughing at him and snorted, then stopped herself. "I made Kayla call Stephanie and shamed Andrew into calling Sylvie, then had it out with Rebecca. She tried to tell me that I never let her do anything."

"That little girl …" he started.

"That little girl had to write down everything she wanted to do that I wouldn't let her do and then she had to write a list of all the things she *got* to do. It didn't take long for her to figure it out. But the best part is that the four of us are spending tomorrow afternoon at the apartment. We're going to get the bedrooms, the living room, and bathrooms clean."

"You didn't." Henry gave her a deep-throated laugh. "But you have to help?"

"It's okay. I was going to have to do the whole thing. At least this way I have a team to work with."

"How long until Rebecca does something stupid so she cleans the other side?"

"I already told her that I was just going to wait."

"You're rotten."

"So you wouldn't have wanted to spend tomorrow afternoon in the office anyway. We'll be making noise. Now you can have fun building your race track in the foyer."

He sat down on the bed and pulled off his boots. "Dad and I had so much fun in the basement at home. When we get more finished upstairs, I want to work on rooms in the cellar for things like that."

"Because there isn't enough space in this huge monstrosity already?"

"You've got it."

Polly leaned in for a kiss and Henry put his arms around her, then pulled her on top of him as he fell back on the bed. "Can we have a little bit of the 'ewww, gross' before I go out and play with the boys?" he asked.

"You can have as much as you want." Polly rolled off and threw her leg over him as she tucked in close. "Thank you for bringing home presents. That was wonderful."

"Doug's enjoying himself and I wanted to be able to give him a little something extra for this."

"He should sell some of these things. He does nice work."

"Let's see how much he can do once things get busy at the shop again. Now that Len's back from Spain, they get through the work pretty quickly."

Andy and Len Specek had gone to Spain the first two weeks of January to spend time with Len's daughter, Ellen. This time, rather than try to see everything in Europe, they'd stayed in Barcelona. Andy declared it was her favorite city in the world. Ellen had enjoyed taking them to her favorite shops and restaurants, offering a more intimate view of the city. Andy was ready to go back any day.

"How are the Schaffers doing in that apartment?" Polly asked. "It isn't very big."

A two-bedroom apartment had opened up just after the new year in the building where Stephanie and Kayla lived. The family moved in, but Polly couldn't imagine how they possibly lived in that small space. Housing in Bellingwood was tight right now, though. The new apartments south of town were filled and new homes were going up, but it just wasn't fast enough. Henry would begin another apartment building as soon as the worst of winter was over, and his company was contracted to build five more homes. When all of this took off, she didn't expect to ever see him again. Until then, she was enjoying the time they had together. And … she was getting as much work out of Henry, Hayden and Heath as she could. She just wanted to finish a few rooms upstairs.

Henry turned on his side to face her. "You left me."

"Oops, sorry. I was just thinking."

"About?"

"About you getting busy with construction again and how I wouldn't see you. And about getting more rooms finished around here."

He snuggled in to her, burying his head under her chin. Polly reached up to stroke his hair.

"It's all going to work out," he said. "Look at us. At least we're here."

"Yes we are. Look what you've done for us."

Polly continued to stroke his head until she realized that his breathing had slowed and he'd fallen asleep. That was okay. She took a few deep breaths to relax herself and kissed the top of his head. This wasn't as exciting as 'ewww, gross,' but it would do.

~~~

Polly and Henry both jumped when the sounds of loud yelling tore past their door.

"What time is it?" Polly asked.

Henry turned to look at a clock on the desk. "Six thirty. What was that about?"

"The yelling or the sleeping?"

He gave his head a quick shake. "I don't care. Either one."

"The yelling sounds like playing, and the sleeping, well, that's on you. I couldn't move."

"I don't nap in the evening."

Polly chuckled. "Interesting. Looks like you do."

He stood and put out his hand to help her sit up. She groaned and rolled her shoulders to loosen them. "We're going to have trouble falling asleep tonight."

"It's your fault. You were warm and snuggly."

"Uh huh. Let's find out what happened to cause yelling."

Henry opened their door and stepped into the hallway. "Nobody's here. It's safe."

The central doors of the foyer flew open and Noah ran toward them, with Andrew right behind him.

"Come here with that," Andrew hollered.

Both boys pulled to a stop in front of Henry.

Andrew glanced down at Noah, then at Henry. "Sorry."

"What's going on?" Polly asked.

Noah ducked behind Andrew.

"It's nothing. We were playing with the racetrack and he stole my car."

"You probably deserved it," Polly replied. She put her hand on Andrew's shoulder. "Run, Noah. I'll hold him for just two seconds."

The little boy looked at her in surprise, but gathered his wits and ran for the kitchen.

"One Mississippi, Two Mississippi," Polly said, then she hugged Andrew.

"What's that for?"

"Just giving him some more time."

He laughed, broke away from her, and cut back into the foyer.

"Can you believe we have a house big enough that the kids can run and play when it's cold outside?" she asked Henry.

"When you start decorating, you'll have to keep the hallway clear of breakables."

Polly nodded. "What shall we do for dinner tonight?"

"Tacos?"

"You think?"

"Yeah. I could run up to the store and get lettuce and tomatoes. You've got hamburger and cheese."

"You'd go?"

"Why not?"

"We need tortillas, too."

He walked back into the bedroom, sat on the bed and pulled his boots on.

"You're awfully good to us," Polly said when he rejoined her in the hallway.

"Remember that the next time you're mad at me." He opened the double doors into the foyer. "I'm going to the grocery store. Anyone want to ride along?"

Noah ran across the room to Andrew and dropped a car in the older boy's hand, then ran over to Henry. "If I put my coat on, can I go?"

Don't forget your shoes," Henry called out as Noah ran toward the door on the north side of the foyer.

The door to Rebecca's room was closed. Polly tapped on it. "Are you in there?"

Kayla opened the door. "It's just us."

When Polly glanced in, she saw Rebecca's hand resting under her pillow. "What are you two doing?"

"Just talking," Rebecca said. "We didn't want to play with cars."

"Okay. We're making tacos for dinner. Henry's going to the grocery store. Do you need anything?"

They both shook their head and Polly headed for the kitchen. She tried not to be hard on Rebecca, but the rule was that phones were off limits until after dinner. If Kayla and Andrew stayed through dinner, their phones were supposed to be in the charger bin, too. They'd had the discussion more than once that those phones were a privilege. Kayla's and Rebecca's were nowhere to be found.

"I'll deal with them later," Polly muttered to herself. She opened the refrigerator and took out two pounds of hamburger. She gritted her teeth. That daughter of hers should know better than to push the envelope after what she'd done earlier. Why was this so difficult? Polly turned the burner on under the pan and went after the ground beef with her nylon chopper.

"Whoa," Henry said as he came through into the kitchen. "What's made you mad again? Leave a little beef for the tacos."

"Nothing," Polly said in a low growl. "Some days I hate being a mother."

"Anything I can do?"

Polly took a deep breath and smiled at Henry. "The worst thing is, I can't blame you for getting me pregnant with her or anything. But I'm fine."

"What did she do this time?"

"Her phone is in her room. She lied to me again and tried to hide it."

He put his hand on her elbow. "I'll handle it."

"It's not that big of a deal. I'm just tired of her behavior."

Before she could stop him, Henry strode down the hallway.

Noah came into the kitchen, dressed in his warm coat, hat and mittens. "Where's Henry?"

"He'll be right back." Polly giggled. The little boy was so adorable all dressed for cold weather.

In just a minute, Rebecca and Kayla came into the kitchen, with Henry right behind them.

"Sorry," Rebecca said. She dumped her phone into the charging station and turned to leave the room.

Kayla murmured some sort of apology and tried to follow Rebecca.

"Nope. Not good enough," Henry said, stopping the two girls. "Why the deliberate bad behavior? You know better."

"We had to cancel tonight," Rebecca replied.

"That would have taken two texts," he said. "Rebecca, your phone is mine until Monday."

"But you can't do that," she protested in a whine.

Polly didn't know whether to laugh or what. Rebecca never pushed Henry.

"Watch me." He grabbed up her phone, popped the back off, and took out the battery. "I don't know what's gotten into you, but this doesn't fly." Pocketing the battery, he put his hand out for Noah. "We'll be back. You two girls might want to clean up that mess in Rebecca's room. I expect to see a clear floor before we eat tonight."

His tone never changed. It was still pleasant and reasonable. When Noah took his hand, the two walked out through the mudroom, Henry asking about the track they'd been setting up in the foyer.

Polly, Kayla and Rebecca all stood in the kitchen, the girls as flabbergasted as she was. Kayla ran over, put her phone into the charging station and headed back down the hallway. Rebecca opened her mouth as if to say something, but stopped before it came out and left the room.

All Polly could do was chuckle and breathe a sigh of relief once they left. Sounds of play and laughter came from the foyer. At least she didn't have to do this alone.

The door from the foyer opened again and Heath poked his head in. "Anything I can do to help?" he asked.

"You're doing it," Polly replied.

"They don't need me. Hayden and Andrew are racing with Elijah. I'm just standing around."

She pointed at the box and wooden items Henry had brought in earlier. "If you could deliver those to where they belong, that would be great. Put Kayla and Andrew's things on the table in the back porch so they don't forget them."

"You want your trivets on the table?"

"Perfect. Thanks."

Heath put everything back in the box. "I could make these."

Oh, that explained it.

"I'm keeping you too busy here at the house to do much creative work at the shop, aren't I?" Polly asked him.

"It's okay. I'll get time someday. These *are* pretty cool. I like the way he glued up all of the different kinds of wood to make the bowl." Heath stopped beside her and pulled it out. "See how it looks on the inside?"

"That's really beautiful."

"I saw something online where a guy glued a bunch of colored pencils together and when he turned it on the lathe, the colorful leads were exposed. I want to try that."

"You know my dad's lathe is in Henry's garage. When we get more finished here, maybe we should put a shop in the basement or build a little shop for you."

His eyes lit up. "Really?"

"Yeah," she said. "Really."

"But I'm a senior. It's not like I'll be here much longer."

"Are you planning to run away?"

"No, but you and Henry and Hayden said I have to go away to college. That means I won't live here."

Polly grabbed his arm and pulled him in so she could kiss his cheek. "You'll still live here. You don't even know where you want to go yet."

His shoulders dropped. "I have to figure that out."

They'd talked through several options this last month, but Heath kept dragging his feet. He and Henry were heading to Iowa State in the next couple of weeks to learn about their Construction Engineering program. Henry was probably more excited than Heath about the possibility of his son having that degree. Polly just wanted the decision made so Heath could quit thinking about it and enjoy the rest of his senior year. He'd had such a rough time through high school.

"You will," she said. "But trust me. You'll always have a home here. No matter where you go."

He looked at her strangely. "I don't want to go anywhere."

This was an old conversation. "I know. We'll talk about it later. Go on and then come back and help me set the table."

Starting your life was never easy. Polly looked around the unfinished kitchen. Sometimes living life was never easy.

CHAPTER FOUR

Not believing her eyes, Polly pulled right back out of her driveway Monday morning after taking the kids to school. Two pickup trucks were parked beside Henry's. This had to mean she was getting her new countertop. They'd been promising to get it here for the last week and if it happened today, she'd forget all about the stalling and cancellations. The cabinets were installed, though they had yet to hang the doors. The sink was still in a box in the mudroom and if today went well, appliances would be ordered and delivered. They were so close.

The quick made-out-of-scrap counter that Henry put in as a stop-gap was torn out last week when he and Hayden brought in the cabinet carcasses. At this point, the room was in worse chaos than before. The refrigerator had been moved to the mud-room and the stove was against the wall to the foyer. Polly just wanted both of those things to be gone. Bill and Marie didn't want the refrigerator back and Polly was sure the stove and oven had been designed for a house in the nineteen seventies. Gold wasn't her color. But she refused to complain. Those appliances gave her the freedom to move into this house. It's just that their time of usefulness was nearly over. She could hardly wait to fill cupboards and drawers again. The pantry was huge, but she couldn't find a thing in there.

If they were working in the kitchen, she was going in the front door. No sense disrupting them. Polly opened the door and stepped inside, then stopped to stare at the unholy mess that had taken over her beautiful foyer. It was truly the only room to be completely finished in the house and she'd managed to destroy it. Things had only gotten worse this weekend. After she and the kids cleaned out the bedrooms, bathrooms, and living room in the apartment, she'd made them help load more boxes from the garage into her truck. By the time they unloaded those boxes, all three kids gave her one more heartfelt apology for lying. They were exhausted. Last night at Pizzazz, Sylvie told Polly that Andrew had gone home and fallen asleep until Sunday morning. He got to spend Sunday afternoon cleaning the bathrooms at his own house.

Kayla and Rebecca had fallen asleep in Rebecca's room until Polly woke them for supper. After Stephanie picked her sister up, Rebecca had no energy to do anything else, so escaped back to her room.

On top of the boxes that had been scattered throughout the foyer, the boys had erected a rather marvelous race track design. Saturday morning, Henry took Noah and Elijah to his parent's house to find more track and his old cars. They'd returned with several boxes and before Polly knew it, there was orange track weaving in and out of balustrades and lying on top of boxes. Whooping and shouting from everyone involved had filled the house. As more boxes were unloaded, they adjusted the track layout. Boxes were shifted back and forth to make it as exciting as possible which meant that Polly had no idea where anything was.

Polly crossed the foyer and pushed open the door to the kitchen. Henry and one of the men were on their knees in a corner.

"I'm back," she said. "Don't get up. Just wanted you to know I'm here."

"We're getting a counter." Henry stood up. "Are you ready for this?"

She laughed. "You have no idea. I won't bother you. Thanks so much."

Polly pulled the door shut behind her and headed up the stairway to the second floor, after draping her coat over the newel post. She was going to forget where that was when she needed it. She'd heard about people taking pictures of their cars in big parking lots so they could remember where they'd parked. Maybe it would work with her coat. If only she could remember that she'd taken a picture.

Last night while she was at Pizzazz with her friends, Hayden, Heath, and Henry ripped apart the walls in another room. Polly wanted to clear the plaster and lath out today. If she could keep pace with them and clear rooms as they went along, things would continue to move forward. They weren't bringing electrical or plumbing in until the studs were bare. The large room over the living room was being expanded out into the hallway at one end and then a wall was going up to split it in two. The master bedroom would be reduced in size so they could put in a large bathroom for her and Henry as well as a normal sized bathroom that opened to the hallway.

Polly tried to convince Henry that finishing those rooms first would make her very happy. Rebecca was taking the room at the front of the house and they would put Noah and Elijah in the next room. Once you turned the corner, there were three more bedrooms along the long hallway. The small bathroom already in place needed to be gutted. Heath and Hayden would take the two bedrooms that shared a closet. The four bedrooms in the wing that held the servant's quarters above the kitchen would be the last thing they worked on.

She couldn't wait to move the younger boys into their own room, returning Heath and Hayden's space to them. Once Rebecca moved upstairs, the office downstairs could be finished. Polly gave herself a small grin. Henry could start working on the library when they moved their bedroom upstairs. Her vision for that room played itself out in her mind's eye whenever she let it. On the nights she had trouble falling asleep, all she had to do was think about dark walnut shelves filled with her books. If Henry agreed, she was going to ask for a bookshelf doorway leading into the bathroom so that it would be hidden to anyone who didn't know it was there. For no other reason than that it would be awesome. The kids would love it.

Polly walked into what would someday be the master bedroom and looked out into the back yard. Okay, it was a little strange that she was staring out into a cemetery, but it was beautiful - always well-manicured, with big trees along the outside perimeter and tidy paths leading from section to section. She could see Andy's house from the upstairs rooms.

These back rooms hung out over the back wall downstairs, giving shade to the porch that needed to be finished. When Henry yanked the rotted floor out last summer, he promised to get it back together soon. Polly was hoping this summer that might happen.

The other day, Elijah asked if he could help upstairs so they could get more done. It was amazing how quickly those boys fell into the rhythms of this family. She hugged her arms around herself. It would give Polly no greater joy than to have this house filled with kids chasing each other and to see them running with her dogs in the back yard. She was grateful to have Hayden and Heath in her life, but they were going to start lives of their own in a few short years.

Hayden was trying very hard not to talk about a girl that he'd been dating. He didn't want to make a big deal of it until he was sure that they were serious. He hadn't brought her to the house yet and avoided any conversation when Polly tried to get him to talk about the girl. She lived in Ames and her name was Tess. Hayden told everyone that was enough for now, with a firm look at Polly. This was when Marie needed to be around. She'd get more out of him, but she and Bill weren't coming back from Arizona for another month.

Bill called Henry every work day, just to keep up on what was happening. He also called Len Specek at the shop every day. Exile was killing him. Well, the heart attack nearly killed him. This was just an annoyance. Marie confided that she was keeping him down there as long as possible so that he could rest and recuperate. The heart attack last September forced Bill to slow down to keep his wife and son happy. Marie had him outside walking every morning and evening and said he was nearly back to normal.

Everyone was ready for their return. Jessie's little girl, Molly, and Marie often spent time on video chat. Marie was the only grandmother she'd ever know. Jessie's father called when he was on the road, but her mother refused to have anything to do with Jessie and Molly. They hadn't even sent the little family a gift at Christmastime, and ignored birthdays. Jessie had tried, but her mother wasn't having any part of a reunion. Molly didn't really know any different. As far as she was concerned, Bill and Marie were her grandparents, while Polly, Henry and Lonnie were her aunts and uncle. The little girl had plenty of family around that loved her. That was what mattered.

Polly walked through the framework separating the two rooms and looked at the big fireplace on the inside wall. They planned to use the fireplace on the main floor, but since this was Noah and Elijah's room, she wanted this one closed off. That meant extra work, but these rooms needed to be done right. Henry planned to take the large wooden mantle and apron off tonight with Hayden and Heath. As soon as everything was cleared out, he'd bring in a mason to brick off the hole in the wall.

Polly put her hand on the handle of her trusted friend, the pretty green wheelbarrow she decided just now to name Hazel. She should have named it a long time ago. They'd become such close friends. Hazel hadn't ever blown a tire or needed extra maintenance. Just the kind of friend Polly liked.

She hauled Hazel into the back bedroom and picked up the first piece of plaster, then dropped it in. The resounding thunk was satisfying. One more day of moving this project along. Lifting, hauling, pushing, dropping. The morning progressed.

While Polly worked, she pictured the changes that would happen to these rooms. With every day of work, the house felt more and more like home. She knew every inch of the place. Well, at least the inches of the rooms she'd worked in. The attic and basement were still alien to her. The only thing she knew about the attic was that it was filled with trunks, boxes and furniture.

Simon Gardner, the owner of the antique store in town, was in the attic last spring, but barely had time to start cataloging the furniture. There was no time to dig into the trunks and boxes. Much of the furniture came from the early nineteen hundreds. He assumed that the Springers stored it up there when they moved in and purchased their own. The furniture from the mid part of the century was in the garage right now. Until they had more space to move around, it was staying there. Polly still didn't know what she wanted to keep and what she was willing to let go.

Polly's phone buzzed in her back pocket and she stood back up. This bending and lifting was killing her back. She refused to complain, but sometimes whining to herself was allowed.

"You should see what we're doing," the text from Henry read.

Half of the floor in the back room had been cleared. She could come back and finish it later. A break was always welcome.

"Be there in a second," she texted back, then went down the main staircase and turned to go into her bedroom. If there were people in her house, she was at least going to wipe the dust from her face and wash her hands.

A few minutes later, she headed down the hallway toward the kitchen.

Three men sat at the kitchen table drinking coffee, while Henry and another man were bent over the end of the counter by the mudroom. She could hardly believe that they were to this point.

"It's gorgeous," Polly said. As much time as they planned to spend in the kitchen, Henry insisted that she choose something hardy as well as beautiful. They'd found a grey marble that didn't feel as if its swirling designs would make Polly nuts in ten years or so. The cabinet doors were made from a gorgeous knotty alder and she was in love with the way it all came together.

"This is going to be nice," Henry said, standing up.

Polly peered at the man standing beside him. "Clark?"

He grinned at her, walked across the room and put out his hand. Just before he reached her, he jerked his hand back and rubbed it on his jeans. "Polly Giller. It's been years. How are you?"

"I'm good. I didn't expect to see you here today. I don't think I even knew what happened to you after high school."

"Got a job working for my uncle's company and been there ever since. When your husband called about the countertops, I knew I had to take the job and see you again. My goodness, girl, you've been busy."

She nodded. "I can't believe you're here." Polly turned to Henry. "I knew Clark in high school." She hesitated, unsure whether it was necessary to announce that they'd dated a couple of times. She could tell Henry about it later, and honestly, it was completely possible that Clark didn't even remember going out with her.

"Took Polly to a couple of dances our junior year," Clark said. "Made a mistake letting that one go. I knew it at the time, too, but it was too late. Then you went away after we graduated. I never saw you again."

"I did," she acknowledged. "Went to school in Boston and came back to Iowa in twenty-twelve. Did you ever get married?"

He shrugged. "Twice now, believe it or not. Married Susie Pierce. Remember her?"

"Yeah? You were dating in high school. She was prom queen or something, wasn't she?"

"Good memory. We got married because she got pregnant. She was going to Kirkwood. Dental hygiene. Come to find out, it wasn't my kid and she up and left with the baby's daddy a year later. That was a bad time."

"I'll bet. But you met someone else?" Polly asked.

A warm smile graced his face. "Karen. You never knew her. She's from down around Montezuma. She had two little boys and ran away from a jackass who liked to hit her. She ended up in town and worked at the grocery store. My best buddy ..." Clark pointed to one of the men at the table. "He and his wife hooked us up. Thought we'd be a good match. We got three more little girls and another one on the way. Karen likes being a mom and if that's what she likes, that's what she gets. She deserves it."

"Do you have pictures?"

Clark took out his phone and swiped to open it, then put it in front of Polly. "That's Karen and the two boys - Destin and Caden." He swiped to the next picture. "Here's Karen with Renna, Albie and Darin. Aren't they just the prettiest things you've ever seen?"

"They're adorable."

He swiped again. "This is my beautiful wife with number six on the way. Took that last weekend. She doesn't like it when I take pictures of her, but she's so damned pretty. I don't know how I got so lucky."

Polly put her hand on his arm. "I'm glad you did."

He stepped back, embarrassed to have exposed himself to everyone. "I think you'll like the counters. Your husband did a great job with the guts here. Made installation easy."

"It's what he does," Polly said. "Is this the first time you've worked with him?"

Clark looked back toward Henry. "Yeah. I guess it is. We don't install much of the good stuff in those apartments and the like. I'm guessing you use the guy over in Humboldt most of the time, right?"

Henry nodded and shrugged. "Didn't know about you until my new guy mentioned your name."

"Doug Shaffer?" Polly asked.

"Yeah, I know Doug real well," Clark responded. "He worked on my brother-in-law's cars all the time. Over there in Boxholm. You remember Beatrice, don't you, Polly?"

Beatrice was Clark's younger sister if Polly remembered right. She nodded.

"She married a farmer. Something she said she'd never do, but she's got two kids and runs a hair salon out of her house. She cuts the girls' hair, so we used to go over on Saturdays. Bump and I'd take the boys and go downtown while the girls did their thing. He always had some car in that garage." Clark turned to Henry. "What's Doug doing down here working for you?"

"His house burned down."

"No way."

"Yeah," Polly said. "They ended up in Bellingwood. Seem like a nice family."

"Doug's a good hard worker. That's too bad about their house. He had a bunch of kids, too, didn't he?"

"Four," Henry replied.

"Man, I don't know what I'd do if my house burned down." Clark looked at his buddies. "Guess I'd have to move in with y'all. Shirley wouldn't mind having eight more people in that big ole house, would she?"

"Let's not find out," the buddy replied.

CHAPTER FIVE

Sometimes it was the little things that made the biggest impact. Polly had promised Noah and Elijah that today they would go to the library for their first library cards. Every day there was something new that she needed to take care of with them. Things that she never really thought about. To celebrate, they were walking from school to the coffee shop to meet her. They hadn't forgotten how kind Camille was to them last summer and loved stopping in to see her.

After a shower and a change of clothes, Polly left by the front door, not wanting to disturb the work in the kitchen. This was going to work out perfectly. The kids usually spent their afternoons around the kitchen table working on homework, but that room was a chaotic mess. Maybe she'd drag chairs into the dining room until things were finished. That was one thing she could talk to Simon Gardner about. He'd look for chairs for her. Polly wasn't sure if she wanted them all to match or to be as different as possible. She wanted wooden straight back chairs. That's all she knew for sure. Jen Dykstra, at the quilt shop, promised to teach her how to make cushions.

Polly had set her sewing machine up on the dining room table after Christmas. The room quickly became a place for Rebecca's crafts along with totes of fabric and notions. Rebecca's stuff was moving out to the little studio when it got warmer. That was another project she and Henry needed to deal with - heating that building for Rebecca. The list was never-ending.

She could hardly believe that in a house that big, they were already out of usable space. How was that even possible? Polly had a bad feeling that no matter how many rooms were available, it would never be enough.

She pulled into a parking space and waved at Jen, who was working on a display in the front window. It was only a quick wave and Polly immediately turned away. She was not getting caught by that woman again. There were already more projects in totes than she had time to finish.

The familiar ring of the bell on the front door and the scent of roasted coffee brought a sense of calm. Camille was waiting on two women Polly knew by sight, though not by name. She nodded and looked around the room to see if there was anyone else here that she recognized. Several people acknowledged Polly, but none of her friends were in sight.

"Hi Polly." Sylvie's assistant in the bakery, Marta, stood up from where she'd been restocking shelves behind the counter.

"Hi," Polly said. "Busy day today?"

Marta shrugged. "Average for a Monday. Sylvie had some big orders, though." She came around the counter. "Secret Woods is selling some of her breads. They just got a big contract with a company up in Webster City to deliver gift packages to their clients. Bread and wine. Kind of romantic, don't you think?"

Polly grinned. "It is."

"I'd better get back there. Only fifteen minutes left in my day and I need to finish this. It's good to see you."

"Good to see you too." Polly smiled at Marta's back. Sylvie had found a gem with that woman. She moved over to stand in line.

"Do you think he left for good?" the woman in the bright red coat asked her friend.

The friend nodded while watching Camille prepare their order. "Shirley Cooper says so. I don't know, though. I think he'll be back. He doesn't know any better. His mother was a worse shrew than she is. He's been putting up with that all his life."

"It's too bad. He's such a nice man and good looking too. All he needs is a sweet woman who understands him."

"Don't we all." The second woman giggled. "Need someone who understands us. I don't need a sweet woman."

The first woman looked at Polly, embarrassment on her face.

Fortunately, Camille stepped forward and put their cups on the tray holding two croissants. "Here you are, ladies. Enjoy."

"Thank you, Camille," the second woman said.

Polly backed up to give them room to walk away.

"Your normal order today?" Camille asked.

"Yeah. The kids are meeting me here. We're going to the library. Noah and Elijah are getting their very first library cards. They can't wait."

"That's pretty exciting. I remember my first library card. It felt like I'd been going there my whole life and then one day, Mama told me it was time for me to take responsibility for my own books. I felt like such a big girl."

The front door flew open, the bell ringing like crazy. Polly turned to see her five charges come in. Elijah ran across the floor when he saw her.

"Walk," Polly said quietly. "No running."

"Sorry," he said.

"How was your day?"

Elijah pulled out a folded piece of paper and put it in her hand. Polly prayed it wasn't a note from his teacher.

"What's this?"

"Read it." His eyes danced and Polly relaxed.

She unfolded it and saw a bright red one hundred at the top with a big smiley face. "You did good," she said with a grin.

"Mr. Phelps told me that I had the best score of everybody." He pulled Polly's hand to bring her closer to him. "He told me that after class so nobody would pick on me. I like him."

"I like him, too," Polly said. "How was your day, Noah?"

"It was okay. Not as good as his, though. But tomorrow, Chief Wallers is coming to class. Did you know my teacher is married to a policeman?"

Polly nodded. "I did. He's a friend of mine and I like him very much. Would you two like hot chocolate today?"

They both nodded and turned their eyes to the bakery display.

She couldn't help herself and chuckled. "And you can pick out one treat to have." Polly turned to include Kayla, Rebecca, and Andrew. "You can all choose a treat and get a hot chocolate."

Camille put Polly's coffee on the counter. "Five hot chocolates?"

"Can I get caramel in mine?" Rebecca asked.

"Me too," Kayla said.

"Me too?" Elijah asked.

Polly glanced around. "Anyone else?"

Noah nodded.

"Andrew?"

"Nah. I like mine straight," he said with a grin.

"Four with caramel," she said.

Camille smiled and winked at Noah, whose eyes grew huge. He looked up at Polly and beamed.

By the time they were finally at a table, the kids were chattering about their day. Kayla thought the student teacher in gym class was really good-looking.

Rebecca caught Polly's eye and winked.

"What's that?" Polly asked.

"Kayla has a crush," Rebecca sang.

Kayla frowned. "I do not. I just think he's kinda cute."

"Is he cute, Andrew?" Polly asked.

Andrew had been leaning toward the book shelf with his head tilted to read the spines. "What? Is who cute?"

"Get him near books and he doesn't hear a thing," Rebecca said. "Whenever we have study hall in the library, I make him sit with his back to the bookshelves."

"You make him?" Polly asked. "What are you, his mother?"

Andrew sat back up. "Sometimes she acts like it. She never lets me do anything fun." He turned to Rebecca and waited.

"That's not true," she protested. "You can do whatever you want. I never ..." she turned to Kayla. "Do I do that?"

Kayla shrugged.

"Do I do that?" Rebecca asked Polly.

"Does she do that?" Polly asked Andrew.

He put his hand on Noah's shoulder. "Does she do that?"

Poor Noah was just lost. "I like Rebecca," he said. "She takes care of me when I need it."

Andrew chuckled. "She takes care of me, too. I was just teasing her."

Rebecca jumped up from the table. "I'll be right back." She ran outside.

"What did I say?" Andrew asked.

Noah looked at him. "Is she mad?"

"I bet she forgot something in her backpack," Kayla said. "We put everything in your truck."

Polly nodded. Rebecca was always planning ahead. That girl didn't like having the world spin out of control around her and did her best to keep things organized. You wouldn't know that by looking at her room, though.

Rebecca came back to the table and put a piece of paper down in front of Polly. "Will you sign this that it's okay for me to try out?"

"For what?"

"For the play. It's about Sherlock Holmes as a boy."

"Maybe Sherlock Holmes should be about a girl?" Polly said.

"That's what I thought. But Miss Hoffman says we're following the script. Andrew's going to try out for Sherlock."

Polly signed the sheet and handed it back to Rebecca. "Are you trying out, too, Kayla?"

"I'm just going to do background stuff if they want me," Kayla replied. "I don't like to be on stage."

Rebecca rolled her eyes. "I tried talking to her. She won't listen. You should at least try, Kayla."

"I don't want to."

"Can't make 'em drink," Rebecca said, putting her hands up in defeat.

Elijah tugged on Polly's sleeve. "I've finished and so has Noah. How long before we go to the library?"

"We can go any time," Polly said. "Hurry. Throw your trash away."

The boys gathered up their cups and napkins and left the table.

"Do you three want to stay here a while and then come to the library?" Polly asked.

Rebecca looked at Kayla and then Andrew. They both nodded agreeably and she said, "Yeah. We'll be there in a while. Thanks."

"Don't be too long. You wouldn't want to miss your ride home," Polly said, standing up. She put her coat back on and waited while Noah and Elijah did the same, then walked with them out to the truck.

"I wouldn't mind being in a play," Elijah said.

"Buckle in, honey. I know it's only a couple of blocks, but put your seatbelt on." Polly turned the truck on and waited while both boys did as she asked. "When you're older, there will be plenty of plays for you to act in."

"We should do one at home someday," Noah said, almost too softly for Polly to hear.

"A play?" she asked, looking in the rear-view mirror at him.

"We have a lot of people. It would be fun."

She backed out of the parking space. "That's an interesting idea," she said. "Where did you come up with that?"

"I just thought of it. That big room in front would be fun or we could do it at your old house on that stage," he said.

Polly drove the three blocks to the library and went around the block to park on the west side. "You are always thinking, aren't you?"

"Yes, ma'am."

"Don't ever stop. It's a good idea. Maybe you should write the play." She unbuckled her belt and turned around to see his face.

"I couldn't do that, but maybe Andrew and Rebecca could."

"What would it be about?" Polly asked.

"I know, I know," Elijah said, standing up. "It could be about two little boys who came to a new town."

"Yeah," Noah said, nodding. "I could be one of them and you could be the other."

Polly opened the truck door. "You two figure out what the story is going to be and we'll see if Andrew might help you write the script. Now let's go inside and see about getting you some books."

"Are there books about how to write a play?" Elijah asked.

"Yes there are," she replied. "But those might be a little too old for you right now. Let's start with books you will enjoy today."

~~~

Polly dropped Andrew and Kayla at their homes and by the time she pulled into her driveway, it was empty of everyone's vehicles but her family's. Noah and Elijah were thrilled with their unlimited access to books. Even though the drive home was short, both boys looked through their stack of books, passing them back and forth and chattering about the stories.

Because they were still sharing a room with Hayden and Heath, the older boys had taken it upon themselves to read with the boys before bedtime. Polly had mentioned it at dinner one evening and the next thing she knew, there was a schedule in place. They were in the middle of C. S. Lewis's Narnia series right now. Heath couldn't remember having read it before and was having as much fun as Noah and Elijah.

"I'm going to read this one right now," Elijah said, brandishing one of his books.

"Homework first," Polly replied. She snapped the locks open. "Put everything in your backpacks before you get out of the truck. You don't want to drop the library's books."

Rebecca shoved her books into the overflowing pack she carried. Polly couldn't figure out what it was she carried with her. Neither Andrew's or Kayla's packs were that heavy.

In a flash, all three kids were out of the truck and standing at the side door, waiting for her to catch up.

"Can I take Obiwan and Han out tonight?" Noah asked.

"Homework," she said patiently. "I suspect that they've already been out since Hayden and Heath are home."

The kids barreled into the back porch, sliding their shoes off and dumping coats everywhere. When they tore into the kitchen, Polly coughed loudly.

"What?" Rebecca asked.

"You all know what. And I was standing right here when you did it," Polly replied.

The three came back into the mud room, picked up their coats to hang them on the pegs in their slots and turned to leave.

"Your shoes, too," Polly said. "You know this."

Slinking dejectedly to their shoes, the kids picked them up and put them on the bottom shelves.

"Did we do it?" Elijah asked.

"You did. Now get busy with your homework. I'm going to check on the big boys and then I'll be back to start dinner."

She waited until they were seated at the kitchen table, ran her hand across the new counter top closest to her, then went into the foyer and up the stairs. Hopefully, Henry was tearing into that fireplace.

Polly entered the upstairs hallway and heard laughter echoing in the empty rooms. She turned the corner and saw why. Heath was sprawled in Hazel, her trusty wheelbarrow, and being pushed across the room by Henry.

"What are you doing?" she asked, startling them all.

Henry tipped the wheelbarrow so Heath could climb out.

"We didn't know you were back," he said. "Did you see the kitchen?"

"It looks great, but you didn't answer my question. What in the world were you doing?"

He laughed out loud. "Hayden challenged me."

"He's faster than me," Hayden said. "The old man can haul ass."

48

"I see." Polly shook her head while she laughed. "You are insane."

"Uh huh."

"Have you gotten anywhere with the fireplace yet?"

"We were just about to pull it off when Hayden got cocky," Henry said.

"Me?" Hayden protested. "You're the one who claimed to be stronger than anyone else in the room."

Henry gave him a look. "Was I wrong?"

Polly pointed at the mantle and apron. "That means you don't need their help to lift this off?"

"Woman," he said. "You're supposed to be on my side."

"I am. You're a big strong man, so you can do it all by yourself."

He shook his head. "Let's show her what *three* big strong men can do. I'll take the center. You two on either end."

"Do you want my help?" Polly asked. "I'm strong."

Henry rubbed his chin. "I know you are." His eyes darted back and forth to the boys. "Of course you are, but I think we've got it."

"Whatever," she said with a shrug. "I'll just stand here and look pretty. It's what women are supposed to do, right?"

"Right," Henry agreed. "And you do it very well." He positioned himself in the center of the mantle and waited for Hayden and Heath to take their places. "Okay. On three we lift and pull. One. Two. Three."

With a heave, he pressed up with his shoulder while the boys pulled the mantle and apron up and back. They took a step and then one more before setting it down on the floor.

"Whoa," Hayden said. "That's a monster."

"Midwestern walnut." Henry patted the top of the mantle. "Good hardy wood, right there. This is well made. Let's lay it down on the floor so it doesn't fall in the middle of the night and scare us to death. We'll separate the pieces another day."

Inch by inch, they tipped it backwards onto the floor.

"Whoa," Polly said.

Henry looked up. "What?"

"No, go ahead. Sorry. There's a metal box in there."

The men finished lowering the piece onto the floor and Polly stepped across the apron to stand in the opening. "There are two metal boxes," she said. "One on each side."

Henry frowned down at the mantle. She reached in for one and he drew out the other.

"Were these built into that mantle piece?" Polly asked.

"I don't know. When we turn it over, I'll see. Mine's heavy. What do you think we have here?"

Polly attempted to lift the lid. "It's locked."

"Mine too." Henry shook the box.

The boys' eyes grew big at what sounded like coins clattering.

"Money?"

"I guess," he said. "I have tools at the shop that will open these."

"Tonight?" Polly asked.

"Aren't you dying of curiosity?"

She shook the metal box in her hands. Nothing rattled and it wasn't nearly as heavy as Henry's. "I'm not dying. It can wait until tomorrow."

"No it can't," Heath said. Then he looked at them. "Sorry."

Henry laughed. "The boxes have been here for decades. We didn't know about them five minutes ago. We can wait until tomorrow. Right?"

Heath sighed a long sigh. "Yeah. Okay. I've got a pile of homework anyway.

"Me too," Hayden said. "I'm going to be up most of the night."

"You boys should have said something earlier," Henry said. "We could have done this another time."

Hayden draped an arm across Polly's shoulders. "Not if we want to keep this one happy. She's rarin' to go."

"Yes I am," Polly said. "I'll run the boxes over to Len tomorrow morning. If there's anything interesting in them, I'll send you all texts and pictures to let you know."

"Send pictures even if it's boring," Hayden said.

Henry took Polly's box from her. "You boys get cleaned up.

We'll let you know when supper is ready. Thanks for helping me get this off the wall."

Heath and Hayden left. Polly chuckled as they bounced off each other while walking away.

"They're such good guys," she said.

Henry nodded. "Are you sure about waiting until tomorrow?"

"I'm sure. My back is killing me, the kids need dinner, and I want to collapse once we get everyone settled. The mystery can wait."

"Who are you and what have you done with my curious wife?"

"She's pooped and I'm all that's left."

"I'll call Jerry Allen and Liam Hoffman and see when their schedules will work," Henry said as they walked through the doorway into the hall. "I need to frame the bathrooms, but the hardest work is done."

Polly put her hand on his arm to stop him. She reached up and kissed his cheek. "Thank you."

"We need to put a hot tub in for you."

She nodded. "Yes you do." Then she laughed. "But I have a big long list of things that need to be done before that."

CHAPTER SIX

"Oof." Polly caught herself on the truck's door as her foot tried to slip out from under her. She hated ice.

She made it to the door of the Sturtz Construction shop and looked back. Of course she'd parked on the only patch of ice in the parking lot. Shaking her head, she went in. "Hello?"

Jessie walked out of a small office at the back. "Hi Polly, what are you doing here this morning?"

"I came over to get some help opening a couple of metal boxes. Henry said there were tools to do it here."

Jessie looked around the space. "I'm sure there are, but I don't have a clue where we'd look or what we'd do if we even found them."

"Where's Len and Doug? Or even Ben?"

"Up at the diner getting breakfast. It's Doug's birthday."

Polly slumped. "Rats. I wanted to know what was in these."

Jessie took one out of Polly's hand. "No key?"

"No. We found them in the mantle that we pulled off a wall last night." Polly shook the heavy box she was still holding. "Henry said it sounds like coins."

Jessie shook it.

"When do you expect them back?" Polly asked.

"I have no idea. They've only been gone about twenty minutes."

"Can I just leave these here, then?"

Jessie reached for the other box. "I'll put them on Len's workbench. When they get back, I'll ask them to help."

Polly let her take the other box. This wasn't working the way she wanted it to work. She had such trouble with impatience some days. "How's Molly doing in daycare?"

With Marie gone for several months, they'd had to come up with a new plan for Jessie's daughter. The toddler was much too active to have around construction. Jessie found a spot for her at the Lutheran Church daycare.

"It was so hard, Polly. Those first two weeks were awful. She was miserable. She missed me, she missed Marie; she even missed Bill and Len. But I didn't have any other options." Jessie smiled. "It's getting better. She's interacting with other kids and adults. I suppose it's a good thing, but I didn't think she'd have to do that at this age. I would have been glad for another year or two of her being just mine. And I'm not thrilled with her getting sassy. She's learned a few bad habits from being around so many other kids, but we'll work through those."

"I'm glad she's settling down. When Marie comes back will you leave her at daycare?"

Jessie shook her head vehemently. "Nope. I don't think Marie would let me. She misses Molly too much. I think a few months a year at daycare is plenty, don't you?"

"Sure," Polly said. "That sounds about right with me. Are you okay by yourself here today?"

"I'm fabulous. It's nice having them all gone for a while. I'm getting some studying done."

"I'm so proud of you," Polly said. "I'll get out of your way, then."

She didn't want to go back home. The crew working on her kitchen was back this morning. She couldn't do anything more upstairs until electricity and plumbing went in and walls went up. Once she was back in her truck, Polly found herself heading for Sycamore House. If nothing else, there was plenty to do in the office. She hadn't been in there for at least a week. Tearing a house apart and managing small children took more energy than she'd ever thought she would need.

As she pulled into the drive and headed for the garage, two men came up out of the creek bed. They acted as if they thought they were protected among the large number of trees.

"Can I help you?" she yelled as she climbed out of her truck.

The two men jumped at the sound of her voice. They looked at each other, back at her and then walked away from her toward the other end of the building.

"Hey!" she yelled. "What are you doing here?"

They picked up speed and she took off at a run, chasing them as they did their best to nonchalantly put more distance between them and her. A blue pickup was parked in the lot and the taller man got to it first and opened the driver's side door. By the time she was in the parking lot, they'd backed out and were heading out of the driveway.

"What in the hell?" Polly opened the door into the addition at Sycamore House, and stepped inside, stopping for a moment to catch her breath.

"Hello there," a woman said, coming out of the addition.

"Hi," Polly replied. She held the door into the main part of the building and the woman passed through.

The woman veered to the kitchen and Polly went into the main office.

"Polly," Kristen said. "What are you doing here?"

"Chasing people who might have been casing the joint."

Jeff came out of his office. "Casing the joint?"

"I just saw two men messing around back by the tree line. When I asked if I could help them, they took off. Do you know about anything going on?"

He shook his head, wrinkling his forehead. "Kristen?"

"No. Nothing."

"Stephanie?" Jeff pushed her office door open. "Do you know anything about a couple of men looking around the grounds?"

Stephanie saw Polly, grinned, and came out into the main office. "Hi there. Thanks for taking Kayla home last night. She had a good time at Sweet Beans and the library with you guys." She turned to Jeff. "Now, what?"

"Polly saw men out by the creek. Do you know why?"

"No. That's weird. Why would they even be there? Don't we own the land on the other side of the creek back there, too?"

Her words made Polly smile. She just loved it that these people took as much ownership of Sycamore House as she did. "Yeah, we do. That's where Eliseo plants sweet corn."

"That's what I thought." Stephanie shrugged. "Maybe he knows something."

"He would have told us," Jeff said. "But they shouldn't have run from Polly." He pushed at her arm. "She's just not that threatening. Especially at face value. Surely they don't already know what she does to men who really make her angry."

"Thank you," a voice said behind Polly. The woman she'd met at the side door stepped into the office and held up a small basket. "I appreciate everything you have available for us." She nodded at Polly and left, heading for the addition.

"Who's that?" Polly asked.

"Margaret Minnis," Kristen replied. "She writes children's books."

"Madge's Minis," Jeff said. "Cute stories about babies who talk to each other and the animals who live in their house, as well as animals they encounter when their parents take them out to play."

"The rooms over there are all full until August," Kristen gushed. "Some really interesting people are coming to Bellingwood. One guy wants Eliseo to teach him how to drive a team of horses for some book he's writing. There's even a couple coming who are writing a screenplay for television." She looked at Jeff. "They didn't tell me what it was about."

"I have no idea." He shook his head. "My mother's coming in April."

The room went silent as every eye turned toward him.

"What?" he asked. "I have a mom."

"I was pretty sure you were dropped from heaven by an angel," Polly said. "Your mother is coming to Bellingwood and you just think to tell us now? And she's staying here? Why not with you?"

"Because I'm not an idiot. She'll redecorate everything," he said. "If she gets just one hour in my house, she'll completely redo my bathrooms. New towels, new shower curtains. Everything. And it will all be fabulous." He rolled his eyes.

"It's been what, four years since you started working in Bellingwood and this is the first time anyone from your family has come to visit?" Polly asked.

"I don't encourage visits. If they must see me, I'll travel to Ohio."

"She's really the nicest person in the world," Stephanie said.

"That's right," Polly replied. "You met them when you two went out after your mother died. So why is she coming now?"

"Her youngest sister has a boy who is going to play football for Nebraska. They're driving out to see the campus. I'll meet them in Des Moines and bring her back here."

Polly chuckled. "So he's not going to Ohio State? That's interesting."

"I don't know anything about it," Jeff said. "I avoid family football talk. They get worked up about these rivalries." He grinned. "Why can't we all just get along?"

"You're weird. But I can't wait to meet her." Polly pointed at Kristen's computer. "Can you pull up the camera feeds from when I got here? Let's see if we can figure out who those two men were and what they wanted."

"I guess those cameras are good for something," Jeff said, teasing Polly.

She swatted at him. "Shut up. I still don't like it, but if we have the system, I don't mind using it for things like this."

Kristen pulled up the program and then turned to Stephanie. "I really don't know how to use the program. How do I go back?"

"I've got it," Stephanie said and leaned over Kristen's desk. The two girls shifted and moved until Stephanie was in Kristen's chair. She tapped and swiped. "Here they are," she said, pointing to the top left video on the screen.

The truck drove around the parking lot twice before it stopped and the two men got out. As they left the camera's view, Stephanie typed and swiped, bringing up the next camera which showed the two men hurrying to the tree line along Sycamore Creek. They walked up and down until disappearing into the creek bed. They were gone a while before re-emerging. There was a great deal of gesturing back and forth, pointing toward the highway and then down the creek beyond where the pasture was.

Everyone laughed as the two men jumped and ran for the front of the building with Polly chasing them.

"I look funny," Polly said. "But what were they doing back there? I can't make any sense of it."

"Would you export that?" Jeff asked Stephanie. "We should probably tell Chief Wallers what's going on, just in case something else happens."

Stephanie nodded before clicking and swiping again.

"You're really good at that," Polly said.

"After my father kidnapped Rebecca, I swore I'd learn that program inside and out," Stephanie replied. She huffed a laugh. "I guess it was good for something, huh?" Stephanie pointed at the desk drawers. "Do you have a DVD I can put this on?"

Kristen nodded and went into the conference room. "I took them out," she said, turning back. "I never use them. We have tons of space in the cabinets in here, so I took over a couple." She returned with a tower of blanks and put them beside Stephanie.

"I'd like one of those," Polly said.

Stephanie nodded and made several copies, then handed them to Jeff and Polly.

A girl and an older woman tapped at the door.

"Hi, Mrs. Ketchum," Kristen said. "Come on in. You're right on time." She escorted the two to the conference room, sending a sideways glance at Jeff as she passed him.

"It seems that I'd best get to work," he said with a chuckle. "A rock star's work is never done." Jeff tapped Kristen as he passed her. "You'll let Rachel know they're here?"

"On it, Boss."

"Polly, do you have a minute?" Stephanie asked, pointing at her office.

Polly nodded and followed her, sliding into a chair in front of the desk while Stephanie closed the door.

"This feels strange," Stephanie said. "Even after all these months, it's weird to have you on that side of the desk."

"This is your office now," Polly said as she looked around. Soft landscapes had been hung on the walls and the shelving that Henry built for Polly's Star Wars collection was filled with plants, pictures of Stephanie and Kayla, books on management and marketing, and dainty tea cups. Stephanie had found many of those at thrift stores and discovered that she couldn't resist them, so started a collection. The office was soft, comfortable and quite feminine.

"It still feels weird."

"What did you want to talk to me about?"

Stephanie took a breath, closed her eyes and then looked up. "I'm worried about Kayla."

Polly nodded. "Because of Friday night?"

"That's just part of it." Stephanie put a hand up. "I'm not blaming Rebecca. Kayla and Andrew were just as much a part of that as she was, but I don't know how to help Kayla be strong enough to stand up for what's right. She's so easily swayed by people. Especially Rebecca. I love that girl so much, but does she understand how much power she holds over Kayla?"

"They're just being kids," Polly said. "I doubt that Rebecca has any idea. Trust me, I understand what you're worried about. Rebecca and I talk about this more than you think. She's a natural leader and it's difficult teaching her to take responsibility for herself and her friends. But I don't know where she'd be without Kayla. She counts on that solid foundation of friendship."

"I just don't want Kayla to be a pitiful puppy, following

Rebecca around with her tongue hanging out. I don't know what else to say to her. When I try to talk about it, she tells me that I don't know what it's like to finally have a best friend." Stephanie's eyes filled. "The thing is, I finally do know that now. Sky and I talk all the time, even if mostly just online or video chat. He knows everything about me. It's nice to trust someone."

Polly leaned forward and reached across the desk to take Stephanie's hand. "I'm happy for you. He's a good guy."

"I have Jeff. He's my best friend, too, I guess. Rachel and I are getting closer too. She's kind of wild and fun."

"But Kayla hasn't ever had a best friend before?"

Stephanie shook her head. "Daddy ..." she stopped herself. "He wouldn't let us have friends." She shuddered. "I don't want to think about it, but the answer is no. Kayla always just had me. She didn't even know Mom that well. Not the way I did."

"You're asking me if Rebecca is trustworthy enough to hold Kayla's heart, aren't you?"

"It sounds so awful." Stephanie nodded. "I guess I am. That thing Friday night really scared me. Kayla doesn't disobey like that and she certainly doesn't lie."

Polly sat back. "I shouldn't even say this out loud, but I'm kind of glad that she did something bad."

"What?" Stephanie frowned, then her forehead relaxed and she smiled. "I get it. Yeah. You're probably right. It means she's trying new things. I see."

"The things that drive me the craziest with Rebecca are going to be the things that serve her well when she gets out in the real world," Polly said. "She's basically a good kid, but she will try to get away with whatever she can. And to answer the question you don't want to ask, she's completely trustworthy when it comes to Kayla. She tried to take responsibility for the entire event so Kayla and Andrew wouldn't be in trouble. She knew what she'd done and knew that it wasn't fair to them." Polly shook her head. "It sounds like neither of those girls knew what friendship was like before they got to Bellingwood. Rebecca found Andrew and then Kayla. She's not really interested in being friends with other kids at school. She trusts who she trusts and has yet to learn to allow parts of herself to reach out to others."

"She's so good with all of your friends, though."

"That's because they don't want anything from her. They don't need her to listen to their stuff or help them. Rebecca keeps them all at a distance. I'm the bridge there, so she's safe with those people. Even with Beryl, whom she sees nearly every week, she confides very little."

"I didn't think about all of that," Stephanie said.

"And you shouldn't have to," Polly replied. "You have enough with Kayla. Is Rebecca going to make some horrible decisions that neither you or I would approve of?" She laughed. "I'd count on it. And those kids are going to get in trouble again. I think we're lucky they haven't done anything more stupid than this."

"You're really smart about this stuff."

"No I'm not. I just have a lot of time to think about things while I haul plaster across floors. Kayla is a sweetheart and I'm thankful she's in our lives."

"I didn't want you to think that I was going to take her away from Rebecca."

"That would kill both girls." Polly put her hand on Stephanie's desk. "You know there's every possibility they're going to fight and break up as friends a couple of times throughout the next years, don't you?"

"No," Stephanie said. "Why would they do that?"

"Because they're kids. We just can't panic. You and I will talk about things and we'll stay calm."

"I hate being calm," Stephanie interrupted. "You have no idea how hard it is for me to not flip out all the time." She sighed. "I guess that's one good thing I learned from my father. I never want to be like he was, so I force myself not to scream and throw tantrums." She opened her desk drawer and pulled out a raggedy balled-up piece of something. "This was a crocheted ball that I found a long time ago. It might have been a Christmas ornament or something. I found it in the neighbor's trash. I don't even know why I picked it up. But it fit in my hand and the next time he ..."

She stopped, her eyes crinkled into tears and she let out a breath Then she gagged as tears streaked her face.

Polly jumped out of her seat and rushed to Stephanie's side, rubbing the girl's back. She reached under the desk for the trash can. "It's okay, honey. You're okay. You're safe. I'm right here."

It took a few minutes, but Stephanie pulled herself back under control, taking deep, gulping breaths. She pushed her hair away from her face, bright red from the exertion.

"I'm okay," she said.

"Yes you are." Polly stood with her hand on Stephanie's back, waiting until she settled down.

"Wow," Stephanie said. "I thought I'd gotten over that. I never told anybody about that ball. It's just become such a habit for me to squeeze and work it around in my hand when I get upset. I always knew when I started it, but I just never said it out loud. I'm so sorry."

Polly hugged her and then went back to where she'd been sitting. "You're absolutely fine. No need to apologize. You are an amazing young woman and I'm proud of you."

"You aren't upset with me for asking about Rebecca?"

Polly smiled. "I keep telling Henry that the reason I don't take any of this personally is that I didn't raise Rebecca. That's someone else's deal, but the thing is, she's a great kid and when she screws up, we have to deal with it. When Kayla screws up, you'll deal with it. We're going to do our best by them. That's all we've got. If you had been unreasonable about those two spending time together, I might have worried, but that wasn't what you were asking. Right?"

"Not at all. I just worry about my sister."

"I hope she and Andrew learned about standing up to Rebecca when she wants to do something they didn't."

"Kayla told me that's why she had to clean on Saturday. It really sank in."

"Good. Maybe next time they'll either stop her or the reason they get in trouble is because they made deliberate choices to do what Rebecca recommends."

"I hope she doesn't do that."

"That's not true," Polly said with a smile. "You want her to be a little rebellious. Just so she isn't disrespectful or does something to hurt someone. A little backbone and a little trouble is good for them."

"You're right. I don't know if I like it, though."

Polly nodded. "Me either. Now, are you okay?"

"I'm fine. Sorry about that."

"I love you, sweetie." Polly stood. "I'll let you get back to work. Don't ever worry about talking to me about Kayla and Rebecca. We'll get them to adulthood if it kills us."

"It just might," Stephanie said. "Thanks again."

CHAPTER SEVEN

Fumbling with her phone to unlock the front door, Polly finally made it into her apartment. It was cold and lonely without anything in there. Every step she took echoed on empty walls. She stepped into the doorway between the living room and her original apartment. Thomas Zeller died where she was standing. Elise Meyers was kidnapped right in front of her in that apartment. Henry put down the floor while she traveled to Boston with Joey Delancy, certain that she would come home and it should be ready for her. She'd slept in that middle room across the way for several months while finishing her apartment. Then it became Rebecca's room. In just four short years, this upper floor of Sycamore House had seen so much life.

Polly ran her hand across the beautiful shelves Henry built for her. He was everywhere in her life. Everything that she had, from the very moment she'd started this project, he'd been part of. Incredible.

They needed one more weekend to finish cleaning the kitchen and dining room. It wouldn't take long. Polly wasn't prepared to discuss the future of this apartment. She didn't want anyone else to live here. Rebecca had been right about not moving the offices into the space. Just those few days of hoisting little Noah up and down the steps last summer had been difficult - she wouldn't subject anyone else to that.

Polly opened the door to the office she and Henry shared. It had been her old bedroom when she lived alone. The back stairs were a fluke discovery by Henry. They had been so useful. All of those trips up and down the steps with her dogs. The number of times she came home and found her animals waiting for her at the top of the steps. Luke had come to love this desk, lying on it every time either she or Henry worked here. He just wanted to be close to them.

Luke and Leia now had an entire house to explore and Polly never knew where they might end up. During the day they were often on their cat trees in the dining room. Sometimes, though, they snuggled into her bed, with one eye aimed toward the back window, just in case a squirrel managed to find them. They'd done their best to get into the second floor, following anyone who was working up there. Those two were better about finding their way back down than Wonder and her kittens.

Polly sat at the desk, turned the computer on and leaned back in the chair.

She loved change. Change was always exciting and yet terrifying at the same time. It nearly always meant that something better was on the way. But this transitional stuff was driving her nuts. First she'd left her office downstairs, thinking she didn't need it as much as Stephanie. This room wasn't her office. It was Henry's. She just used it. The things she loved were all in boxes. If she and Henry continued to share an office, her things might never come back out again. That was actually a little sad. He didn't want her Star Wars toys around, but she wasn't ready to give up that part of her life. Not yet. Really ... not ever.

When the computer finally warmed up, Polly slid the DVD in that Stephanie had made for her and watched the video of those two men in the back yard. She could not imagine what they were doing. Nothing made sense.

She dragged the file onto the computer desktop, then into a cloud drive so she could access it anywhere. The disk was going to Chief Wallers this afternoon. She opened the shared finances folder to check outstanding bills. Jeff had made notes on several with explanations as to what they were, others came with notes from Stephanie and Kristen. There were bills for the bakery that Sylvie hadn't approved yet and two that Polly was certain were for the catering business. They had only been entered, not checked yet, so she left them open.

A soft rap on the door at the bottom of the stairs preceded Rachel's voice. "Polly? Are you busy?"

"Come on up," Polly said. She was finished with this task anyway, so she closed the file. That action alone would alert Kristen that she'd worked on it. Not that the girl wasn't in the middle of things all the time. She'd worked out well in the office. Jeff was happy, Stephanie was happy; that was what mattered.

Rachel walked in.

"What's up?"

"Jeff said I should talk to you first," Rachel said.

"Talk to me about what?" Polly pointed at the chair and Rachel dropped into it.

"We've been discussing a catering van. I do an awful lot off-site and I don't mind using my car, but it would be convenient if I had a van. Sometimes I have to make two trips because it won't all fit."

Polly smiled. "It's a great idea. Do you have the money?" She'd just been in the program, but hadn't checked balances. They kept the different businesses separate now that each was growing on its own.

"Things might be a little tight for a couple of months. I can wait. It was just a thought. No big deal."

"No, no, no," Polly said. "I'm not saying you can't do it. I just wondered if you had any idea whether the business could do this as a cash transaction. What does Jeff say?"

"He said that we could borrow from the general account if things got too tight after the purchase."

"Have you found what you want?"

Rachel smiled as she opened her phone. She swiped a few times and put a picture of a van in front of Polly. "I found it a couple of months ago. There's a perfect van in Ames and it's still available. I was thinking we could also design a wrap for it that would tell everyone it was Sycamore House Catering."

"That's a great idea. Who would you get to design it?"

"I have a friend at Iowa State. She works for a design company there. This is kinda what they do."

"Through the university?"

Rachel nodded.

Polly stood up. "Let's talk to Jeff together. If the two of you think now is the right time to do all of this and we can afford it, then I'm in full agreement."

"Really?"

"Look at me," Polly said with a laugh as she waved her hand around the room. "I bought an old school. I bought an old hotel. I bought an old house. I built a barn. If I worried about buying a van, you need to just commit me today. Let's talk to Jeff."

She grabbed up her phone and followed Rachel down the back steps, through the kitchen and across to the offices.

"You're back," Kristen said. "I got your approvals on the checks. I'll print those in a few minutes and send them out."

"Thanks," Polly replied. "Is Jeff available?"

"I'm always available for you, sweet stuff."

"Oh," Polly said. "I thought you might be in your meeting."

Jeff came to his door. "No comment on my term of endearment for you?"

Polly shook her head. "I don't even know what to say. Can Rachel and I steal a few minutes?"

"Will you give them back?"

"Nope." Polly pushed past him into his office.

He stepped back for Rachel and joined them at his table. "Is this about the van?"

"Polly says it's okay."

"Of course she does. She knows what's right."

"And you're totally on board?" Polly asked.

"Rachel found a good deal. If you want Henry to look at it and make sure that it's not a lemon, I'm fine with that. But there's no reason not to step it up and look a little more professional when she takes catering jobs."

"And the wrap?"

"The what?" Jeff asked.

"You know," Kristen said. "The design work on the outside of the van."

"Oh. The wrap," he replied. "Yeah. Isn't that cool?"

Polly chuckled. "So the next thing we do is get you a little Mini Cooper and wrap it with the Sycamore House logo?"

"I'd drive that," he said. "But I'll bet you can't get Eliseo to drive a pickup truck all painted up."

"That would be awesome," Polly said. "Sycamore House with a barn and horses."

Jeff put his hand out. "You should probably stop right there. We can be happy with a catering van for now."

"Let me know what you need me to do, then," Polly said. She put her hand on Rachel's shoulder. "It looks like you're about to step up in the world. But let's make sure it says Sycamore House Catering and Bakery. That way Sylvie can use it if she needs it for deliveries, too."

Jeff nodded and they both looked at Rachel.

"Okay." Rachel looked at her hands and chewed her upper lip. "That sounds right."

"What's wrong?" Polly asked.

Rachel shook her head. "I was just being selfish. I wanted it to be here when I need it. But if Sylvie uses it too, the van will be busy and that's a good thing. Don't mind me. I wasn't thinking."

"You two can work this out, right?" Polly asked.

"Seriously. I was being stupid," Rachel replied. "It's a great idea." She put her hand on top of Polly's. "Don't worry. I'm sorry I said anything."

"When you double the business," Jeff interrupted, "you each can have a van. One of these days we'll have a whole fleet of Sycamore House vans running around the county. Okay?"

Rachel smiled. "Sounds good." She stood. "I'd better get back to work. Thanks."

She left and Polly turned to Jeff. "Is she okay?"

He nodded. "We might want to talk about sending her to school to get her degree, too. She wants so badly to be respected in this job. It's a big deal to her. She went out and did the research before talking to me. Rachel took ownership of the project and now she has to sacrifice some of that, but she'll be fine."

"I don't want to lose her."

"If we lose her over something like this, then she wasn't worth keeping. But that's not who Rachel is. Things will be fine."

~~~

Polly laughed when she walked out to the driveway and found her truck parked halfway up the drive, aimed toward the yard. At least she'd closed the door when she took off running. She climbed in, turned the truck back on for warmth and pulled her phone out, then dialed the police station.

"Bellingwood Police."

"Hi Mindy, this is Polly. Is Ken around today?"

"He's in town. I can find him. What do you have for us?"

"I chased a couple of guys off the Sycamore House property and we have video. I just want him to have this in hand. You know ... because things happen around me." Polly laughed as she said it.

"Oh Polly," Mindy said, echoing her laugh. "You do keep us entertained. Did you at least use a shovel or rake to threaten them?"

"I just asked if I could help and they ran for it."

"You are scary or so I've heard. Do you want to meet Ken here or at the coffee shop?"

This time Polly laughed out loud. "I have a choice? I'd really like to choose the coffee shop, then."

"He's probably there right now. I'll let him know to wait for you if you're on the way."

"I'm on the way," Polly said. "Thank you." She put her phone on the console beside her. Small town life was funny.

Since she was in such a strange position in the driveway, it took a few turns to get her truck aimed toward the highway, but she did and waited as cars went past. The sky was gray. Even though the forecast didn't threaten snow, it looked and felt like a dreary winter day.

Polly pulled into a parking space across the street from Sweet Beans. As she walked down the block, she grumbled about how it figured that on a day like today, she couldn't park in front of the coffee shop. As soon as she opened the door, the warmth of the room and the smell of coffee and baking, cast all grumbling and mumbling aside.

Ken Wallers stood up from where he'd been bending over talking to an elderly couple at a table. He caught her arm and walked to the counter with her. "Mindy tells me you had prowlers."

"I guess that's what you could call them," Polly said. She handed him the disk. "The video is on there."

"Aren't you glad you have the system?"

She glared at him. "Don't you start with me. I'm glad to be able to give this to you, but overall, I'm still not happy that we need to have those cameras. So there."

"This one's on me," Ken said to Skylar.

The young man looked at both Polly and Ken, confused. "Okay?"

Polly laughed. "You're a terrible man."

"He won't let me pay," Ken said. "And I know you never pay. But it's fun to watch him react."

"That really wasn't fair, sir," Sky said. "Your regular, Polly?"

"Yes sir, and one of those cream cheese brownie things." She was hungry and didn't know yet what was happening for lunch. Polly missed the days when her friends were footloose and fancy free, with time to meet her at the last minute. Since today was Tuesday, Lydia and Andy would be busy at church. Sal had a baby and a schedule that went with that. There was no way that

Joss could pack her little ones up in a hurry and Henry was wrapped up with the kitchen remodel today. She needed more friends.

Ken slipped several dollars into the tip jar and followed Polly to a table. "I saw one of your boys this morning. Noah. Right?"

"He said you were going to be in his classroom today," Polly replied. She took a sip of her coffee. Skylar even got the temperature perfect for her.

"How are they doing?"

She took a breath. "I think it's okay. They're very happy at home. I just worry about them at school. I'm thankful that your wife has Noah this year. Next year he'll have Mrs. Hastings. Both of those women are terrific so I know he's safe in the classroom. He's so quiet. He never complains, but all of this change hasn't been easy for him."

"Maude always tells me that the kids who succeed are those whose parents love them and are involved with them at school. You make it easy for her to do her job, even if the kids are troublemakers."

"Noah is a troublemaker?"

Ken laughed. "Oh no. I didn't mean that. I was speaking in general terms. She hasn't said much about him. There are a few in the classroom that I tend to hear about on a regular basis, but so far, not Noah. He seems like a good boy. Listened attentively while I read to them and was polite to me and to Maude."

"They've had such varying associations with law enforcement," Polly said. "He's young and wants desperately to trust you, but the way he grew up - no one trusted the police."

"That's why I do this," Ken said with a nod. "If I could put all of my crew in that elementary school on a regular basis, just getting to know the children and letting the kids get to know them, I would." He smiled. "You have no idea what it means to me to have one of Maude's children come up to me on the street just to shake my hand. I don't want them to be afraid of us."

Polly reached out and put her hand on top of his. "You are an amazing man, Ken Wallers. Bellingwood is lucky to have you."

He took his hand back and tapped the DVD. "Tell me what else you know about these men."

"The video is in black and white so you can't see that their truck is blue, but other than that, I don't know anything more. No one in the office knows why they were there. That's all I have."

"I'll see what we can find out. Let you know?"

"Thanks." Polly's phone buzzed and she looked at it. "That's Jessie at Henry's shop. She's telling me that Len is back. We found something at the Bell House last night."

"Yeah? What's that?"

"Henry pulled the mantle and apron off an upstairs fireplace. When they put it down on the floor, we found two heavy metal boxes hiding inside. I took them to the shop to see if they could figure out how to open them."

Ken shook his head. "We haven't done anything about that symbol you discovered. I feel bad. Do you suppose it's all connected?"

"I don't know," Polly said with a shrug. "I have to think it is. Would there really be that many different mysteries in that old house?"

"This is *your* house," Ken said with a smirk. "There could be this many and more. I'm just glad you found metal boxes rather than a body when you pulled that mantle off the wall."

She shuddered. "Don't even say that. I found one old body on that land. That's enough. Though ..." Polly's eyes twinkled. "We haven't broken up the hearth yet. Maybe we'll find bones."

"You call Aaron, then. I don't want to know about it. Why don't you give me a call when you know what is in those boxes? If it feels like it might be part of the mystery we've already got in hand, then we'll call a meeting and push forward. No letting it go this time."

"Let me tell Jessie I'll be there after a while. I want to enjoy my coffee for a few minutes first."

"I'm heading out. Let me know what you find."

"I will. Thanks, Ken."

CHAPTER EIGHT

Turning as she heard someone say her name, Polly put her brownie back on the plate as Sandy Davis approached. The woman's face was drawn and she looked as if she could break into tears at any moment.

"Hi Sandy. Sit down."

"I shouldn't. I just stopped in to get some coffee. I needed a break."

"What's going on?" Polly pointed at the chair that Ken Wallers had vacated.

Sandy sat. "I left Will with JoAnne. He doesn't need to see me fall apart."

"Honey, what's going on. Is everything okay with Benji?" Polly had met Sandy Davis last year. An architect, Sandy helped the women at the quilt shop design their new space. She'd taken freelance work when their baby had arrived. Her husband, Benji, was a lawyer and had known Henry in high school.

"Benji's fine." Tears streamed down her face.

Polly took Sandy's elbow, helped her stand and led her to one of the tall-backed booths. Sandy sat down and scooted across, while Polly sat beside her. "Now tell me what's happening. Is it Will?"

Sandy nodded. "He's got cancer. My little boy has cancer, Polly. What did I do wrong?"

Polly knew better than to say anything. She slipped her arm around Sandy's shoulder and the woman fell into Polly, doing her best not to sob and create a scene.

"He's not even two and he's going to spend his childhood in the hospital. All of his little boy years are gone. Why him?"

Sandy cried and cried. Skylar came over to the table and put a glass of water and a stack of napkins down in front of Polly. She smiled at him and held on to Sandy.

"This isn't fair, Polly."

"I know." Polly handed her a napkin. "It isn't fair at all. Where's Benji?"

"He went back to work. JoAnne and I brought Will home. She's putting him down for a nap and told me to just go somewhere to cry if I needed to. I can't believe you're here. I needed to talk to someone. Will doesn't know yet what's going on. He's been sick. All of those tests." She looked at Polly again and her eyes filled to overflowing. "They want us to bring him back tomorrow to start treatment. It's going to be really aggressive. He's going to get so much sicker. Oh Polly, what if I lose him?"

Polly brushed Sandy's hair back from her face. "Your doctors are going to do their very best for Will. I'm so sorry that you have to go through this."

"It's not me. My precious little boy has to go through this."

"It's you, too, Sandy. You're going to lose sleep and your entire life is about to be disrupted. It's okay to feel a little sorry for yourself. This is scary. How did Benji handle it?"

"He's so freaked out. I told him to go to work. At least he can find some distraction there today and he has to close things out so he can take time off. He offered to come home with us, but it's okay."

"You and he are going to have to really pull together, you know," Polly said. "You can't do this alone and neither can he."

"I don't want to do this at all," Sandy said. "I want someone to pinch me and tell me that it's just a horrible nightmare."

"I wish I could."

"We woke up this morning and the world was normal," Sandy said. "I barely remember what that feels like now. Everything is upside down. I don't know how I'm going to finish the jobs I have going. I can't think about anything. I can't think."

"There is nothing that demands you think today. You can think in a couple of days and then you've got friends who will step in and help you manage your life."

Sandy slumped. "I wouldn't have any if I hadn't met you last year. You introduced me to everyone. How am I going to tell Cooper and Sophie? Will loves playing with them."

"Joss will tell her children," Polly said. "That's not on you. We'll get you through this, Sandy."

Sandy's phone buzzed. She looked at it and smiled. "That's Tab."

"Tab Hudson?"

"We're supposed to have lunch with her, Sal and Alexander tomorrow. I need to cancel it. I don't know what to say."

"Do you want me to tell them?"

"I'll just cry. I can't ask you to do that, though."

"Sure you can. Tab and Sal are my friends, too. I talk to them all the time."

Sandy handed her phone to Polly, who swiped the call open. "Tab? This is Polly."

"Hello?" Tab sounded confused.

"I'm sitting with Sandy at Sweet Beans. She's not going to be able to have lunch with you tomorrow. They have to take Will back to the hospital. He has cancer."

Just the word was enough to bring more tears from Sandy's eyes. Polly scooted closer.

"Oh no," Tab said. "What can I do?"

"Maybe give her some time to process this and then call her back?"

Sandy nodded.

"Maybe Thursday after they've figured out what's going on at the hospital," Polly said.

Sandy nodded vigorously.

"Yeah. She says that's good," Polly went on.

"Okay. Tell her I'm sorry and I'm praying for her," Tab said. "We'll be there for her. Tell her that, too."

"Got it. Thanks." Polly put the phone back down on the table. "She says she'll be there for you. You have friends, Sandy."

"I don't know what to say."

"I'll call Sal later. Don't worry. Tomorrow is handled."

"I'd totally forgotten about lunch until right now."

"Nothing else is important today. Just you and your family."

"I'm sorry I made such a mess on you." Sandy brushed at Polly's shoulder. The shirt had definitely taken a beating.

Polly pushed the glass of water toward Sandy. She wasn't sure why water was the go-to remedy for tears, but it always worked. "Don't worry about my shirt. It'll wash. What will you do now?"

"I've cried. I've thrown a tantrum and I should probably go home and relieve JoAnne. Will is as important to her as he is to us. This broke her heart. But I thought I was going to choke if I just sat there watching him. She and I don't talk very much about personal things. I should let her go home. Then I'll call Benji and tell him I'm pulling it together. He knows that I have to think about all of the worst things in the world first. Then I start trying to figure out what the next moves will be."

She shook her head. "The last big crisis was when we found I was pregnant with Will. Damn, I threw a fit over that. I didn't want to be pregnant. I didn't have time for a kid. What a child I was. I'd love to go back and change all of those feelings now."

"You're fine, Sandy," Polly said. "In fact, you're doing better than a lot of people would under these circumstances. If you want to call me later, go ahead. You can do that any time you need to."

"Thanks. I probably won't, but thanks." Sandy looked toward the door. "I should go."

Polly backed out of the seat. "Get yourself a coffee and maybe something sweet. Both for you and for JoAnne. I'll text you tomorrow. If you want to talk, you can call. If you ignore me because you have so many things going on, I won't be offended. Okay?"

Sandy stepped out of the booth and reached up to pull Polly into a hug. The two women held each other while Sandy breathed deeply several times. "I'm so glad you were here today. Thank you."

"Take care of yourself today and love on your little boy."

Sandy nodded and walked up to the counter while Polly headed for the bakery. She needed to talk to Sylvie.

~~~

Marta was alone in the bakery. Sylvie was running errands. Polly wasn't ready to do anything but process on Sandy's news, so she waved goodbye to Skylar. The brisk walk in freezing temperatures to her truck didn't do anything for her disposition. What Sandy Davis was going through right now was one of the worst things a young mother could face. Polly didn't know how she'd get through something like that. What she really wanted to do was drive over to Sandy's house, scoop both her and Will into her arms and hold them until this was all over. As fast as that, tears flowed down her cheeks. She was in the process of brushing them away when her phone lit up with a call from Sal.

"Hey," she said after swiping the call open.

"Tab just called me," Sal said. She sounded as dejected as Polly felt. "I'm glad you were there for Sandy."

"Me too. Are you okay?"

"I'm a little freaked out. Alexander is taking a nap and now I just want to hold him. Oh, please let nothing happen to him."

"I know," Polly said. "It's impossible not to think of this coming into your own family."

"What are you doing?"

Polly huffed a small laugh. "Sitting in my truck down the street from Pizzazz, crying my eyes out."

"Come over."

"Are you sure?"

"Yeah. I need a hug and it sounds like you do, too."

"What are you doing for lunch?"

Sal laughed. "Probably eating Cheerios. I don't feel like making anything."

"Do you want anything from the diner or a sandwich from Sweet Beans?"

"Sweet Beans? Would that come with coffee?"

"It could."

"I wouldn't hate turkey on a croissant. Skylar knows what I like."

"Let me go back in and pick up food and coffee for us. Then I'll be over."

"Thank you. I just need a hug and you can get back to your day."

"I don't even know what I was going to do with my day at this point," Polly said. "Everything went flying out of my head when Sandy used the word cancer."

"What a horrible word that is."

"Scariest one I know. Okay, let me hang up and I'll be over in a few."

"I love you, Polly."

Those were the only words that seemed to mean anything right now. "I love you, too."

~~~

By the time Polly arrived at Sal's front door, she was much better. A fun conversation with Skylar, who didn't ask a thing about Sandy, a few more drinks of coffee and she felt like she could handle anything - even a disheartened friend.

If Sal's dachshunds were inside and barking, that meant that Alexander was up and awake. He was such a little cutie. Just starting to crawl, he had his eyes on everything. The dachshunds wanted to play with the new moving target and he wanted to play with them, too. His little fingers reached for their ears and tails, anything he could get his hands on. They'd learned to climb to the back of the sofa and chairs to avoid him, because of course Sal had steps everywhere for her favorite pups.

The inside front door was standing open by the time Polly got there. She opened the storm door to more barking. "Hello?"

"Come on in," Sal called out. "We're in the kitchen."

Polly pulled the storm door closed as both dogs ran to greet her. Felix jumped up to look out, imitated by Oscar not a moment later.

"Come on, boys. Let me shut the door." She put one of the cups on the table and brushed them back.

Felix wasn't going to be denied. He stood back up to look out the window and barked at something Polly couldn't see. Oscar joined him and soon the two were raising quite a cacophony of sound.

"Sal?" Polly called out. "Help?"

"Felix!" came Sal's voice. "Oscar. Come."

Their tails wagging, the two dogs ran to the kitchen and Polly shut the door, laughing. How could you be in a bad mood with that much fun and love in the house?

When she got to the kitchen, Alexander reached out for her from the high chair. His hands were covered in something gloopy.

"Not yet, sweetie," Sal said. "You eat, I'll clean you, and then you can sit in Polly's lap."

He pushed the bowl back and reached for Polly again.

"Are you really finished?" Sal asked. "Try some more bananas." She turned to Polly. "I thought we'd be finished by the time you got here."

"Baby food bananas?" Polly asked.

"Yeah."

"Those were always my favorite."

"You remember from being a baby?"

Polly laughed. "No. Why do I know about that? I didn't have babies in my life." She pursed her lips. "It must have been one of my friends with their baby sister. But I remember loving mashed banana baby food."

"There are more jars in the cupboard if you want one," Sal gestured with her head toward the cupboard beside the refrigerator.

"Yeah. I'm good," Polly said. She watched Sal scrape food from Alexander's cheek and put the spoon back toward his mouth. "That has always been the weirdest thing I've ever watched."

"What?"

"Scraping his face clean and feeding it to him. I get it. But it's just weird."

Sal laughed and put the spoon back in the dish when Alexander wouldn't open his mouth for another bite. "Let me tell you. There are a lot of things I've learned to do because of a baby in the house. This doesn't even come close to the weirdest." She pulled the bowl back when he thrust his little hand at it again. "Are you finished yet?" She scooped more onto the spoon and aimed for his mouth. He turned his head. "I guess so. Let's clean you up so you don't mess Polly's shirt."

Polly patted her shoulder. "It's been sobbed on already. I can take a little baby mussing."

"But I can't take it," Sal said. Within moments she had his arms and face wiped clean and Alexander was on the floor.

He crawled to Polly who bent down to pick him up while Sal cleaned up the rest of his lunch.

"I can hold him while you eat," Polly said.

"We'll go out to the living room so he can play." Sal touched her son's head. "Daddy brought you a new toy. Will you show it to Polly?"

The little boy heaved himself away from Polly and she caught him before he fell, her heart in her throat. "What in the heck?"

"Oh. Sorry. My fault," Sal said. "He's a little independent and when he wants to go, he wants to go."

Polly put Alexander on the floor, every nerve ending in her body on alert. "I need to breathe. That scared the crap out of me."

Sal laughed. "Yeah. It does me too. Every time. We're learning not to talk to him about doing anything unless he's already down, because of this. Are you going to be okay?"

"A few more deep breaths and I should be good to go."

Sal picked up the bag of sandwiches from Sweet Beans and the coffee Polly had put in front of her. They passed Alexander who was making his way as fast as he could to the blanket in the middle of the living room floor.

"He wants to walk so badly," Sal said. "He doesn't quite have the whole standing up thing going on yet, but as soon as he does, everything in the house will need to be put on the top shelf."

Alexander had stopped on his blanket to pick up an immense stuffed brown horse. He held it out to Polly.

"What am I supposed to do?" she asked. "Take it?"

"Sure," Sal replied. "See what he does. I told him to show it to you."

Polly sat down on the floor beside the blanket and put her hand out. She was close enough that Alexander could give the horse to her and he did just that. She snuggled it to her face. "This is a very pretty horse. Did Daddy give it to you?"

Alexander beamed and made a few noises as he bounced up and down.

"One of these days real words will come out of that mouth," Sal said. "Mark keeps working on Daddy."

"Da," Alexander said.

Polly looked from him to Sal. "Did I just hear that?"

Sal had a bemused look on her face. "I don't know if it was just a syllable or if he's trying to participate." She bent over. "Did you say 'Daddy'?"

"Da." He bounced up and down again and grabbed at the horse.

"Say it again," Sal said. "Daddy."

"Da."

This time Polly handed him the horse and he held it out to Sal. "Da."

"Well, I'll be," Sal said. "Mark is going to be disappointed that you got to hear it before he did."

"That really just happened?" Polly asked. "Right now? While I was here?"

"I think so." Sal brushed her hand across Alexander's head. "Is the horse from Daddy?"

He bounced a few more times on his bottom and said, "Da."

"You're my bright boy," she said and picked him up to her lap. "Do you mind?" Sal handed Polly her phone. "Take a video. I want to send it to Mark." She bounced Alexander a couple of times. "Please be a good boy and do it again. Please."

Polly was thankful that Sal used the same phone she did and quickly set it up to record. Sal nodded and Polly tapped the button.

"Who gave you the horse?" Sal asked. "Daddy?"

Alexander burbled over the stuffed animal and smiled at his mother.

"Is the horse from Daddy?"

He burbled again, speaking nonsense.

Sal gave Polly a piteous look. "Please Alexander. Say 'Daddy.' Just one more time. Is that from Daddy?"

He shook the horse and said "Da" as clear as could be.

Sal turned to the camera. "He said it a bunch of times with Polly here, Mark. I think he's got it. Right, Polly?"

Polly reoriented the camera so she was in the frame. "He really did. I promise. Your boy knows your name."

"That's good," Sal said and Polly tapped the button to end the recording.

She handed the phone to Sal, who put her son back on the floor.

"He's just not going to believe it." Sal swiped the video to send it to her husband. "He'll be all over this when he gets home tonight."

"You can hardly blame him. That's just the coolest thing," Polly said.

Sal opened the bag from Sweet Beans. "You didn't."

"The brownies? I ate one while I was there. Those are for you."

CHAPTER NINE

Her day had been completely turned upside down. Polly started out this morning trying to get those two metal boxes open. The kids would be home from school in less than a half hour and she wasn't sure whether to head to the shop and ask them to open the boxes or just go home. There was no plan in the works for dinner tonight. She certainly hadn't intended to be out of the house all day.

She took her phone out and called Henry.

"Hey there, beautiful wife of mine."

"Hey there, yourself."

"Did you get over to the shop?"

"Uh. No. It's been a weird day."

"Good weird or bad weird?"

"A little bit of both. Where are you?"

"Where do you want me to be? I can be in bed in just a few seconds if that's what you want."

"Henry!" Polly scolded.

"What? You know we men think about it all the time."

"Being in bed? Do you need a nap?"

He laughed. "Where do you need me to be?"

"Nowhere really. I was just wondering if I should go over to the shop and deal with those boxes now. The kids will be home soon and I haven't given a single thought to dinner tonight."

"I'm north of town at the Winters'. I can drive somewhere and pick dinner up if you want."

"No. I don't want any more takeout. Are the counters done?"

"All done. Len is working on the rest of the cabinet doors this week. You should be able to fill them up this weekend."

"That's just crazy," she said. "Now we need the appliances."

"I told you it would come together."

She laughed. "You said no such thing. You just kept working."

"Well, you knew it would. That's the same thing, isn't it?"

"I love you."

"Do you need me to do something? If you want me to, I can go open the boxes at the shop when I'm done for the day."

"No!" she said, much too loudly, startling even herself.

"Why not?"

"Because I want to be there when they're opened. My curiosity is getting a little out of control."

"I don't know how to help you now."

Polly chuckled. "I'm confused myself. Maybe I just needed to hear your sweet voice."

"Oh my dawling," he purred. "You are mah heart and my so-uhl."

"That's exactly what I was hoping for," she said. "Don't worry about anything. Just come home when you do. I'll go over to the shop and bug Len, then text Rebecca to make sure everyone is working on their homework. A quick trip to the grocery store and I'll come up with something clever for dinner. It might be spaghetti, though."

"I'm always good with spaghetti. I love you, you know."

"I do know." Polly smiled as she hung up and backed out of Sal's driveway. She wound through the back streets of Bellingwood until she ended up at Henry's shop.

No one heard her walk in. Doug Shaffer was working at a

sander and Ben was pushing boards through what Henry had called a jointer. The sound was deafening with the machines and their dust collectors on. She slipped to the side of the shop and headed for Jessie's office. Len was nowhere to be seen and he was who she wanted to open the boxes.

Polly rapped on the door and Jessie looked up from her computer, surprised, and then with a grin. She jumped up to open the door and closed it right behind Polly, shutting out the sound of the shop.

"I didn't realize it was so loud out there," Polly said.

Jessie nodded. "When all of them are working, it gets ridiculous. Bill won't let anyone work in here without hearing protection though. He's a real stickler about it. When they built this office for me, he put in a lot of insulation. The only sound that really gets in is through the door and it's not bad. Are you here so we can open the boxes?"

"I'm sorry it took me so long to get back. The day just went crazy."

"I can ask Ben or Doug to do it. Len's gone for the day. He and Andy have something in Des Moines with one of her grandkids."

"Henry told me to have Len do it."

"That's what Len said, too. He didn't know if the other guys had used the grinder before."

"Will he be back tomorrow morning?"

"Yeah. It's not an overnight or anything. Are you sure you can wait that long?"

Polly laughed. "I suppose. It's not like the contents will change overnight. They hid in that mantle for a hundred years, they can wait another day." She dropped into a chair. "Now I have to figure out what to do for dinner. I told Henry it was going to be spaghetti."

"Molly loves spaghetti. It's just 'sketti' to her, though."

"You two should come to dinner. I always make enough to feed an army. The new counters are in the kitchen and you can ooh and aah over them."

"Really?"

"Why not? Noah and Elijah would love to play with Molly. In fact, so would Heath and Hayden. They set up race car tracks in the foyer. Those things are all over the place. On top of boxes and furniture. Everything."

"I haven't seen it like that," Jessie said.

"Between my dad's house, Rebecca's mother's stuff, things from Hayden's apartment and everything from Sycamore House, that place is stacked. I don't know if I'll ever get through it. I guess I have to have it cleared out by next Christmas or the party will be a bit of a problem." Polly gulped. "Damn."

"What?"

"I just now realized that Heath is graduating in May. I have to have the place ready for that." She gripped her forehead with her right hand. "I don't know how I'll get everything cleared out in time."

"You can have the party in the back yard," Jessie said.

"Not if it rains. I think I just gave myself a stroke."

"Why don't you use the auditorium at Sycamore House?"

"Yeah. I could do that, but it gets snapped up by parents who actually remember that their kids are graduating. I'm a horrible mom."

"I don't think so."

"This is embarrassing. I'm glad I figured it out now rather than April. When did my life become this insane mess?"

Jessie chuckled.

"You're laughing at me. Stop laughing at me."

"I can't help it. You aren't a mess. You aren't insane. You have plenty of time before May and nobody else but us has to know that you didn't think about this until now."

"Right. You're right." Polly stood up and put her hand on the door handle. Then she stopped. "But really. Come over and eat with us. We'd love to have you."

"About six?"

"That's perfect. See you later." Polly left the shop and got in her truck. There was so much planning ahead for Heath's graduation and she hadn't given it a single thought. What kind of a mother was she? Rebecca would be good help for this. They'd sit down tonight and sketch out plans. At least they could put ideas on paper.

Polly was at the elementary school when she realized that she'd driven past the grocery store. She had nothing at home to make dinner. She didn't even think there was any pasta in the pantry. She turned the corner and drove around until she finally ended up where she needed to be. Her mind was whirling with all that had happened today. Then it hit her, she'd completely pushed the contents of those metal boxes out of her head. Who had time for a damned mystery anyway?

~~~

"How are classes going?" Henry asked Jessie as he picked up her plate.

"It's okay," she replied. "I miss having Marie around to talk to. She's always practical when I'm in the middle of an idea that's really big. She's the one who taught me how to break those down into pieces and then put them back together. And statistics? That class makes my head spin. I wish I'd taken it while she was here."

"But she'll be back before you're finished with the class, right?" Polly asked.

"Thank goodness."

The decibel level in the foyer grew as the little kids squealed and screamed.

"I'm sorry she's so loud," Jessie said. "She's not usually like that."

Polly laughed. "She's in a good place here. You can hear that the boys are having fun too."

Rebecca crashed through the door holding Noah's hand. "He fell and hurt his arm. It's bleeding."

"What did he fall on?" Polly asked. She stood and then stopped in place. At Sycamore House, she had first-aid items spread all over, but she had no idea where things were right now.

"Come here, buddy." Henry picked Noah up and plopped him

on the counter top next to the brand new sink. "Let's see what's going on."

Noah's eyes were filled with tears, but he wasn't crying. That was a good sign.

"He ran into a dresser and bounced off it into a box," Rebecca said. "Nothing was sticking out of the box, so he must have caught the corner."

"Was this the arm you broke last summer?" Henry asked, knowing full well Noah had broken a leg.

Noah shook his head, his lower lip trembling. "Did I break something else?"

Henry grinned at Polly, telling her that everything was fine. "Let's see." He tapped Noah's elbow. "Does that hurt?"

The pouty little face turned to the right and left, just once.

Henry tapped Noah's wrist. "How about that? Does that hurt?"

Noah shook his head again, his lip still wavering, ready to cry.

"Does anything hurt except where you scraped it?" Henry asked. "Stretch out your arm for me."

Noah did.

"Now wiggle your fingers."

When Noah wiggled his fingers, Henry tickled the boy's palm. Noah giggled.

"We'll clean this up and put a bandage on the scrape and you'll be good as new. Nothing to worry about." He looked at Polly. "Bandages are in the cabinet in our bathroom."

"You're such a good husband," she said with a laugh. "I'll be right back."

Polly took the long way and walked through the foyer.

Heath was on the floor with Molly while Elijah held two cars in his hands at the top of a long slope. "Are you ready, Molly?" Elijah asked.

She squealed and clapped her hands. "Go!"

He released the cars and she ran to follow them along the tracks.

"Wearing 'em out?" Polly asked Heath.

"I don't think we can. Noah okay?"

"He's fine. I just need a bandage."

"I don't know how he did it, but one minute he was running and the next he was on the ground."

"Sometimes he doesn't pay attention where he's going," Elijah said, accepting the cars from Molly. "He watches everything else. Maybe he shouldn't play baseball."

Polly laughed. "Where did that come from?"

"I like baseball, but Noah might hurt himself. The ball comes right at him and he doesn't see it."

"He doesn't see it?"

Elijah pointed at his eyes. "Noah's eyes aren't so good."

"What?"

"I told him that he should tell you. He's going to be mad at me. I wasn't supposed to say. You can't play baseball if you have to wear glasses."

"That's not true. Does Noah want to play baseball?"

Elijah shrugged. "Not as much as me."

Noah never complained about anything, making it difficult for Polly to grasp what his needs and wants were. She couldn't convince him that they were there to help him and he didn't need to hide things that bothered him. Thank goodness for Elijah, who was just so upfront with her.

Polly walked past Elijah, snuggled his shoulders and went on through to the door leading to the hallway in front of their bedroom.

Hayden had begged off playtime with the kids. He had a heavy class load this semester. Once the kids were all asleep, she often found him in the family room wrapped in blankets, with books spread everywhere. This was another reason she pushed so hard to get the rooms finished upstairs. If she could get Rebecca, Noah and Elijah into rooms away from the main floor, that would allow Heath and Hayden privacy and freedom of their own.

The bathroom had doors on either side - one to her bedroom and the other to Hayden and Heath's room. When she went in to look for the bandages, the sound of keys clacking told Polly that Hayden was madly writing.

"Is that you, Polly?" he asked.

She stepped through the open door. "Yeah. Getting bandages. Noah fell and hurt himself. How are you doing?"

He stretched and yawned. "I'm good. Sorry I'm not social tonight with Jessie here."

"She's not here for you. She's here just to enjoy a night with friends and to give Molly a chance to run and play. You're fine."

"Thanks. You didn't say anything about those metal boxes at dinner tonight. What's up with them?"

"They aren't open yet. I'm going over tomorrow morning when Len is back in the shop. I'll let you know when I do." She turned to head back into the bathroom.

"Hey, Polly?"

"Yes, Hayden."

"Can I bring Tess to dinner sometime?"

Polly spun back around. "Your girl?"

"Yeah. I don't want to make a big deal about it."

"It's taken you long enough," she said. "How long have you been dating?"

"Not very. But we've known each other for a while. It was just never the right time."

"And now it is?"

He shrugged. "It's good."

Polly sat on the bed. "How good? Are you in love with her?"

Hayden had never blushed like that before. "I think about her all the time. She's wicked smart and makes me laugh."

"Where's she from? Have you met her parents? Is she in school? Come on, boy. I have questions. I want answers."

"I met her in school. She's only a junior. In political science."

Polly looked at him in horror.

Hayden laughed. "I know. But what better time than this to be studying that? The world is all over the place right now. She wants to go to law school after she graduates."

"A poli-sci lawyer? Hayden, you are a crazy man."

He nodded.

"You find out when she can come to dinner and we'll be on our best behavior. I'd love to meet her." Polly pushed at his shoulder. "I can't believe I didn't know how serious this was. When do you have time?"

"It's mostly been lunch and coffee. Sometimes we video chat late at night, just to catch up."

"I can't wait to meet her." Polly stood up and shook her head. "A poli-sci major. Is she considering a political career?"

"I don't think so. But who knows. Maybe. It's a long time before she gets to that."

Polly looked into the bathroom and laughed at seeing Rebecca standing there.

"What?"

Rebecca sighed, then said, "We're waiting for bandages. Did you forget about Noah?"

"I didn't forget him. I just got distracted. And speaking of distractions, Missy, you and I need to have a chat."

Rebecca wrinkled her forehead. "What did I do now?"

"There," Polly said. "That'll teach you to give me trouble. No. I need your help with something. We'll talk after Jessie goes home."

"She says she should leave now," Rebecca said. "Molly needs a bath and Jessie needs to study." She peeked into Hayden's room. "Is that what you're doing or are you chatting with your girlfriend?"

"What girlfriend?" Polly asked, grinning at Hayden.

Rebecca smiled. "The one he pines for when he thinks we're not looking. The one he talks to late at night in the family room."

"You can hear me?" Hayden asked.

"I can't hear you, hear you. Just your voice," Rebecca said. "It has to be a girl. Who else would it be?"

Polly pushed Rebecca back into the bathroom. "Go back to your studying. I'll deal with her," she said to Hayden and shut the door. Opening the cupboard, she found the bandages on the first try and handed the box to Rebecca. "Take that to Henry. I'll be right behind you."

When Rebecca was gone, Polly leaned on the counter and peered into the mirror. "Time is moving too quickly," she whispered to herself. "I'm not ready for Hayden to fall in love. He's going to leave us and I love having him here. Then it will be Heath. And then Jason is going to graduate and move on. How do I make this slow down?"

"You enjoy every moment for what it is."

Polly jumped at the sound of Henry's voice. "How long have you been standing there?"

"I came to see what was taking you and then Rebecca so long. My lord, woman, all I wanted was a few bandages. It shouldn't take an epoch and an eon to get them. Then when I get here, I find you eulogizing your life. What's going on?"

She took his hand and whispered again, "Hayden has a girlfriend and he wants to bring her to dinner. This one sounds kind of special."

"Good for him."

"But now there's this new woman in his life and she'll be the one he talks to about everything."

"Uh huh. That's the way it's supposed to work."

Polly patted his chest. "You aren't helping."

"Sorry. Come on. Jessie wants to gather Molly up and go home. You need to be hostess-like."

"Do you know that Heath is graduating in May?" Polly asked.

Henry tugged her toward the hallway. "Yes. Is that freaking you out, too?"

"A little bit. But even more is that huge mess in the foyer. I have to figure out a big graduation party for him by May."

"There's my practical girl. You scared me with all that philosophizing I heard in there. You worrying about this stuff? That's what I'm used to."

She dropped his hand as they entered the kitchen. Jessie was on her knees, putting Molly's coat on the little girl.

"I'm sorry to eat and run," Jessie said. "But I have a paper to finish."

"We're so glad you came over," Polly said. She took Molly's hat off the shelf and knelt beside the girl to put it on her head. "Thank you for coming to dinner, Molly."

Molly waited patiently for her mother to pull the zipper up on her coat, then turned and threw her arms around Polly. Obiwan and Han stood behind Polly and the little girl rushed to Obiwan to give him a hug. Han bounced beside the older dog until Henry clicked his tongue and said "Sit."

"Bye, doggies," Molly said.

Her mother picked her up. "Thank you again. Will I see you in the morning, Polly?"

"I'll be there."

Henry opened the back door and walked outside with Jessie.

"I'm dying," Rebecca said. "What did you want to talk about?"

"Come over to the table."

"I really am in trouble, aren't I?"

"Not at all." Polly sat across from Rebecca and pushed a stack of dirty plates to the side. "We need to talk about Heath's graduation party."

Rebecca's eyes lit up. "That's fun. Where are we having it?"

"I think we should have it here, but the foyer is a mess and I'm worried about organizing things."

"And you came to me because I make such great parties?"

Polly chuckled. "Yes you do. I thought that between the two of us we could pull off something amazing. Are you up for this?"

"I'm so up for this. I'll start working on it tonight."

"Did you finish your homework?"

"Yeah. I'm all done."

"What are you two cooking up?" Henry asked.

"Heath's graduation party. Polly's going to let me help plan it."

He smiled. "She's a smart woman. I'm taking the dogs out. Anyone want to join me?" When he didn't get a response, he continued. "No one? Fine. I'll be back."

"He's such a good guy," Polly said. "I feel a little guilty, but dang, it's cold out there."

"So what are we going to do with everything in the foyer?"

Polly shook her head. "I've got nothing."

CHAPTER TEN

Frustrated, Polly closed her laptop and let her hand hang down beside her. Obiwan reached up to give it a quick lick and she rubbed his head. She'd already taken the kids to school and rather than getting coffee at Sweet Beans or heading to the shop to watch Len open those metal boxes, she was at the house, waiting for a load of lumber to arrive.

The lumber coming in this morning would be used to frame the bathrooms and Rebecca's room upstairs. As soon as Henry, Heath and Hayden finished that, Liam would plumb those two bathrooms and Jerry Allen would send Doug and Billy over to start wiring the upstairs. When things started moving, it didn't take long to finish the work, but wow, it seemed like forever. They'd been working on this house for a year and it would be at least another year before they'd feel completely settled.

The beeping sound of a truck backing up alerted Polly to the arrival of lumber. She'd already made sure the doors to the foyer were closed and all felines were accounted for. She felt ridiculous counting them off as she saw them, but it was the only safe way to ensure everyone was where they belonged. She slipped into the foyer, checking that she wasn't followed, and went to the front doors. Not only were they dropping stacks of two by fours and two by sixes, but there were loads of drywall to drop as well. Polly waited until they were finished and opened the door before the driver knocked.

"Quite a place you have here," he said as he put a clipboard in front of her. He pulled a pencil out of his pocket.

"It's a lot of work," Polly replied.

"This for upstairs?" He pointed at the back of the house.

Polly nodded. "Framing in bathrooms and splitting a room in half."

"You must have a really big family. I ain't never seen a house this big. Well, except some of those million dollar mansions. But I ain't ever been in one of those. Your husband rich?"

She laughed. Apparently he didn't know who her husband was. "No. We got a good deal on it and my husband is a contractor. We're doing most of the work ourselves."

"He did this?" He pointed around the foyer.

"Our sons and he did the work. I did the painting."

"Wow. You should go into business. This is nice."

"Thank you, but he is in the business."

"What's his company? Do I know him?"

"Probably. Henry Sturtz."

"This is Henry's house? I thought he was living in that old school building with …" The man stopped and looked at her. "You're his wife. Sorry. I didn't know he'd moved over here."

"We bought this last year and moved in over Thanksgiving. It's pretty rough. Some of the rooms are finished, but most are still under construction."

"I'd sure like to see it when it's done. Henry's a good guy. Tell him Jonah said hey."

"I will." Polly handed the clipboard back to him after signing the invoice. "Thanks for bringing this in."

"Sure will be a nice place when it's finished. I shoulda known it was Henry. The ticket says Sturtz Construction, but I didn't know he was living here too. He's one of the best here in Bellingwood."

94

As far as Polly knew, Henry was the only full-time contractor in Bellingwood. There were plenty in the area, but he was the only one who lived in town. "I think so," she said.

"I'll get outta your hair. Tell him hey for me, will ya?"

"I will. Thanks, Jonah."

He looked around the room again. "You guys got a lot of stuff. Gonna fit in here when it's done?"

"I sure hope so. Otherwise we'll have to buy another house."

His eyes grew wide. "You kidding me? This isn't enough of a house?"

"I was kidding. We'll make it fit," Polly said with a laugh.

"How many bedrooms you got up there?"

He was never going to leave and the thing was, he had two guys waiting for him in the truck. "I think we'll end up with ten rooms upstairs. They won't all be bedrooms unless we have a lot more children show up."

"You said you had sons. You're not old enough to have sons who can do this work."

"We adopted."

"Oh. Yeah. I heard about that. The boy whose buddy was killing people. Didn't you adopt a little girl, too?"

"Yes we did."

"Somebody said Henry had two little boys from Chicago now, too. That right?"

"It is."

"That's gotta be hard. Nobody around here who's like 'em."

Polly set her teeth. "The good thing is that everybody is like them. Color of skin doesn't mean anything. Right?"

"Yeah. I was just saying. Sometimes folk don't see it that way."

"Well, I hope they do. They're just little boys who want to grow up and have good lives. Just like your kids. No difference."

His eyes darted around the room, landing on the front door. "I better be going. We got more loads to get out today. Tell Henry hey."

"I will. Thank you very much." Polly held the front door as he left and when she closed it, she leaned against it and breathed out.

"Now I really do need a cup of coffee. He wore me out." She took her phone out and called Henry.

"Hi there," he said. "Did you get lumber?"

"Jonah says 'hey.'"

"Ohhhhh," he said, a rumbling laugh coming over the phone. "Did he try to talk your ear off?"

"Uh huh. You didn't warn me."

"I didn't know he'd be driving. He had an issue and was off the road for a while. I guess they needed him back."

"Their customers must be so happy."

"He usually delivers to work sites and folks just ignore him. He had a captured audience with you. Sorry about that."

"It's okay. I called him out on being a bigot and he ran for his life before we could go down the rabbit hole."

"A bigot?"

"Yeah. You know he heard about you getting two little boys from Chicago."

"Oh. I see." He chuckled. "You're pure entertainment sometimes."

"Yeah. You're paying for this one, buddy."

"If I build bathrooms and a wall for Rebecca's bedroom upstairs, will that be enough?"

"Nope. You're going to have to pay in other ways."

"Then let me be the first to announce that I'm a bad, bad man and you're my judge, jury and executioner."

"Off with his head." Polly giggled. "Okay, that sounded dirtier than I intended."

"Like I said. Pure entertainment. What are you up to now?"

"Coffee and then those stupid boxes are mine. I can't believe I still don't know what's in them. What is wrong with me?"

"Life?"

"Something like that."

"Call when you know what's in them."

"You know it's going to be something stupid, don't you?" she asked.

"Then we'll know that it is and move on. I love you."

"I love you too. And next time you see Jonah - tell him hey for me, okay?"

"Got it."

~~~

She couldn't very well go to the shop without goodies, so Polly purchased muffins and croissants to take with her. When she got back to her truck, she took a long drink of her coffee. There was never enough of this stuff in her day. A tap on her truck's hood pulled her upright and Dylan Foster, the owner of Pizzazz, waved as he went into the coffee shop. It never failed to surprise her how easy life was in a small town. People said hello and smiled and were generally willing to go an extra step out of their way for you. When things fell apart, someone always stepped in to help. She knew that was probably an exaggeration, but some days the immense difference between living here and living in Boston was obvious. She wouldn't be able to live there again if she had to. The idea of staring at the ground when you walked down a street, or ignoring people because you didn't have time to be pleasant was alien now. It didn't take long to learn that behavior. It had taken longer for her to unlearn it when she returned to Bellingwood.

Jen Dykstra opened the door of the quilt shop as a customer left, saw Polly and waved, then went back inside. Polly knew these people. They were friends and neighbors. She backed out of the parking place and drove through the main area of town. She recognized Marla Singer's van in front of the hardware store and saw Jean Gardner coming out of the grocery store. Jean didn't look up. It was cold and she had the hood of her coat up against the wind. Nate Mikkels would be behind his counter, serving up medication and humor. She and Henry needed to invite them over for dinner soon. Sophie and Cooper loved playing with Rebecca and the boys.

Polly drove past the police station. Mindy would be in there, drinking from her never-empty cup of coffee. That woman was on fire. The veterinarian's office was just down that way. Marnie

Evans was one of the nicest people Polly had ever met. That would be a hard job, though. Worrying over people's pets every day. Polly was attached to her animals, but she knew people who were much worse. She chuckled. If she hadn't married Henry and filled her life with kids, there was every possibility she'd be that person. You have to pour your love out somewhere.

She drove into the parking area in front of the shop and took one more long drink. Her coffee would be much cooler when she returned. It would still taste amazing. She grabbed the bag of treats and headed for the door. She was nervous about this. If they found something important, she didn't know what she'd do. If it was nothing, Polly was almost certain she'd be disappointed about that. Talk about a catch-22.

There were no machines running when Polly walked in. The three men were sitting with Jessie at a work bench in the back.

"Hello, Polly," Len Specek said, standing up. "We just stopped for a break."

"Then my timing is perfect." Polly brandished the bag she'd brought with her. "I have treats."

He met her halfway through the shop. "Put those three-day-old brownies away, boys. She brought the good stuff."

Polly handed Len the bag and he peered inside. "Lots of the good stuff."

Ben Bowen dragged another stool over. "Coffee, Polly?"

"I'm good. Thanks."

Len tore the bag open and placed it in the middle of the workbench. "Jess told me to wait until you were here to open those boxes. Our curiosity is killing us. What do you think is in them?"

"I have no idea," Polly said with a shrug. "If I hadn't been so busy the last couple of days, I would have been hovering over you until they were open."

"Well, let's see what we've got now that you're here. We'll just head over to the angle grinder and cut into the locks."

Polly nodded. She had absolutely no idea what he was going to do, but she was happy to have him do it.

Len handed her a pair of the goggles hanging from a hook and put another pair on. "Do you want hearing protection? This will get loud."

"I'm good," she said.

"Why don't you stand back a little. I don't know what I'll hit. We'll start with the box that rattles."

He cut right through the lock and handed the box to Polly.

She pulled the goggles to the top of her head and opened the box, then stuck her hand inside. When she brought it back out, she was clutching a handful of gold coins.

"Gold," Doug Shaffer breathed. "Is it all gold?"

Polly looked around for a container.

When Ben realized what she was looking for, he produced a wooden bowl that had been sitting on a shelf by the lathe.

"Are you sure?" she asked.

"Yeah. This is a test piece. Go ahead."

She upended the box into the bowl. Sure enough, all gold coins, and more than she expected.

"That has to be worth a lot," Jessie said.

"We don't even know if they're real," Polly said.

Doug reached out toward the bowl, then thought better of it and looked at Polly. "I heard that if you bite down and leave tooth marks, it's real. Should I try it?"

"I'd hate for you to hurt your teeth," she said.

"I won't bite that hard."

She shrugged. "Go ahead."

He picked up a coin and after brushing it off, bit it with his front teeth. He peered at the coin and said, "Bite marks. I'll be."

Jessie had been digging through her phone. "This site says that if gold is covering lead, it will show bite marks. Lead is soft, too."

"You should take these up to Gordon at the jewelry store. He could tell you," Ben offered. "If they're real, he'd put you in touch with someone to buy them, too."

Polly nodded. She didn't want to get too excited. So far that house hadn't produced anything other than bills to be paid. To think that it was going to offer her a windfall was ridiculous.

"There are about seventy-five coins in there," Doug said. He peered at the coin he held and turned to Jessie. "See if you can find a nineteen-hundred, five - maybe that's a five dollar gold coin. What's it worth?"

They waited as Jessie swiped and typed into her phone.

She gasped and turned her phone around so they could see the numbers. "About two thousand apiece. That's a hundred and fifty thousand dollars right there."

Doug dropped the coin back in the bowl and everyone backed away as if they might be bitten.

"This can't be real," Polly said.

Len pointed at the coins. "If it is, you need to get those locked up right away. Maybe you should go straight to the bank."

Polly shook her head. "It isn't real. There's just no way."

Jessie headed for the office. "I have a bank bag in here. Just a second."

"Okay," Len said. "Shall we see what treasures are in the other box?"

Polly nodded. She felt sick to her stomach. If there had been only a few gold coins in the box, she'd have had fun with that. This was a lot of responsibility. Who did the coins really belong to? She knew that legally they were part of the house, so she and Henry had ownership, but it felt wrong to just have something like this show up. She glanced at Doug Shaffer who was doing all he could to pull his family out of a financial hole that he'd been unable to escape. They were still living in a two-bedroom apartment. His wife's sister had left town with some man she'd met while waiting tables at the Alehouse. But that meant her income was gone, too. He was saving money to move into a home, but there just weren't that many low-priced homes on the market in Bellingwood. Why would Polly have this influx of cash and not him? And Jessie. She was paying for as much college as she could, but there would be student loans by the time she was finished.

Polly shook her head. Henry would tell her she was thinking too hard about this. One step at a time. The coins were probably counterfeit anyway. Right?

Len brought the second box to her. "Here you go. This one doesn't have much in it. It's lighter than that other one."

She took a breath and opened the lid, then lifted out four books and a sheaf of papers. After all those years, they were still intact.

Jessie had returned and filled the bank bag with the coins, putting it in front of Polly. "The first thing you should do is count how many there are," she said quietly. "Don't let them out of your sight until you know."

Polly nodded. "Thanks." She flipped open the first book and realized that she was looking at a ledger, the pages filled with names and numbers. Her heart stopped when she turned to the inside back cover of the book and saw the symbol that had been found throughout the Bell House. A star with the sword and plow on either side. "There it is again."

"What?" Len asked. "What's that?"

"It's the symbol that was all over my house when we stripped it to the frame. It was painted across the ceiling in the foyer and then I found it etched into door and window frames in other rooms on the main floor."

The four of them looked at her. "That's kind of creepy," Doug said.

"I know. We can't figure out what it's about." Polly opened the other two ledgers and found the same symbol inside the back of each. When she riffled through the loose sheaf of papers, she realized she was looking at contracts, all with that same symbol sketched at the end of the contract, just under a signature.

"I need to spend time with these," she said.

"Can I help?" Jessie asked.

Polly shook her head. "That's okay. I promise to tell you what's going on when I know, but you have enough with work, school and Molly."

Jessie laughed. "But this would be so much more fun."

"Is it always this interesting with her?" Doug asked Ben Bowen.

Ben nodded. "And more."

CHAPTER ELEVEN

Polly knew her reaction was strange, but the anticipation and curiosity at opening those boxes had given way to malaise. She didn't know whether she wanted the coins to be real or counterfeit. She sat in her truck with the metal boxes beside her - one filled with the ledger books and contracts and the other containing the bank bag full of coins.

The only thing she knew to do was call Henry, so she took out her phone.

"Hey there, what did you find?" he asked.

"Where are you?"

"Oh no. What's wrong?"

Polly looked at the boxes again. "Nothing's really wrong. I might have a hundred and fifty thousand dollars sitting in the truck with me."

"You might have what?"

"Gold coins. Maybe seventy-five of them. At least that's what we estimated. I haven't counted them."

"Why not?" he asked. "That's exciting."

"Is it?"

"What's wrong with you? Of course it is."

"It just makes me nervous. I don't know where these coins came from."

He interrupted. "The mantle in our house."

"Yeah. I know. The other box was full of stuff that has that sword and plowshare symbol all over it. I wish I knew what it meant."

"This really has you freaked out, doesn't it?"

"A little bit. It feels bigger than just a couple of boxes. And nobody can tell me what's going on."

"What do you want me to do?"

Polly just needed to hear him ask that question. "Where are you?"

"I'm actually on my way back into town. Where do you want me to be?"

"I think we should get a safety-deposit box and put everything but one or two of these coins in there. Would you meet me at the bank?"

He chuckled. "You're awfully practical sometimes. That's a good idea.."

"Then I want to go see Ken Wallers again. This mystery with the symbol is driving me crazy. He and his buddies don't get to slough it off any longer. We're digging in and looking for answers."

"Back out of the parking space and head for the bank, Polly. I'll be there shortly."

"Are you telling me to stop it?"

"I'm telling you to focus on one thing at a time. We're in no hurry."

"Except I want these coins out of sight."

"I love you. Hang up and drive."

"I love you, too. Thanks, Henry."

Polly dropped the phone into the box with the bank bag and backed out of the driveway. She wound around a few blocks until she was across the street from the bank. Every time she passed this place, she remembered the night Cindy Rothenfuss stormed out of this building, screaming at someone inside. Then she remembered Beryl telling the story of how she gave the bank a painting because Cindy hated it so much. Cindy's husband, Barry, who had been president of the bank at the time his wife was murdered, was gone. Rumor was he'd moved back to the Quad Cities and was living with Cindy's sister. Polly hoped it all worked out for him. He was a nice guy and hadn't deserved that shrew for a wife.

Henry hadn't said how long it would take for him to arrive, so Polly pulled out the bank bag and dumped the coins back into the metal box. She counted them one by one as she added them back to the bag. When she finished, she had counted eighty-two coins. She took a photograph of them in the bag, then placed two of them side by side on her console and took close-up photographs with her phone. Eighty of these would go in a safety-deposit box, two would stay with her. If they needed more than that to identify their authenticity, she'd come back.

When she'd found the Iranian vase and the cash those soldiers were looking for in her barn a few years ago, she knew right away that it didn't belong to her. It had a home. If this was real, it was really and truly hers. She and Henry could ... Polly shook her head. They didn't need the money. Oh, they could use it, but they didn't need it. At some level, she hoped it was counterfeit and she wouldn't have to think about it any longer.

Henry bumped his horn as he drove past and parked in front of her. She waved and smiled. That man made her happy no matter what. He got out of his truck, waved at someone who drove past, then walked back and opened her door.

"Heya, beautiful. Let's see our loot."

Polly chuckled and opened the bag.

"Whooee," he said. "Even old and dull, that's some shiny stuff there. Do you want to run away to Hawaii with me?"

"Yes sir, my handsome boy. Let's pack it in and run until we can't go any further."

"Now you're talkin'." He pointed at the bag. "Did you count them?"

"There are eighty in the bag." Polly pulled two out of her pocket. "I want to keep these so we can have them checked."

"Good idea. You took pictures already?"

She nodded.

"See, this is why I love you. You're smart. Let's go in and rent us a box and get this loot off the streets." He dropped into a drawl. "You know those wild rustlers are bound to be ridin' up the street on their horses."

"You're such a nut." She handed him the bag while she climbed down.

Henry slammed the door and escorted her across the street. "Don't mind me, ma'am. I'm just your bodyguard today."

"Thankee, kind sir."

It always surprised Polly when there was a line to get to a teller. No matter what time of day it was, people had business to do at the bank.

"Hello, Henry," a young woman said when they approached her at the counter.

"Hi Lou. Have you met my wife, Polly?"

She nodded. "I've seen you at Sycamore House. But I don't think we've met. I'm Lou Wymore. My dad works for Henry."

"We need a safety deposit box," Henry said. "Can you help us?"

"Sure. What size?"

He held up the bag. "About this size. And can I get another one of these from you?"

She pushed a card in front of them. "Fill this out. I'll get things started."

~~~

"Do you feel better now?" Henry asked as they walked back to their trucks.

"Some," Polly acknowledged. "Ben said I should take a coin to Gordon at the jewelry store. He'd know what it is."

"I'll ride with you. Let's go now."

"Really?"

"I have time." He handed her the new bank bag. "That needs to go back to Jessie, doesn't it?"

"You're smart too."

"I recognized Dad's writing on the other one. Figured Jessie had given it to you."

He got into the passenger side of the truck. They could have walked to the jewelry store, but Polly was tired of being cold whenever she was outside. The truck was still relatively warm. "Are we going to talk about this?" she asked.

"About what?"

"About what to do with the money if these coins are real?"

Henry put his seat belt on. "That money isn't going to find its way into our coffers. I already know that. What I don't know is exactly where you'll put it. If we desperately needed it, you'd have already talked about what bills we should pay or something the kids needed. Right now you're trying to figure out how best to put it to use. It's found money. You didn't earn it."

"You think you know me so well." Polly wrinkled her nose at him before pulling out onto the street.

"Am I right?"

"I didn't earn Dad's inheritance."

"And you didn't use any of it until you bought Sycamore House. That was an investment. You could have used that money to do any number of things, but you didn't."

"Well, don't go getting all self-confident about knowing me. I might surprise you."

"You surprise me all the time, but not about your basic personality." He pointed at a parking space and Polly pulled in.

"Thanks for doing this with me today," she said.

"For once in your life, I can actually be there when you're caught up in the middle of something. I'm taking advantage."

"Of me?"

He reached out and took her hand. "I'll do that later."

"I'm so glad you put extra insulation in our walls," she said. "Last night Rebecca said something about hearing Hayden talk to his girlfriend through the walls between her bedroom and the family room."

His eyes grew big.

"I know!" she said. "Thankfully, Rebecca has never looked at me funny and she didn't say a word about us."

"I'm tripling the insulation upstairs then."

Polly laughed. "That sounds like a great idea."

~~~

By the time they finished with Gordon at the jewelry store, it was lunchtime. Gordon kept one of the coins and told them he'd call by the end of the week with news. They went back outside into the bitter cold and Henry pulled her close.

"Diner?" he asked.

Polly nodded. "Tenderloin."

"You're so predictable."

"What if I take you back to your truck," she said. "I want to see Ken Wallers and maybe Simon Gardner this afternoon. I really need to find out what happened in our house a hundred years ago."

"I can walk over there," Henry said. "It's only three blocks."

She slipped her arm in his and rubbed her hand up and down his arm. "You're such a tough, strong man."

Henry flexed under her hand. "Don't you forget it, little missy."

The warmth and familiar smell of the diner welcomed Polly in ways she couldn't believe. Lucy waved at them and pointed to a table tucked against a wall. The place was busy, yet she slipped between customers and tables with the agility of a dancer.

"Coffee or soda today?" she asked, putting her hand on the table.

"Hot coffee," Henry said.

Polly smiled. "Me too."

"Back in a minute." She was gone as soon as the words were out of her mouth.

"I know what I want," Polly said, closing the menu. She pushed it to the side. "I always look and I always order the same thing."

"Taking the day off?" They looked up to see JJ Roberts, one of the owners of Secret Woods winery approach. "Shouldn't you be building something?" He clapped Henry on the shoulder.

"Good managers don't have to be on the job every minute," Henry said. "We hire people that we trust. What are you doing in here today?" He stood and shook JJ's hand.

"Sit," JJ said. "Sit. Not much to do in the middle of winter. Patrick went back to California to raise capital for another software project. He always has something going. He's got Ryan in Vegas at an electronics show and I've been left behind to keep an eye on things." He nudged Henry's shoulder. "Maybe I should sell out to you two while they're gone. Do you want a winery?"

Polly looked into his eyes to see if he was joking. She couldn't tell one way or the other. "You're kidding, right?" she asked. "Aren't things going well over there?"

"They're great. But if those two get bored with this, I don't know where that will put us. I never wanted to be in business by myself." He shrugged. "I hope this is just one of Patrick's notions. I was kinda getting used to living in Iowa again."

"You could do it on your own, JJ," Henry said. "Don't kid yourself." He turned in his seat and snagged a chair from the empty table behind him. "Join us."

"You sure?" JJ asked. "I'm not interrupting?"

"You're fine," Polly said. "Are you worried they're moving on?"

"Just some things Patrick hinted at. He's never really been happy coming back here. You know he doesn't get along with his family and after Annalise left him, he never really ..." He shrugged. "He's just not happy. And Ryan, well, he'll do whatever Patrick wants him to do. "

Lucy brought coffee for Henry and Polly and bumped her hip against JJ's arm. "Boy, you've got to find someone else to feed you. You'll get fat if you eat here every day."

"Yes, ma'am," he said. "Better make it a salad then."

They both laughed at that.

"Your regular?" she asked.

He nodded.

"What about you, Polly? Anything other than a tenderloin?"

Polly handed her the menu. "I need a tenderloin today. And fries. I need those too."

Lucy chuckled. "Tough day already? How about you, Henry?"

"The meat loaf special. That sounds warm."

"It *is* cold out there," she said.

"Hey, Lucy." Polly put her hand on the woman's arm. "Any chance I could talk to your husband sometime about history stuff from the Bell House?"

Lucy patted her shoulder. "I wish you would. Since Ken asked him about it last fall, he's been reading up. But then it seemed like you all dropped it. He hasn't, though."

Polly glanced at Henry, who just smiled at her. "Really? Could I bring Simon and Ken with me one of these days?"

"Of course you could. Greg would love to see them again. You know he's got a computer that lets him communicate now. He's been practicing with it and he's doing much better. I think he'd like to show off."

"If I come over will you cook me dinner?" JJ asked.

"Honey, you have got to get yourself a girlfriend." Lucy turned to head back to the front, then spun back around and tweaked his ear. "Or a boyfriend. Whatever makes you happy." She sauntered off after flashing Polly a grin.

"She really does like you," Polly said.

"I love her. Just wish I could do more for her and Greg. He was always good to me, too. When I was a kid, Mom and Dad dropped me at their house so Lucy could babysit. Greg taught me how to play board games. He was the one that taught me all about strategy. And he read everything. I think the only time the television was on was when I was there. But he'd just sit back in his recliner and read while I watched TV. Such a good guy. I kinda miss him."

Polly looked at JJ. "Did you buy that computer for him? Ken was talking about it, but Lucy shut them down.

JJ gave her a funny look. "Don't ever tell her. She has no idea where it came from. I overheard Chief Wallers talking about it in here one day. When she said no to him, I went back to the office and called some friends. They just shipped one to the house and nobody knew where it came from. The chief was genuinely surprised, so Lucy couldn't make him take it back."

"You're a good kid," Henry said. "No matter what anyone else tries to tell me."

"You and the Parkers were some of the few that believed in me." He smiled. "But it's getting better. That's why I don't want Patrick and Ryan to screw this up. I'm finally doing something good for this town and I like that people stopped looking at me like I'm a loser."

"Can you run the place without them?"

JJ shuddered. "Probably. But it wouldn't be any fun."

"Can you afford to buy them out if they want to leave?" Henry asked.

"I don't know. Patrick has the numbers. We've been doing good, but I don't know if it's been that good."

"You're the idea man," Polly said. "Go out and sell yourself. Bring on new partners if you have to. Don't run away from something you enjoy just because your friends do."

"I don't even know if they will. It's just been feeling kind of weird over there lately."

She looked up when Lucy came back with a soda for JJ. After Lucy walked on, Polly said, "Talk to someone before you make any decisions, okay?"

"Who? You?"

"Yes, me," she replied. "Or Henry. Or even Greg. Or go talk to Jeff. He knows people around here and I can tell you right now that Sycamore House and Sycamore Inn would be much less successful if Secret Woods wasn't around. We're better together."

Lucy was back with their meals. After making sure they had what they needed, she patted JJ's head and took off.

"You live in an apartment in Ames, right?" Polly asked.

"Just moved there before Christmas," he replied.

"You should come over for dinner some night. Have you seen what we're doing there?"

He stopped mid-bite. "No. I know everybody talks about it. Sylvie told me what a nice job you did in the foyer. She said you were the one who painted it and everything."

"We're just finishing the kitchen this week and starting on some of the upstairs bedrooms. Maybe one day next week. What evenings are you free?"

He closed his eyes, thinking, then pulled out his phone and swiped through to a calendar app. "There's a meeting Tuesday afternoon and I'm always there every Thursday, Friday and Saturday evenings. Most Sundays, too."

"So Tuesday. You can come for dinner on Tuesday?"

JJ looked at Henry. "She's kinda tenacious."

"You don't know the half of it, my boy," Henry said. "You might have just become her next project. Are you sure you can't claim a girlfriend somewhere so Polly doesn't start looking for one?"

The young man looked at Polly in a panic. "You wouldn't."

"No," she said. "I wouldn't. Unless of course, something perfect comes up." She pursed her lips. "Wait. Maybe I do have a good idea. Do you want kids?"

"What?" he gasped.

"Kids. You heard me. Do you want kids?"

"I suppose. Someday. Are you serious?"

Polly grinned across the table at her husband. "Tab."

"That's mean," Henry said. "You can't do that to her."

"Unless she wants me to set her up. Come on, it would be fun. And we have all those hooligans that live with us to keep everyone entertained at dinner. If it ends up being a terrible idea, no one is harmed."

"You're seriously setting me up on a blind date?" JJ asked.

"I'll find out if she's interested. If she says yes, will you come?"

His shoulders sagged. "I suppose. It's not like I've been doing any good on my own. Sure. Who is Tab?"

"You'll see next week if it works out. I'm not going to say anything more." Polly pulled the imaginary zipper across her lips.

"You two are scary," JJ said. "So far, in one meal, I've told you a secret, been ordered to look for potential partners and now I'm about to have a blind date."

"Pretty productive lunch," Henry said. He pushed the ticket toward JJ. "This one's on you. You can claim it on your taxes."

JJ took the ticket. "I should pay anyway. You guys are always doing stuff for people. I can do this."

"I was kidding," Henry said.

"No sir. This one's on me."

CHAPTER TWELVE

A quick stop at the police station and Polly discovered Ken Wallers wasn't there. The next stop she made was Simon Gardner's antique shop. From the warm heat and smell of grease at the diner, to the warm and slightly musty scent of his shop, Polly marveled at how much she loved Bellingwood.

"My dear, how good to see you," Simon said. He came out from behind his counter and took her hands in his. "You should wear gloves. It's bitter out there."

"I left them in the truck," Polly said. She was glad to let him hold her chilled fingers in his very warm hands.

"Come away from the front door. I have a space heater behind the counter. We'll just pull up this rocking chair and you can tell me why you've come to visit me." He helped her remove her jacket, then placed it neatly on a dresser.

Polly reached into her pocket and took out the gold coin she'd kept for herself. Simon put out his hand and she dropped it into his palm.

"What's this?" He looked at her curiously. "I don't see these very often."

"Gordon at the jewelry store is checking on their authenticity."

"You have another?"

"I have eighty-two."

"My, my my. That's quite a find. Where did you come up with eighty-two five dollar coins?"

"At the Bell House."

He frowned. "In the basement with the other things?"

"No, these were in metal boxes that had been built into a fireplace mantle upstairs. Henry and the boys pulled it down on Monday." She looked out the front door. "I should have brought that other box in."

"Do you have the coins in it?"

Polly shook her head. "I put the rest of the coins in a safety deposit box at the bank. The second metal box contains contracts and ledger books. Simon, that symbol was on everything. We have to figure out what it is."

Simon looked at the floor. "I've been remiss. Every once in a while, a thought flits into my head and I remember that I intended to dig out mother's journals, but then other thoughts take over and before I know it, months pass and I've done nothing. Now here we are, and I still have done nothing about it. I apologize."

"I'm no better," Polly said. "Once we started packing and moving, I just let it go. If we hadn't found those metal boxes, I might never have brought it up again.

The front door to the shop opened and Polly understood why Simon was so happy behind his counter with the space heater blowing. Cold air rushed in, bringing Paul Bradford with it.

"I thought I saw you come in here, Polly Giller," Paul said. "Your husband called last week and asked me to order hardware for him. I have it here. Can I send it with you?"

"Hardware?" she asked.

Paul brought a box over to Simon's counter and opened it. "Said this was for your kitchen cupboards. Pretty stuff, isn't it?"

Henry hadn't said a word to her about what he was using for hinges and handles on the cabinet doors, but she trusted him. Polly peered into the box and smiled. The burnished steel would be perfect. "That's really nice. He's got good taste."

"He picked these out?" Paul asked.

She nodded. "The kitchen design is all his. He asked for my opinion on a few things, but otherwise, he did it."

"You're a trusting woman."

"I'm a smart woman. He's good at what he does. I'm glad to take these. Do I need to come next door and pay you?"

"Oh no," Paul said. "Henry's on account with us."

Polly wasn't going to argue and try to tell him that they kept the business and personal stuff separate. Whatever Henry did with Paul was his business. All she needed to do was ask Henry where these were to be delivered - the house or back to the shop. "Thank you, Paul."

Simon held the coin out to her surreptitiously. She nodded.

"Polly brought something in that she discovered at the Bell House," Simon said, holding up the coin. "Gordon Berkley is checking it out for her."

"Is that gold?" Paul asked.

"Might be," Polly said. "But you two have to promise not to say anything to people. I don't want this getting around town."

Simon chuckled. "You've told the wrong two people, then."

"What?"

"Well, I'm a terrible gossip, and between Paul and his wife, the whole town will know by the end of business today."

She looked at them both. "You're kidding, right?"

"Not really," Paul said. "This is interesting stuff. If you aren't finding bodies, we have to have something to talk about."

"You... You... You..." Polly stammered. "Don't tell people until I know something. Please."

"We'll try," Simon said with a shrug. "Paul, did you ever look for more information on that plow and sword symbol? Polly said she found ledger books with it in there."

"Nah. Sorry, Polly."

"Well I'm back and even more curious than before. Are you two going to help me this time or not?"

The two men looked at each other and smirked. "I guess so."

"I just talked to Lucy and she said that Greg got that computer to help him speak."

Simon wrinkled his brow. "He did? Where did that come from? Last I knew he said no."

"I don't have all the details," Polly replied. "But he has it and he's willing to see us. Just because you fellas forgot about me doesn't mean he did. She says he has information."

"I haven't talked with Greg in years," Paul said. "It would be good to see him again. He's always been such a quiet thinker."

"And someone has to help me find that stuff from Ken Wallers' friend that ended up in the basement of the library. I asked Joss about it and she has no idea where to start. It sounds like things are a real rat's nest down there."

"They should really put someone to work down there that likes to organize," Paul said. "It ain't me. Unless it's got a price tag on it, I don't want to file it."

Polly's face slowly broke into a grin. She knew the perfect person and that woman was already spending time at the library. She was surprised that Joss hadn't picked up on it yet.

"What's that look for?" Simon asked.

"Andy Specek. She is the grand madame of organization." Polly stood up. "You." She pointed at Simon.

He responded by giving her a querying look and pointing at himself.

"Yes. You are going to find your mother's journals. And you," she pointed at Paul.

He backed up a step.

"Don't run away from me. You're going to find whatever it was you thought your father and grandfather had. It's probably already there in the shop. You just need to put your hands on it."

"You know that means I have to go down to my own basement," Paul said, complaining.

"I don't care what it means. You both should feel horribly guilty that you've done nothing about this when I was asking for your help." Polly waited for them to catch her teasing them, but they didn't.

"You're right," Simon said. "I do feel awful."

She laughed. "I was kidding. I try not to use guilt to manipulate people into doing things. But I would appreciate it if you could at least put your hands on these items. I'm going to ask Andy to help me find things in the library basement and then dig into those ledgers and contracts from the other metal box. Gordon said he would have an answer on the coins by Friday. Once we have more materials in hand, I think we can set up a time with Greg Parker. We'll figure this out, yet."

"What if you've gone to all this trouble and it's nothing?" Paul Bradford asked.

"Then it was fun getting to know you better. But what if it's really something?"

He put his hand out. "Let me see that coin."

Simon dropped it into his hand and Paul took it up to his mouth and bit down on it gently. "I heard that you will leave an indentation in gold."

"If it was lead, you'd leave the same indentation," Simon said scornfully. "You old fool. Gordon will tell Polly what it is and what it's worth. She's doing this the right way." He took the coin back and handed it to Polly. "Tuck that away before the boy swallows it."

"I don't know if I can find anything by Friday," Paul said, ignoring his friend.

"Then we'll say early next week. That gives you the weekend, right?"

"I was going ice fishing this weekend."

"Paul Bradford, you will help this young lady out. You do nothing but sit on your bottom in that store anyway."

"Yes sir," Paul said, pursing his lips. "I'll see what I can find."

"Thank you." Polly stood and reached for her coat.

"Do you need to leave so soon?" Simon asked. "Maybe I could convince you to walk with me over to the coffee shop. I could use a break. I've been working hard all day long."

"You were just there this morning," Paul said.

Polly shook her head. "I'm sorry. I should get going. I have kids coming home from school and ... I should just get going. Thank you both for everything."

Simon nodded and gave her a sad smile. It occurred to her that he might get lonely sometimes.

"One of these evenings you should come to my crazy household for dinner," Polly said to him, taking his hand. "You can see what we've been doing to the place. The foyer is a mess right now, but it's coming along."

"I'd enjoy that. I haven't yet spent much time with your little boys, and that young daughter of yours is growing up much too quickly."

"Yes she is," Polly said. "What about Monday evening?"

"I'll put it on my calendar. Thank you."

"You never acquiesce to our invitations that easily," Paul said.

Simon huffed. "That's because she invites me as a friend. You and your dear wife think I'm too feeble to take care of myself."

"We do not."

"I'll see you two later," Polly said, heading for the door. They were still bickering at each other as she went back out into the cold.

Polly got up into her truck and called Henry back.

"Did'ja miss me?" he asked.

"So much. Say, Paul Bradford just handed me a box of hardware for the cabinet doors. Do I take this home or back to the shop?"

"Home is fine. I'll deal with it. How was Simon?"

"Good."

"I meant, is he going to help you?"

Polly chuckled. "I guilted him into it. Paul, too. They said they forgot. I also invited Simon to dinner on Monday."

"Simon on Monday and JJ on Tuesday? Do you have a woman in mind for Simon, too?"

"I wouldn't ..." Polly stopped. "Okay, I guess I did with JJ. I need to call Tab and see if she's at all interested. She's going to have my head, you know."

"With good reason."

"I'm heading to the house now. I want to spend some time with those books before the kids come home."

"I love you. See you tonight."

Polly backed out of the parking space and headed home, but an empty parking space beside Sal's car in front of Sweet Beans pulled her in. Surely she could use more coffee.

"Hi, Polly," Skylar called from the front counter.

She smiled and waved, looked around the room and found her friend sitting with Tab.

"I knew you two would be together," Polly said. "I was just talking about you."

"Who, me?" Sal asked.

"Not this time." She pointed at Tab. "No, you."

"What did I do?"

"Are you interested in a blind date?"

Tab was shocked. "Uh." She looked at Sal.

"Take her up on it," Sal said. "Look what happened with me and Mark."

"Uh, with who?"

Polly lowered herself into the seat and then stood back up. "I'll be right back. I want more coffee." She gave them an evil grin as she sauntered up to the counter.

"What's up today?" Sky asked.

"Just a cup of coffee, dark roast."

"Nothing fun?"

She shook her head. "I've had enough fun. I just need more coffee."

He filled a mug and handed to her. "If you need this to go, come back."

"This will be perfect. Thanks."

By the time Polly got back to the table, Tab had Alexander in her arms and was pacing back and forth behind Sal.

"That was mean," Tab said. "Now what do you mean by blind date?"

"I'd invite you, Mark, and Alexander, too," Polly said to Sal. "Now that the kitchen is nearly finished, it's more fun to invite people over. The foyer is still a complete mess, but I can ignore that."

"Hey," Tab whispered. She nuzzled Alexander's face. "She's being mean to me. Would you go over there and spit up on her hair?"

"We'd love to come for dinner. Alexander likes playing with Noah and Elijah, and Rebecca is always so good with him. He loves it when she and Kayla babysit."

Tab moved so that she was standing between Polly and Sal, blocking their view of each other. "You two stop it. I'll arrest you both for harassing an officer of the law."

Polly leaned around her. "I think we're in trouble."

"Wouldn't be the first time. Do you remember ..."

Tab spun on Sal. "Stop it. This isn't fair. And remember, I'm holding the baby."

"Okay," Polly said. She blew across the top of her mug and took a sip. "Still too hot. Maybe I should get an ice cube and cool it down."

"If you walk away from this table one more time, I'm slapping cuffs on you."

When Polly looked up into Tab's face, she decided she was one move away from going too far.

"JJ Roberts."

Sal leaned around Tab. "The owner of Secret Woods?"

"Yeah. One of them. He's a good guy. Henry and I just had lunch with him."

"And you told him about me?" Tab asked.

"No. I asked if he would be interested in a blind date with a friend of mine. Next Tuesday. Dinner at my house. There will be kids and noise and no pressure."

"No pressure, hah. What am I supposed to wear, my uniform?"

Polly lifted an eyebrow. "Well, you know what they say about uniforms. No, just wear jeans. I'm not doing a dress-up thing. Can you come, Sal?"

"I'll ask Mark. I don't think we have anything going on. What can I bring?"

Both Polly and Tab burst out laughing.

"What?" Sal protested. "I can make a salad. I make a great salad. And Dylan makes fabulous garlic bread. I'll buy it from him."

"No. Just bring your family," Polly said. "And Tab, don't worry about finding the perfect thing to wear. You are free next Tuesday, right? Not on duty?"

"He's willing to do this?"

Polly nodded.

Tab turned and handed Alexander to his mother. "I'm so flustered right now, I don't know what to say."

"Say yes," Sal said. "I'm telling ya, Polly is rarely wrong."

"I'm not ready to settle down, though. I love living in my quiet apartment all by myself. After a long day, I like coming home, taking my bra off and wandering around in a night shirt. I don't want anybody in my space. No. I don't want to do this."

Polly sat back, surprised. "Really?"

"Not if Sal's telling me this is the beginning of the end. I don't want to fall in love with some guy. I like my life just the way it is. Just me. Nobody else."

"I don't know how to respond to that," Polly said to Sal. "It's a genius shutdown."

"No it's not," Sal said. She sat forward, placing Alexander's bottom on the table. "You are going to go out on this date and you are going to enjoy yourself. And if he asks you to go out on another date, you're going to agree and do that, too."

"Why?"

"Because I said so and I'm the mommy. Got it?"

"That's not fair," Tab protested, but with a hint of a smile.

"If you don't want to meet him because you're afraid of meeting someone new, that's unacceptable. Is that why you're being disagreeable?"

Polly didn't see this side of Sal very often. She liked it.

"Maybe."

"No one is asking you to get married and give up your single life," Sal said.

"Not yet."

"So Tuesday evening. My house," Polly said.

"Fine," Tab agreed.

"Have either of you spoken with Sandy today?" Polly asked.

Tab pulled out her phone. "We've texted a couple of times. They are just in hell trying to get Will admitted. A lot of tests and tons of doctors and everything."

"How's Benji holding up?"

"Sounds like he's doing okay. I think they both are going through the motions and trying to take in as much information as they can as fast as they can. He's taking next week off."

"Good," Polly said. "I was worried when she said he went back to work yesterday. I didn't think about him having to rearrange his schedule so he could take time off."

"Will's going to be okay, though, right?" Sal asked.

Tab gave a small shrug. "The doctors say it's going to be rough, but they've had good success with treatment. Sandy won't give up."

"I love that you two have gotten to know her," Polly said.

"Tab more than me," Sal replied. "Maybe when Alexander is a little older, the boys can play together. I like her."

Tab smiled. "She isn't like anybody else I know."

"What do you mean?"

"Well, you had a baby and were ready to be a mom even though you're all career-oriented. Sandy wasn't ready at all. She didn't think she'd ever have kids. They were going to be a power couple. Then Will came along and all of a sudden, she decided that her life was going to be different. It's been a big change for her and I think it still surprises her that it happened. And now this. She told me today that she was glad they made the choice for her to stop working full-time. It all worked out for the best."

"Are you going over to see her?" Sal asked.

Tab shook her head. "Not for a few days. They've got so much to deal with right now. I told her to let me know if she needed something from the house. I know her code. Otherwise, I'll text her. If Will is feeling okay after the first treatment, they'll bring him home. Probably this weekend. I'll stop by her house after my shift.

"You're going to have to move to Bellingwood if you keep making friends up here," Polly said.

Tab scowled. "It's only fifteen minutes. I like my apartment."

Polly finished the coffee in her mug. "I'd better go. There will be small children piling into my house any minute. See you Tuesday?"

"I'll be there." Tab sighed out a loud breath. "With bells on."

CHAPTER THIRTEEN

Standing up after breakfast Friday morning, Rebecca pointed at Polly. "We've all talked," she announced.

"About?"

"About you and Henry."

Polly chuckled. "Are we in trouble?"

"No, but you should get a night off from us."

Henry had already left for the day, but the kids were all there.

"I like spending my evenings with you."

"Well not tonight. I talked to your friends and you're going to Beryl's house at six o'clock. Then I talked to Mr. Mikkels and he wants Henry to come over and work on cars. Joss has some library thing, but he said they'll hire a babysitter." Rebecca pointed at Hayden. "I know you have a date, so you're off the clock until midnight. When you come home, you have to check on all of us and make sure we're in bed."

He laughed. "I can do that."

"Andrew, Kayla, and I are going to take care of Noah and Elijah tonight. We'll make dinner and we have a whole bunch of things to do with them. If it's okay, Kayla is going to spend the night with me. I think Stephanie and Sky are going out on a date, too."

Polly nodded.

"Heath is going to drive you, just in case there's wine. And you're supposed to call him when you want to come home. He'll come get you and won't make any judgment."

"You've got this all figured out. What if I don't want to spend the evening with Beryl?"

Rebecca's face transformed into a look of shock. "Are you two fighting?"

"No," Polly said with a laugh. "I'm kidding. Have you talked to everyone?"

"Even Sylvie. She doesn't have to work tonight at Sycamore House. Rachel just has a small party and doesn't need her help. If Sylvie needs a ride home, Heath will take her."

"You've thought of everything. Did you decide on the theme of our party, too?"

Rebecca sat down. "I thought you guys could figure that out. I just wanted to do something nice. I felt bad all week for what we did to you last Friday night. Is it okay?"

"It's perfect. Do you want to call Henry and tell him what he's doing tonight or should I?"

"Mr. Mikkels said he'd call."

"Awesome. And what are you making for dinner tonight?"

"Hot dogs!" Elijah yelled.

"And potato chips," Noah said.

Polly looked toward the pantry. "Do we have everything you need?"

"I took hot dogs out of the freezer," Rebecca said. "If we don't have buns, we'll use bread."

"Tell you what," Polly said. "I'll make sure you have what you need for a party. How about popcorn and M&Ms for a movie treat?"

"Yay!" Elijah yelled again, jumping up from his seat. "Can we stay up late?"

"That's up to Rebecca and Kayla," Polly said.

"Please?" he asked Rebecca. "Pretty please?"

She nodded. "But we have to be in bed before Hayden comes home from his date. Deal?"

"Deal."

"If you're finished, go brush your teeth, boys," Polly said. "I'll get your dishes."

They pushed back from the table and ran down the hall.

"Thank you for organizing this, Rebecca," Polly said with a smile.

"I really am sorry about last Friday. I can't believe I did that."

Hayden picked up the little boys' plates and stacked them on his. He patted Rebecca on the head as he walked past. "Someday you'll quit making bad decisions. Right, Heath?"

Heath rolled his eyes. "When it happens, I'll let you know."

"So you don't have anything to do tonight?" Polly asked Heath.

"Jason said something about playing games at Sycamore House. Up at Doug's place? But I don't really know how to play those games."

"You should totally go," Rebecca said. "Jason will teach you. He taught me and Kayla. Sometimes we play Sword Lords with him and Andrew. He says it's just so he can level up. You could use my character. That way you wouldn't have to start at the beginning." She smirked. "And if you level it up for me, I'll be even better the next time I play."

"You're still playing that?" Polly asked. "I'd have thought people moved on."

"No," Rebecca replied. "They totally upgraded it and added in these new great levels and more characters and really cool evil guys. There was just a new release a few months ago."

"Huh. We're having JJ Roberts here for dinner on Tuesday night."

"The winery guy?" Rebecca asked.

"And one of the guys who started Sword Lords."

"Seriously?" Heath snapped his head to her. "He lives in Bellingwood?"

"Yeah. They sold the game company and moved here to open the winery. I thought everybody knew that," Polly said.

Hayden walked past his brother and popped the back of Heath's head. "Unless you were living under a rock. I was going to talk to you about Tess."

"Yeah? When can she come to dinner?"

"I was going to ask about Monday night. She's not working. But if you're having people over Tuesday night, that's too much."

Polly shook her head. "No, that would be great. I already invited Simon Gardner from the antique shop to dinner on Monday, Tess would be more than welcome. She'll love him. His background is in anthropology and he is so smart about everything."

"Are you sure?"

"Unless she's not comfortable meeting another stranger, it would be terrific. Is there anything she doesn't like to eat?"

"Tess likes everything."

Polly dramatically brushed her hand across her forehead. "Whew. I worried you might bring home a vegan and I'd have to learn an entirely new type of cooking."

"Not Tess. She's easy."

"Then be sure to let her know we'd love her to join us on Monday."

He bent over and gave Polly a quick hug. "Do you want me to take the littles to school today?"

"You have time?"

"Sure. Rebecca, are you about ready?"

"Yeah. Let me get my stuff." She hugged Polly on her way past. "Thanks for agreeing to do tonight. I wanted to do something nice."

"This is great. Thank you. Now hurry. Don't make Hayden wait and don't forget your flute."

"I know," Rebecca called out as she ran down the hall. "I have a lesson this morning."

"You're not in a hurry?" Polly asked Heath.

"Late morning today. Some in-service thing."

"I should probably know that, shouldn't I?"

He laughed. "It's on the calendar."

"Yeah. I was afraid you'd tell me that. So will you go to Doug's tonight?"

"I guess. He's a lot older than me, but Jason says it's cool. His girlfriend is going to be there, too."

"Whose? Doug's?"

"Well, yeah, her, but Jason's, too."

Polly sat forward and leaned on the table. "Jason has a girlfriend?"

"It's just Mel. But they're together all the time. She's even started going to the barn with him, and Eliseo's teaching her how to ride."

"This is what I miss about being at Sycamore House all the time. I don't get in on the scoop anymore. Nobody tells me anything."

"So I've been thinking about college."

Well, that was a change in topic. Polly just flowed with it. "Yes?"

"I know you and Hayden think I should live on campus, but I don't really care about that. I looked at a management program at DMACC. It's an AA degree. That would let me work for Henry too."

"I get that you don't want to live on campus," Polly said. "That isn't a requirement from us. We'd love to have you stay here."

He nodded.

"Would you hand me my laptop?" Polly pointed to the other end of the table.

Heath reached down and pushed it toward her.

"Do you think you can't do the work?" she asked.

He shrugged. Words were a problem for this boy when he was on the spot.

"When you moved in with us, what was your grade point?"

"It was only two-point-six."

"And what have you raised it to?"

He lowered his eyes. "Three-point-six."

"To raise it like that, you've had an awful lot of A's, haven't you?"

"Yeah. But the classes are easy."

"No they aren't," Polly said.

"I'm not smart like Hayden."

Noah and Elijah ran into the kitchen, their faces flush with excitement. "We get to ride with Hayden. Where is he?"

"Right here, guys," Hayden said, coming in from the foyer. "Where's Rebecca?"

Polly picked up her phone and texted her daughter. *"I'm not yelling down the hallway. Hayden's ready to go."*

"Coming," Rebecca yelled from her doorway.

Polly stood and helped Noah and Elijah put their coats on, hugged them both, and kissed their foreheads. "Remember how much I love you and how proud I am of you, okay?"

She hugged Rebecca. "I love you and I'm proud of you, too. Have a good day and thanks again for tonight."

Once everyone was out the door, Polly turned on Heath. "Now I can lop your head off."

"What do you mean?"

"Don't ever tell me that you aren't smart like Hayden. Ever. You can do anything you want. You're bright and you motivated yourself to work these last two years. Look what it got you."

"But..."

She put her hand up. "But nothing. You aren't interested in academics like he is. I get that. You don't want to do the science stuff that he loves. I get that, too. It's like how much I love all of you. I don't love any of you more than the other one, but I love you differently because you are each unique. Henry would like you to get this construction management degree at Iowa State. If you want to be in business with him, and he'd love that more than anything, you want to bring your A-game. This degree will teach you things you are just beginning to comprehend right now."

"But I could learn it all from him while I'm on the job."

"Or you could learn it in new and different ways and teach Henry what he doesn't know yet." Polly pointed at the screen where she'd brought up a course list. "Look at what you'll learn. This is practical stuff, Heath. With this information, you'd increase Henry's business knowledge exponentially."

"He really thinks I could do it?"

"We've talked about it. He's willing to pay for your education. And if you want to live here, we're fine with that. I think you'll be missing out on some of the college fun, but okay."

Heath put his head in his hands, his fingers massaging his scalp. "It's just so much to think about."

"Henry always tells me to take it one step at a time. You have the grades and your ACT scores were good. You can do this."

When he looked up at her, there were tears in his eyes. "I can't believe this is my life."

"Crazy woman pushing you to go to college?"

"Yeah, that too. When Ladd killed that girl at the coffee shop, I thought I was going to end up in prison just like my aunt always said I would. Now I'm talking about this crazy future."

Polly took his hand in hers. "You have so much to look forward to."

~~~

The last few days had been busy enough that there hadn't been a single moment to sit down with what Polly found in the metal box. In fact, she'd forgotten about them, having tucked them behind the driver's seat in her truck. Now, here it was Friday and she was supposed to go to the jewelry store to see what Gordon had discovered about her gold coins. Polly could hardly blame Simon, Paul and Ken for not digging more deeply into her mystery when she couldn't remember it moment to moment.

When her phone rang, she picked it up and heard laughter on the other end. "Did you get managed too?" Henry asked.

"I did. I take it Nate called you."

"We just got off the phone. Apparently I miss him desperately and have been pining for a little motor oil under my fingernails."

"Well, haven't you?"

He huffed a laugh. "I do feel guilty about leaving that Woody at his house. We haven't worked on those…"

"Since we bought this place?" Polly interrupted.

"At least that long. Maybe even longer."

"You told me it was going to take forever to finally finish them. At this rate, I'll be old and gray before I get to drive it."

"You and I can race each other down main street at twenty-miles an hour, just to give the young folks a thrill," Henry said.

"Are you okay with these plans?"

"It sounds like fun. I'm sorry you and Joss won't be able to spend time together. It sounds like she has something going on."

"Oh, you didn't hear."

"Hear what?"

"I've been set up with Lydia, Andy, Beryl, and Sylvie. We're having a party at Beryl's house. And Heath is in charge of getting me there and home safely. You know, just in case I have a little too much to drink."

"I might have heard about that."

"You knew?"

"I just knew that I wasn't supposed to let you get busy with anything else tonight. The rest is all Rebecca's."

"She is the queen of parties."

"You're pretty good at letting her get away with the fun stuff."

"When Rebecca is thinking about other people, she is an amazing person. It's only when she focuses on herself that I want to lock her in a dungeon."

"I'm glad that doesn't happen very often."

Polly laughed. "It's true, you know. She is good ninety-five percent of the time. And yet, I focus on those moments when she's just horrible."

"Who said that thing about being good?"

"What do you mean?"

"When I'm good, I'm very, very good … what was the rest of it?"

"But when I'm bad, I'm better?" Polly chuckled. "I think Mae West. Let's not encourage Rebecca with that one, okay?"

"Got it. Are you going uptown?"

"Yeah. Gordon opens at ten. I might have to have coffee before I see him, though."

"Do you always run into friends at Sweet Beans?"

"Most of the time."

"Think about that."

"What?"

"You always run into friends when you go to the coffee shop. Do you remember feeling bad because you didn't know enough people in Bellingwood?"

"It's wonderful, isn't it?"

"I probably won't see you until late tonight, then."

Polly thought about that and realized it made her sad. Then she realized how happy she was that it made her sad.

"Polly?"

"Sorry. I was thinking."

"You do that a lot. Sometimes I worry about you."

"I love you. I'll miss you this evening."

"Me too, but if you come home tipsy, you know I'll be waiting."

"What are you saying?"

"You know exactly what I'm saying. There's something about a tipsy Polly that makes my nights more fun."

"You'd better go to work."

"I know," he said, laughing. "Or I might have to come home."

She laughed as they hung up. What a wonderful life she led.

Polly wandered through the house, making sure that she had a head count on all of the animals. Cats were on cat trees, snuggled into Rebecca's pillows, and wrestling on Hayden's bed. Obiwan and Han followed as she made her rounds. "I'm leaving you here," Polly said. "Be good and keep those cats in line. Don't let them get in trouble. You hear me?"

Obiwan cocked his head and wagged his tail as she spoke. Whether or not he understood her, at least he knew she was speaking to him. Han, on the other hand, just wagged and followed along like the big goof that he was.

She put her coat on and went outside. Polly was ready for a few days of warmer weather. The forecast kept promising they'd see days in the upper thirties and lower forties, but it hadn't happened yet. The weekend was supposed to be nice. She could hardly wait.

As she drove down Beech Street and turned west to head for town, she saw a very small girl walking along, carrying a backpack. The school was just down a few blocks, but it was much too cold to be without a coat or jacket. Polly slowed and turned her window down.

"Honey, are you okay?"

The little girl stopped and looked at Polly. "I'm late for school."

"Where's your coat?"

"I couldn't find it."

"What about your mommy?"

The little girl scrunched up her face and looked as if she was about to cry. "I don't know."

Polly was pretty sure this little girl lived across the street from her. There were a million children in and out of those homes, so she wasn't sure who belonged where. They still hadn't had time to get to know their neighbors. Now she felt really guilty about that.

"Do you know who I am?" Polly asked.

The little girl, whose lower lip was out about a mile, nodded.

"Would you like to get in my truck and warm up? I'll take you to school." Polly opened her truck door and jumped down, then opened the back door. She saw the metal box on the floor and shook her head. She'd forgotten about it again.

"What's your name?" she asked, as the child approached.

"Rose Bright."

"Well, Rose, let's warm you up and take you to school. Were you all alone in the house this morning?"

Rose nodded again. "I looked in Mommy's bedroom and everywhere. I couldn't find her."

"Did you have breakfast?"

"I made a mess and had to clean it up when I made cereal." Rose looked at the floor.

"I'm sure no one will be upset about that. You did just fine." Polly pulled a blanket over the little girl. "You warm up. It's only a few blocks to school." First things first. The girl needed to be in a safe place and then Polly was calling Ken.

"Did you lock the door when you left?" she asked Rose.

"No. We never lock the door." Rose put her hand over her mouth. "I shouldn't say that, should I? Somebody could break in."

"It's okay. I'll keep an eye on things. I'm proud of you for going to school, though. What grade are you in?"

"First grade. Mommy says I'm a big girl now."

"You are. Your mommy will be proud of you." Polly climbed back into the driver's seat and turned up the heat. She was thankful this truck warmed up fast. "Do you have any sisters or brothers?" She looked in the rear-view mirror to watch the girl's response.

Rose nodded. "But they don't live with us. They live with my other daddy."

"Where does your daddy live?"

"My daddy doesn't live with us either. But my other daddy lives in Algona."

Polly couldn't even fathom what makeup this family had. She pulled in front of the school. "Let's go inside. Are you ready?"

"It's warm here."

"I know. Do you want to take the blanket with you?"

The hopeful look on Rose's face told her enough. Polly got out, opened the back door and helped Rose to the ground, then wrapped the blanket around her. They went inside and headed for the office. The secretary, Sharon, looked up.

"Hi Polly. What are you doing here today?" Then she saw Rose, wrapped in the blanket. "Well, Rose. I wondered where you were. It's good to see you." She gave Polly a questioning look.

"Do you think that Rose could find a warm place to sit while I talk to you, Sharon?" Polly asked.

"That's a great idea. Come with me, Rose. I'll bet Mrs. Welch has some juice she'd share with you." Sharon came around the desk, took Rose's hand and guided her to the nurse's office. Once the door was closed, she came back with the blanket and handed it to Polly. "What's going on?"

"I don't know. I found her walking to school with no coat. Fortunately, she recognized me and let me pick her up. She doesn't know where her mother is. I thought I'd call Chief Wallers and ask him to check the house. If we can't find her, do you have other contact information so you can reach somebody?"

Sharon nodded. "I have her father's information and her mother's first husband, too. He's in Algona, I think. I just have a cell number for her dad, though. Let's hope you find her mother and everything is okay."

"Either Ken or I will be in touch," Polly said. "Thanks."

Polly tossed the blanket into the back seat and took out her phone.

Ken responded right away. "Hi Polly, I still don't have any information for you. I was going to work on that this weekend while Maude and the girls are gone."

"No, that's not it. I just took a little girl to school and she doesn't know where her mother is."

"Please no," Ken said.

"I found the daughter, not the mother. I'm hoping that means something good," Polly said. "And I called you, not Aaron. Positive steps, right?"

He gave a pained chuckle. "What's the name?"

"The little girl is Rose Bright."

"Oh. They live right across the street from you."

"So you know them?"

"Not well. But yes. I'll head right over."

"Do you mind if I meet you there? I'd like to help. If they need anything, I'd like to be part of that."

"You're a good person, Polly. I'll be there in less than ten minutes."

CHAPTER FOURTEEN

Turning around in her driveway, Polly sat in her truck while watching for Ken's police car. Instinct told her to start looking for Rose's mother, but good sense told her to wait. To be honest, Polly wasn't exactly sure which house Rose lived in. Shawn Wesley and his family lived on the corner close to where Polly picked Rose up, but there were four other homes in various states of disrepair directly across the street from the Bell House. Many of the homes in this part of town were old and run down. It wouldn't take much to make them look better, but as far as Polly could tell, parents were working long hours and probably living paycheck to paycheck. She knew how lucky she was. She also knew that the state of the outside of these homes didn't tell the whole story about whatever was going on inside the houses. Most of the yards were as tidy as could be expected. Lawns were mowed and kids were called inside for dinner during nice evenings. She really needed to make more of an effort to get to know these people. Hopefully when spring and summer arrived, they'd be outside more and could host fun events on the block. The street back here was pretty quiet. It would be a perfect place for a block party.

Ken pulled up in front of a small dingy brown house with old gray shutters in the middle of the block. A driveway led to a matching garage in the back past a big old oak tree. The front porch steps sagged on one side and the door's screen was torn in several places.

She walked across the street to meet him. "Rose says the house is unlocked. Should we just go in?"

He walked up the steps, pulled open the screen, and rapped on the door. "Mrs. Bright? This is Chief Wallers from the Bellingwood Police Department. Are you here?"

They waited for a response and when there was none, Ken tried the door handle. Just as Rose had said, it opened into a small living room.

"Mrs. Bright?" Ken called out again. "My name is Ken Wallers. I'm the Chief of Police and I'm just here to check on you. Are you here?"

The living room was neat and clean with throw rugs scattered across worn carpeting. A sofa with a slip cover on it sat along one wall and a rocking chair and red plaid recliner were the other two seating options. A relatively new television stood in a corner and a bookshelf filled with knick-knacks, photographs, and books took up another corner.

"Why don't you go up and check the bedrooms while I look around down here," Ken said.

Polly nodded and went up the stairway. There were two bedrooms and a bathroom upstairs. Rose's room had been painted a light green and her mother had filled it with pink and red flowered decor - from the curtains on the windows, to the bedding and fabric covered lampshade. Her mother's room was also warm and inviting in tones of browns and green. A large knitted blanket covered the bed. The bed had been quickly made, much like Polly's own on busy mornings when all she did was fling the comforter up toward the pillows. She checked the bathroom, but no one was there.

"There's no one up here," she called out as she descended the stairs.

"Nothing on the main level either," Ken, standing in the kitchen doorway.

"Have you found the basement?" Polly asked. She opened a door beside the stairs and flipped on a light. "How about I check this and you check the garage. Make sure her car is there."

He smiled and headed for the back door while Polly negotiated her way down the steep open stairway. Before she reached the bottom, though, she yelled for him. "Ken! I found her."

Polly hurried to the woman's side. "Mrs. Bright, can you hear me?" She looked around the woman and didn't see any blood, but the light was dim and she wasn't positive of anything. Polly hesitantly picked up the woman's wrist. Her body felt warm, giving Polly hope that this wasn't going to turn out badly. She felt for a pulse and nearly dropped with relief when she found it on the first attempt.

Ken stopped at the bottom of the steps and took out his phone. "Mindy, I need an ambulance right away. Polly, don't let her move. If she fell off the steps, she might have hurt herself badly."

"She's not responding yet," Polly said. "But there's a pulse. You're good luck, Ken Wallers. This time I found someone who was still alive."

"I'll be right back." Ken went up the steps and Polly took the woman's hand in hers.

He returned with two blankets that he'd taken from the sofa and with Polly's help, covered the woman.

They both startled at the sound of moaning.

"Mrs. Bright?" Polly asked, kneeling down again. "Don't move. You've fallen off your basement steps."

"Rose," the woman said.

"She's at school. She's worried about you, but she's safe at school."

"How?"

"Mrs. Bright, I'm Polly Giller. I live across the street. I found her walking and when she said she didn't know where you were, I called Chief Wallers and we're both here. An ambulance is on the way."

"No. Too expensive."

"You can't worry about that now," Polly said. "You're hurt."

"Rose's coat." She attempted to move and Polly squeezed her hand.

"Please don't move. I don't know where you've been hurt. Is Rose's coat in the dryer?"

"Yes."

"That makes sense then. She couldn't find it, but knew she was late for school."

"I'm so embarrassed."

Polly chuckled. "I get that. But things happen all the time. Rose is in good hands and soon you will be, too."

"I can't go to the hospital."

"Let's see what the EMTs say before you make any decisions."

Ken took off up the steps. "I hear the siren." He stopped halfway up. "I don't know why I'm even here, Polly. You handled everything just fine."

Polly pursed her lips at him and he chuckled, then went on.

"Everything hurts," the woman said.

"What's your first name?" Polly asked.

"Mona."

"Do you know what happened?"

"I was in a hurry. So stupid. I didn't even turn on the light. There's plenty of light over by the dryer. I came running down the steps. I shut the door because I don't want Rose coming down here. She knows she isn't supposed to. I must have gotten too close to the edge and I just fell off the steps. It was like slow motion and then you were here."

"You need a banister on that open side of the stairway."

"I need a lot of things in this house. Maybe someday." Mona closed her eyes.

"Why don't you keep your eyes open," Polly said. "You scare me."

The woman started to laugh, then stopped herself. "That hurt. You're the one who finds dead bodies, aren't you?"

"Yes. And I'm very glad you aren't. You have to stay awake

and alive or I will never invite you and Rose over to see my house."

That elicited a smile. "If I had my wits about me, I would have been worried when I realized who you were," Mona said. "I need to call work and tell them that I'm not coming in today."

"Is there anyone else that needs to be contacted?"

Mona shook her head. "Not really."

The sound of footsteps above them preceded the door opening and people coming down the stairs.

"I'll get out of their way," Polly said. "But I'll just be upstairs. We can talk when they're finished."

"Thank you for finding me." Mona squeezed her hand.

Polly smiled at the EMTs and backed away, giving them room to work. As soon as the path was clear, she went up the steps. Once she was in the living room, she dropped into the recliner.

It took a half hour, but soon Ken Wallers came up the steps, followed by the two EMTs, with Mrs. Bright strapped to a gurney. They dropped the wheels and Polly jumped up from her seat.

"What happened?" she asked.

"I broke my collarbone and have a concussion," Mona said. "They're also worried about maybe a broken rib. I don't know what to do with Rose if they put me in the hospital."

Ken put his hand on the woman's arm. "Take a deep breath," he said with a chuckle.

"What?"

"Because I'm about to step in," Polly said. "Let Rose stay at our house tonight. I'm sure she knows my two little boys. My daughter, Rebecca, and her friend, Kayla, are in the eighth grade. I'm more than glad to pick you up when you're ready to come home and if it takes longer than an overnight stay, Rose and I will visit you."

"That's too much to ask."

"No it isn't," Polly said. "That's what neighbors are for. Even if I haven't come over to introduce myself yet. Rose will be safe with us. She can come here after school and pack up a few things for an overnight stay."

"She's going to be pretty scared," Mona said.

"We'll figure that out. Maybe I can bring her down after school so you can reassure her."

"You shouldn't be doing all of this."

"Yes she should," one of the EMTs said. "And we have to get you to the hospital. It's time to start fixing what you broke."

Polly shook her head and grinned. "Do you have her phone?"

"It's by the television," Mona said. "And my purse is beside it. That's where my insurance card is."

Taking a business card out of her own phone case, Polly handed it to Ken who was gathering up the phone and Mona's purse.

He slid the card and phone into the purse and tucked it in beside the woman. "Don't worry. We'll close up the house."

"Thank you both," Mona said as she was wheeled away and out the front door.

"I'm going back downstairs to grab Rose's coat. It was in the dryer," Polly said. "That's why Mrs. Bright was in the basement this morning."

"I'll check the back door and make sure lights are turned off. You do get yourself involved in people's lives, don't you?"

Polly nodded. Now she wasn't sure what to do about the party Rebecca had planned this evening. She didn't feel comfortable leaving Rebecca and Kayla at home alone with a child they barely knew. It would have been one thing if Heath or Hayden had been there, but a frightened child was too much responsibility. Polly opened the dryer door and took out a coat, scarf, hat, and mittens that had been freshly laundered. She was glad that Rose had chosen to walk to school just as Polly drove by, but couldn't believe the child had gone out in the cold with none of her usual protection.

~~~

Polly went back to the school and took Rose's coat in to the office.

"Did you find Mona?" the secretary, Sharon, asked.

"She'd fallen off the basement steps. Rose would have had no idea where she was. She'd gone down to get Rose's coat out of the dryer." Polly put it on the chair in front of Sharon's desk. "Would you see that she gets it?"

"What's going on with Mona?"

Polly moved the coat and sat down. "She's gone to the hospital. Probably with a broken clavicle and a concussion, maybe bruised ribs. I'll pick Rose up this afternoon when I get the rest of my gang." She stopped to think about how she was going to get one more child into her truck. There weren't enough seatbelts. That problem could wait until later.

"I should tell Rosie what's going on," Sharon said. "When you find out how long Mona has to stay in the hospital let me know. If she comes home this weekend, I'll make sure we get some meals to her and Rosie." Sharon blew out a breath. "This is going to be rough on them financially. Those ambulance rides are expensive." Then she nodded. "But we'll do a little fund raising around here. We can help her manage this."

Polly grinned. She loved it when other people dug right in. "Let me know. I'll help out, too."

"Oh, Polly, you're already doing something. Mona is a really nice woman. Whenever she has a vacation day, she comes in to help us. If she isn't in Rosie's classroom, she comes to the office to run the copier or put files together. She just likes to be around us. I wish we could afford to give her a job, but there's no money."

"Sharon?" Miss Bickel stood in her doorway.

"I'd better get to work," Sharon said. "Thanks for letting me know. I'll talk to Rosie."

Polly nodded at the principal, who acknowledged her with a curt shake of the head, then got up and left. Sharon was a saint.

She went back out to her truck and decided that she could really use more coffee now. Lydia's Jeep was parked across the street from the coffee shop. Polly couldn't believe her luck. She parked and headed in, relieved to see Lydia and Andy sitting in a booth together.

The two women waved and Polly acknowledged them, then pointed at the front counter. Lydia nodded and went back to her conversation with Andy.

"How are you?" Camille asked.

"I'm good," Polly said. "Have Lydia and Andy had anything to eat?"

"Just coffee."

"I need my regular, then, and three croissants."

"Chief Wallers was ordering coffee when you called this morning. Is everything okay?" Camille asked.

"One of my neighbors fell down her basement stairs. I needed him to help me get into her house so we could take care of her."

"But she was alive?"

Polly grimaced. "I hate that you have to ask that, but yes. She was very much alive."

"Well, what a great day. That calls for a celebration."

"Aren't you the funny one."

Camille chuckled. "I thought so." She handed the plate of croissants and cup of coffee to Polly. "Go celebrate with your friends. A live body is always better than a dead one."

Polly shook her head as she walked away, then slid into the booth beside Lydia.

"What did you do?" Andy asked, reaching to the other end of the booth for the napkin dispenser.

"I brought treats. Apparently I should be celebrating. I found someone alive rather than dead."

"That does call for a party," Lydia said. "Good thing we have one planned for tonight."

"About that," Polly said.

Andy lifted her hand and waggled her forefinger at Polly. "Oh no you don't. We're looking forward to this."

"I am too, but I am going to have a little girl staying with us tonight that doesn't know anybody. Her mother doesn't even really know me."

"The woman who is alive?" Lydia asked.

Polly nodded. "Mona Bright."

"Oh yes, your neighbor. She's a nice girl. Had a rough time of it, but she's got a sweet daughter," Andy said. "Mona's parents are in the cemetery, not too far from my back door. I see her out there quite often. What happened?"

"She went downstairs to get Rose's coat out of the dryer, fell off the steps onto the concrete floor and knocked herself out. A broken clavicle and a concussion."

"How did you find this out?" Lydia asked, putting a croissant on a napkin and setting it in front of Polly. She took the last one for herself.

"I found Rose walking to school without a coat."

"On a day like today?" Andy was aghast.

"Exactly. Rose told me she couldn't find her mother, but she didn't want to be late for school. I called Ken and he met me at the house. We went inside and I discovered her on the floor in the basement. She hadn't turned the light on or anything. And ... she told Rose to never go into the basement. The child wouldn't have known to look down there."

"You have to come play with us tonight," Lydia said. "What can we do to help you?"

"Rebecca and Kayla were going to babysit the boys and I know they'd be fine with Rose, too, but Mona doesn't know my family. There really needs to be an adult in the house."

"Where's Henry?" Andy asked.

"He's going out to Nate's to work on the Woody. Hayden has a date and Heath made plans to go up to Doug Randall's apartment for a big game night. I want all of them to have fun tonight."

"You just need an adult." Lydia put her hand out on the table. "Andy, who do we know?"

"You aren't going to let me bail on tonight, are you?" Polly asked.

"No way, Jose," Lydia responded. "Now think, ladies."

Polly put her hand on Lydia's arm. "I'll talk to Jessie. If she doesn't have a big deadline, she and Molly can come over and spend the evening. The kids all like her. If she can't do it, I'm out. Deal?"

Lydia frowned. "Not a good deal, but okay."

"Has anyone talked to you about cataloging the items in the basement of the library yet?" Polly asked Andy.

Andy shook her head. "No. It would be a good project, though. Things are in complete disarray down there. Why?"

"I need help finding boxes from some woman who was the unofficial historian of Bellingwood. Simon Gardner seems to think that her children donated them to the city and they ended up in the basement of the library."

"Margie Deacon?" Lydia asked.

"Yeah. That's her."

"What are you looking for?"

Polly was still carrying the gold coin in her pocket. She took it out and put it on the table.

Andy picked it up first. "What is that?"

"A five-dollar gold coin. Maybe. Gordon Berkley is authenticating it. I'm going to see him when I'm finished here."

Lydia took the coin as Andy offered it to her, turning it back and forth. "He knows his stuff. Where did you find this?"

"In a metal box tucked into a mantle on the second floor. I counted eighty-two coins."

Andy leaned forward and whispered, "How much are they worth now?"

"If they're real, over a hundred and fifty thousand dollars," Polly said. "If they're counterfeit, nada."

"Let's hope they're real. What will you do with all of that money?"

"I have no idea. It doesn't feel right to just uncover money and then use it willy nilly. If it's real, I want to do something good with it."

"That's my girl." Lydia patted Polly's hand. "You just can't enjoy some good found money."

"It's not right."

"Sure it is. But I won't be able to convince you of that."

"What does this coin have to do with the boxes from Margie Deacon?" Andy asked.

"Oh yeah." Polly laughed. "There was another box with ledger books and some kind of contracts. They all had that symbol of the plow and the sword. Simon, Ken, and Paul Bradford think that Margie might have information in those boxes that will help unwind the mystery of what it means. And I also need to go see Greg Parker. Lucy says he wants to talk to me."

"Greg wants to have you come over?" Lydia asked in astonishment. "Really?"

"I guess."

Andy reached out for the coin again. "I'll be in the library this afternoon. I was going to help Joss with a shipment of new books, but I can head for the basement and see what I might uncover. It would be good to get a handle on how much work there is to do down there. I might have to enlist all of my helpers to get the task complete."

"That's a great idea," Lydia said. "Let's call Beryl and invite her to help."

CHAPTER FIFTEEN

"'Lo, Mrs. Sturtz," Gordon said when she walked into the jewelry store.

Polly didn't feel the need to correct him. "Hi there. Did you find anything out?"

He nodded and smiled, then reached under the counter and pulled out a small plastic bag containing her coin. "I certainly did. This is the genuine article. I didn't know that so many of them were still out there. That quantity will drive their price down but you will still be much wealthier than you are now."

Polly swallowed. Now that she knew the truth, she didn't know whether to be excited or what.

"That's good news, isn't it?"

"It is," she said. "You're sure?"

"Couldn't be any more sure." He put a piece of paper on the counter. "There's a certificate stating its worth as of today and asserting its purity and authenticity. If you want to sell the coins, I would be glad to handle the transaction for you. I have a few buyers that would be interested. If you want to take them somewhere else, that certificate will make it easier for you to make the sale."

"I need to talk to Henry," she said.

"In this day and age, people like to keep gold around, too. It's always a safe form of currency."

She huffed a small laugh. "I doubt we'd do that. What do I owe you for the work you did?"

He put his hand up to stop her. "I would appreciate the opportunity to sell these coins for you. There would be a small handling fee involved and that would cover this as well."

"Thank you." Polly scratched her head. "I don't know what we're going to do."

"I understand. It's quite a lot to take in, a windfall of this magnitude."

"Yes it is," she agreed. "Thank you."

"Mrs. Sturtz, if I may?"

"Yes?"

"If you find anything else like this while you're clearing out that old house, please allow me participate in any verification you might need."

"Oh. Sure," Polly said, still processing on what it meant to be holding these two coins. Nearly four thousand dollars was tucked into her pocket and she barely felt its weight. "Thank you so much for your time. I'm sure we'll be in touch."

"Thank you."

The front door opened and an elderly couple came in. Polly smiled at them as she went back out into the cold. She turned right before remembering her truck was across the street. Polly wandered over to it, climbed in, and turned the truck on. She took the coins out of her pocket, passing them back and forth in her hands. This was absolutely ridiculous. Of all the strange things she'd encountered since moving to Bellingwood, none of them felt as surreal as this. She'd heard about people uncovering treasures in their attics, but that was the last thing she expected at the Bell House.

Bellingwood was probably just waiting for her to discover something interesting. As if Franklin Bell's body in a hole in her back yard wasn't enough. But what was that hotel really used for? The overly romanticized notion that it was a speakeasy during Prohibition and that Bell had provided whiskey to Al Capone was the stuff of stories and tall tales. Was this money part of that enterprise or was it something else? She just wished she had an inkling of what had gone on during those early days of the last century. But no one had any knowledge of the symbol that was such a big part of her home. Who was involved and why was it only at the Bell House? Surely if those who used it to mark their work were part of the community, it would have shown up in other homes from the same era.

She slammed the base of her hand on the steering wheel. Nothing made sense. And to top it off, she had to figure out how to take care of another little girl this evening while still attending a party with her friends. She really wanted to go, but didn't feel comfortable leaving Rose with two junior high girls. Mona would probably be glad of two junior high girls to babysit her daughter, but not in a strange house and not while she was stuck in a hospital.

Polly's phone rang. She didn't recognize the number, so she answered tentatively. "Polly Giller."

"Hi Polly, this is Mona Bright."

"Oh hello. How are you?"

"Better than I should be, I guess."

"What do you mean?"

"I did break my clavicle, but the concussion is light and they aren't keeping me overnight. I won't need to bother you to keep an eye on Rose this evening."

"We were glad to do it," Polly said. "When will they release you?"

"No need to worry. One of my friends from work will pick me up on her way home."

"I'd be glad to come down to get you."

"That's not necessary, but I appreciate all that you did for me. That was very nice."

Polly smiled. "I just feel bad that we met this way instead of something a little more neighborly. I spoke to Sharon at the school and she has Rose's coat, hat and mittens."

"Oh, thank you. I'd forgotten all about that. I'll call Sharon and let her know that everything is okay."

"How will Rose get home tonight?"

"We use their afterschool program, so she'll stay like she always does. My friend and I will pick her up. Again, thank you so much for everything you did this morning."

"I don't feel like I did all that much. Would you mind if I stop in tomorrow to check on you? If you need me to do anything, just tell me. I broke my clavicle a couple of years ago. It was a terrible time of not being able to do what I wanted to do."

"That would be very nice. Thank you for everything."

"You have my number. Please call if you need anything. No matter the time of day. I'm right across the street and have a house full of very helpful young people."

"Yes you do," Mona said. "I'll keep it handy."

Polly ended the call and entered Mona's name as a contact. It hadn't taken that long to deal with that issue. She was surprised they weren't keeping the woman overnight, but could imagine that Mona had been quite adamant about going home to take care of her daughter.

She realized she was parked just down from the grocery store. Now would be a great time to pick up food for the festivities. Polly climbed back out of her truck and braced herself against the wind as she headed down the sidewalk. The warmth from the grocery store enveloped her as she walked in. Grabbing a cart, Polly proceeded to fill it as she wandered through the aisles.

"Hello, Miss Giller," a woman said.

"Hi." Polly peered at the woman, trying to identify her. She'd met her at least once before and worked to come up with where.

"I'm Julie Shaffer."

"Oh. Julie. Hi," Polly said. "How are you?"

"We're good. Doug really enjoys his job. Your husband was so nice to help him out."

Polly chuckled. "The truth is, Doug is helping Henry. He

needed to find someone for that position. Doug showed up at just the right time. How's Cameron?" She was proud of herself for remembering their oldest son's name.

"He has good days and bad days. He misses his old friends and hasn't made many new ones in Bellingwood yet, but we're hopeful. Doug thinks we'll be able to get into a small house sometime this summer and he promised Cameron that we would get another dog. I think Cameron misses his dog as much as any of his friends."

"That's so hard," Polly said. "I don't know where I'd be without my pets."

"Everyone in Bellingwood was so nice when we landed here. Pastor Dunlap told us they would be. I can't wait to get into a house, though. Maybe I can start my daycare again. That was how I got to know some of the other mothers. But it all takes time and we're grateful for a roof over our heads and food on the table." She pointed down the aisle. "I should probably finish my shopping. I didn't want to bother you, but since I saw you, I wanted to say hello and thank you."

"I'm glad you did." Polly reached into her pocket, took out her phone and drew another business card from the case. "If you ever need anything, please call me. And maybe one of these days, Cameron could come over after school and play with our dogs and the kids."

"That would be very nice," Julie said, taking the card. She dropped it into an immense overflowing purse. "I'll be seeing you."

Polly finished her shopping and carried the bags out to the truck. She climbed back in and turned it on again, waiting for the heat to blow on her. Taking out her phone, she texted to Henry. *"The gold coins are real. Gordon wants to sell them for us. I told him I had to talk to you."*

"Wow," he texted back. *"Wait. You had to talk to me? Because you can't make a decision without your big, strong husband?"*

"Exactly."

"That's what I thought. Glad I'm here for you."

"Me too. I sent our neighbor to the hospital this morning." Polly laughed out loud as she pressed send.

Sure enough, her phone rang.

"You did what?" Henry asked.

"The neighbor across the street. I picked up her daughter who was walking to school with no coat. She didn't know where her mother was, so after I turned the little girl over to Sharon in the school office, I called Ken and he met me at the house. We found the mom lying on the basement floor. She broke her collarbone."

Silence greeted Polly's words.

"Are you there?" she asked.

"I don't know how you do it. But she was alive when you last saw her, right?"

"Yeah. I told Ken he was good luck. It's Aaron that gets the calls when they're dead."

"Which neighbor is this?"

"Mona Bright. She lives in the little brown house."

"The one where all the kids go in and out?"

"Yeah. I think most of those kids live with her ex-husband in Algona. She just has the one little girl at home with her."

"Weird."

"She's very nice and the little girl is a sweetie."

"Is another child staying with us while this woman is in the hospital?"

Polly chuckled. "Nope. I just talked to her. She's coming home this afternoon. My duties are all wrapped up with that one."

"For now."

"Shut up."

Henry laughed. "You're going over to check on her tomorrow, aren't you?"

"Didn't you hear me? I said shut up."

"Got it. Fine then. I'll shut up and get back to work. I love you."

"I know."

Polly went straight home. Her kitchen looked so different with the counter tops in. Even though the cabinet doors weren't hung yet, this room was finally coming together. She hefted the grocery bags up onto the counter beside the door.

Polly was a little tired of having the stove and refrigerator spread between two rooms. They were out of the way of construction, but she looked forward to having appliances fill the empty spaces where they belonged. Marie and Bill didn't want their old refrigerator back. Henry recommended that Polly keep it. The way their family kept growing and with as many kids as seemed to come over, she'd need the extra storage. There was plenty of room for it on the side porch with the washer and dryer. The old stove had to go, though. Henry had picked it up cheap. They just needed to find it a new home.

She opened the door to the pantry and cringed. Once they cleaned this room out, she was certain they'd find groceries they forgot they had. All she wanted was a couple of bags of chocolate chips. Polly moved a bag of cat food and some boxes of crackers off a shelf, shifted empty plastic containers around and finally discovered what she was looking for.

Polly opened the refrigerator and took out butter and eggs, then went back to that horrid pantry for flour, sugar and brown sugar. Once those were on the counter, she headed back in for her mixer.

"I swear," she said to Obiwan, who had followed her back and forth across the room. "When Henry gets my fancy cabinets installed and I can clean out that room, I'm going to be content."

He chuffed a bark.

"Oh, so that's the way it is," she said. "You don't believe me."

Obiwan barked again.

"I know, I know," Polly said. "I'll never be content. There will always be something else that needs to be dealt with."

This time Obiwan walked over to the pantry and barked one more time. Polly looked at him and then she laughed. "So you weren't talking to me about my problems; you were asking for a treat." She rubbed his head and opened the container of treats, taking two out. Flipping one in the air, she waited for him to catch it, then tossed the second up for Han.

The younger dog watched the treat go up and when it hit the floor, he jumped high before pouncing on it.

Obiwan barked at the pantry door again.

"No," Polly said. "You've had your treat. I'm making cookies now."

By the time she had the mixer going, every single animal in the house had made its way to the kitchen. She'd taken Luke, Leia and Wonder off the counter at least three times. The kittens were too small to jump up yet, but they whined and whimpered around her ankles, looking for attention.

"Look, you guys. There are more of you than there are of me. You're supposed to play with each other." For good measure, she bent over and picked two kittens up, snuggled them, then returned them to the floor and looked around for Arrow. Unlike his television namesake, Rebecca's Arrow was a tubby little monster who loved to eat. Polly found him nosing around the floor of the pantry, looking for anything that might have dropped to his level. She scooped him up, grabbed two cookie sheets, and after kissing his cute little head, put him back down and shut the pantry door.

"This place is a regular zoo," she muttered.

Leia had jumped back up on the counter to bat at the dishcloth someone had draped over the faucet. It was too much work to fight with every cat every single time, but Polly gave it one more shot and put Leia back on the floor. That earned her an annoyed tail twitch and the cat left for the dining room to watch her daily back yard entertainment.

When it was time to get the kids, Polly lifted the cooling trays of cookies to a middle shelf in the upper cupboard and put the mixing bowl in the refrigerator, moving things around for space. She'd finish when they got back.

"You boys be good. Andrew will be here soon and he'll take you on a walk around the yard." Polly rubbed Obiwan's head and scratched Han's neck before putting her coat back on.

She glanced at the Bright's home after she backed out of the driveway. Maybe one more batch of cookies this afternoon. That would be a nice treat to take over. It sounded like friends from school would take care of other meals for them. She turned the corner. When the weather turned warmer, she wouldn't worry about the kids walking five blocks home, but this wind was bitter. The line of mothers and fathers waiting for their kids was long today. At least Polly's kids knew where to look for her. Pretty soon, Elijah and Noah came running toward her truck. They jumped into the back seat and buckled in.

"It's really cold," Elijah said.

"Yes it is," Polly agreed. "Did you have a good day today?"

He dug around in his backpack and took out a piece of paper, then unbuckled himself and handed it across the seat to her.

"What's this?"

"I had a spelling test. Look."

Polly tapped the one hundred percent mark. His teacher had drawn a smiley face beside it. "Good job, sweetie. I'm proud of you. Anything else happen today?"

"Jimmy Newlon cut his hand and had to go to the nurse."

"He did? That's too bad." Polly smiled to herself. It was fun listening to what these kids remembered from their day. "How about you, Noah? How was your day?"

He caught her eye in the rear-view mirror and smiled. "Mrs. Wallers asked me to help Ben Jorgenson with his math."

"She did!" Polly said. "Was that because you were good at it?"

Noah nodded, still smiling.

Polly wondered if Maude Wallers had any idea how much that meant to the little boy.

Rebecca, Kayla, and Andrew ran up to the truck. Kayla usually got in the back seat with the little boys so Andrew and Rebecca could sit together up front. Polly thought it was sweet of her, even though the two were together all the time. Besides, if they tried anything in front of her, she'd kill 'em both.

"Did you hear about our neighbor?" Rebecca asked. "Her little girl came to school without a coat or anything because she couldn't find her mommy. And she was almost dead in the basement."

"I heard that she was drunk and fell down last night and was there all night long. The little girl didn't have any clean clothes or anything," Kayla said.

"Do you know who the little girl is?" Polly asked, grinning to herself.

"Rose Bright," Andrew said, sitting forward to look around Rebecca at Polly.

"I know Rose," Elijah said. He stood up and leaned across the front seat.

Polly patted his head. "Sit back and buckle in. We're going home. Do any of you know which house they live in?"

"I think it's that blue house on the corner," Rebecca said. "It looks like someone who is drunk all the time lives there. It would be nice if they painted it, you know."

Polly listened to the kids gossip about the story as she drove home. Just before she pulled into the driveway, she pointed to the little brown house across the street. "Look at that house," she said.

Everyone followed her finger.

"Yeah?" Rebecca asked.

"Just get a good look. I'll tell you why when we get inside. Andrew, will you take the dogs out for a run?"

"But I won't hear why you wanted us to look at the house."

"I'll wait. Everyone else will put their things away and get into weekend clothes. Speaking of weekend clothes, Kayla, do you have an overnight bag?"

"Stephanie is bringing it over later."

"Got it." Polly popped the locks open on the truck and the kids jumped out and ran for the house. Andrew had the dogs on their leashes and in the back yard before she got to the side door.

"Go on," she said, when she got inside. The other four kids were sniffing around the cookies. "Hang your coats up, leave your shoes on the porch, put your backpacks away and change your clothes. This will be here when you come back.

Polly had a plate of cookies, napkins, glasses and milk on the table by the time everyone returned. Andrew came in, flushed from running with the dogs.

"They did everything, but we'll go back out later and take more time." He dropped his coat on the floor, saw Polly's look, picked it up and slung it over Rebecca's before rushing to the table. "What did I miss?"

Obiwan looked longingly at the pantry door and Polly chuckled before opening it and taking out two more treats for the dogs.

"Okay, why did we look at that house?" Rebecca asked.

"Because that's where the Brights live."

"Oh. Okay." Rebecca reached for a glass and the milk.

"I'm not finished," Polly said.

Rebecca's hand paused in mid-air.

"You know gossip is a terrible thing because you never really get the whole story. I let you kids get it all out on the way home and now I want you to know what really happened. Mrs. Bright wasn't drinking. She takes very good care of her daughter and she'd fallen off the steps this morning as she went to the basement to get Rose's coat, scarf, hat and mittens out of the dryer. Not only were they clean, but she intended for them to be warm and snuggly when Rose put them on to go outside. Rose wasn't on the same floor when Mrs. Bright fell and didn't know where her mother had gone. She was scared when I picked her up and took her to school."

At that, she had everyone's attention.

"I called Chief Wallers and the two of us went over to their house. I found Mrs. Bright in the basement. She wasn't nearly dead. She wasn't drunk. She'd hit her head and blacked out. She's a nice woman and this weekend we'll take cookies over. It's my fault that I haven't been a better neighbor, but that changes now."

Noah put his hand up.

"Yes, sweetie?"

"Chief Wallers was at my school this week."

Polly smiled. "I know that. Do you like him?"

Noah nodded.

"For the rest of you, how do you feel about the gossip you participated in today?"

Kayla looked up. "I just said what I heard."

"That's pretty much the definition of gossip," Polly said. "We don't repeat things that are speculation or stories. In fact, we just don't talk about other people in negative ways. Okay?"

Kayla turned away.

"I'm not mad at any of you. I just wanted you to know the difference between gossip and truth."

"You really found her?" Andrew asked. "And she wasn't dead?"

Polly laughed. "Now you stop that. She was very much alive."

"That's why you called Chief Wallers instead of the sheriff, isn't it?" Rebecca asked.

"We'll just call Chief Wallers good luck. Eat your cookies. I'm going to make another batch and get ready to head over to Beryl's house."

Rebecca passed the milk to Kayla. "You're going to let Heath drive you, aren't you?"

"I think I'll be fine."

"But he really wanted to do that."

Polly smiled. "I guess I can let him, then."

CHAPTER SIXTEEN

Easing between Lydia's Jeep and Andy's car, Heath pulled in to Beryl's driveway. Polly put her hand on the truck door.

"Thanks for doing this," she said.

"What time do you think?"

"I'll try to be early."

He laughed. "That's not what I meant. I don't care. I was just wondering if I should leave Doug's house early."

"Oh. No," she said. "Why don't you send me a text when you're about to leave and if I'm ready here, I'll let you know. Otherwise, Sylvie can take me home and pick up Andrew. We'll figure it out."

He patted the grocery bag on the console between them. "Thanks for this."

Polly had packed up cookies for him to take and a couple of bags of potato chips. She knew how those kids ate. She gave his hand a squeeze. "Have fun tonight. Don't be nervous."

"It will be fine. Thanks."

She grabbed up her own bag of goodies, jumped out of the truck and headed for the front door. Loud music was coming from inside, something Beryl never did. Polly pressed the doorbell and waited. Heath hadn't backed out of the driveway yet. She pressed the doorbell once more, looked back at him and shrugged. Then she tried the door and when it opened, waved goodbye and went in.

The music was incredibly loud and the hallway light was off, but lights were strobing ahead of her. She flipped it on and looked up. The bulb had been replaced with a black light bulb. "Huh," Polly said to herself. "Gonna be one of those nights."

She walked past Beryl's front room and into the living room where a strobe was bouncing light off the walls. Beryl was sitting in a chair, holding a glass of wine.

Inch by inch, Polly took in the room, her eyes landing on Lydia who was seated on the sofa, smiling at her.

"Hello," Polly yelled.

Lydia nodded, but didn't say anything.

"Where's Andy and Sylvie?"

Lydia nodded again.

Polly tapped her ear. "I can't hear anything," she yelled. "Can we turn the music down?"

Beryl jumped up and went down the short hallway to the kitchen. In just a moment, she returned with another glass of wine and handed it to Polly.

Polly grabbed Beryl's wrist. "I can't hear anything."

Beryl nodded and sat back down.

"This is a little freaky." Polly rubbed her forehead and then jumped when she felt a hand on her shoulder. She spun around to see Sylvie standing there, her eyes big.

"What's going on?" Sylvie asked, yelling into Polly's ear.

"I don't know. They aren't talking," Polly yelled back.

Beryl jumped up again and disappeared into the kitchen, then returned with another glass of wine, which she handed to Sylvie.

"Where's Andy?" Sylvie asked Polly.

This yelling thing was getting old, but Beryl and Lydia didn't seem flustered in the least.

Andy came up the stairs from the basement, her face lighting up at the sight of Sylvie and Polly. She glanced at Lydia and Beryl and her face broke into a grin.

"Drink up," she yelled at Polly. "Trust me. The whole glass."

Polly wrinkled her forehead and Andy mimed pouring back a drink. She looked at Sylvie and the two downed their wine in several gulps.

As soon as they were finished, Beryl jumped up again, grabbed their glasses and headed for the kitchen. When she came back into the room with refills, the decibel level dropped significantly.

"Ohhhh," Polly said with a sigh. "That's better."

Beryl, Andy, and Lydia all pulled ear plugs out.

"You rats," Sylvie said. "What was that about?"

"It's seventies night at The Studio," Beryl announced. "That's what I'm calling my party house. Does it work for you? I thought we'd start with a rave." She nodded and the decibel level went back up.

"Stop it!" Polly yelled. "You're killing me."

The music returned to a more decent level and Lydia laughed as she held up a remote control. "This is fun. I like having power."

"If I'd known we were doing seventies, I would have dressed more appropriately," Polly said.

"Now that would have been a good idea," Beryl said. "Why didn't I think of it? You two girls take your coats off." Beryl put her hands out. "What did you bring? You weren't supposed to bring anything."

Polly handed her the plastic tub. "I just made cookies. If you're plying me with wine, I return the favor with cookies."

"Mmmm, these are fresh, aren't they?" Beryl said. She opened the carton and tossed a cookie at Lydia, who expertly grabbed it out of the air. "Don't spoil your appetite, though."

Lydia simply nodded.

"And what did our sweet baker bring?"

Sylvie opened the Sweet Beans bakery bag and Beryl peered in. "What's this?" She drew out a roll. "Looks like bread. Is it bread?"

"It is," Sylvie said, nodding. "Marta and I tried out a new French roll recipe this afternoon."

"So we're nothing more than your guinea pigs?" Beryl asked. She chomped down on the roll, spreading flakes everywhere. "Oh wow. That's crispy on the outside and moist on the inside." She tossed the roll at Lydia, who fumbled it because of the wine glass she'd picked up. "Come on, Toodles. You can do better than that."

Lydia shook her head and smiled.

Polly slipped her coat off and dropped it on a chair. "You're being awfully quiet, Lydia."

"I'm letting the star have her turn." Then she grinned wickedly. "Mine's coming later."

Beryl snatched the bag from Sylvie, pirouetted away from them and handed the tub of cookies and bag to Andy. "Are we ready down there?"

"Yes, Mistress."

"See," Beryl said. "That's the way I like my help. Obedient and polite. Come on, ladies. Dinner is served."

Skylar Morris stood at the bottom of the stairs, dressed in a tuxedo.

"What's this?" Polly asked.

"This is our waiter for the evening," Beryl replied.

"I thought you had a date with Stephanie, Sky."

He smiled. "She has to work until eight. Then we're going out." He swept his hand down. "And we're dressing up, too."

"This is crazy." Sylvie gave Skylar a hug. "You kids are nuts."

He shrugged. "Ms. Watson asked if I'd be interested in a job for tonight. I said yes before she told me who I was serving. If I'd known it was you …" He paused and smiled at them. "I'd have asked for more money."

"We'll be nice," Sylvie said. "Won't we, ladies?"

Skylar moved as quickly as possible and managed to catch everyone's chair but Polly's as they sat down. She winked at him. "Better luck next time."

"May I fill your glass?" he asked.

Polly held up her nearly empty wine glass.

"The first course tonight is a hearty butternut squash soup with curry and roasted chicken," he announced. He emptied the bag of rolls into a basket and placed them on the table. "I believe Sylvie's rolls will make a perfect accompaniment." With a flourish, he lifted a napkin from the top of a tray filled with steaming soup bowls and put one in front of each woman.

"Wow," said Polly. "I feel underdressed and outclassed."

"Drink more wine," Beryl said. "You'll become less dressed and less classy in no time." She snickered. "Did I say that?"

"Ladies, please," Skylar said. "Maintain decorum and keep your clothes on. I do not want to be a victim of one of your parties."

"What have you heard, young man?" Beryl asked.

"Enough. And that's all I'm going to say."

Polly tasted her soup. "This is incredible." She blinked. "Okay, there's the curry. But still, it's wonderful. Where did it come from?"

"I made it, of course," Beryl said. She snorted with laughter. "I can't believe that got out of my mouth without choking me. Especially with the heat of that curry."

Sylvie looked around. "Where are your cats? I half expected them to be in my lap during dinner."

"They're upstairs in my bedroom," Beryl said. They're so poorly behaved that I didn't want you to deal with them tonight." She looked pointedly at Lydia. "Some of you aren't animal people."

"I like animals," Lydia protested. "I like them just fine. But you're right. I don't like to have them eat with me."

Polly sighed. "At my house, it's a constant battle. Luke and Leia have learned that they don't get to be on the table with us, but the kittens are so curious. One climbs up, we put it down and before you know it, another finds an empty chair and sneaks up. We put it down. It usually takes two or three times per kitty before they give up. Arrow is more persistent and I have to put him down several times before he gets distracted by something else and runs off."

Lydia shuddered. "I couldn't do it."

"Then you should get a dog," Sylvie said. "Padme is awesome.

If something falls on the floor, she has it cleaned up before I even realize it's gone from the table. It really put a dent in my mopping schedule."

Lydia looked at her in shock.

"I'm kidding," Sylvie said. "Kinda. She's polite at meal times, though those are the saddest eyes you'll ever see when she thinks she should have part of what you're eating."

"You don't give it to her, do you?" Lydia asked.

Sylvie darted her eyes back and forth between Polly and Beryl, then pressed her lips together in a tight smile. "Uh, no. Absolutely not. That would be wrong."

"Who does she sleep with?" Beryl asked.

"Depends on the time of night. She starts out in Andrew's room, but he tosses all over the place. By about midnight, she ends up in Jason's room. As he's gotten older, it's like his body temperature has gotten warmer. She can only take so much of that before she's out of there and in with me. She gets to me about three thirty and for the last hour of my night, I relax against a furry warm beast."

"She's not talking about Eliseo. He's not that furry," Beryl said.

Andy chuckled. "I wasn't going to tease her about him until someone else started it. Can we go now?"

Sylvie put her fork down hard on the table. "Okay. Here it is. Before you even begin. We see each other nearly every day. He comes up to the coffee shop after Jason heads to school and the horses are out. Then he usually tries to take time to see me after I'm done with work in the afternoon, as long as there isn't a big catering event coming up. We go out on Monday nights when things are slow. He's had dinner with me and the boys quite often. They really like him. We kiss a lot, but so far we haven't had sex." She giggled. "Too many people in our lives and not enough privacy. Is that enough information for you?"

A quiet cough from behind the counter of Beryl's bar reminded them that Skylar was still there.

Sylvie clapped her hand over her mouth, flushed bright red, and gulped.

"Drink, woman," Beryl said, handing the half full glass to her.

"Oh my god," Sylvie said. "I'm so sorry, Sky."

"It's okay. I heard nothing. Isn't that the way waiters are supposed to act?"

"But ..."

He brought out a tray with small shrimp cocktail dishes and put them at each person's place. Polly was finished with her soup and offered the bowl to him. He took it and then picked up everyone else's bowls. Skylar took the empty basket off the table, filled it with different rolls and put it back, then went around the table and refilled empty wine glasses.

"After that, I really need to have two glasses of wine for every one of yours. I'm so embarrassed." Sylvie paused. "Maybe I should stop drinking and I'll be better able to curb my tongue."

"How can you be embarrassed about not having sex?" Andy asked.

Sylvie just shook her head and dipped a shrimp into the cocktail sauce. "I need a hole to crawl into."

"You need sex education courses if you think that's the way the whole thing works," Beryl said.

"Huh?"

"You aren't the one who crawls into a hole."

"Beryl Watson," Lydia said. "You stop that right now."

Beryl laughed. "Honey, I started drinking wine when the food showed up this afternoon. I've had a buzz on since you got here. Ain't nothing gonna stop this tongue from flying."

"So is it good with you and Eliseo?" Andy asked. "He's such a nice man."

Sylvie nodded. "It is. There are some things I need to figure out how to do better. When he gets overwhelmed or highly stressed, he shuts down. It's almost like he leaves and his mind goes somewhere else. I know it's a coping mechanism, but it isn't something I'm used to. Really loud noises shut him down, too. We went to a movie theater for the last Star Wars movie and had to leave before it was over. There was just too much input. He silently started to shake beside me and I just knew I had to get him out of there. I don't know how long he'd been like that before I noticed. When I whispered that we should leave, he didn't respond. I had to physically force him to stand up and then he was like an automaton. I drove his truck home that night and it wasn't until we pulled up in front of my house that he really came back to normal."

"I can't believe he let you see that," Polly said.

"Me either," Sylvie replied. "That was the worst it's ever been." Her eyes glistened. "You know, because we only see him a few hours a day here and there, he can hide most of his PTS from us. Jason said he's seen it a couple of times. Not real bad of course. Those horses really calm Eliseo down. But when they've been in Boone before, Eliseo jerks and reacts strongly to things like cars backfiring or loud bangs. He handed Jason the keys one time and asked him to drive home. Jason said he didn't shut down or go away, but it shook my boy up."

Skylar came back to the table, put his hand on Sylvie's shoulder and picked up her empty dish, then moved around and cleared the table. "The main course will be family style," he said. "And then it will be time for me to take off. Ms. Watson, dessert is already plated and in the refrigerator behind the bar. I'll take the dishes upstairs and they'll be clean for you to put away."

"Thank you, sir," Beryl said. "The tickets are in an envelope on the kitchen table."

He smiled and re-set each person's place with dinner plates and silverware that was neatly wrapped in cloth napkins.

Andy unwrapped her silverware and put the napkin in her lap. "When are you and Eliseo getting married?" she asked, and giggled.

"What?"

"I've had wine, too." Andy took a drink and put her glass back down. "Do you have an answer?"

"No," Sylvie replied. She picked up her glass and clinked Polly's. "We have work to do to catch up to these three."

"Will he move into your house and leave his sister and her family out on the farm?" Lydia asked.

Sylvie turned pleading eyes toward Polly.

"Don't look at me," Polly said. "They tortured me until Henry and I finally just found a judge."

Lydia frowned. "It wasn't that bad, was it?"

"Yes," Polly said. "You were relentless."

While they talked, Skylar had filled the table with serving dishes. "Bon appetit," he said. "I've got two bottles ready to be uncorked and there are more behind the bar." He chuckled. "In fact, there's an entire case back there. Secret Woods must do a boom business when you ladies have a party."

Beryl reached out and took his hand. "Thank you for your time tonight. Have fun."

"I'll do this again any time you ask," he replied. With a flourish and a bow, he said, "Good evening ladies. The pleasure was all mine." He carried a tray filled with dishes up the steps and was gone.

"How did you get him to do this?" Polly asked.

"Good cash and tickets to a concert in Ames that were impossible to snag," Beryl replied. "I overheard him talking about it last week when I was in the coffee shop. I might have a few connections that no one knows about. I rented the tux for him, got the tickets and paid him a little extra. He can show his girl a good time."

"Must be a late concert," Lydia said.

Beryl nodded. "It is." She leaned forward and picked up a bowl filled with roasted potatoes. "Take something in front of you and pass it around. We don't have all evening."

"Where did you get this food?" Polly asked again. She served herself from a bowl filled with mushrooms and asparagus.

Lydia started a tomato and onion gratin around the table while Andy lifted the lid from a chicken dish.

"What is this?" she asked.

"Chicken Marbella," Beryl said. "At least that's what I think it is. It's what we discussed."

"Who is we?"

"I recognize green olives," Andy interrupted. "What else?"

Beryl grinned and lifted her glass. "Wine."

"No, the other little brown things?"

Beryl chuckled and took a drink, then said, "Prunes."

"Huh. Okay, I'll try anything once."

The food went around and before she knew it, Polly's plate was full. "Are you really not going to tell us?"

"Rachel at Sycamore House Catering," Beryl said, with a huff. "Who else do you think I'd use?"

"How long have you been planning this party? Rebecca just told me about it this morning."

"Your Rebecca felt terrible for what she'd done last Friday night, so while we were inking in her latest comic book collaboration with young Andrew, she and I discussed an evening of frivolity for you. Since you have a tendency to get too busy, I told her to wait until today to present you with any details."

"What if I'd been busy?"

"Rebecca and I have been communicating all week long. Henry knew about this, too. He wasn't going to let anything come up. It was pure fortune that Rebecca managed to find a fun activity for him tonight. We're all quite grateful that you like surprises."

"It's a good thing," Polly said. "You people keep coming up with new ways to shake up my world."

"Whatever happened with your neighbor?" Lydia asked.

"She came home this evening, I guess. Told me to leave Rose at the after-school program and not to worry. Rebecca and I will take cookies over this weekend and check on them." Polly took a bite of the chicken dish. "This is amazing. Sylvie, she is doing so well."

Sylvie nodded. "I'm proud of her. We need to hire another person to cook with her a few days a week, but it's going well."

"What about Hannah?" Hannah McKenzie had helped Sylvie in the early days at Sycamore House. Her husband, Bruce, was a high school friend of Polly's. With three small children, Hannah appreciated having something fun to do for additional money every once in a while, but Polly hadn't seen her in quite a long time.

"Their youngest, Tyler, has been diagnosed with autism,"

Sylvie said quietly. "It was hard on Hannah. She lost her bright, bubbly boy and couldn't stop the change." Sylvie smiled. "But she's wonderful with him. They have a long way to go, but everyone is helping. Bruce's mother is extremely patient and believe it or not, his father is part of Tyler's team, too. Tyler loves the big tractors. Lyle helps him up into the front of the tractor and they travel all over the fields together. They fitted Tyler with special headphones to block out the worst of the noise and once he's inside the cab, he just hums along while Lyle works."

"I never would have believed it of that old man," Lydia said. "Guess he has a heart after all."

CHAPTER SEVENTEEN

All the food she'd eaten made no difference. Polly was happily buzzed. They managed to get the dishes upstairs and into the kitchen without anyone falling up the steps - a feat they all toasted once the food was put away, the dishes stacked in the sink, and the cats released to the house.

"Who's ready for dessert?" Beryl asked.

"What are we having?"

"Well, this is something I didn't ask Rachel to do since Sylvie would have been required to work for her party, so I went to a cute little bakery in Ames and ordered a beautiful caramel apple cheesecake." She lifted plates out onto the counter and Polly took them to the table.

She was already full, but the cheesecake looked amazing with drizzled caramel over curled thinly sliced apples and topped with candied walnuts. "This looks like heaven."

"Wait until you taste it."

Sylvie poked at her piece. "I don't do many cheesecakes. In fact, I've only done one or two for customers who asked. Do you think I should make them more often?"

"I think tonight is not the time to talk about business, little missy. We need to get back to asking why you aren't having sex with Eliseo."

"You really don't," Sylvie said. "I'll never tell you whether we do or not. It isn't your business."

Beryl sat down at the table. "Isn't our business? Well of course it isn't. But that won't stop me from asking." She reached back to a side table and picked up a large envelope. "You all might need a little more wine before we enter the fun part of our evening. Polly, would you do the honors? I think you're the least sober. Lydia has quit talking. She might need to stop."

"That's not it," Lydia asked. She shook her head. "I'll be good. Let's party."

Polly stopped as she prepared to pour more into Lydia's glass. "What's going on?"

"We're having a party tonight."

"Did something happen between the time I saw you this morning and tonight?" Polly asked.

Lydia nodded slowly.

"You've been a sourpuss all night," Beryl said. "What's up? Did you fight with the big man?"

"No. We're fine. Girls, I ran into something this afternoon and I don't know what to do about it."

"Can we help?" Polly asked.

"You could, but Polly, I feel like I always come to you four when I need something." She took another drink of wine. "Let me mull this over. For now, we should drink."

"The last time we drank wine while you were upset about something, we had so much none of us could go home," Andy said. "Are we doing that again tonight?"

Lydia gave a half smile. "I'm not that kind of upset. Aaron's fine. He's got a lot going on, though."

"Like what?" Polly asked. "I haven't called him in a while."

"I know. He almost misses you. I think that if you were involved in the latest mess, at least he would be confident it might get solved. As it is, this has been hard on him."

"What has?"

"People are breaking into homes around the area again. But this time, they aren't going after farmers, they're attacking older women who live alone."

Beryl gasped and clutched at her chest. "Oh dear. Might they attack me?"

"Anyone who considers attacking you is a fool," Andy said. "You'd hurt them."

Polly put the half empty bottle down in front of Lydia and twisted a corkscrew into another bottle. "We're going to need more. I can tell."

"Older widows?" Andy asked.

Lydia nodded. "And if the woman protests, one of them smacks her around."

"What are they stealing?" Andy asked.

"Anything of worth. Some jewelry. They've taken computers and any cash they find in the house. So far it hasn't been a large amount of money, but it's like they're waiting for that one woman who hides all her money at home. They've been tying the poor old ladies up and then they trash the house or apartment."

"Does Aaron know how they're finding these women?"

Lydia put her glass back down and shook her head at Polly. "No. Anita is working on patterns - trying to figure out what each of them have in common, but right now they're from all over the county and even a few up in Hamilton County. They live in houses and apartments, rural homes, in town; big towns and little towns." Lydia shrugged. "I guess at least they aren't going after women in nursing homes and care centers."

"Is this what you're worrying over?"

"No, that's not it, but I wish Aaron could figure it out. He doesn't know where they're going to strike next, so he doesn't know how to protect people."

Beryl swatted at Polly. "He should hire our girl here to teach those little old ladies how to go for the balls and the eyes. You know, grab 'em where it hurts and then kick 'em when they're down."

"Can't you see that?" Polly asked. "An army of white-haired little old ladies standing in their doorways with hands raised in a martial arts form. 'Come and get me, suckas.'"

Beryl jumped to her feet and settled into a fighting stance. "Like this?" She wobbled and put her hand on the back of the chair. "Remind me not to do that when I've had too much wine. This conversation is depressing. I don't want to be a victim and now you're telling me that a lot of people just like me are being tormented by a couple of stinking punks. That makes me mad."

"Aaron doesn't have anything?" Polly asked.

"Not that I know of," Lydia said. "Somebody thought they might have seen a pickup, but they don't know the color or anything. The women are letting them in and then it's all over."

"What I want to know," Andy said, "is why I haven't seen this on the news yet. They should be warning us to be careful."

"You'll see it tomorrow in the paper and maybe on tonight's news. This just started. The men hit six houses last weekend. Then it's been a couple every day. Aaron and his team are just digging in."

"You have to tell us about the other thing that happened today," Andy said.

Lydia rubbed her forehead. "There's a young family whose furnace is dying on them and they can't afford a new one. They can barely afford to bring someone in to repair it. He works two jobs, but both are minimum wage. She works, too, but she might as well not. The daycare for their little ones eats up her paycheck. I don't know how to help them. He's really proud and doesn't want to accept charity from us."

"How did you find out about it?" Beryl asked.

Lydia laughed. "Aaron checks on them. He actually checks on a bunch of families in Bellingwood who are right on the edge financially - just to make sure they're safe and things are working okay." She looked at Polly. "Do you know that Henry helps him out?"

Polly looked confused. "Uh. No. I had no idea. Henry's never said anything."

"Would he?"

"I guess not."

"Yeah. He's looked at this furnace a couple of times. I know he's put doors up for people and he's put windows in. All at cost with no labor. Aaron feels badly about calling him, but Henry insists. One day last fall he insulated a house and put drywall up for a family, then dropped off two pails of paint. They'd never finished the inside of their home. It was only a little house, but still. He changed their whole lives. Now they'll be warm this winter. At least warmer than they were the last few years. They pretty much just lived in one room that had a wood stove."

"How can that even be in this day and age?" Andy asked.

"You know this is why no one can ever run against Aaron and think to win," Beryl said. "These people that he never talks about helping will always vote for him."

Sylvie put her hands out. "What can we do?"

"That's what I'm trying to figure out," Lydia said. "I know we could raise the money tonight with just the five of us, but this man wouldn't take it. I have to find another way to get it to them."

"It bothers me that people in town live like that at all," Sylvie said. "I was close, but at least I could afford the apartment."

"There is more of this out there than you realize," Lydia said. "If you heard half the stories Aaron tells me, you'd be shocked. People are working and doing all they can, but it isn't easy."

"If you figure out a way, let us know," Sylvie said.

Andy tapped Polly's arm. "I've forgotten to say something five times tonight." She looked sheepish. "I know this is the wrong time, but it crossed my mind again. I found boxes at the library today that you might want to look at. Are you busy tomorrow afternoon?"

Polly sat down. "That's fantastic. Do you think I could take them out of there? That way I could look through them when I have time."

"You're best friends with Joss. I doubt anyone will care. I'll be up there between one and four."

"Then I will too," Polly said. "Thank you. I'm excited."

Andy turned to Lydia. "I apologize. I shouldn't have interrupted the conversation."

Sylvie chuckled. "I'm just glad we aren't talking about my sex life anymore. I was tired of that."

"You wouldn't be tired of it if you were getting any," Andy said, then covered her mouth and giggled. "That was me. I said that!"

Lydia chuckled. "You're always so nice. Nobody ever expects you to be lewd. And we never talk about your sex life."

"Yours either," Andy retorted. "But mine's great, thank you very much."

"So is mine."

Beryl waggled her fork at Polly. "So tell us that you're having incredible sex."

"For a woman who is glad to be single, you're sure interested in our sex lives," Polly said. She grinned. "And by the way, it's great."

"I like other people to have great sex lives," Beryl said. "It gives me hope that someday I will find a male form so incredible I can't resist it." She lifted her eyebrows. "So far, the pretty boys have no brains and the brainy boys aren't interested. Maybe someday. But until then, I'm a perfectly happy single woman." She giggled. "With her three cats."

"I'll take my big warm man," Lydia said.

Beryl cackled. "Well then. I have just the thing."

Lydia groaned. "Oh no. What did you do?"

"Pour more wine in her glass, Polly," Beryl said and opened the package. "Do you remember that conversation we had about tattoos?"

"You can't have a tattoo artist in there," Lydia said. "You aren't making us go somewhere tonight, are you? I'm not ready. I haven't thought about if I really want to. What have you done?"

"Calm yourself, woman. I have something even better. Check this out." Beryl took sheets of paper from the package. "Temporaries."

Polly snorted with laughter. What?"

"Yeah. I bought temporaries. Sheets of them. When one comes off, you can put a new one on. Nobody's getting out of here tonight without their tattoo. I ordered them specially for all of you." Beryl took a sheet out of the package. "Let's see. This one is for you, Lydia." She turned the sheet of images for everyone to see.

"Are those?" Polly started.

"Handcuffs?" Beryl nodded. "Absolutely. Two hearts hooked together with handcuffs. And there's Lydia's name in one and Aaron's name in the other. And we're going to put this right on her rump."

"No we're not," Lydia protested.

"Oh yes we are." Beryl stood up after placing the rest of the sheets face down on the table. "You can finish your cheesecake in a minute. Come with me. I've already tested it and know what to do."

"I'm not going anywhere with you."

"Wanna bet?" Beryl tickled Lydia's sides until Lydia batted her hands away.

"Stop that."

"I will torture you until you follow me over to the sink. I have everything there."

Lydia looked at everyone else in a panic. "Stop her. I don't want to get naked in front of you all. This isn't fair. Make her stop."

Polly put both hands up and sat back. "I'm not getting in the middle of it. I think it's a great idea." She turned to Sylvie. "You getting involved?"

"No way. I kind of dread what Beryl has planned for me."

Andy reached toward the stack of papers and Beryl jumped around behind her and snatched them. "Cool your jets. It's not your turn."

"Are you coming peacefully or do I have to get brutal with you?" Beryl asked Lydia.

Lydia pouted at the rest of her friends. "No one is going to help me?"

"Not a chance," Polly said. "But you don't have to get totally naked. Does she, Beryl?"

"Only if she wants to. I don't need to see her pasty white legs, though. Just that pretty rump."

"Why do I have to go first?" Lydia asked.

Beryl took her arm. "Come on and quit whining. It's going to be awesome and in three or four days it will have washed off and you'll be over it."

Lydia let herself be pulled up and out of the chair. She put her napkin down beside her plate and followed Beryl into the bathroom.

In seconds, Andy, Polly, and Sylvie jumped up and headed that way.

As they jostled to make room, Beryl laughed. "I brought her in here for privacy. I can see that was ridiculous." She poked Lydia's back side. "I'm thinking right here. How's that?"

"It's a little low," Lydia said. "I don't want to sit on it."

"Because it will poke you?"

"No, I just don't want to wear it off tonight. If I have to have one, I want it to stick around at least until Aaron sees it." She turned and looked at everyone, then waggled her eyebrows. "He *will* see it tonight, even if he's asleep when I get home." Lydia reached around, feeling her bottom with her hand and then pointed. "Right there. We shouldn't have to pull my pants down too far for that, right?"

"Whatever you say. Unzip 'em, baby."

Lydia sighed, unzipped her pants, then pushed them down. "I can't believe I'm doing this."

"How much more embarrassing would it be if you were in a tattoo parlor?" Andy asked. "At least this way it's only us."

"Whatever."

"This is going to be cold," Beryl said. She soaked a cotton ball in alcohol and wiped it across the area to be tattooed, then winked at Lydia in the mirror, bent over and blew on it.

"What in the hell?"

"Just need to make sure it's dry."

Beryl snipped off one of the tattoos and peeled away the clear protective covering. "Are you ready?"

"Just do it."

Waving her hands around in a grand flourish, Beryl pressed the tattoo to Lydia's rump and gently held a damp wash cloth over it.

When she didn't move away, Lydia craned her neck. "How long do I stand here?"

Beryl chuckled. "We'll wait a full minute before I peel the backing off. Then you have to let it dry for at least ten minutes."

"I have to stand here holding my pants halfway up my bum for ten minutes?"

"That's why we did yours first. I knew you'd never let me get away with this otherwise."

"Damn right. I'm going to kill you."

"No you're not. You're going to go home and show Mr. Snugglebum what you've got and then you're going to be a very contented lady tonight."

"That still might be, but you are going to suffer."

"Bring it, baby. I'm ready for anything you have to offer." Beryl giggled as she peeled off the backing. "It's perfect. Now stand right there. Don't move. I'll be back." She passed between Polly and Sylvie in the doorway. "You all stay put, too. If we're going to play in here, then I'm all for it."

"We can come back out," Andy said. "There's more room."

"I'm not coming out there like this. What if somebody else shows up?" Lydia asked.

"Who else would possibly show up?"

"I don't know. But I'm not going anywhere until I can zip up my pants."

Beryl returned and took Polly's arm. "You're next. And I think you should unzip your pants, too."

"This is a little risqué, even for you," Polly said. "What did you find?"

"This." Beryl held a sheet covered with multiple copies of the same purple image.

Polly peered at it. "What in the world is it?"

"Don't you see?" Beryl asked. "Purple panties. Pink bows. The word 'friends' right there above the panty crotch."

"You can't put that on any part of your body that people will see," Andy said.

Sylvie chuckled. "Her boob,"

"No," Polly said. I'm not putting purple panties on my boob."

Beryl tapped Polly's tummy, just below the waist. "I was looking for your pelvic bone. We should put it right there."

"You are a very scary woman, Ms. Watson."

"I've had wine. It's what happens. Now drop 'em."

Polly shut her eyes and then burst out in laughter. "You aren't going to believe it." She unzipped her jeans and lowered them just a shade.

"They're purple," Andy exclaimed. "The same ones?"

"No. Those are gone. I can't believe I have purple panties on tonight, though. I didn't realize it was such a popular color in my lingerie drawer."

"Those panties are low enough that you can leave them on. Do you want to do this or do you want me to?" Beryl asked.

"By all means," Polly said.

"Really?" Beryl snickered and soaked another cotton ball in alcohol.

Polly grabbed it out of her hand. "No. I've got this. You stay away from me, you crazy old lady."

Beryl cut a tattoo off the sheet and handed it to Polly, along with the damp cloth. "At least a minute. Then you have to let it dry."

She held up another sheet. "I bought red roses for us to put on our boobs. Let's see what else I have in here. Oh look. Sylvie, it's a horse wearing a chef's hat. I guess that one is for you. And Andy, I found just the thing for you." She turned around a sheet with a large beautiful butterfly on it.

"That's huge."

Beryl cackled. "I'm putting this on your lower back. It's a perfect tramp stamp, am I right? What will Len think?"

"He'll think I've lost my mind." Andy took the sheet. "Let's do it. What did you buy for yourself?"

"I thought this was pretty," Beryl said. "I want to put it on my wrist. I might actually get this one for real." She turned over the final sheet of tattoos - a beautiful image of a paint palette with a brush. "Maybe not quite this big, but I love it. Shall we?"

Lydia turned so she could look at her rear end in the mirror. "This is really neat."

Sylvie giggled. "You said 'neat.'"

"I ran out of good words. I think I've had too much wine."

CHAPTER EIGHTEEN

Vowing once again to not do that again any time soon, Polly woke the next morning to bright sunshine. That meant she'd been asleep far too long.

Eliseo had come to pick Sylvie up the night before, returned Polly to the Bell House, and gathered Andrew to take home. The boy had been asleep on one of the sofas in the foyer, with Noah and Elijah asleep on the other. Kayla and Rebecca were sound asleep in Rebecca's room and Hayden was still up, watching movies in the family room.

Polly had texted Heath to tell him she was home and safe and that he could come home whenever he wanted. It had been another hour before he arrived. She'd long since climbed into bed with Henry, who loved her pretty new tattoo, by the way. But Heath texted her to let her know when he was home and that he'd had a good time.

The door to the bedroom was closed and no dogs snuggled her. The thing with good insulation was not just that no one could hear what was happening inside this room, but with the doors closed, Polly had difficulty hearing what was happening in the rest of the house. Hoping that it was empty of everyone but her family and maybe Kayla, Polly pulled her heavy winter robe on, slipped her feet into slippers and stepped into the hallway. Laughter and noise echoed down the hallway from the kitchen. She smelled sausage, coffee and toast. Whatever they were doing, she needed some of that coffee.

"Hello, Polly." Rebecca jumped up from the table. "Did you have fun last night?"

"I did." Polly tried to completely open both her eyes, but they refused to work well, so she squinted with one eye closed. "Where's Henry?"

"He told me to tell you that him and Hayden are getting the rest of the cupboard doors this morning. They've been gone a while. Should be back pretty soon."

"He," Polly said. "Good morning, boys."

"He what?" Noah asked.

"Not him and Hayden. He and Hayden."

"You need coffee," Noah said quietly.

Polly laughed and reached down to hug him. "I love you, little man. You are so very smart. Did you have fun last night?"

"We played until I fell asleep on the couch," he said proudly.

Rebecca put a cup of coffee in Polly's hand. "Do you want eggs? Kayla and I are cooking this morning."

"That sounds wonderful," Polly said. "Thank you." She kissed the top of Rebecca's head. "How was everything last night?"

"We had a blast," Rebecca said. "We played Sorry and Checkers and then we played Twister. Andrew taught Noah and Elijah how to play Battleship. I told them that we couldn't play video games until eight o'clock. But we didn't play those at all. We watched the first Harry Potter movie."

"I never saw that before," Noah said.

Polly sat at the table beside Elijah. "What are you doing?"

"I'm making a comic book like Andrew and Rebecca." He nodded toward Rebecca. "She told me she'd show me how to make some pictures. First I have to draw the boxes. Isn't that a good square box?"

"It's great. What's your story about? Do you have a superhero?"

"His name is Little E. He can fly."

"How did he get that power?" Polly asked.

Elijah looked at Rebecca, but she was working at the stove. "Rebecca?"

"Yes."

"How did he get flying power?"

She smiled. "I don't know. You have to tell the story. What do you think?"

"Maybe he was flying a kite and it got zapped by lightning."

"Like Benjamin Franklin?" Polly asked.

Elijah smiled at her. "I read about him last week. He was electric. Maybe that's what Little E's super power is. He can turn things on by zapping them with his finger."

"And if someone has a heart attack, all he has to do is zap them and shock them back to life," Kayla said. She popped toast out of the toaster and put it on a plate before bringing it over to Polly.

"That would be so cool. He could save lives and people wouldn't have to go to the hospital," Noah said.

Polly rubbed his back. "You've got a great start on the story. Keep going. Did you have fun last night?"

He nodded, but didn't look up, his focus on the paper in front of him.

"Where are the dogs?" Polly asked. She didn't have to ask about the cats. Though she couldn't get a good count, it seemed like they were all over the kitchen.

"Henry took them, too," Kayla said.

"And Heath?"

Rebecca turned and laughed. "He's still in bed. Hayden said that we should leave him alone."

"Good." Polly took a drink of her coffee. "Oohhh, that's good."

"I don't like coffee," Noah said. He'd taken the chair at the end of the table, but pulled it closer to Polly.

She reached over and took his hand. "When I was your age, I didn't like it either."

Rebecca brought the pan over and slid an egg on to Polly's plate. "She told me that I can't drink coffee until I'm in college." When Rebecca walked back to the stove, she sashayed across the room. "Nobody will be able to tell me what to do then."

"Really?" Elijah asked, looking up in awe. "Nobody?"

Rebecca spun. "Polly still can. I was just being funny. I didn't mean it."

"That's okay," Polly said. "College is when you start testing your freedom. You have to take responsibility for yourself, but it's still pretty safe. We'll be there to back you up."

"What if she does something really bad?" Noah asked.

"I won't," Rebecca said. "I don't want to go to jail."

His eyes grew huge. "You would do something to go to jail?"

Rebecca brushed his shoulder and sat down across from Polly, then scooted forward so Kayla could go around her. "I wouldn't do anything like that. Polly would be really disappointed."

"You bet I would," Polly agreed.

They looked up as the back door opened and two dogs flew across the floor, wagging and yapping at each other. Obiwan pulled to a stop in front of Polly, his tongue hanging out.

"Good morning, bud," she said. "It's good to see you, too."

Henry came in, followed by Hayden, both carrying stacks of wooden cabinet doors.

"Wanna see?" he asked Polly.

She brushed her hands on her robe and stood, waiting for Obiwan to move. "I do. What do they look like?"

He tipped one of the knotty alder doors up.

"These are really beautiful. I can't believe you're about to put this all together."

"We're almost there," he replied. "The appliances will be delivered and installed on Monday. We're taking this old stove to the shop. Dad wants to do something with it when he gets back."

She turned and smiled at the kids who were sitting at the table. "I'm going to have a finished kitchen. Can you believe it?"

"We've got another couple of loads in the truck," Henry said. "Finish your breakfast."

Noah had followed Polly to look at the cabinet doors. He pointed at one of the knots he could see. "Is that what makes it pretty?"

She lifted a door down so he could see the face of it. "That's called a knot. Most of these are formed when the trunk of a tree grows out and around where a branch is. When a tree is turned into wood they slice right down and expose these beautiful marks. I chose this type of wood because it's not perfect. The marks make it interesting and unique."

Noah pointed at an old scar on his forearm. Polly didn't want to think about where it had come from. "I have marks," he said, then lifted the bandage from the scrape he'd received the other night.

Polly took the bandage. That wound wouldn't leave a mark. "Those make you interesting and unique," she replied, giving him a hug. "We each have marks that make us different from everybody else. No matter how we got them, they tell part of our story. Right?"

Rebecca put a hand on Noah's shoulder. When he looked up at her, she swiped a sticky finger down his cheek. "I just marked you."

He laughed and ran back to the table to wipe his face with a napkin.

Heath came into the kitchen as Henry and Hayden walked in with more stacks of door faces. "You should have woke me up. I could have helped."

Hayden smiled at him. "You were out later than me. And when was the last Saturday you got to sleep in?"

Polly reached out and took Heath's hand. "Just when you were getting used to him being a rotten older brother, he does something nice like this."

"I know," Heath said, yawning. "It confuses me."

"Did you have a good time at Doug's last night?"

He nodded. "We played a lot. Jason let me be the newbie with him, so I leveled up pretty fast. Mel hadn't ever played before either."

"Was Anita there?"

"She's really good. And she's so smart."

"Do you want eggs?" Rebecca asked. "I'm cooking."

Heath grabbed his throat and pretended to choke. "Your cooking might kill me."

"Fine then," she said. "Cook your own eggs."

He reached over and mussed her hair. "Sorry. I'd love some eggs. What should I do?"

"You can make your own toast. How many eggs?"

"Three."

That didn't faze Rebecca at all. No one was surprised at how much those boys could eat. She went back to the stove as Hayden and Henry returned with yet another load of doors. Hayden took his coat off and Henry went back out to the truck.

When he came back in, he brandished a Sweet Beans cup. "Polly?"

She looked up from her plate. "You didn't."

"Of course I did. We stopped on the way back. I couldn't leave with nothing for you."

"You sweet and wonderful man. I'm gonna owe you big."

Henry choked back a laugh. "It's okay. You're paid up in full." He leaned over and whispered something in Noah's ear.

The little boy looked at Polly in surprise. "What's on your arm?" he asked, reaching out.

She pursed her lips at her husband and pulled the robe's sleeve back. "Just some fun that we had at Beryl's last night."

"That's pretty." Noah traced the rose that she'd placed on the underside of her forearm.

Since she was hiding one of her tattoos from everyone but Henry, rather than putting this one above her breast, she placed it somewhere that her kids could see. The other tattoo just didn't need to be part of any conversation with people in this room.

"What is it?" Rebecca asked from across the room.

"Beryl got temporary tattoos for us."

"Oh. Those. You know she designed and drew them all, don't you?"

Polly looked at her forearm and thought about the purple panties. "Really?"

"Yeah. You can order them somewhere on the internet. We should do that for a party sometime."

"We really should." Polly looked at her forearm again. "I can't believe I'm wearing Beryl's artwork. That's really cool." She caught Henry's eye and he grinned.

"Don't you grin at me, Mr. Man," Polly said. "I learned something new about you last night. I can't believe you never told me."

"Told you what?"

All eyes were on her, waiting for the big revelation.

"Your dad is a pretty cool guy," Polly said. "He fixes people's furnaces and puts up walls and helps people who can't afford to do those things themselves. Lydia ..." She turned to Elijah. "Mrs. Merritt told me that her husband calls Henry when he finds somebody who needs help and your dad always shows up."

"It's no big deal," Henry said. "I just do what I can."

"It's a big deal to me," she replied. "I'm awfully proud of you."

He shook his head. "Not a big deal. If you have a skill that you can use to help people, you should. I have plenty of customers who pay me well, I can turn around and do things for others."

Rebecca put a plate down on the table where she'd been sitting beside Kayla. "Here you go, Heath. Breakfast is served."

"You were sitting there."

She moved behind Polly to sit on the other side of Elijah. "I'll just sit here and help Little E work on his comic book."

~~~

Polly parked across the street from the library and flicked the door locks open. One thing she was grateful for with two boys from the city was that they didn't jump out of the car until they made sure the street was clear. Not that it was usually a problem in Bellingwood, but anything could happen. They clambered down from the back seat and looked up at her.

"Go," she said. They looked both ways then ran across the street and up the steps of the library. They'd only been here once, but Joss had made them feel so welcome, they couldn't wait to be back. "Run your little hearts out, my boys," Polly said under her breath as she crossed the street. "Burn away that excess energy."

By the time she stood in front of Joss's counter, the boys had found their way to the books they wanted. Polly had told them she'd be at the library for a while and they assured her that they would find a good place to read while they waited.

"There's nothing I like better than seeing children rush to the library," Joss said. She patted the stack of books they'd returned. "Are these too young for them?"

Polly shook her head. "I don't care right now. I'll let them choose their own reading for a few months. Little by little we can introduce higher level books. I just want them to enjoy it."

"They're such bright boys," Joss said.

Giggling and quiet laughter came from an aisle to Polly's right and she leaned enough to see the two boys kneeling in front of a set of shelves as they pulled books out and flipped through them. A young girl was standing nearby, reading through a book until a woman who was obviously her mother grabbed the girl's arm, removed the book and shoved it onto the shelf.

"We're leaving now," the mother said loud enough for Polly to hear.

"But I wanted to read that," the girl protested.

"We'll come another time when there aren't so many ..." The woman looked directly at Polly's sons. "Other people here."

Polly seethed. The woman couldn't possibly be insinuating what Polly thought she was.

As they passed by Joss, the woman dropped a book on the counter. "We'll get our books another time." She sneered at Polly, who had had it.

"Excuse me," Polly said. "Did my boys do something to upset you?"

The woman was startled at being accosted. "It's just too busy in here."

There were a few other people in the library, but since it had only been open about fifteen minutes, the place could hardly be called busy. Polly glanced around and slowly nodded her head. "Busy, huh?" She looked at the little girl. "What grade are you in, sweetie?"

"Third grade."

"Is Noah in your class?"

The girl shook her head. "He's in the other third grade class. He has Mrs. Wallers."

"Have you ever talked to him?"

"Sure," the girl said. "He's nice. Aggie's in his class. She said he's shy, but he helps her with her math problems sometimes. He's really good at math."

Polly put her hand out and the girl shook it, then Polly reached toward the woman. "It's nice to meet both of you, Mrs.?"

"Come on, Lia," the woman said. "It's time to go."

"But we just got here."

"We'll come another day." The woman guided her daughter out the front door, leaving Polly there with her hand out.

"Ferguson," Joss said. "Celia and Marianne Ferguson. Celia's dad teaches down at Iowa State. They're divorced."

"Duh," Polly said. Then she chuckled. "That was mean. What in the heck was up with her?"

Joss shook her head. "Little towns in the middle of Iowa are such great places to raise kids, but then you run into someone like that and you understand why anyone with children who aren't white move to bigger cities. At least there is a higher percentage of kids that look like you. I can't understand why she thought that it would be okay for her to be so obvious about it in here. Celia isn't."

"I hope she stays that way," Polly said. "Is Andy around?"

Joss grinned. "She's already in the basement. You're supposed to go down there when you're ready. Are you ready?"

"How bad is it?" Polly asked.

"Even though people call it the catacombs, we haven't found any dead bodies." Joss looked up at Polly and started to laugh uncontrollably. "And I'm sending *you* down there. The library board will never forgive me if you find someone."

"I'm looking through boxes." Polly glared at her friend. "I'm looking through boxes that Andy has already opened. I won't go any deeper into the bowels of this place than what she's exposed. I promise. If there's anything dead down there, it will have to wait for another day."

Joss shuddered. "Can you even imagine? I've been here almost seven years and I've never spent much time down there. What if something horrible is tucked back in the deep dark recesses of that basement?"

"Is it really that bad? I thought you sold off your books regularly."

"Since I've been here, we have," Joss said. "But it's not all books. There are paintings and sculptures, and boxes of historical things. Anything that has to do with Bellingwood has ended up either down there or in the basement at Memorial Hall. That place isn't much better."

"The town needs a historical center if we have so much," Polly said.

"And they need someone with the organizational skills of Andy and the energy of a five-year-old to deal with everything that's been collected."

"I just want the little bit that has to do with the Bell House," Polly said sheepishly.

"Hopefully Andy found something that helps you. Do you know what you're going to do with those gold coins yet?"

Polly shook her head. "I have to figure out something. For now they're safe, but I don't want to just let them sit there." She grinned. "Maybe we should talk about this at pizza tomorrow night."

"Sandy isn't back in town yet, is she?"

"I should ask Sal," Polly said. "I think they were coming home this weekend after Will's first treatment was over. Hopefully she feels like she can leave him for a couple of hours and eat with us. I'm glad you said something."

Noah ran over to Polly and handed a book to her. "Do you think Hayden would read this to us at night? Andrew said it was a good book."

Polly took it from him and held *Treasure Island* up for Joss to see. She smiled. "I think Hayden would love to read this to you boys. It's a great book. Do you want to leave it here with Miss Joss?"

He nodded and before running back to his brother, stopped and said, "Thanks."

"They're good boys," Joss said.

"I love that their book influences are coming from Andrew," Polly said. "Okay, point me to the stairs. I'm ready to dig into boxes."

CHAPTER NINETEEN

Every horror story Simon Gardner had told Polly about the dreaded depths of the library's basement was a lie. She was surprised at the bright fluorescent lights hanging from the ceiling. There were hundreds of boxes stacked everywhere, but it was nothing like she imagined. Wooden filing cabinets stood along one outer wall, while others were lined with immense steel shelving units filled with labeled filing boxes. Plastic bins and boxes were stacked to make aisles and pathways. She stood on a step halfway down and looked out over the large open space. Off to the left she saw doors marked as restrooms, to the right were three closed doors, and in the back were doors leading to yet more rooms. However, right at the base of the stairs was an open space with three eight foot tables. Andy had set herself up at the farthest table, her travel tote of organizational office supplies by her side.

"You're here," she said.

"I was expecting something much worse," Polly replied. "This isn't so bad.

"It is if you realize that we have no idea what is actually in some of these cartons."

"I was picturing dank, dark and musty. So you found Margie Deacon's boxes?"

Andy snapped the lid back onto the marker she'd been using, stood up, and beckoned to Polly. "Over here. I don't know if you'll find what you're looking for, but these came from her house."

Polly did a quick count of the boxes in front of her. When she got to twenty-four, she cringed. "This is going to take forever. Ken Wallers said the woman had an unconventional organizational style. How am I going to find anything?"

"Don't panic until you get into them. The first box I opened was filled with newspaper clippings from the late nineteen-thirties. I found a few about the new tuberculosis sanatorium being constructed in the old hotel."

"Oh, that's cool. So it's organized by decade?"

Andy chuckled. "I wouldn't go so far as to say that it's organized. I think she did her best, but much of it was just tossed into boxes without any thought as to maintaining what she'd originally put together. Grab a box and bring it to the table."

"I have to start somewhere, I guess," Polly said. She pulled the top box from a stack and carried it back to Andy's table. "What do I do now?"

"Don't worry about organizing and classifying," Andy said with a smile. "I won't take up your afternoon like that. Nobody loves this type of work as much as I do. You're going to just do a brute search. Try to keep the items you pull out as close together as possible. If you want to take something with you, I have a notebook for you to jot down a general idea of what it is you're taking." Andy handed Polly an envelope file. "Use this for what you want to keep. When you're finished with a box, tear off the page of things you took, put it on top, close the box and put it back in the stack. If you want to make any marks as to what's in the box, do it, but I have no expectations."

"You're awfully calm about me digging into these without organizing them," Polly said.

"I'm a very nice person," Andy replied with a grin.

They worked in silence for a while. Polly found nothing in the first box she checked. It was filled with programs, pictures, and newspapers from around the time of Bellingwood's centennial celebration fifty years ago. She made a quick notation on the top of the date and contents and set it to the side before pulling another box.

What the woman upstairs had done still bothered Polly. She couldn't put it out of her mind.

Do you know a Marianne Ferguson?" she asked Andy.

Andy nodded. "Yeah. She and her husband were divorced a few years ago. They have a couple of kids."

"I know of a daughter in third grade."

"How do you know her?"

"I just met her upstairs." Polly put the stack of papers down that she'd been riffling through. "Andy, am I paranoid or would she have been upset because Noah and Elijah are black?"

Andy smiled a sad little smile. "That sounds like her. She's not as bad as her parents were. When the high school closed and the kids had to go to school in Boone, they nearly came unglued at the thought that their children would be associating with colored kids." Andy emphasized the last two words with air quotes. "And it wasn't just about black kids. They didn't want their kids to come into contact with Asians or Mexicans or even a Jewish family that had kids their age. It was pretty ugly. As I recall, they finally pulled Marianne and her brother out and put them in a private school. I don't know where they ended up going to high school. I didn't have either of them in class."

"That's awful. You would think that we'd be past that by now."

"That's not the worst of it." Andy paused. "I don't mean it that way, but poor Marianne would. Her ex-husband got married last year and the woman is black. She's a professor at Iowa State, too. Rumor is she's pregnant." She giggled. "Can you imagine how Marianne is going to feel knowing that her kids have a half-sibling who is mixed race? Sometimes karma just slaps a person around."

"Wow. Do Marianne's parents know about this?"

"You know," Andy said. "I haven't heard much about them in years. Her mother didn't work, but her father was some kind of a salesman. I don't know what he does. Maybe he's retired."

Polly picked her stack of papers back up. "Noah and Elijah are going to face this type of thing every day, aren't they?"

"Unless you keep them at home, it will always be something." Andy sighed. "All you can do is make sure they grow up with self-confidence and the knowledge that you love them. Just like you'd do with any kid."

"I had no idea what I was walking into when I fell in love with those boys," Polly said. "They were just little boys to me."

"And that's as it should be. We just hope that every year the world gets a little less hateful about differences."

Polly was idly flipping through the papers when something caught her eye. She backed up through the pages and took a breath. "Here it is."

"Here what is?"

"That symbol that's all over my house. Nobody acted like it existed anywhere else." She split the stack of papers, turning the top batch face down and exposing the symbol.

"What do you have there?"

"A bill of goods from a lumber supplier in Fort Dodge. It looks like someone was doodling the symbol on the page." She brought the paper closer to read the faded writing. "It's dated September twelfth, I think that's nineteen fifteen. I can barely read the name. It has to be Franklin Bell. I can take this?"

"Sure," Andy said. "Just make a note. What are the other papers around that?"

Polly looked at the next invoice in the stack. "This is for kitchen appliances at the Bell House," she said. "But the name on it isn't Franklin Bell, it's an Arthur Bradford. Do you suppose that's Paul's grandfather? Why would he pay for appliances over there?"

"Maybe it came through his hardware store," Andy said.

"I suppose." Polly nodded. "That makes sense. But this doesn't. All of these building invoices are made out to different people, but the address is the Bell House. I thought this was all Franklin's." She backed up through the papers that had been on top of the one with doodling until she came to a three by five card with a handwritten note on it.

"*The Bell House was home to racketeering and murder. Each man involved with Franklin Bell hid the fact that among them was a serial killer. Evidence is mounting. Someday I will expose these men's guilt. It may embarrass some of the leading families in Bellingwood, but the truth will prevail.*"

Polly took a breath after reading this to herself. "You have to hear this," she said.

"What did you find?"

"I assume Margie Deacon wrote this." Polly read it out loud and Andy's eyes grew big. "Serial killer? I don't know anything about a serial killer in Bellingwood." She grinned at Polly. "Except the one you brought to town."

"Hey," Polly said. "That's not fair. I didn't invite him. He just showed up."

"I know, honey. Nobody blames you." Andy capped her marker again and set the stack of papers she was sifting through into the box lid and laid it atop the box. "I'm not spending any more time on this. Your story is much more interesting. Let's get digging." She carried the box to the front table, then retrieved another from the stack. "Show me that symbol again," Andy said.

Polly sketched it out on a blank piece from the notebook Andy had given her, then ripped the page out and put it on the table. "That's close."

"Swords into plowshares," Andy said. "What does that have to do with anything, much less a serial killer?"

"We need to find news articles from those years," Polly said. "Anything that talks about a serial killer or maybe even just a bunch of deaths."

Andy nodded. "We can access old newspapers online. We're going to need more help than just us, though."

"Do you really think that these boxes contain much more information about all of this?"

"Who knows?" Andy asked.

Polly's phone rang. Though the number was local, she didn't recognize it. "Hello, this is Polly."

"Hello, my dear. Simon Gardner here. How are you today?"

"I'm good. How are you?"

"Perfectly wonderful. I'm calling because I've found my mother's diaries. I have only begun to read through them, but I believe there will be information of interest to you."

"That's terrific, Simon," Polly said. "I'm actually in the library basement with Andy Specek. We're going through Margie Deacon's boxes."

"You found them, did you? I'm surprised."

"It's not as bad as you made it sound, Simon."

He chuckled. "I do tend to exaggerate."

"Would you bring those diaries with you to dinner on Monday?"

"I'd be glad to. My mother wrote of a group of men who met in an upstairs room on a regular basis. Franklin Bell was part of that group, of course, but she spoke of secret meetings. She was a young girl and the intrigue was exciting."

"Can I ask one strange question?"

"Of course, my dear."

"Did she write anything about a serial killer?"

"A serial killer? My goodness. That sounds ominous. I will read on with that in mind. What made you ask?"

"A note that Margie Deacon left with a stack of invoices for building the hotel. Franklin Bell wasn't the only one who paid to build the Bell House. Paul Bradford's grandfather purchased the kitchen appliances and Ken Wallers' grandfather's name is on another invoice. There are invoices here with other names."

"Well, well, well. That certainly makes for a more interesting mystery. I will speak to young Paul and find out what he knows. I look forward to our dinner together."

"Hayden is inviting his girlfriend as well," Polly said. "It's the first time we'll meet her. I did it on purpose, thinking she'd enjoy meeting you. Maybe take some pressure off the evening for her."

"If you're sure I'm not an intrusion into your family dynamic, I'd certainly enjoy it."

"I look forward to having you there," Polly said. "It's always interesting, that's for sure."

"Thank you for the invitation. I do anticipate an entertaining evening, and I wish you luck as you continue to search through the boxes. I hope to hear that you've solved the mystery before we meet."

"Thank you, Simon." Polly smiled as they ended the call. "I really like him," she said.

Andy nodded. "I never got to know him. Bill knew his brother, Sam, but Simon wasn't interested in agriculture." She smiled. "I never had need of additional antiques. I think it's wonderful that you've gotten to know him so well, though. I'm sure he'll be a great help when you want to sell any of the pieces the Springers left in the house."

"I don't know what I'll sell yet," Polly said. "There are some beautiful pieces of furniture. It kinda kills me to let it go. Especially when all it might take is some lemon oil and elbow grease to bring it back to life."

"Don't you have enough of your own furniture?" Andy asked. "I mean, what with your father's home and your home."

"That's a pretty big house we're living in. I don't have nice dining room pieces, so we'll refinish the things that were originally in there. And yes, some of the bedroom furniture is horrid colors, but if it can be repainted and used, I'll be glad to. It is much more fun than buying new."

"Most people like to buy new furniture."

"Not me. I guess I'm just a big believer in rescue and repair."

"Which is why you renovate. I'd never have the patience for that," Andy said.

Polly gestured around the room. "I don't have the patience for this." She looked at the time. "I need to keep moving. Those two little boys are patient, but they won't last forever upstairs."

The two of them dug through boxes as fast as they could, sorting out things that had anything to do with the Bell House.

"Here's something," Andy said and held up a newspaper clipping. "It's an article about building the high school. Do you want a copy of this?"

"I'd love that," Polly said, reaching out to take it. She skimmed through the article and took a breath when she read many of the same names that had been associated with building the Bell House. "That's really weird."

"What is?"

"The same people were involved in building the school as the hotel."

"That makes sense, don't you think?" Andy asked. "They were probably families who had money and invested in the town whenever they could."

Polly nodded. "I guess it was only fifteen years later. I wonder what else they did."

Andy handed a stack of clippings. "Here, take these, too. It's all about building the gymnasium, and there are articles about when that was torn down and when they closed the school." She smiled. "There's even a small article in there about when the school hired me."

"She really saved everything, didn't she?" Polly tapped the pile. "Henry never said anything about seeing that symbol when he was renovating the school."

"But if it was as hidden as you say, he might not even have realized it was there."

"That's true," Polly said. "If we hadn't pulled the plaster off the ceiling in the foyer, I don't know if I would have ever made the connection. It was just so big and bold." She took the file folder that Andy handed her and slipped the stack of school articles into it, then closed the box she was working through. She'd found nothing in this one. It was filled with articles, pictures and notes from city meetings in the late nineteen-eighties. Bellingwood was pretty boring back then. The population was shrinking and community leaders were desperate to find a way to bring fresh growth to town. They'd failed, since it was only ten years later that the school finally closed. Polly marked the box and set it aside, then took another from the stacks. They weren't even halfway through the boxes and she was already bored to death.

"Polly?" Joss's voice came from the top of the steps.

Polly jumped up and ran over. "Is everything okay?"

"Your boys are getting tired up here. Can I send them down?"

"Absolutely. I'm so sorry."

Joss smiled. "It's really okay. They were great, but when I saw Noah lying down on the floor, I knew he was wearing out."

"Of course he was." Polly beckoned to the two boys. "Come on down. I want to look at one more box and then maybe we'll go see Miss Camille at the coffee shop."

Elijah attempted to slide down the banister, but a stern look from Polly put his feet back on the steps.

"We found a lot of books," Noah said. He patted the stack he dropped on the first table.

"Good for you. Can you two wait just a little longer while I look through this box?"

"Can we look around?"

Polly glanced at Andy, who shrugged. "I don't think they can hurt anything," she said.

"You can't touch stuff," Polly directed. "If you think you need to touch something, come back here and we'll find paper and pencils for you to draw. Okay?"

"If you need to leave," Andy said, "I can finish looking through these boxes and save anything I think pertains to your mystery."

"One more box. It's killing me that there is so much here and I can't get to it." Polly took the lid off the box she'd brought to the table. "This is it," she said breathily as she sat down.

"What?"

Polly held up a three by five card. *"Early twentieth century serial killer in Bellingwood and surrounding areas"* was written in what they'd come to recognize as Margie Deacon's handwriting.

Andy replaced the lid on the box she'd been digging through and moved to stand over Polly's box. "Okay. That's a big sign."

"I know," Polly said. She took out a stack of newspaper articles that had been jumbled together. Some were folded and others were crumpled. "Do you want to look through these or dig through the box?"

"I'll start with these." Andy pulled the pile back to where she'd been sitting and flattened the first article. "This is about a hobo they found dead by the train tracks in Boone. The article doesn't mention anything about a serial killer."

Polly nodded. She took out a ledger that looked awfully similar to those she still hadn't looked at. That metal box was still sitting behind her car seat. She flipped the book open. Signatures filled the first page, all of whom had been part of the group who paid for the building of the Bell House. The strangest thing was that brown smudges followed each signature.

"Do you suppose it's blood?" she muttered to herself.

"Is what blood?" Andy asked.

Polly held the book up for Andy to see. "Did they just sign this ledger and seal it with their own blood? What in the hell was happening in Bellingwood back then?"

Andy shook her head. "I have no idea. Polly, these articles are about deaths, but none of them seem to be connected. I can't understand why Margie assumed these were connected to a serial killer."

"I want to know where she got hold of newspapers from those days."

"She'd been collecting information for many years. Who knows. If you think about it, the nineteen forties weren't that far removed from when all of this happened. If she started researching it then, the old newspaper office might have had plenty of extra newspapers."

"I suppose. If feels like a hundred years was so long ago, but yeah, it wouldn't have felt that way when she was young."

"We should ask Ken or someone who knew her better. I have a niggling memory that she worked for the newspaper at one time."

"That makes sense," Polly said. "She'd have known exactly where to look." Polly waggled the ledger. "What I don't understand, though, is how she got her hands on this and why she never said anything to anyone."

"What's in the ledger?"

"I can't tell. It's just lists of numbers and then a tally of costs. I don't know if this was money that was paid out or money that came in. There aren't any notations to signify. But it's a lot of money. There are thousands of dollars moving around." Polly continued to flip through the book. The ledger ended about halfway through the book and there was nothing else until she turned to the back cover where the familiar symbol had once again been sketched.

She also found another note card and read out loud. *"Whiskey money may have built the hotel, but it also paid off this cabal. Which one was the murderer?"*

"Margie just insisted that someone in this town was a killer," Andy said.

The sound of crashing toward the back of the room sent both women to their feet. Polly ran toward the sound and found Noah and Elijah looking up at her sheepishly.

"What's going on?" she asked.

"I'm sorry," Noah said.

Elijah's lower lip trembled. "Me too. We were just trying to look at that lion up there."

She looked up to where he was pointing and saw a stone lion.

"One of the library's old gargoyles," Andy said. She righted a chair that had tipped over while Polly picked up two boxes that had fallen.

She grinned at their designation. "Centennial programs. Fifty cents apiece. Looks like they had extras."

"So many extras. Are you two boys okay?"

They nodded.

Polly put her hands on their backs and guided them to the tables. "We should get going. I've kept you here too long." She pointed at the box. "Do you mind if I take this box with me?"

"Not at all," Andy said. "But you must tell me what you find."

"I promise." Polly gathered up the rest of the things she'd culled from other boxes and set them inside before replacing the lid. "Thanks for your help today, Andy. I'm sorry to leave you."

"You made the afternoon fun."

"Where are your coats, boys?" Polly asked.

Elijah's eyes grew big. "They're still upstairs." He ran toward the steps and turned back to the table to get his books. Noah picked up his stack and followed his brother up the stairs.

"They're going to wear me out," Polly said. "But good heavens they're fun."

"Enjoy it," Andy said with a laugh. "You do know that it's going to get harder."

"I know." Polly let out a sigh. "Rebecca broke me of believing I had angelic children. Love her to pieces, but she's going to bring more gray hair than I'm prepared for."

Andy smiled as Polly turned to go up the steps.

CHAPTER TWENTY

Polly headed out Sunday evening, fully ready to be away from the house. She'd hoped to have time to look through the box of things she brought back from the library, but when she walked in the door yesterday, Henry had finished with the cabinets and was ready to help her organize and fill them. They'd spent the rest of the evening sorting through things in the pantry and deciding where things might fit the best. She'd stopped him in the middle of unpacking to make dinner. As usual, there was a small army to feed. Andrew and Kayla were at the house since Stephanie and Sylvie were tied up with a large event at Sycamore House.

At some point in the evening, Kayla and Rebecca had gotten into a snit. Kayla sulked at the dining room table while Rebecca ran to her room to pout. Hayden was out again with his girlfriend. Henry and Heath escaped to the upstairs rooms to build the framework for the bathrooms and Rebecca's new bedroom. That left Andrew to entertain Noah and Elijah, but he'd used up most everything in his bag of tricks the night before. To top it off, he didn't know what to do about his friends.

Fortunately, Stephanie showed up to take her sister home and soon after, Sylvie texted Polly to send her son outside. He'd knocked on Rebecca's door to say goodbye, but all she did was yell goodbye to him from within.

Polly smiled at the memory of Noah and Elijah who were completely stupefied by Rebecca's behavior. They were certainly seeing it all. At one point, Noah lightly tapped on Rebecca's door to ask if she was okay. Polly waited for her to snap at him, but instead, Rebecca opened the door and invited the two boys into her room to play with the kittens. If that was what it took to bring the girl back to normal, Polly was all for it. She wasn't going to step in until absolutely necessary.

Heath and Henry came back downstairs about ten o'clock and Polly sent the boys off to take showers and get ready for bed. Once they were gone from Rebecca's room, Polly finally waded in.

"Do you want to talk about it?" she asked.

"Not really."

"Are you going to pout for the rest of the weekend?"

"I'm not pouting," Rebecca announced. "I was fine with Noah and Elijah."

"Uh huh. So you're done?"

"Yeah," Rebecca said. "I'm done."

"Do you want to tell me why you and Kayla fought?"

"She's being dumb about the play."

"What do you mean?"

"She heard from Missy Lohman that I was going to be Mrs. Butterworth and Andrew got to be Lestrade."

"Okay?"

"Now she's mad that she didn't try out."

"But I thought she didn't want to."

"I know!" Rebecca set her jaw. "That's what I told her. She had every opportunity and now that it's all decided, she's mad because I didn't force her to do it. What am I, her mother?"

"You didn't say that, did you?"

Rebecca looked at her in horror. "No, that would be awful."

"Okay. Good. So she's mad at you because she made a decision and you didn't encourage her to change it."

"Exactly."

Polly almost couldn't believe that Rebecca wasn't somehow at fault. This was terrific.

"Why were you mad at Andrew?"

"I wasn't until he asked me if I wanted to give Kayla my part. What in the heck was he thinking?"

Polly chuckled. "He said that out loud? In front of her?"

"Boys are so dumb sometimes."

"No kidding. What did Kayla say to that?"

"Oh she got all pouty because Mrs. Butterworth has so many lines and she couldn't ever memorize that many."

"I'm sorry you two fought about this."

"We'll get over it tomorrow," Rebecca said. "She'll think about it and realize that she doesn't really want to be on stage. It would scare her to death."

Polly sat on Rebecca's bed and patted it beside her. "I am sorry, but ..." Polly turned and grabbed Rebecca's upper arms and grinned. "Congratulations on getting the part! You should have told me earlier."

Rebecca looked down after giving Polly a small smile. "I wasn't going to say until I knew for sure. Missy Lohman is probably telling the truth, but I want to see my name on the piece of paper on Monday. Then I'll know that I really got it." She let Polly hug her. "And Polly, it's like the most lines in the whole play."

"I'm so proud of you for trying out and for doing well. This is exciting. We should celebrate."

"And that's the other reason I didn't want to tell you while Kayla was here. I knew you'd be excited and I didn't want her to feel even worse."

"I get that." Polly hugged Rebecca again. "Let's go tell Heath and Henry. They're going to want to know this."

"But what if it isn't true?"

"We'll deal with that later. What do you think the odds are that you didn't get the part?"

"Not very ..." Rebecca looked at Polly. "I don't know how to phrase an answer to what you asked."

Polly laughed. "I'm not sure what just happened there either. What's your confidence level that you got the part?"

"Like ninety-five percent?"

"That's a great answer. Come on, let's go tell them."

~~~

Sunday had been more of the same insanity around the house. After church and Sunday school, they'd come home. While Polly took the dogs for a walk, Henry, Hayden and Heath went back upstairs. They wanted to finish framing the rooms so electricity and plumbing could go in.

Rebecca talked Elijah and Noah into watching a movie with her, hoping they'd relax enough to fall asleep. That certainly didn't happen and as soon as Polly and the dogs returned, the boys were ready to play. Instead, Polly had them help her find boxes in the foyer that looked like they contained things for the kitchen. She had more than enough cupboard space now and was ready to fill it with everything that she'd been missing for the last two months. The afternoon quickly passed as they held their own scavenger hunt.

In the middle of unpacking boxes, Polly suddenly remembered that she had wanted to check on Mona and Rose Bright across the street. She took a container of chocolate chip cookies out of the freezer and called for Rebecca.

"Do you want to go across the street with me?"

"Do I have to?" Rebecca asked.

"No, but it would be nice."

"You go be nice. I'm working on a project for school."

"Really?" Polly asked. "What class?"

Rebecca had been surprised by the question. "Fine. I'm drawing a picture of Wonder for art class."

"Come with me, then."

"But I don't want to. It's cold out there."

"You have a very nice coat. We won't be there very long. Come with me."

Rebecca put her hands on her hips. "You just don't want to go alone, do you?"

Polly laughed. "Maybe a little."

"Take Noah and Elijah. They're closer to Rose's age."

The two little boys were watching a movie in the family room; neither of them dressed to go out.

"Fine. I'm mad at you, but you don't have to go," Polly huffed.

"Really mad?"

"No. Just middling mad."

"I can live with that."

Polly had put her coat on and headed across the street.

When Rose opened the front door to her, she smiled. "Hi. You found my mommy."

"Yes I did. May I come in? I have cookies."

"Mommy, can the lady from across the street come in?" Rose yelled. "She has cookies."

Polly gave a little wave. "Go stand in front of her and ask so you can hear her response."

Rose ran into the living room and then came back. "She's been sleeping, but she said it's okay."

Polly stepped into the house, walked past the front closet and into the living room. Mona Bright was propped up on the couch.

"How are you doing?" Polly asked.

"I'm making it. Rose has been a big help." Mona smiled. "So have my friends from the school. There is a lot of food in the refrigerator."

"Well, I just brought cookies. Sharon said they were going to make sure you had food."

"She's a good friend. Thank you for the cookies. Rose, would you take those out to the kitchen table?"

Polly held out the container and Rose took it. "Is there anything I can help you with?"

"No, I'm fine. Thank you. My friends come over to help with lunch and dinner. They're the ones who figured out how to make me comfortable." She pointed to her shoulder. "This is awful. I can't do anything."

Mona hadn't invited Polly to sit, so instead of lingering, Polly moved back toward the front door. "I won't stay. I know it's hard to have people you don't know around when you feel awful, but if you need anything, please call. I can be right over."

"Thank you so much. I feel like I'm being rude, but between the pain and the drugs, I don't have all of my senses about me. Maybe next week."

"I'll check on you again, then," Polly said. "And really. I'll do anything. If you need help with laundry or cleaning or getting Rose to school, let me know."

Mona nodded as Polly stepped backward. "Thank you again."

Rose had returned to the living room and followed Polly to the door, shutting the inside door as Polly stepped outside. It was one thing to be proud and try to stand on your own, but she hoped Mona really did have enough friends to help her get through this.

Construction was finished about four o'clock and Hayden escaped to his room to study. Polly had checked Noah and Elijah's backpacks and left strict orders for Henry and Rebecca to make sure they finished their homework before going to bed. She kissed them good night and left the house. She could hardly wait to get to Pizzazz.

The threat of coming snow kept enough people home that the downtown area was fairly empty. Polly parked closer than usual and walked into Pizzazz to find Joss and Sandy Davis at their table.

Polly hugged Sandy. "I'm so glad you're here tonight. How are things going?"

"We're making it. He's a tough little boy. The doctors are so good and they try to help him be strong and not afraid. I'm glad he listens to them when I'm scared to death." She pointed at the table. "Benji made me come. He said I needed to see real people."

"Benji's a smart man. How's he doing?"

"Fine. It's so much to take in, but we just do it step by step."

Polly winked. "Kind of like designing a building, right?"

"I suppose. I hadn't thought of it that way, but that's exactly right. I just have to stay in the moment."

Sal came rushing in the front door. "Wow. It's blowing out there. I nearly lost two dachshunds when we went out for a walk tonight."

Joss came around the table. "I totally just had an image of your dachshunds lifting into the sky while you held on to their leashes. Pretty soon all of you were floating away."

"Don't laugh. It could happen," Sal said. She hugged Joss, then stepped up beside Polly and reached for Sandy. "I'm so glad you came. You weren't sure yesterday."

"I'm here," Sandy said, nodding. "Thanks for encouraging me."

Tab and Sylvie came in at the same time, followed by Elise Myers and Camille Specht.

"Everybody's here," Polly said. She and Joss headed for the back of the table and Sal slid in on Polly's other side.

She reached over and took Polly's hand. "I feel like it's been forever. It's good to see you."

Baskets of cheese bread arrived and the waitress took drink orders. Everyone usually ordered the same thing, but she'd been tripped up a couple of times and double checked now. The cheese bread was just a given. The women chattered about their weeks and listened as Sandy described what she'd been through. Tab told a story about a little old lady whose daughter was worried that she had too many cats in the house, so she called the sheriff's office. Even though the daughter was told there was nothing they could do, she insisted they check on the woman. Tab had gotten that duty. When she arrived at the home on the outskirts of town, the woman was polite and proceeded to introduce her by name to her nine cats. Their litter boxes were clean and the house didn't smell bad at all. While there were cat beds and scratching posts all over the main level, the woman mentioned that she didn't have many visitors.

"Where does the daughter live?" Sal asked. "Around here?"

"No, she lives in New Mexico."

"And the woman is alone? No other family?"

Tab shook her head.

"Well the poor lady needs her friends, then."

"That's what I thought," Tab said. "She was clean. Her house was clean. The cats were clean. They looked like they were well fed. I saw a veterinarian's business card on the refrigerator and a half full bag of cat food on the back porch. I don't know what the daughter's problem is, but there was nothing wrong that I could see."

"Lydia tells me that Aaron checks on a lot of people," Polly said. "I think he sees quite a few sad stories around town."

"In Bellingwood?" Sal asked. "That surprises me."

"Why?"

Sal shrugged. "I guess I just assume that the cost of living has to be reasonable."

"But pay is low for some of these jobs."

"Yeah. You're right."

"And insurance costs are ridiculous," Joss said. "You can't afford not to have it, but it takes a huge chunk out of your salary every month."

"If you get sick, not only are you paying high premiums, but all of a sudden you have a deductible to pay and the out of pocket hits you immediately, too. It's scary," Sandy said. "We're lucky, but if Benji didn't work where he did, we'd be in trouble with what Will has going on right now."

Polly nodded. "Lydia told me that Henry helps Aaron with house repairs for some of these families. I had no idea. He just said it's the right thing to do."

"He's right," Sylvie said. "That was one of the reasons I didn't move into a house before I came to work for you. I couldn't afford everything *and* worry about a furnace going out or a roof needing to be replaced."

"Apparently, there's someone Aaron is trying to help who needs a new furnace. Henry's been over a couple of times to fix it, but Aaron is worried it won't make it through the winter."

"That's not right," Elise said, startling everyone. She was usually very quiet. "Is this a family?"

Polly nodded.

"Nobody should have to worry about whether or not their kids are warm. We should help."

"Lydia says he won't take help."

"If his furnace goes out and his kids are cold, he'll take help," Camille said. She looked around the table. "My mother started something like this back at home. Hear me out before you jump in." She waited while everyone nodded. "What if we started a fund? Mom has about thirty or so women who contribute something every month and then they do good things in the neighborhood. If they hear about a family that needs food, they use money from that fund. If something big like a furnace comes up, they've got money saved to take care of it. Every six months or so, the women all meet and discuss upcoming needs. I think they even bought a drum set for the high school jazz band when the school couldn't afford it. A little neighborhood grocery store needed a new freezer because theirs was always breaking down. The ladies voted and bought them a freezer."

Sal grinned. "When you talk about thirty women donating a hundred dollars every month, that kind of money grows really fast."

"We could do that," Sandy said. She stopped. "I'm sorry. I don't know about the rest of you. I could do that, though."

"Who'd manage it?" Joss asked.

No one said anything.

"Maybe it's not one of us," Polly said. "And we're only eight, but Lydia has a big group of friends. She might know someone who would take responsibility for keeping track of the funds." She stopped and sat back. "Oh, I wonder if that's it."

"What's what?" Joss asked.

"That money that was in the ledger. Do you suppose it was the same type of thing as we're talking about here?"

She had everyone's attention.

"Sorry. I've been processing on a mystery I uncovered at the Bell House."

"Does it have anything to do with those gold coins?" Tab asked.

"How do you know this?" Polly asked, laughing.

"Everyone knows," Camille said.

Sandy looked back and forth. "I don't know. You found gold coins?"

Polly nodded. "In a hiding place at the house. And there are ledgers with numbers and money logged in them. And there's a weird symbol and I can't figure it out. It's driving me nuts."

"What are you going to do with the money that comes from the coins?" Elise asked. "Camille was telling me about it."

"I don't know yet. It isn't my money. I don't want to just use it for something in the house. I want it to be used for something ..." Polly looked around and smiled. "Something like a little water park in that empty space down the street. That's it." She waved her hand. "I want to be part of this group - whatever we're going to call it and I could seed it with some of that money. But I talked to Rachel last fall about doing something to remember all of the people I've found since I got here."

Sylvie looked over her glasses. "The dead people?"

"Yes," Polly said. "The dead people. I feel bad that I don't even know all their names and there isn't a way to remember them. Rachel told me about that empty space where the building burned down. What if I bought that and put one of those water spray things in there for kids? With picnic tables and park benches. I wouldn't have to make a big deal about it, but maybe put each name on a brick, just so they're remembered."

"That's kind of cool," Elise said. "The kids would love it. There's one of those not far from where my parents live. It's always full of kids in the summer time."

"You could hire someone to paint big murals on the walls around it, too," Sal said. "Brighten it up and make it fun."

Polly smiled. "I love this idea." She pointed at Camille. "I'm sorry. I interrupted what you were talking about. I love that idea too. So how fast can we raise money for a furnace? I don't even know how much it would cost."

"Say three thousand," Joss said. When the women turned to look at her, she put her hands up. "I just built a house and did a lot of research. If it's a little house, three thousand should cover it."

"That means we need thirty women."

"So no men?" Sylvie asked.

Camille shook her head. "Do we need them?"

"No way," Sylvie replied with a grin. "I like having them around, but I don't need them. We can do great things on our own, right?" She put her hand into the middle of the table and waited.

When everyone had followed suit, she said "Girls Rule!" and they all cheered.

"That's what we'll name it," Camille said. "Girls Rule. We can take care of some of the problems we hear about in Bellingwood on our own. And when we come together like this, it makes it feasible. Will you call Lydia tomorrow, Polly?"

"Absolutely. She's going to love this."

Camille picked up her purse and took a checkbook out. "I'm writing you a check for my part. Do you mind taking our money for now?"

Polly laughed. "I knew this was going to happen to me. Of course I don't mind. I'll open a separate account and put this in there until we can get an account for Girls Rule." She sighed. "I'll call my accountant tomorrow too. He can help me do the work. If we want to start a non-profit foundation or whatever, he'll figure it out. Heck, maybe before the end of the year we can deduct this from our taxes. I love you guys. All I did was tell you about a problem and now I get to call Lydia with a solution."

"Do they have to do a hundred dollars a month to be part of this?" Tab asked.

"Good heavens, no," Polly said. "Why?"

"Because I think that we could get a lot more women involved. Especially some of the younger girls like Anita. She can't afford this much every month, but she could do something."

"Invite everyone you can think of," Camille said. "At whatever level they're comfortable. We can change this town."

CHAPTER TWENTY-ONE

"Remember the box," Polly said out loud. She'd just dropped the kids at school and would be stuck in the house all day. Not only were her kitchen appliances being installed, but Doug Randall and Billy Endicott would be here to take electricity to the rooms upstairs. She got out of the truck, started to walk away and shook her head before turning back to open the door of the back seat.

She'd made a second pot of coffee before leaving. At the thought of that, Polly stuck her lower lip out in a pout. There hadn't even been time to stop at Sweet Beans today.

Hopefully, she was one of the first installations on the list. Her plan was to attempt Sylvie's fried chicken for dinner tonight. It was going to be a big deal with Hayden's girlfriend and Simon there as well as celebrating Rebecca's selection as Mrs. Butterworth in the school play.

Last night after dinner at Pizzazz, Sylvie had not only stayed to write out the recipe for her, but made notes about where there might be pitfalls. That was the kind of tutoring Polly appreciated. This would be her first time attempting fried chicken and hoped it wouldn't be her last.

She'd put the box from the library on the big dining room table and set the small metal box down beside it. Her sewing machine looked forlorn in its place with several piles of fabric beside it, all in various states of completion.

"I'll get to you, I promise," she said.

Obiwan looked up at her and wagged his tail.

"I'll talk to anyone around here, won't I?" Polly went back out to the kitchen and stopped to take it in. Things were going to look so different this afternoon. Ovens in the wall, a range in the island, a beautiful new refrigerator, and a dishwasher tucked into its new home. Now, if everything would just fit perfectly and work as soon as it was hooked up. That was all she could ask for. Her biggest concern was the range. She needed that to make the chicken.

Polly opened a cabinet door beside where the range would be placed and pulled out the shelf filled with her pans. On the other side of the range was a custom spice drawer with the things she used most often. Just below it was a drawer with her favorite cooking utensils. Everything had a place. Henry had designed pull-out cutting boards under both sides of the range as well as beside the sink. He'd created an appliance garage along the west wall, allowing her to hide the mixer, bread machine, toaster and her coffee pot. The best part was that he'd added an on/off switch to manage the power for all of those things. Polly appreciated knowing that she could simply switch it off when she left the house and alleviate any worry that something might burn the place down. Not that there weren't a million other potential fire issues in this big old house.

She picked up the stack of mail and other papers that had already accumulated on the corner of that counter. Until they had an office here at the house, everything was collecting on the dining room table. This was the last time Polly was ever going to move. She stamped her foot on the floor, making Han jump.

"That's it," she said. "I just put my foot down. Never again."

He wagged his tail and put his head back down on his paws.

"Don't act like that. I mean it this time." Polly poured a cup of coffee, then opened the cupboard above the appliances. She loved having so much space. Most of the cupboards were still empty, but her pump thermos was sitting right where she'd placed it. Polly filled it with the freshly brewed coffee and made another pot, then brought down disposable coffee cups and packets of sugar. If the installers were going to be here for a while today, she'd at least make sure they had coffee.

Pounding at the back door preceded Doug Randall's voice yelling, "Hello? Are you here, Polly?"

"Come on in." Polly stuck her head around the door into the mud room. "I'm just making coffee."

He came in, rubbing his hands together, then stopped at the threshold into the kitchen. "Wow. This is something."

"I know," she replied.

"Heath says your appliances are coming in today. Really?"

"Any time now. I'm just making coffee for anyone who wants it."

"I miss that about working for you at Sycamore House. You made good food for us."

"Do you need something to eat?" Polly looked around him.

"Billy's on his way. He's got everything for upstairs. And I'm fine. I had breakfast at the diner this morning. Got up way early."

"Because you had company?"

He had the grace to blush.

"Heath said he had fun at your place Friday night." Polly let him off the hook.

"He's a good guy and figured out the game really fast. It's not the same over there without your family around, though."

"It has to be weird without Rachel and Billy there, too."

Doug chuckled. "Billy's at my house all the time. Whenever Rachel works late, he just hangs out with me until she's ready to go home. It's like he never left. Except that I don't have to share the bathroom with him in the morning now."

"No, you just have to share it with a girl."

"Not all the time. Just once in a while." He dropped his head. "It's weird to talk about this with you."

"I'm sorry."

Doug laughed. "No you're not. You think it's funny to embarrass me."

Polly rubbed her hand up his sleeve. "Honestly, Doug, if you had to find any girl, I'm glad it's Anita. I adore her."

Honking in the driveway spun Doug around. "That's Billy. Can we go in the front door so we can haul everything upstairs?"

"Sure. I'll open it. Would you ask him to pull way up so the truck with my appliances can back in?"

Doug nodded and left while Polly went into the foyer. She unlocked the front doors and looked around to make sure no cats were in the immediate vicinity. She'd need to corral as many as possible when they started hauling appliances in. It was always something with those little ones. Fortunately, the windows looking into the back yard offered plenty to keep them occupied.

At a slight tap on the door, Polly flung both open. "I hope you can find your way through all the junk," she said, motioning to the piles of furniture and boxes. Things had gotten much worse over the weekend, even though they'd emptied as many boxes tagged for the kitchen as they could find. Empty boxes and packing paper had been strewn around the room, making a perfect playground for cats and dogs. Boxes had been shifted and moved and furniture shoved out of the way to get to renegade stacks of containers. Polly intended to simply ignore the mess until it either became dangerous or began to reduce in size. Around the first part of May she'd hit the panic button and dig in.

The two boys went up the north stairs.

"We're just going to set up," Doug said. "Jerry will be here about ten to make sure his plans are correct."

She closed the doors. "Thanks. I'll be back in the dining room if you need anything."

"Yes, ma'am," Billy said, sliding into the upstairs hallway with a grin on his face.

He was never going to stop teasing her about that term. There was something wonderful about having these young men in her life.

No sooner had she walked into the kitchen then she heard the familiar beep of a truck backing up. Henry's bobcat made the same sound. Such a little machine, but it had dreams of being a great big truck. Polly took a quick look around the kitchen and didn't see any cats, so she closed the door leading to the dining room from the kitchen, then went through and closed the double doors to the hallway as well. A quick head count tallied five cats. Leia was missing, but that only meant that she was lying in a sunbeam on the floor somewhere.

Polly shook her head at the boxes still sitting on the dining room table. Sometime today she was going to dig into those. She didn't know what she'd find, but there had to be something more. Andy had only just started going through the articles about the deaths during the years the serial killer supposedly worked. The older woman wasn't ready to believe that they were associated in any way, but Margie Deacon had seen something. Even though Ken Wallers thought she was eccentric, that didn't mean the woman hadn't seen a pattern.

She managed to get to the side door before a young man came up the steps to knock.

"Good morning," she said.

"Do you want us to bring these in back here?" he asked.

"You can. If you think it would be easier to come in the front door, that's fine, too. You wouldn't have to go around corners or come up so many steps."

"Can I see what we've got going on?"

Polly stepped back to let him in. Just as she was about to close the door, another young man came up the steps and she waited for him to enter as well.

The two stood inside her kitchen and looked around.

"Where's the front door come in?" the first young man asked. "Over here?" He pointed at the double set of doors leading to the foyer.

Polly nodded and walked over to open them. "Sorry for the mess. We're still moving."

"Can we come across that floor?"

If there was one thing Polly had confidence in, it was Henry's floors. They couldn't hurt these floors. "Absolutely," she said and led them across the foyer to the main doors.

"This would be a lot easier if you don't care."

"I don't care at all. I'm just glad you're here."

The second young man pointed at her yard. "Can we back up? That would easier too."

The ground was frozen. After the damage Liam Hoffman had done to her front yard last fall, this couldn't make it any worse.

"Sure," she said.

"You wanna guide me in, Dar?" the second asked.

Dar nodded and waved his partner off. "If you don't mind, we'll bring everything inside and unpack it here. That way we won't have your doors open for very long."

"You're taking the boxes and packing stuff away, aren't you?" Polly asked. That just about scared her to death. She couldn't have more boxes in the house. Then it occurred to her that Noah and Elijah would love some of those immense boxes. No, what they didn't know wouldn't hurt her.

"You bet." He stepped onto the porch and then moved so that the driver could see him as he backed the truck into her yard. Now all Polly worried about was that they wouldn't hurt her porch with the truck. She shook her head. They'd been doing this for a long time. Surely they knew what they were doing.

It didn't take long for the truck to be exactly where they wanted it. Dar had yelled to his buddy to stop and he stopped. Polly didn't want to watch them take her expensive appliances off the truck, so she went back into the kitchen. She was still trying to get enough caffeine in her system. But once again, she crossed into the kitchen to the sound of knocking at her side door.

Polly grinned through the window at Jerry Allen. She'd gotten to know him well over the last few years. He was a good man. With the growth that had occurred in Bellingwood, not the least of which were her big projects, he'd steadily grown his business.

"Good morning," she said as she opened the door. "Your boys are already upstairs setting up."

"How are you doing today? Looks like you're getting a delivery."

She showed him into the kitchen. "The appliances are here." He'd wired this room months ago, but he stopped to look at how everything was laid out.

"This is nice," he said, pointing to where she had her small appliances. "Henry said he was doing this. I didn't have a good picture in my head. "I really like the tambour door. That's nice work." He pulled it down and pushed it back up. "Keeps the counter open so you can work."

Jerry ran his hand along the counter, then stroked the wood on a cabinet door. "Henry is so good at this."

"Actually, this was Len Specek and Ben Bowen," Polly said. "And they have a new guy over there."

"I met him. Doug something-or-other. Nice young man."

"Schaffer. Yeah. He's working out really well."

"Are you going to have an open house when this place is all finished?"

Polly chuckled. "That might be in ten years. It feels like we're never going to be done with all the things that need to be renovated."

"That means I'll be able to afford to take my wife to Paris," he said with a laugh.

"Yeah, guh-reat," she replied.

"She'd take you, too."

"I don't have time for that," Polly said. "I have to keep coming up with projects so you can afford to travel."

He laughed and pointed at the doors into the foyer. "That way?"

"Yeah. I'm not watching them bring my appliances in. If you see those guys are screwing up, yell at them for me, okay?"

"Got it."

Polly picked up her coffee mug and took a drink. Fabulous. Tepid coffee, and her microwave wasn't installed yet. Henry had taken the microwave over to the shop for storage yesterday. She just wanted this to be finished. Polly poured half the coffee down the sink, then refilled it from the thermos. If she'd been the only person drinking it, she might have been tempted to pour it back in the pot and stir it around.

She took a long drink and walked to the dining room door. No. She didn't dare go in there yet. Not until the truck was unloaded. If the cats thought they were stuck in one room, they did everything in their power to escape. As soon as she opened the door, she'd be assaulted by very annoyed felines. This morning wasn't turning out quite the way she'd planned.

Polly went back to the kitchen table and sat down. She really didn't want to be in here either once they started shoving appliances into small spaces.

"Mrs. Sturtz?"

Dar came into the kitchen.

"Yes. Is everything okay?"

"Yeah. Do you have something to hold these doors open?"

Polly looked at him. All of the doors just stayed where you opened them. There were no springs on any door inside the house. "What do you mean?"

He turned and looked at the door he'd just come through. "Oh. Sorry. No worries."

"I'm worried now," she said to herself after he left the kitchen. Polly did not want to supervise this process, but began to worry that if she left the room, things would go very badly.

The first thing they brought into the room was the dishwasher. That made sense since it was small, but it certainly wasn't what she would have worked on first. They pushed it into the space and left the room again.

Polly took out her phone. *"I don't want to supervise the installers. Are you sure they've got this?"* she texted to Henry.

Her phone rang.

"Hello?"

"Are they making you nervous?"

"A little bit," she said. She got up and walked into the hallway, then whispered. "He asked for something to prop the interior doors open."

"Those don't have springs to cause them to shut on their own," Henry said.

"Exactly. They backed up to the front porch and brought everything inside. They're unpacking things in the foyer."

"It's cold outside. That makes sense. They got in without hurting the porch?"

"Yeah. I watched, but it makes me nervous. I don't know what they're doing and I wouldn't know how to fix it if they did something wrong." Polly went on into her bedroom with both dogs following her. "These boys are awfully young, Henry."

He laughed. "We're getting old, honey. Everybody is young these days. Are Doug and Billy upstairs?"

"Yes. Jerry just showed up. He says I'm paying for his vacation to Paris."

"That's probably right. But back to Doug and Billy. Do you trust them to do the electricity in your house?"

"Yes."

"Are they younger or older than the two installing the appliances."

"Hush up. You're right. I'm being ridiculous."

"Everything is ready for them. They don't have to do anything but hook things up and make sure they work. The only thing I'd ask you to do is make them turn everything on and show you that it's working correctly before they leave."

"But if it isn't, you can fix it, right?"

"Polly!" he said.

"Right?"

"Of course."

"I think that's why I married you."

"Because I can fix things?"

"Yep. You're my fix-it superhero."

"Here he comes to save the day," Henry sang.

"I wonder if I can get some of those extra boxes from unpacking the kitchen onto their truck. That foyer is a mess."

"You don't want to save the refrigerator box?" he asked. "Noah and Elijah would love it."

"Hush. I thought about it and put it aside. I don't need anything else in that foyer. You could put your hands on one of those boxes if we ever wanted one, though, right?"

"I can get you as many as you want. Are you okay there?"

"Yes. But I'm not getting anything done."

"What do want to get done?"

"I wanted to spend time going through that box I brought back from the library. Especially with Simon Gardner coming here tonight."

"That's right," Henry said. "I just thought we were meeting Hayden's new girlfriend. This is going to be a wild evening. Did Rebecca text you yet about if she really is that character in her play?"

"Mrs. Butterworth. Not yet."

"Will you let me know as soon as you do?"

Polly heard a crash coming from the vicinity of the kitchen. "Damn it."

"What?"

"Something crashed in the kitchen."

"Go look and take me with you."

She ran down the hallway and came to a stop when she got to the kitchen.

"Sorry," Dar said. "We dropped the cart on the floor when it came off the fridge."

"Okay," Polly said, breathing heavily. "It was just the cart," she said to Henry.

"Do I need to come home?"

"I'm fine. We've got this." She looked at the two young men who were staring at her. "We have this, right guys?" she asked them.

Dar nodded. "Sorry about that."

"We've got it. I'll let you know. Thanks, Henry." Polly ended the call and put the phone back in her pocket. She sat down at the kitchen table as the two young men went back into the foyer. This was going to be a long morning.

CHAPTER TWENTY-TWO

It was so damned frustrating. Polly stood in the middle of her kitchen with tears streaming down her face. Dar and his buddy had been going along just fine. Then the refrigerator was missing a hose for the ice maker. She told them not to worry, they could deal with that another day. The next thing she knew, though, as they lifted the microwave into place, it slipped out of Dar's hand and while crashing to the floor, scratched the front of the oven and scarred two cabinet doors.

Yes, she'd told herself earlier that all she really needed was the range, but right now it felt as if nothing was working right.

Her phone buzzed with a message from Henry. *"Is it all in? Does it work? Everything look awesome?"*

"Sort of. No. No," she sent back. It was her own fault for having high expectations.

Dar insisted that this had never happened before. They'd done tons of installations and he'd never had so many things go wrong. He and his cohort were so freaked out, they even forgot to haul the cardboard out of her foyer. Of all the damned days for her to have people come for dinner, why had she been so stupid as to make the invitation on a day when everything new was being installed.

Her phone rang.

"I'm sorry. I'm a little pissed right now."

"What happened?" Henry asked.

"Missing a hose for the fridge and they dropped the microwave. Scarred the oven and two cabinet doors."

"They what?" he demanded.

"It was awful. I watched it happen and could do nothing to stop the outcome. It was slow-motion chaos."

"Did they leave?"

"Oh yeah. They were totally freaked out. I didn't yell or anything though."

'You should have. I'll yell. I do business with these people. There's no call for this."

"No. It's okay. We'll deal with it another day." Polly knew she sounded despondent, but right now, she couldn't do anything else.

"They just left?"

"Yeah. Something about another delivery they had to get done."

"They left to go somewhere else?"

"What were they going to do, Henry? Stand here and magically fix the microwave and repair the stove door?"

"No," he spat. "They should have driven back to the warehouse and picked up a new microwave, gotten the damned hose they needed and swiped a door for the oven to replace it. And they should have it done by four o'clock. I'll call you right back."

Before Polly could protest, he was gone. She was still mad as hell, but it made her chuckle. She was no shrinking violet, but it was kind of satisfying to have Henry get angry and rush to her rescue.

Polly knew it was ridiculous, but right now, she just wanted to order pizza for tonight, she was so mad. No matter that the chicken was thawed and she'd already peeled and cut up the potatoes. They were soaking in a pan in the old refrigerator. Since she was being pissy about the whole thing, she didn't even want to look at the new refrigerator. It wasn't fully working anyway.

She didn't have to start supper for a couple more hours. Now would be a perfect time to do something other than stand around in the kitchen and feel sorry for herself. Polly went out to the mudroom, opened the freezer, and took out an ice cream sandwich. That would teach those rotten installers. She'd inhale some ice cream and get over herself.

Her phone rang again as she walked into the dining room. She tugged it out of her pocket, placed it on the table and swiped the call open, then pressed the speaker button so she could eat and sort papers at the same time. "Hey," she said to Henry.

"There's a miserable supervisor right now. Apparently, he hadn't yet been told about what happened."

"It's no big deal, Henry. I'll get through tonight and when they fix it, they fix it."

"Oh, they're fixing it today. He's coming over himself."

"I didn't want to get those boys in trouble."

"Why? Because they didn't want to carry the appliances into the house so they backed up onto our lawn? Or because they unpacked everything in our foyer and then didn't haul away the boxes? Or how about not having extra items they might need for a refrigerator install. We haven't even gotten to running out on you and not calling their supervisor after they ruined a stove front and scarred cabinets. Yeah. They made their own trouble and today, I'm just the man to dish it out."

"I love it when you get all protective of me," she said with a smile.

He chuckled. "I don't get to do it very often. You manage to take care of yourself quite well, but damn, this made me angry. I paid extra so this would all come in today and be ready for us to use right away. Are Doug and Billy still working upstairs?"

"Yeah. They left for lunch and got back just before all hell broke loose in the kitchen."

"Did you cry?"

Polly laughed. "That's not fair. You know I did. I waited until they drove away, though."

"I hope that I've been able to make a miracle happen. I'm sorry this messed up your day."

"It's okay. I'm eating an ice cream sandwich and about to finally open the box that I wanted to look through before Simon got here tonight."

"You're going to be okay with someone else disturbing your afternoon?"

"I'll be fine, Henry. Stop worrying. Thank you for taking care of it, but it would have worked out." She chuckled. "Heck, I could probably have taken the pie over to Mona Bright's house and used her oven."

"You made a pie?"

"It's one of those apple pies I made over Christmas and put in the freezer."

"You had an apple pie in the freezer? Who are you?"

"The woman who bought too many apples and had to do something since no one was eating them. Did you even know I was so domestic?"

"I'm a little scared right now."

"Not impressed?"

"Impressed would imply that I might have expectations of you as a housewife. I will never do that. You are amazing in everything you do."

"Seriously, Henry," Polly said, laughing. "I am not mad at you about this install. You're my hero in the whole thing. You can quit trying to make points with me."

"Oh baby," he said with enough of a leer that she could hear it in his voice. "That's not why I'm working to make points."

"Horndog."

"Every day." His tone returned to normal. "Okay. I need to get back in there. Let me know when people show up again. Will you?"

"Sure. Thanks." She looked at her phone after they ended the call. Ryan Gosling had nothing on her husband.

Polly emptied the top layers from the box onto the table and picked up the stack that Andy had been looking through on Saturday. These were the deaths that had occurred during the time period Margie Deacon thought the killer was active. She put the box on a folding chair beside her, then spread the articles out on the table. Margie had identified twenty-two different people's deaths as belonging to the serial killer, who she named "The Invisible Killer." The woman had meticulously noted the date and which newspaper the articles had come from, so Polly sorted them by date and started at the beginning with an article from July twentieth, nineteen-thirteen, three years before the Bell House was built. A young woman was found dead in the back yard of her parents' home. There was no sign of foul play, the medical examination didn't find signs of poison and she hadn't been suicidal. Milly Burstyn was found lying crumpled on the ground in front of a wooden swing.

The second death happened less than a month later. This time it was Lester Black, aged 68. He'd had heart issues and his wife found him when she returned home after visiting her sister in Des Moines. It was assumed he died of a heart attack.

The names and dates became unimportant as Polly continued to read. She marked each down on a blank piece of paper, just in case she saw a pattern in that information later. The one significant thing about each of these deaths was that there was no apparent cause. None of them had been caused by accident and each death had occurred when the person was alone, only to be found by someone close to them within just a few hours.

This information wouldn't have raised any red flags, since the deaths occurred quietly and spanned a time period of more than five years. Polly checked her notes once again before sliding the articles back into the folder Andy had provided. Margie Deacon wasn't nuts. This felt like something bigger than just random deaths. It might have been interesting, though, if Polly could have seen a listing of all the deaths in the county during those years. How many more might Margie Deacon have missed? Polly didn't have any foundational information for the case that Margie was building. All she had available was exactly what Margie was feeding to her. Polly wished she'd gotten to know the woman before she died, if nothing more than to be able to confirm for herself that she had integrity. It didn't matter to Polly that Margie was eccentric and odd.

She thought about some of the interesting characters that she'd grown to know while working in the library in Boston. There were many eccentric and odd patrons. Some of them were so weird, nobody liked dealing with them, but she'd gotten to know two wonderful people whose eccentricities made them stand out from the crowd. Both were exceptionally brilliant. While a few of the other librarians saw them as arrogant and condescending, Polly soon realized that they didn't feel those things at all. They were genuinely grateful for her help if they needed it, but were so highly focused on the work they were doing, it was as if they'd disconnected from the real world. The two people didn't know each other and were rarely in the library at the same time. Over the years she'd gotten to know each of them well, especially since her coworkers tended to find other places to be when they approached the main desk. One of her friends, Ilsa, tried to ridicule Polly for being the nice girl from Iowa, who didn't know any better than to be nice to mean people. Polly reminded Ilsa that she was just as nice to mean coworkers.

The next stack of papers and notes were in a fat file folder with two rubber bands around it that disintegrated when Polly took them off.

The three by five note card taped to the inside of the folder read, *"Uncle Deke's personal notes."*

Okay, who was Uncle Deke and what was his role in this story?

It didn't take Polly long to discover that Margie's uncle had investigated the deaths himself, even though he wasn't part of law enforcement. She looked at the names on her list of the dead. How was he connected? How was any of this connected? Polly kept the pages of articles, notes and paperwork in order, flipping one after the other over. Some were duplicate articles, others were similar, coming from different news organizations. He'd attached notes about what the victims had been wearing, their activities the day of their death, and details he uncovered about their families and friends. It was going to take much longer than Polly wanted to spend to understand how any of this was connected. She chuckled as she considered what Henry might say if she built a murder board in this room.

Polly took out her cell phone. Her mind was just reeling with possibilities.

"Chief Wallers," came from the other end of the phone.

"Hi Ken, it's Polly."

"More news on your trespassers?"

Polly had to stop for a moment to think about what he was asking. "What? Oh, no. I'm working through this mystery from the Bell House. Who was Margie's Uncle Deke?"

He chuckled. "That was a great-uncle, I think. Maybe her father's uncle. He was quite a character from what people said. I think he died in the early fifties. By that time he was nothing but an old drunk. He lived alone in an old run-down house over by you, from what I remember folks saying. Why do you ask?"

"She has a folder of stuff here. It looks like he was investigating those deaths she was so worked up about."

"That sounds right. I'd need to ask some other people who have better memories than me, but I remember my dad talking about him. Polly, I think he lived in the Bright's house now that we're talking about it. Dad used to drive around town with me in the car and tell me about some of the people who'd lived in the houses we passed. Let me think. It seems that Deke Deacon ... What was it Dad told me about him? Something about his girl dying two weeks before they were supposed to be married. Dad always said that was what killed him in the end." Ken laughed a little laugh. "You're making me focus. Yeah. Maybe it was in her back yard. Anyway, Deke couldn't let it go. He was sure that she'd been murdered. He searched his entire life for the murderer. Some say he knew who it was but couldn't get enough evidence to prove it."

Polly reached across the table and picked up the stack of

articles with the one about Milly Burstyn on top. "That's the first murder," she said quietly.

"Murder?" he asked.

"Okay, death. It doesn't even look suspicious, I suppose. She was found in her back yard on the ground in front of a swing. No outward signs of an altercation, she was just gone. He has a list of twenty-two deaths, Ken. I can't figure out how they're connected, except that none of them look suspicious and every person was found dead."

"That's usually what happens, Polly."

"Stop it. I know. I just mean that in each death, there was a span of time when they were alone and that's when they died. It's too bad we can't get medical records from back then."

"A hundred years ago? Doubtful. Especially if nobody thought there was anything wrong."

"Have you seen this list of deaths he collected?"

Ken huffed a laugh. "No. Margie alluded to something in the past, but I assumed she was attempting to make a big deal out of nothing."

"Do you have a minute that I could read you the list? Maybe you'll recognize some other names."

"Sure."

Polly read through the list until Ken said, "Stop. Back up. What was that name?"

"Booker Earl."

"I remember Granddad talking about him. They were best friends when Granddad was a kid. Did everything together. Booker died pretty young. Granddad wouldn't talk about how he died, just that it was so unnecessary."

Polly noted Ken's name beside Booker Earl's on her list and went on through it. He didn't recognize any others.

"I'm going to keep digging," she said. "Are we meeting with Greg Parker tomorrow?"

"Yeah. It will be interesting to discover what he knows. That man has a steel trap for a brain. Anything that goes in, he retains. And he's really good at assimilating it and making sense of data."

"I can't wait to meet him. Thanks for your time, Ken."

"I'm glad we aren't dealing with a current serial killer. You're dogged."

"I just don't like unanswered questions. I can set them aside for a while, but sooner or later, I need to know."

"You'd make a good investigator."

The doorbell at the side door rang. Henry had finally fixed it to be different than the front doorbell. "Except for the fact that I always have something going on." Polly was already out of the dining room when she said goodbye.

"Ms. Giller?" a good-looking man about her age asked.

"Yes."

"I'm here to finish installing your appliances. I spoke with your husband and understand there were several issues."

"Come on in." Polly stepped back. "I wouldn't have made a scene today," she said. "I'm sorry you had to come out."

"It's no problem, ma'am. Just sorry my boys couldn't get the job finished." He wiped his feet on the rug and stepped into her kitchen. "Henry does nice work." His eye caught the scarred oven door and he walked around to look at the damage done to the cabinet doors. "I'm very sorry about this. We'll work with Henry to pay for new doors."

"Those aren't my biggest concern." Polly grimaced. "I don't have a biggest concern. It was just a bunch of messes all at once."

He nodded. "It should take me about a half hour to deal with these messes. Hopefully that will relieve some of the pressure."

Polly smiled at him. He got it. One thing was easy to manage. Even two, but when more than that happened at the same time, it became less easy to focus on the fixes instead of the problems.

"I have the hose right here to fix the fridge. We'll start with that so you can use one thing right away. I want to doublecheck the dishwasher too."

"Thanks," she said. When things had spiraled earlier, there was no time to ensure that everything was working correctly. The young men had panicked and run.

The door from the foyer opened and Billy walked in. "Polly," he started, then said, "Joe. What are you doing here? I thought you got promoted away from customer installs."

"Hey, Billy. What's up, man. Good to see you." Joe walked around the island and shook Billy's hand. "I'm just here to do some repair work. Our boys had a few issues this morning."

Billy pointed at the stove. "That's not good."

Joe shook his head. "No. Not good at all. They've done a lot of installs for us, but ran off the rails today."

"You're going to clean up her foyer, too," Billy said. "Right?"

"The foyer?"

"They left all the packaging in there."

Joe rolled his eyes and blew out a sigh. "Yep. Guess so. What are you doing here today?"

"Running electrical in rooms upstairs. Doug's up there, too. I just need to get some more things out of the truck."

"I'll walk out with you," Joe said.

Polly had no idea what Billy was planning to ask her, but that was okay. At least her kitchen was coming together and before too long she'd have three bedrooms upstairs.

CHAPTER TWENTY-THREE

"Now, are you sure I can't help you with anything?"

Hayden's girlfriend was a sweetheart. Polly had fallen in love with the girl the minute she walked in the back door. Her dark brown eyes sparkled with life and she knelt down to embrace Noah and Elijah when they crashed through the foyer doors at the sound of Hayden's voice.

"I've heard so much about you two," she'd said to them. "Hayden tells me you're two of his favorite little brothers."

Hayden stopped to give Polly a quick hug. "I promise to introduce you as soon as they release her."

"She seems like a terrific girl," Polly said. "I hope you bring her over often."

He'd given her a small smile and she wondered what that meant. Polly hoped it wasn't an 'I've already asked her to marry me' smile. A graduation was all she could pull off this year.

Polly turned around twice in the kitchen. "I don't remember where we've put the glasses," she said to Tess, and then pointed to the corner cabinets near the refrigerator. "Maybe look in those. They're in one of them, I'm sure of that."

"Hayden said you just moved everything in this weekend. I can't imagine living out of boxes."

"It's been entertaining."

"This kitchen is huge and amazing, though." Tess opened the upper cabinet closest to the refrigerator and then moved to the next one ... where she found the glasses. "How many do I need?"

"Yeah, I don't even have a good number in my head yet. This family keeps changing." Polly used her fingers while she silently ticked off all the people who lived with her now, then added two more for Simon and Tess. "Nine should do it." She ran through the names in her head one more time. "Yes. That's right."

Polly had been at a loss without Rebecca, who had stayed after school for something to do with the play. If they were starting rehearsals, that teacher did not waste any time. After that, she, Andrew, and Kayla were going to Kayla's apartment. Since Stephanie took Mondays off, she enjoyed having the kids there every once in a while. Jason picked his brother up after he was done working with Eliseo, and Henry would be home any minute with Rebecca. Heath was going to arrive just before dinner. He'd had to go to Fort Dodge to pick up supplies for one of the work sites.

After the installer left this afternoon, Polly went back to the spot where she'd stood and cried and turned around a few times, taking in the expanse and beauty of the room. Everything was here and it was all hers. Until she emptied the refrigerator on the porch into this one, those extra steps were going to be annoying, but it really was coming together. She'd gone right to work. The potatoes had been put on to boil and she chopped vegetables for the salad. Polly had dredged the chicken and mixed dough in her bread machine for rolls.

Sylvie's fried chicken was easy, but it still took time. Polly could hardly believe that the first thing she was cooking in her brand-new kitchen would splatter grease everywhere. Why couldn't she have just made a meatloaf or something simple?

The mashed potatoes were in the oven, along with a corn casserole and a smothered asparagus dish. She covered the chicken platter and slid it into the warming oven drawer that she still couldn't believe Henry had purchased for her. She'd read through the directions for that one. He hadn't told her that it was coming in and the installer had to explain what she'd received.

Polly wiped down the range top and put the last of the dishes into the dishwasher. She dried the stock pot she'd used to boil the potatoes and returned it to a lower cabinet. That might not be where it would always live, but for now that's where she had space.

"Hayden said that you had a friend coming tonight?" Tess asked.

Polly nodded as she flipped open cupboard doors looking for the plates. "Simon Gardner. He owns the antique store uptown. A fascinating man. His study was in anthropology, but when he was young, his life turned upside down. So here he is, observing life in a very different manner. His brother was a botany professor at Iowa State. He's retired now."

"He sounds interesting." Tess took the plates from Polly's hands.

Polly smiled and pulled drawers out looking for the silverware. This was ridiculous. She finally found it and counted out knives, forks and spoons. "He is and he's a lovely man, too. We're in the middle of trying to understand a mystery I've discovered here at the house."

"What's that?"

Polly chuckled as she followed Tess around the table, placing silverware where it belonged. "Honestly, it might be more than one mystery. I just don't know. We found a strange symbol on the ceiling of the foyer after Heath and Hayden pulled the plaster off the ceiling. Then I found it on window and door sills on this level. And it was also on some ledgers I discovered."

"Hayden told me about the boxes in the mantle. That's crazy."

"It's pretty crazy. So I have that symbol and a bunch of names from a hundred years ago. Some of them are related to men and women I know today. I just thought those people were associated with the moonshine whiskey that was being made in town. But there's more to it. I found information this weekend that might point to a serial killer working in this area during the early part of the nineteen hundreds. If so, somehow these same men are involved. Probably not as murderers." Polly shook her head. "I just don't know what to think."

She turned back to see Tess opening more cupboard doors. "What are you looking for?"

"Napkins."

Polly laughed out loud and pointed at the door next to the mudroom. "In the pantry. On a shelf just to your right when you walk in. There should be a glass pitcher in there, too. Would you bring that out?" She took Tess's place and opened more cupboard doors looking for serving dishes. She was sure she'd seen them here somewhere. If she thought about it, the organization of the kitchen would probably make sense. More than likely, Henry had patterned it after his mother's house. It certainly wasn't set up like the apartment at Sycamore House. But he'd never had anything to say about that. Polly had filled the cupboards when she moved in and never made an effort to streamline them. Though there was plenty of room, that kitchen was still small enough that it took very few steps to get from one side to the other.

"Hayden also told me that you lead a pretty exciting life when it comes to finding dead bodies." Tess put the pitcher on the island and gave it a little push to move it closer to Polly.

"He did, did he?" Polly asked. "I don't know that it is exciting, but yes, it gets the blood pumping." She shrugged. "It's been quite a while since I've found anyone. I keep hoping that at any moment my streak will be over and I can go back to living a boring life."

Tess pointed at the foyer. "You don't seem like the type of person who will ever lead a boring life."

"I hope not. So tell me where you're from, Tess. Hayden hasn't said much."

Tess chuckled. "He told me that would give me something to talk about tonight; that he hadn't spoiled all of my stories by telling them first."

"That's an interesting way to look at it," Polly said with a laugh. "Good for him."

"My mother is from the Dominican Republic and Dad grew up in Ohio. She was here on a student visa and they fell in love. They live south of Indianapolis in a little town. Dad's a lawyer and Mom's a nurse."

"Do you have any other siblings?"

"I'm the oldest. I have a brother who is a junior in high school and then the family got a surprise five years ago, so I have a little sister too."

"And your mom's a nurse?" Polly asked, chuckling.

"I know, right? She should know about that stuff. I teased her, but it's kinda cool."

"What brought you to Iowa State?"

"I hate to even admit it," Tess said, "but it was a boy. I thought we were going to be together forever. He's an engineering student and got a scholarship, so I followed him." She gave her head a quick shake. "We broke up in October of my freshman year, but I loved my roommate and was making friends on my floor. There was no reason to go home, so I stayed. I'm glad I did." Tess smiled at Hayden as he came through the door.

"We were just talking about you," Polly said.

"About what a gorgeous young man I am? Or maybe it's my over-the-top brilliance." He patted his head. "No, I get it. My beautiful head of hair."

"You're a strange boy." Polly handed him the pitcher. "Would you please fill that with ice?"

When he headed for the new refrigerator, she pointed at the back porch. "We don't have much in here yet. Let's empty the bin in that fridge. Then would you fill it with water and fill glasses?"

"What if I just came in to ask you a quick question?" he asked.

Polly caught his wink at Tess, but rushed to his side and took the pitcher back. "I'm so sorry, my brilliant, gorgeous, hairy son. What was I thinking? You are lord of all and shouldn't be asked to do demeaning work."

"Uh. Okay."

She chuckled. "What did you want?"

"Do you care if the boys go upstairs with me to look at what's happening in those rooms? One of them is their room, right?"

"That would be fine. If they're with you, they can go up any time. I just worry about nails and splinters."

He took the pitcher back from her. "I'll fill this with ice first, though."

"No," she said, grinning. "You go be with the boys. I've got this."

Hayden released the pitcher to her and left the room. Polly stepped onto the back porch and opened the freezer as the back door opened.

"Hello there," she said.

Rebecca shook out of her coat and started to drop it on top of her backpack, but checked herself, put the backpack into her cubby and put the coat on its hook. "What a day," she said.

"Congratulations on getting the part." Polly hugged Rebecca's shoulders. "I'm really proud of you. Come in and meet Tess. Is Henry coming?"

"He's just getting something out of the truck." Rebecca went into the kitchen and walked right up to Tess. "I'm Rebecca. Are you in love with my brother?"

Tess lifted her eyebrows and looked at Polly.

"Rebecca," Polly scolded.

The younger girl laughed and put her hand out. "I'm sorry. I am Rebecca. That would have been funnier if Hayden had been in the room. But your face wasn't bad."

Polly filled the pitcher with water and brought it over to put into Rebecca's hands. "Fill the glasses on the table."

The dogs had gone back and forth between the foyer and kitchen, but they'd been fairly quiet. The cats were quite interested in all that was going on, but had grown tired of constantly being put back on the floor so had escaped to parts unknown. When Han and Obiwan rushed past everyone to the back door, Polly knew Henry was there.

"Look who I found," Henry said.

"I'm so glad you're here." Polly rushed to the door to greet Simon. "Let me take your coat."

"My dear, I am in love with your kitchen. What a beautiful room. It was quite dingy and frightening the last time I was in here. I could only imagine those poor women who had to serve the hotel's guests while working in the steamy heat of this room. Mother had several entries in her journal about working here in the heat of the summer." He shrugged out of his coat.

Polly took it from him and placed it on top of the washing machine in the mud room.

Henry put his on a hook after handing her a package.

"What's this?"

"I'm sorry you had to put up with such a crazy day. I thought you might need something to remind you that I love you."

"You're a nut. You were my hero today. I always know you love me."

Rebecca had come to get Simon and introduce him to Tess, so Polly unwrapped the gift Henry had given her.

"I don't know what this is," she said.

"It isn't perfect, but Len helped me carve it." Henry turned it so that it faced the other way. "It's a pineapple. You're supposed to hang it near your door. It's a symbol of hospitality."

"Really?"

He nodded. "I think the idea came from the South, but yeah. Didn't you notice Mom's?"

"I just figured she liked the pineapple or wanted a reminder of Hawaii or something."

"No. It's symbolic. I thought it would be perfect here. We could even hang it on the door sill just outside the back door."

Polly reached up and kissed him. "Thank you. I love it."

"No Heath yet?"

She shook her head.

Henry took out his phone and sent a quick text, then put it down on the counter. "Introduce me to Tess."

"She's a wonderful girl, Henry." Polly whispered at him. "I think she really does love our boy."

"That's nice. I like her already."

They walked across the room. "Tess, this is Henry. Henry, Tess."

He put his hand out. "It's nice to meet you. Might I ask your intentions toward our son?"

The girl looked at Henry, surprise on her face.

Polly stepped between them and took Tess's arm. "I'm so sorry. I guess they like you. They're not usually this offensive. Tell her you're kidding, Henry."

"About what? I want to know what she's intending to do with Hayden."

Polly wrapped an arm protectively around Tess's shoulders. "Tell her."

He laughed out loud. "Nobody lets me have any fun around here. Simon, do you see the struggle I put up with every day?"

"It appears to be quite a difficult life."

"That's what I'm saying." Henry reached across and touched Tess's elbow. "Welcome. I'm a very nice man. I promise. Where are Hayden and the boys?"

"They're upstairs checking on the work in their future bedroom," Polly said.

"I'd like to see that too. Then I want you to give me a full tour of the new kitchen appliances." He stepped forward to look over the island. "Those scratches on the doors aren't awful."

Polly nodded. "They don't bother me."

"Maybe we should leave them so in ten years we can remember today's events."

"That's not the worst idea," she said. "Scars and imperfections are memorable."

"That's my girl." Henry smiled. "It's one more story you can tell about re-building this house."

"No shortage of those."

The dogs followed him out and Polly turned to Simon. "We'll eat soon. We're just waiting on Heath to get home. If we have to start without him, we will. Would you like to see the downstairs? It's not nearly what we want it to be, but at least we're in."

"I'd love to see what you have done."

"Tess, you can join us on this short tour," Polly said. She opened the tambour that covered the corner counter leading to the dining room. "This was a cool idea they had for serving into the dining room. Henry replaced the tambour and I love it. The table was probably built in this room. There's no way, even with those double doors, that it's coming out on its own. Until we finish more rooms in this house and I can refinish some of the original furniture from here, I'm just using it as a catch-all." She pointed at the box from Margie Deacon. "Simon, that's the box I'm working through."

He picked up the pad with the list she'd made on it. "What's this?"

"Margie Deacon seemed to think that those people were all killed by the same person." Polly pointed at the first name. "Ken Wallers told me that Milly Burstyn was Deke Deacon's girlfriend and that he'd investigated this as a murder for the rest of his life."

"He died a sad man," Simon said.

Polly scrolled down the list with her finger until she came to Booker Earl's name. "Ken also said this man was a close friend of his grandfather."

"I wonder what other connections we can make to names on this list." He put the pad back on the table. "I'm sorry to distract you. Please show me the rest of your home."

They went through the double doors into the hallway and Simon looked down, then up and around. "A long Persian runner would be a beautiful addition to this hallway."

"That's a grand idea," Polly said. "I thought about throw rugs, but those things skid all over the place, even with that rubber stuff underneath."

"You could install it much like carpeting so that it stays. You might not want to damage the floor, but it would cut down on the sound and be quite attractive. I'm certain that at one time there was something like that here."

"How do you know that?"

He frowned in concentration. "It seems that I've seen a

photograph of this hallway. But I don't know where. Let me think on that."

Heath had arrived home before they returned to the kitchen. Polly was generally embarrassed about the state of her foyer, but she just decided to own it. At least the monster boxes were gone.

"Is Heath here?" Elijah asked as he ran down the steps. "I want to tell him about our new room. It's going to be awesome."

"He's home," Polly said. "But we should have dinner first, don't you think? You can take him upstairs after we're done eating."

Elijah ran back up the steps, yelling, "It's dinner time. Come on, everybody."

He spun around on the landing and tried to jump up to put his leg over the banister.

"No," Polly snapped.

He looked at her in shock.

"You do not slide down that banister. Not today. Not ever," she said. She took a breath when she saw his face and turned to Simon and Tess. "I'll be right in. We'll have dinner in a moment."

As they left the room, Polly walked up the steps to meet Elijah. "I'm sorry I snapped at you. Do you understand why I might worry?"

"Because I could fall off and hurt myself?"

"You could hurt yourself really bad," she said. "Okay?" Polly put out her hand.

Elijah put his hand in hers. "I'm sorry."

"It's okay. Let's go eat." When they got to the bottom of the steps, she pointed to the back of the house. "First, go wash your hands, though."

He slapped them on his jeans. "They're kinda dirty."

"I know they are. Go on. I love you."

When Henry, Hayden and Noah came out onto the landing, Polly smiled up at them. "I just sent Elijah in to wash his hands for dinner. You three should do the same. Everyone is home, our guests are here, and dinner is about to be served. Hurry."

CHAPTER TWENTY-FOUR

Tess had only required a few minutes last night to get comfortable with the strange sense of humor Polly's family exhibited, but once she did, she dropped right into the fun and games. Polly and Simon had no time to look through the box of things she'd brought back from the library, but they were all meeting at Greg Parker's house this afternoon once Lucy finished work at the diner.

Polly was a little frustrated with herself for scheduling another dinner party this evening. And this one was important. She really wanted Tab and JJ to have a good time. Whether they ended up doing anything further together was their decision, but dinner could at least be fun. With Polly's family, nobody had much time to be uncomfortable.

The boys loved meeting new people. Last night, they had attached themselves first to Tess and then to Simon, asking questions of the guests and telling tales as tall as any Rebecca or Henry could come up with. They'd met Tab before, so were already comfortable with her. JJ was enough of a scoundrel that he should get along with all of them.

Hayden wouldn't be at dinner tonight. He had an exam that was stressing him out, so planned to stay in Ames to study. He told Polly he'd spend the night with friends and packed a bag. She'd given him a sideways glance when he told her his plans, but he insisted he was staying with friends and not Tess. She chuckled. The boy was not her son and he was an adult. She loved that he still felt it necessary to answer to her. What a good kid.

Sal and Mark also weren't coming to dinner. He had a continuing education class and she realized that one of her deadlines was closer than she'd thought.

Doug and Billy were back at work upstairs. They planned to be finished by the end of the day and were perfectly comfortable working without anyone else in the house. Doug even offered to take the dogs out when they got back from lunch. That meant that once she left for the day, she had nothing to worry about.

Polly had done her best to have everything prepared for dinner. No more fried chicken. At least not for a while. It had been a huge hit and Henry declared that it was going to be his request for every birthday henceforth. The rest of the family echoed his assertion and Polly knew she was in trouble. Honestly, it hadn't been that difficult, it was just tedious and required that she stand over it and pay attention - something she didn't love having to do.

Tonight she was serving beef tips over noodles. The beef was in the slow cooker and the noodles would cook in a hurry. She had a quick stir-fry green beans with mushrooms side dish to make and would toss the dried ramen noodles in with the broccoli salad she made earlier this morning. The ingredients for the rolls were already measured and tucked in behind the tambour with the appliances. Rebecca had been instructed to start the machine when she got home from school. By the time Polly arrived, the dough should be ready for her to shape into rolls and drop in the oven. Since she'd served apple pie last night and Rebecca's favorite dessert was chocolate cake, Polly called the bakery early this morning and ordered a dozen cupcakes. That would be a nice celebration dessert. They had plenty of ice cream in the freezer, so she felt like everything was ready to go.

Polly texted Doug that she was leaving and headed out to her truck. She'd cleaned up after the first pot of coffee and put everything away. It had been just enough for her, Henry, and Hayden to get a start on their day. It was not enough, by far, to keep her energy level up. Fortunately, she knew exactly how to take care of that.

The smell of coffee when she walked in the front door of Sweet Beans greeted Polly like a long-lost friend. She still couldn't believe they had a coffee shop in this little town.

"Good morning," Camille said. "Something fun or just black?"

"One of each," Polly replied.

"That bad?"

Polly shrugged. "Not really. I just didn't get enough coffee before I left the house this morning."

"You are definitely one of my most addicted customers," Camille said.

"Let's not say that too loudly. How about I just have a mug of dark roast right now and before I'm ready to go, I'll order my regular."

"Got it." Camille pulled a mug off the counter behind her. "I talked to Marta yesterday and she'd like to be part of Girls Rule. Elise is excited, but she's sad because she doesn't know anyone except us, so she can't invite people to join."

"I think your idea was fantastic. I haven't had a chance to tell Lydia what we're planning yet."

Camille pointed to the door. "You have your chance now. She comes in early every Tuesday morning before she goes to church for her meetings."

"She has women's meetings every Tuesday?" Polly asked.

"I guess."

Lydia came inside and smiled as she approached Polly. "I'm so glad you're here this morning. How was your dinner last night? I understand you met Hayden's new girlfriend. Is she wonderful?"

Polly nodded. "I love her and so does everyone else. I hope she sticks around for a while."

"Just a mug of whatever flavored roast you have today," Lydia said to Camille.

"You have women's meetings every Tuesday?" Polly asked. "That sounds awful."

Lydia chuckled. "I have meetings two out of four Tuesdays and the other two I help in the office. That way I keep a schedule."

"You're amazing." Polly pointed at a table. "I have something I want to talk about with you."

Lydia paid Camille and dropped money into the tip jar. "What's up?"

"Do you remember telling us about that family that needs a furnace?"

They sat down and Lydia held her hands over the steam coming off her mug. "What about it?"

"We're going to take care of it."

Lydia frowned. "Who's we. He won't take charity."

"He might not have an option. I talked to the girls at Pizzazz the other night and Camille came up with an extraordinary idea. Something her mother set up in Omaha. We're going to organize a group of women who contribute a hundred dollars every month to a fund. Right now it's just the eight of us, but we're hoping to bring more and more women in. Camille called us 'Girls Rule.' And of course we'll let women in who can't afford that much every month, but it's kind of a base so we can actually raise some funds."

Lydia opened her purse and took out her checkbook. "May I join?"

"Of course. I was hoping you would. And I was also hoping that you might know of others who would want to participate. We're just getting started and the eight of us voted to do something right away." Polly patted her back pocket. "I have everyone's checks and I'm going up to the bank to open a checking account. It will be attached to mine at first. I want to talk to my friend in Story City about how to do the finances for this and set it up as a non-profit organization. And I'll supplement the fund to pay for whatever the furnace costs."

"This should help." Lydia handed her a check for five hundred dollars. "Beryl and Andy will be part of it immediately, too. I can drop off their checks to you later today."

"Don't worry about that. I just need to get the account open so I have a place to deposit these things. They all decided I'd be the perfect person to manage the funds." Polly flattened her lips. "Joy."

"You'll be fine."

"I know. But still. Anyone else could have done it." Polly smiled. "I haven't told Henry yet, but I'm hoping he can find a good price on the furnace and help install it. Your family won't have to know whose idea it was to give them a furnace, they'll just know that they're going to be warm for years to come. Once we get organized, we'll start a wish list and discuss items in town that need to be funded."

"Like wheelchair access and accessible seating at the ball fields," Lydia said. "And speaking of wheelchairs, Mr. Denison's ramp is in terrible shape. I'm so worried that he's going to fall into a rut and not be able to get out of it."

"Henry would fix that right now for him. It's probably just a couple of boards."

Lydia nodded. "I know, but he's proud. If it came from something like Girl's Rule, he wouldn't be able to say no."

"I don't get it," Polly said. "We're supposed to take care of each other. Why is it so difficult?"

"People are uncomfortable being indebted to each other."

Polly blew out a breath. "That drives me nuts."

"That's because you are on the giving side," Lydia said patiently. She blew across the top of her coffee and took a tentative sip, then smiled and took a bigger drink. "Perfect."

"That's not it," Polly said. "Generosity is in the giving and the receiving. That's what Dad always taught me. You just have to learn how to say thank you with grace and not embarrassment."

"That's a virtue that's been lost in the past for many of us," Lydia said. She pushed her check closer to Polly. "I'm excited about this group. You'd be surprised at the number of women who will want to participate. It's been easy for us to see the men of the community as the philanthropists. The only problem some of them will have is that they'll want their names attached to the gifts."

"Then I don't think they want to be part of this group. The women who participate will be anonymous." Polly nodded as she thought. "And that tells me that I need to talk to the bank about making these payments for things anonymously. I certainly don't want any accolades coming back to me. It wasn't even my idea. I'm just going to make it work."

"I'll call Aaron and tell him what you're doing. He won't believe it. I'm sure he knows of quite a few other things that need to be taken care of in town. Hopefully they won't all be as expensive as a furnace and we can do more than one good thing each month." Lydia glanced at her watch. "I usually only come in for a quick cup. I'd better get going. Maybe Camille will put this in a takeout cup for me." Lydia jumped up from the table and went back to the counter.

Camille poured Lydia's coffee into a cup and filled it up from the thermos.

Lydia was at the front door before she realized she hadn't said goodbye and rushed back to the table. "Sometimes my body gets ahead of my mind. That was so rude."

"You're fine," Polly said with a laugh. "Have a good morning and if you think of any women who would be a good fit, just collect their checks. They can write them to Girl's Rule or to me. I'll have the account set up by the end of the day."

"I love you, sweetie." Lydia gave her a quick hug and was gone in a flash.

"Is she on board?" Camille asked, walking by Polly's table with a cloth in hand.

"All in," Polly said. "When you're finished, I'll need that coffee to go. I'm heading to the bank to deposit the funds."

"I'm glad you said that. I have a check from Marta. I'll just sign it over to you."

"If you collect any more, just have them write the checks to Girl's Rule. Do you want to be a signatory on the account?"

Camille looked at her in horror. "No way. You're going to do just fine with that."

"I need at least one more person on there," Polly said. "I'm not going to be the only one responsible for it." She walked with Camille back toward the counter.

"Why don't you wait and see who else joins us. Maybe a perfect cohort in crime will come along and you'll have your sidekick."

"You really don't want anything to do with the finances, do you?"

Camille shook her head. "I watched my mother take that on. You're just like her. You have the perfect temperament to deal with crazy ladies. I get all defensive and want to kill them."

"I don't hate the idea of killing crazy ladies," Polly said.

"See, you think it's funny. I'm completely serious. Some evenings when I go home it takes me at least a half hour to get over the stupidity that I encounter here. Those are the nights I make meals for an entire month. Elise usually ends up taking food to work for everyone's lunch the next day."

"Oh Camille, I'm so sorry."

Camille put her hands up. "That's not it. It's just the way I handle it. Badly. You laugh about the crazy ladies. I don't. Apparently you aren't afraid to tell them off. I try to ignore what they say or push it aside."

"I'm not good with ignoring. Especially when they're being stupid."

"That's why it's better that you take this on and not me. I'll always be right there supporting you and I'll even say so out loud, but I don't want to be on the front lines. Otherwise there'd be more bodies for you to find." She handed Polly's coffee to her. "Now go take on the world. I'll be here making coffee for you."

"I love you, Camille," Polly said, laughing. "You have a good day. If all goes well, I'll be back later for more. I'm picking up cupcakes this afternoon."

She was still laughing as she climbed up into her truck. She knew the greatest people.

Polly drove down to the bank, parked, looked at her hot coffee yearningly, and sighed. "You're going to be cold when I come back. That was some poor planning on my part."

She went inside and glanced at a man sitting on a bench off to the side. He looked familiar, but she couldn't place him. Giving her head a quick shake, Polly walked up to the counter.

"Hi, Ms. Giller," the young man - David was on his nameplate - said.

"Hi, David. I need to speak with someone about opening a new account. Can you do that?"

His eyes darted back and forth. "I'm new. Just a minute and let me get someone else to help you."

Polly smiled at him and he walked away.

An older woman was standing in front of the counter next to her and when Polly took a good look, she not only saw fear in the woman's face, but her hands were trembling as she filled out a check. Polly realized that she knew this woman. She lived on the other side of the creek behind Sycamore House. Polly and Obiwan had walked back there several times over the years and she'd gotten to know some of the people, especially when they walked on warm summer evenings. Mrs. Olson lived alone. Her husband had died several years ago, but left her with a nice home and a healthy retirement. She loved to travel with her friends. They had great fun taking bus tours around the state. The last time Polly had seen her, she was leaving for a cruise with five of her girlfriends. It was her first trip on a ship and Mrs. Olson could barely contain her excitement.

Polly turned to look back at the man who was sitting on the bench and recognized him as one of the men she'd encountered in her back yard. What was he doing here?

She stepped close to the older woman. "Mrs. Olson? Are you okay?"

The woman looked straight forward. "Don't talk to me. He'll see."

"Is he trying to hurt you?"

"Please step away. I don't want him to hurt you, too."

Polly bent over. "I'll be fine. You just need to sag as if you are fainting. I'll make the scene and he'll leave. Trust me. Now go."

Surprisingly, Mrs. Olson obeyed and sagged into Polly's arms. Luckily for both of them, she was a petite woman who weighed practically nothing.

"Oh my gosh, Mrs. Olson," Polly cried out. "Are you okay?" She looked around for the teller who had been working with her. "Someone get some help. I need a doctor. Is there a doctor in the building?"

People from all over rushed to Polly's side and within seconds, the man who had been waiting got up and left by the front door.

"It's okay," Polly said to the woman. "You can get up now. He's gone."

Mrs. Olson used Polly's arm to steady herself as she stood back up. "But he'll be back."

Polly used her loud voice again. "It's fine. She was just a little woozy. Cancel the call for a doctor."

"What do you mean he'll be back?" Polly asked Mrs. Olson.

"He showed up at my front door. Did you see the way he's dressed?"

Polly thought about it. "Black pants and a jacket."

"He and his friend look just like those missionaries that come around all the time. You know the ones. They're always dressed so nice and they are so polite. I enjoy talking to them so whenever they knock on my door I invite them in and we have coffee and a nice chat."

"These men aren't so nice?" Polly asked.

"They pushed their way in and shoved me to the floor, then ransacked my bedroom. They stole all of my jewelry." Her eyes filled with tears. "They even took my wedding ring. I heard them saying it wasn't enough. That's when they picked up my Trixie and told me that they'd kill her if I didn't get them money. He had my bank book and knew exactly how much I could withdraw." Tears flowed down her face. "My Trixie is gone."

Polly and the bank manager, Floyd Eldridge, escorted the woman into an office where she could sit down. "Just a second,"

Polly said and took out her phone. She placed a call to Ken Wallers.

"It's not quite time yet, Polly. Are you getting excited?"

"Could you get someone over to Mrs. Olson's house on South Willow? She's here at the bank. A man just held her up at her house. His partner might still be there holding her dog hostage while she was supposed to withdraw money for them."

"Oh my god," he said. "I'm going there right now. Tell her to stay put and I'll send Bert to you. Is she okay?"

Polly heard his car start up. "She's okay. A little shaken up and terrified that she just killed her dog. Will you call me as soon as you know?"

"I will. I'm only a minute away. Take care of her."

He ended the call and Polly smiled. Only in small town Iowa could the police chief already be out and that close to the scene of trouble. She went back into the office and knelt in front of Mrs. Olson. "Chief Wallers is going to your house now. He's going to call me back when he knows about Trixie. My guess is that they're already on their way out of town."

"What if they come back? They're going to be so angry."

Polly took the woman's hand. "Do you have a friend you can stay with tonight?"

"I don't want to put any of them in jeopardy."

"Would you like to stay at the hotel? Or at Sycamore House?"

"But Trixie ..."

"In my world, dogs are always welcome," Polly said. "Wherever you will feel the safest, we'll find room."

"I'll feel safest when those men are caught." She dropped her head to her chest. "It's an awful feeling when you know there is nothing you can do to stop someone from hurting you."

"I know that. But you're safe now," Polly said. "We'll take care of you."

Mrs. Olson squeezed Polly's hand. "I miss seeing you and your Obiwan. Are you enjoying your new house?"

"It's a lot of work," Polly acknowledged. "But it is nice to have plenty of room for my family. It keeps growing, you know."

"I heard that. I'd love to meet your new little boys someday. Would you bring them over to visit?"

"I'd love to." Her phone rang and she picked it up. "Ken?"

"Trixie is just fine," he said. "There's no sign of anyone here, though."

Polly stood up and said, "Chief Wallers tells me that Trixie is fine. The men are gone. Would you like me to take you home so you can pack a few things?"

"Would you?"

"Can I bring her home?" Polly asked Ken. "She wants to pack some things and then she'll be moving into the hotel for a few days."

"That's probably a good idea. Tell Floyd that Bert will be there to talk to him. He'll want surveillance tape if he can get it."

"I'll do that." Polly glanced up. "Bert's here now. We'll see you in a few minutes."

CHAPTER TWENTY-FIVE

Still shaken, Mrs. Olson agreed to leave her car at the bank, as long as it was locked. Polly helped the woman into her truck and drove to the house.

Ken Wallers came outside with Trixie in his arms. It broke Polly's heart to see Mrs. Olson sob at the sight of her dog. She ran around to help the older woman out and Ken put the dog on the ground, holding its leash.

"Oh Trixie, I was so frightened for you. I thought I'd killed you." Mrs. Olson bent over and the small white terrier jumped into her arms.

"She was just fine when I got here, Verna," Ken said. "I doubt the other man stayed in the house long after you left. More than likely he was outside the bank waiting for his buddy."

Mrs. Olson's face went from fear and sorrow to fury in a heartbeat. "Those sons-a-bitches," she said. "How dare they threaten me and my dog. Damned cowards."

Polly attempted to suppress her laughter at the foul words coming from this sweet little lady. She caught Ken's eyes and he smiled at her.

"I still think it might be a good idea for you to stay somewhere else tonight," Ken said.

"I won't deliver my friends into the hands of those jackasses," Mrs. Olson returned, "but Ms. Giller here has offered a hotel room to us and I believe that's as safe as I'm going to get." She looked at Ken. "Unless your dear wife wants to put me up in the guest room."

He opened his mouth to speak, shut it, glanced around, then opened it again.

Mrs. Olson put her dog back on the ground and swatted at Ken's arm. "I'm teasing you. But I would greatly appreciate it if you would please stay with me while I pack a few things."

"I'd be glad to," Ken said. "I need to ask you some questions about your experience."

"I was scared to death," the woman said as she walked up the steps to her front door. "I thought they were a couple of those nice young men who come around. I certainly enjoy their company. They always have interesting things to tell me about where they're from and it does the soul good to talk about God even if they don't go to my church. Gotta be respectful and courteous to everyone, right?"

Polly trailed behind as the two went inside the house. She wasn't sure what to do next. She was glad to take Mrs. Olson over to the hotel and it would be no problem for her to round someone up to move the car wherever Mrs. Olson wanted it.

"Have a seat," the woman said as they passed into the living room. "I didn't have much time to tidy up this morning. Those young men came in just after Trixie and I returned from our morning walk. The breakfast dishes are still on the table."

Looking around, Polly shook her head. Everything was neat and clean. Horizontal surfaces were dust-free and a sweet little red doggie bed was nestled into the corner of the sofa with a blue dinosaur toy lying in the middle of it. Even the magazines on the coffee table were artfully arranged. Music was open on the stand of the piano at one end of the room. The bench had an embroidered floral cushion on it.

After dinner last night, Simon Gardner had commented on the fact that the Bell House needed a beautiful old grand piano. Polly didn't disagree. Rebecca was probably too old to dive into piano lessons with a passion, but both Noah and Elijah had potential. There was no reason Rebecca shouldn't take lessons so she had some background, but the boys were a different story. Polly and Henry had talked about it. She hadn't wanted to haul a piano up to the apartment. They considered an electronic keyboard, but the timing just hadn't been right. Now was the right time to make this happen. She'd like the piano to end up in the living room. That wouldn't happen until Hayden and Heath were out of there and upstairs, and their rooms wouldn't be ready until the next round of demolition and reconstruction.

It killed Polly to think that Hayden wasn't long for their home. After spending time with Tess last night, Polly wouldn't be at all surprised if they were married after the girl graduated. That all depended on where she chose to go to law school. She shook her head. Thinking about that was too overwhelming. Thinking about where to put a grand piano was much easier. When the first round of rooms was finished, she and Henry would move upstairs and the piano could go into the future library.

The double doors on the rooms made it easy for her to consider a piano that large. She'd played a little when she was young. Her dad wanted her to do more but Polly wasn't interested. However, she believed in the importance of music for kids. As much as Rebecca fought against practicing, she enjoyed being in the band. Music lessons were a big commitment. Polly didn't want the boys to start taking piano lessons and then quit after a year or two. If she started with them down this path, it was going to be long-term, no matter how much they whined. While her dad had let her quit piano, it was only after she assured him she would continue playing the flute. There *would* be music and there would be lessons in her life. No options. And look, here she was still playing that crazy instrument, even if it was only in the summer.

Maybe Jeannie Dykstra would teach the boys. Polly heard the name in her head and realized that Jen and Jeannie had to be married to brothers. She'd never met either of their husbands. The surname was unique enough that there couldn't be two random families in Bellingwood with it. She was going to have to ask.

"Polly?"

She jumped up from the piano bench.

Ken was standing in the doorway leading to the kitchen where he and Mrs. Olson had gone to talk about her experience.

"Yes," Polly said.

"You were working on something there."

She chuckled. "Just thinking about a piano and lessons and kids and ..." Polly took a breath. "Oh my lord, Ken. I have kids in my life and now I'm responsible for them. What was I thinking?"

"You're a grownup?" he asked, laughing at her.

"I was just going to move into a small Iowa town, renovate an old school house and maybe invite people to stay there while they did creative things." She flung her hand in the air. "Everything has changed and now I'm responsible for children."

"Thinking about piano lessons caused this panic?" he asked.

"It's all moving so fast. Do you know that I have to go to school with Rebecca next week to help her choose a class schedule for her freshman year in high school? What's happening to me? Heath is graduating and Henry's taking him to Iowa State to meet with advisers and ..." Polly took a deep breath. "I can't think about it. Especially when I'm standing in someone else's living room while talking to the Chief of Police. Am I crazy?"

"Maybe a little. Verna is upstairs packing a bag. Thank you for taking her to the hotel."

"I'll ask Grey to put her in the room closest to his apartment. That way he can keep an eye on her tonight. Do you know who these two are?"

"This is the first I've heard of them."

She pursed her lips. "You need to talk to Aaron."

"Yeah. I do. I saw that on the news the other day. I hate to think that they've moved up here to Bellingwood."

"Lydia didn't say that they'd forced any of those people in Boone to go to the bank," Polly said. "That's new."

"I don't like it. That means they're getting bolder. Probably not finding enough ready cash or easy-to-pawn items in these homes."

"Do you think they were watching Mrs. Olson that day I saw them at Sycamore House?"

He nodded. "Now that I know this, it's exactly what they were doing. I wonder who else they've targeted."

Polly shook her head. "But how did they know to target her?"

"It could be any number of things. Maybe they saw her outside with Trixie or followed her home from the grocery store. All they had to do was watch the house for a few days to make sure she lived alone. I'll talk to Bert. We'll keep an extra eye on some of our more vulnerable citizens. That's all I can do right now."

Mrs. Olson came into the room, carrying a small suitcase and a train case. She pointed at the dog bed on the sofa. "Would you mind carrying that for me, sweetie? Trixie loves to sleep with her dino."

Ken took the bags from her. "I'll carry these."

"He's such a good boy," Mrs. Olson said to Polly. "Come, Trixie. We're going to have an adventure." She snapped the leash on the little dog and handed it to Polly while she donned her coat and picked up her purse. Taking the leash back, she led the small processional out of her home and down the steps. Once at the bottom, she turned. "Just trip the lock, Ms. Giller. The house will be all buttoned up until I return."

"Polly, Mrs. Olson," Polly said, locking the door.

"Then you must call me Verna. That Mrs. Olson nonsense makes me feel old."

Ken put her bags in the back seat of Polly's truck. "If you give me your car keys, Verna, I'll make sure your car is taken wherever you'd like it."

"If I have it at the hotel, those nasty men might know I'm there. Maybe I should just have you bring it home and put it in the garage. The garage door opener is in the console."

"We can certainly do that. I'll leave your keys with Grey at the hotel."

She took the key ring out of her purse and handed them over. "You've been very kind to me. Thank you."

"I'll never forget all the kindnesses you and your husband did for me when I was younger. I'm just glad that today worked out as well as it did." He helped her up into the truck and then handed Trixie to her. "Take care and I'll be in touch."

Polly got in and after putting her seat belt on, said, "You don't have anywhere to eat supper tonight. I'd love to have you join my family."

"At the Springer House?" Verna asked. "That would be lovely. I'd enjoy seeing what you've done with it. My goodness, but you've gone out of your way to take care of me today."

Polly smiled. "We're calling it the Bell House nowadays. There has been quite a bit of history come out about it."

"That's right. A young Bell built that hotel. My daddy used to talk about some of the goings-on over there. You know, he made whiskey moonshine. He loved to tell tales of those wild days in Bellingwood."

"Your father?" Polly stopped at the stop sign and turned her right blinker on. "What was your maiden name?"

"Monroe. Why?"

"I have tally boards in the basement of the house with names of people who made whiskey." Polly thought back through the names she'd seen. "D. Monroe."

"That was my daddy. Daniel. He was just a young man back then. And a bit of a rapscallion. He and mother weren't married yet. He always claimed that he was ten minutes too late to have met Al Capone one evening. Mother said that was a good thing or he might have ended up in Chicago and then in prison."

"Why?"

"He didn't settle down until he met Mother. He liked to spend evenings at the hotel, drinking as much whiskey as he could. Not only did he brew the stuff, but he drove the wagon that went to all of the farmers who brewed for Bell. Everybody knew daddy. He was tough, too. He carried Bell's money to pay the farmers and no one ever tried to rob him. They knew he'd beat the hell out of them if they tried anything. He always carried a gun under his seat, just in case somebody tried anything." She shook her head. "And to think, I was nearly done in by a couple of cowardly fools this morning. My daddy would have been ashamed of me. But they scared me something fierce."

"Was your father part of a secret society at the hotel?" Polly asked.

"A secret society? What do you mean?"

Polly pulled in front of the entrance to the lobby and stopped, then took out her phone. She flipped to a picture of the symbol and showed it to Mrs. Olson.

"Oh my," Verna said, her hand flying to her throat. "I thought that died out years ago."

"What is it?"

Verna shook her head. "A pile of foolishness. That's what it was." She put her hand on the truck's door. "I don't really want to talk about it and I'm quite worn out."

"But it's all over everything at the Bell House," Polly protested. "I'm just trying to figure out what it's about."

"Best not to bring those types of things back up. Bellingwood really never knew what was happening in the underpinnings of the community. I wish I'd never been told."

"Who told you?"

Verna pulled the handle on the door so that it opened, then put her foot on the running board and climbed down. She lifted Trixie off the seat and put the dog on the floor. "I'm sorry, Polly. Not today. I've had enough for one day. I don't want to think about this."

Polly frowned in frustration, then breathed to let it go. "I understand." She really didn't understand. What could have happened that long ago that still haunted people to this day? She reached into the back seat and gathered up the dog's bed, toy and the train case. A little extra maneuvering and she had the suitcase in her hand as well.

They went inside and June Livengood looked up from the computer. "Well, hello there, Verna. How are you today?"

"I need to spend a night or two in your hotel," Verna said.

"Are they fumigating your house?"

Verna shook her head. "No. There are a couple of bad men who might be looking for me."

June looked at her and then at Polly, who nodded.

"You're not kidding me?"

"Not at all. They broke into my house this morning and then tried to force me to withdraw cash from the bank. Polly here recognized that something was wrong and talked me into faking a fainting spell so she could surround me with all sorts of people. It worked. The bad guys left, Chief Wallers rescued my dog, and now I'm here. Polly says you might put me in a room where your manager could keep an eye on me."

"Of course we will. My goodness, Verna. That's quite frightening."

Verna set her jaw. "I shouldn't be frightened. I should have fought back. While we were driving over here, Polly helped me remember what a fighter my daddy was. He taught me better than this."

June chuckled. "You aren't twenty-five any longer."

"But I'm not a weak old lady," Verna said. "I refuse to be a weak old lady." She scowled at Polly. "I was a weak old lady this morning. I don't know when it was I got so frightened of things."

June put a card in front of Verna. "Just sign here."

Verna put her purse on the counter and took out her wallet, then handed over a credit card. She turned to Polly. "I suspect you were about to let me stay here free of charge or at least pay for it yourself. I'll have none of that. You saved me several thousand dollars this morning. I can afford to treat myself to a room for a night or two."

"The least we can do is give you our friends and family discount," June said. "Have you met Mr. Greyson?"

"I've seen him out walking his dogs," Verna replied. "But I've never met the man."

"Just a moment." June knocked on the door leading to Grey's apartment, listened, then stepped inside.

Verna spun on Polly. "You were going to pay for my room, weren't you?"

Polly chuckled. "I wouldn't dream of it."

"I'm sorry that I became so uncomfortable talking about things at the Bell House," Verna said. "Let me rest today. Maybe by this evening I will have been able to come to grips with discussing it again. I understand that you have questions. There are probably still people in town who have a better understanding of everything than I do."

"I don't even know who those people are," Polly said. "I've identified a few names, but that was only because they had sons who had sons."

"Chief Wallers," Verna said, nodding.

"And Paul Bradford."

"Oh yes, of course. The Bradfords. At the very least, I might be able to help you identify more families."

"That would be wonderful. Thank you."

Grey came out with June. "Hello, Polly. How are you today?"

"I'm great."

He strode out from behind the counter and put his hand out to Mrs. Olson. "June tells me that you're moving in for a couple of nights. I'm glad to have you. My name is Alistair Greyson. Please call me Grey."

"My name is Verna Olson. And you can call me Verna. This is Trixie."

He bent down and put his hand out for the small dog to sniff. In mere moments, she was licking his hand and wagging her tail.

"She likes you," Verna said. "She's picky about the men she likes. She didn't like those two gentlemen this morning at all. I had to put her in the bathroom and she still wouldn't shut up."

"Trixie is a smart girl," Polly said.

"That she is."

Grey stood and reached for the suitcases Polly was carrying. "I'd be glad to take you through my apartment and out the back door over to your room," he said. "That way you don't have to walk all the way around. He gestured to the dog bed. "That too?"

Polly nodded and put it in his free hand.

"You can go on, Polly. We've got it from here."

"Are you sure?" Polly looked at Verna for affirmation.

"I'm in good hands."

"Either Henry or myself will be here about six thirty to pick you up for dinner," Polly said.

"I'm looking forward to it." Verna put her hand out to take Polly's. "You've been so generous with your time today. I don't know what I would have done if you hadn't been there for me. I'm afraid I distracted you from your own errands, but I appreciate everything. I promise to put all of my thoughts into words so that I can explain to you what that symbol meant to so many in Bellingwood."

Polly smiled and gave the woman's hand a small squeeze. As they left through the door behind the counter, she realized that she still had those checks in her back pocket and no bank account to deposit them in.

"Thanks, June. I'll see you later."

"Take care," June called out.

Polly got back in her truck and headed downtown. She'd give this bank thing one more try.

CHAPTER TWENTY-SIX

Not wanting to be late, Polly hurried over to Greg and Lucy Parker's home. She breathed a sigh of relief when Ken Wallers was waiting for her outside. At least he'd know which door to use.

"Did you get Verna settled?" he asked.

Polly smiled, then opened the back door of her truck. "I left her with Grey and June at the hotel. She's in good hands." She tucked the smaller metal box under her arm and lifted the cardboard box that she'd been carrying around for the last several days.

"Let me get that," he said, taking the cardboard box.

She pushed the door closed. "I showed her that symbol. It affected her. Her father was part of that group of people that made whiskey."

Ken peered at her. "I guess I don't know what her maiden name was." He chuckled. "I thought she was born married."

"Monroe. She said her father was the one who paid the farmers who were brewing whiskey. He was also the pickup and delivery guy."

"That's information I didn't have." He stopped in front of the door while Polly reached for the doorbell.

Lucy greeted them with a smile. Polly didn't remember ever seeing her without her uniform on. The house was warm and cozy, done in browns and blues.

"Paul and Simon are here," Lucy said. "They're in the dining room with Greg. Can I get you anything? Some coffee?"

Polly smiled as she shrugged out of her jacket. Lucy already had her hand out to take it.

"You serve coffee all day long," Polly said. "Surely we could help."

"It's my pleasure." Lucy took Polly's arm. "It's so wonderful to see Greg interacting with people again on an equal footing. Go on in, Ken. Polly will help me."

Ken held out the box he was carrying and Polly put the metal box on top of it.

"That's what you wanted, right?" she asked.

"No," he said with a mock scowl. "I wanted you to carry it in for me."

Lucy swatted at him with the dish towel she was holding. "Get going. We'll be right there."

"Yes, ma'am."

Lucy's kitchen was bright and cheery, all in whites with pink, blue and yellow floral patterns along the chair rails and in the tile pattern behind the sink.

"This is lovely," Polly said.

"We redid it just before Greg's accident. That was years ago. It stays nice because I do so little cooking in here. I'm a slob, you know."

"No way."

Lucy took a tray out from a lower cabinet and placed it on the table. She pointed at a cupboard. "Cups are in there. Would you mind?"

Polly opened the door and took down six cups and saucers, then placed them on the tray.

"I hate cleaning," Lucy said. "Greg has a home care aide who stays with him during the day. She helps with most of his physical care, but she can't bear boredom, so if he doesn't need something, she cleans. I feel so fortunate. We adore Donna. I don't know what we'd do without her."

"Do I know her?" Polly asked.

"Probably not. She lives between here and Stanhope. That's where her life is. Her kids go to school in Jewell, so she doesn't participate in Bellingwood activities." Lucy poured the coffee into a thermos and closed the lid, then put sugar and a small pitcher of milk on the tray. She took two cups away. "Simon already has tea and Greg won't drink coffee with us." With a smile, she opened a bag from Sweet Beans. "I don't get a chance to buy Mrs. Donovan's bakery items very often, but when I have the time, I go a little wild." She filled a plate with brownies, scones and croissants. "I was bad this afternoon."

"I never get enough of her baking." Polly put her hands out to pick up the tray just as Lucy did the same.

"You go ahead," Lucy said. She pushed the door open into the dining room and Polly followed her.

"I'm so glad to see you here," Simon said. "I wondered if you'd gathered us all together for no other reason than to have coffee with Lucy and Greg."

"Would I do that?" Polly asked. She placed the tray on the table and Lucy took her arm.

"Greg, this is Polly Giller. Polly, this is my husband, Greg."

He nodded at Polly.

She was used to putting her hand out at introductions, but forced herself to hold it at her side. "It's nice to meet you, Greg. I know people always tell you how wonderful your wife is, but she really is."

"I love her." The mechanical voice coming from his computer was a little strange. That would take some getting used to.

"I love you, too," Lucy said. She gestured to an empty chair at the end of the table for Polly and then sat beside her husband.

Simon was at the other end of the table, with Ken across from Greg and Paul Bradford across from Lucy.

"I understand you finally got into the bowels of the library," Paul said to Polly.

She pointed at the box Ken had carried in for her. "There are many more boxes from Margie Deacon down there, but when I landed on this one, I knew it had some information we needed to see." Polly pulled the top off and looked around the table. "I'm sorry. I'm being rude. Let's eat goodies and drink coffee first." She put her hand on the pitcher's handle. "I can pour."

When Greg Parker looked at her, she swore she saw him wink, but he turned away too quickly. "You aren't rude. Just excited," he said. "Me too."

Lucy took the cups from Polly after they were filled and passed them around. "I forgot napkins," she said and stood up. "Does anyone need anything else?"

"Do you have a few pencils?" Ken asked. "I completely forgot to bring one. I'll bet Polly will share paper from that notepad."

"If you're good," Polly said.

Paul Bradford backed away from the table, took his phone out and swiped it open. He stood and walked out of the dining room. "Upper shelf in aisle four on the right. Look all the way in the back. Got it? Okay. I'm going to be busy for a while. Unless you're desperate, try not to bother me, okay?" He came back in and sat down. "That's why I don't like to take vacations. There are too many things in that place that nobody would ever find unless they tore it all apart."

"What will they do if you get sick?" Simon asked.

Paul crossed himself. "Let's just hope that never happens. Hush, old man."

Lucy returned with napkins and passed them out, then put a stack of notepads and a tall mug filled with pens and pencils in the middle of the table. "Will that help?"

Ken took one of the notepads with the logo of Joe's Diner at the top. "I've never seen these."

"That's because the address is wrong," Lucy said. "I couldn't let Joe throw all that good paper away so I brought them home. We've used them for years. I may never run out of paper. Joe got mad at the printer and refused to make any more." She shook her head. "Sometimes he just cuts off his nose to spite his face."

"I believe I will have one of these brownies," Simon said, reaching for the plate.

Paul pushed it closer to him.

"Please help yourselves," Lucy said."

Greg tapped his hand on the table. "It was not swords into plows, but plows into swords," he said.

That caught everyone's attention. "What do you mean?" Ken asked. "I just assumed."

"They had good intentions." Greg shook his head slightly. "No."

Ken sat back, his mouth poised to take a bite of a croissant. "I can't believe that. Granddad was a good man."

"Not part of the club."

"But the symbol was on each of those tally boards," Polly said. "They weren't part of what was going on?"

"No. Hostages," Greg said.

"He's been barely able to contain himself," Lucy said. "Greg has been researching this for the last few months with information from his own family and other things he's collected over the years. His mother was part of the team gathering information for the centennial fifty years ago, but there were things no one would tell the community. It was just hidden away because so many of that generation were still alive at the time."

"No longer, though," Greg said, turning to his wife.

Polly nodded. "That's what Verna was trying to tell me. Something really upset her about that symbol."

"Verna Olson?" Lucy asked. She turned to Greg.

A moment later, he said, "Monroe."

Polly had written the names from the tally boards on another sheet of paper and tore it from the pad, then pushed it over to Greg. Lucy picked it up and put it on the table in front of him. He scanned through the names and nodded.

"All hostages."

"But who was behind this plows into swords thing?" Paul asked.

Simon picked up a leather satchel that had been sitting beside him and drew out several small leather bound books. "These are a few of my mother's journals," he said. "I wish I'd read them more thoroughly when I was younger. These three are the years nineteen-fourteen, nineteen-fifteen, and nineteen-sixteen, which is when she went to work at the hotel." He flipped through the last journal to a page which had been marked with a small piece of paper. "I believe she's writing about that room where you found the journals, Polly. She says that she delivered refreshments to a group of men who were meeting up there. She only recognized Franklin Bell and his partner, Reginald Adams."

"The man who killed Franklin Bell," Polly said quietly. "Who were they with?"

"The scuttlebutt was that one of the men with them was from the federal government, but the other two were from Chicago."

"Capone's organization?"

"She believed it was a competitor."

"Holding the local men hostage," Greg interrupted. With the knuckles of his left hand, he pushed a book toward the center of the table.

Lucy picked it up. "Greg's mother bound up some of the notes that she'd taken. These men from Chicago came into town to encourage the building of the hotel. They wanted a central distribution location between Chicago and Omaha and they wanted it far from large cities such as Des Moines." She looked at Greg and he gave her a small smile, so she continued. "They came to Bellingwood and connected with young Franklin Bell. He had money and a desire for notoriety. He also had connections with a large group of men, both business people and famers - men who were willing to ride on the edge in order to make extra money."

Ken shook his head. "Granddad would have been that person."

"Mine too," Paul said.

"Verna Olson said that her father was a bit of a scoundrel before he got married. He liked living a wild life," Polly said.

"Each man had to make an initial investment into the company," Lucy said.

"Wait." Polly took the folder with the receipts out of the box. "I found these. They look like they're receipts for different items around building the hotel." She handed it to Lucy, who opened it and put it in front of Greg.

He pushed the papers around. "Laundering," he said. "Bell had the money to build the hotel."

"There was to be a large return on their investment, or so they were told," Lucy continued as Greg continued to peer at the invoices and receipts. "Then things got more difficult. This group from Chicago, along with a federal employee, got greedier and greedier. They made regular visits to each of these men at their homes, usually with three or four mobsters who carried guns. They didn't always want money. Sometimes it was something as simple as providing a night's stay and a few meals for one of their friends. Other times the men were asked to carry satchels of cash from Bellingwood to other locations around the state."

"I don't understand why these men continued to do things that made them uncomfortable," Polly said

Greg's computer said, "The Fed."

Lucy nodded. "By that point, he had something on each of the men; whether it was making moonshine, carrying money for the mob or providing a room for an escaping criminal. They were all small crimes, but he reminded each of them regularly that they were on the hook and could be taken to prison for any of those crimes."

Polly blew out a breath. "So why those small tokens in their tally boards."

"Greg and I've talked about that a lot," Lucy said. She turned to her husband.

He gave a small shrug. "Maybe a bond."

"Some small reminder that they were all in it," Lucy said. "If any one of them tried to deny their part in it, those tokens would be brought out to prove that they'd been corrupted, just as everyone else had."

"I can't believe no one ever broke under the pressure," Polly said. "If just one of them had gone to the sheriff or the state police."

"Too much corruption everywhere," Greg said. "Nobody knew who was safe." He pushed one of the receipts out of the pile and Lucy picked it up.

"What am I looking at?" she asked.

"Sonny Barnes Construction Supplies," he replied. "Federal officer."

She tilted her head. "He owned a construction company?"

"No," Greg replied. "Payoff money."

"Who was that invoice made out to?" Polly asked.

Greg pushed his hand toward Paul. "Arthur Bradford."

"Gah," Paul said. "Of course he did. That makes sense. The local hardware store would buy construction supplies. I can't believe you found those invoices."

"Margie Deacon did," Polly said. "I've barely gotten through that box. So tell me more about that symbol, Greg."

"Reminder. Warning."

Simon tapped a different diary. "The whole town was excited about the new hotel, mother said. They hired mostly local men to do the work, but supervisors were from out of town. She thought they might be from Chicago. She mentioned something about the ceiling in the foyer. Just a moment, let me find it." He flipped through to different bookmarks in the journal and stopped. "Here it is. She writes that when they were working on the ceiling, only a few of the local men were allowed into the building. She thought it was odd because most of those men weren't plasterers and she mentioned your Granddad, Ken. Joe Lemon, Cecil Renner, and Kenneth Moyers."

Polly recognized each of those last names from the tally boards in her basement.

"Mother wrote that Joe Lemon was a farmer, Cecil Renner was the optometrist in town and Kenneth Moyers was a butcher. It didn't make sense to her that they were doing that work. Apparently, it didn't make sense to a great many people in town, but they all just left it alone."

"Sonya Biederman at the quilt shop was a Lemon," Lucy said quietly.

Greg tapped at his computer.

"Sometimes it's faster for him to type out names," she said. "JoAnn Davis. Oh, you know who that is, Polly. That's your friend Sandy's mother-in-law. She was a Renner. That's a big family. They're all over the county." Lucy patted her husband's arm. "Do you know any of the Moyers's?"

He tilted his head, then shook it slightly.

"Do you suppose that they were expected to paint that symbol on the ceiling and then cover it up?" Ken asked.

Paul sighed. "Probably so that every time they were in the hotel, they knew that it was hovering over them."

"It was burned into window sills and door sills, too," Polly said.

Ken gritted his teeth. "I was never going to tell anyone this." He scratched the back of his head. "I didn't tell you guys the truth earlier."

"What do you mean?" Paul asked.

"I had seen that symbol once before, but I was sworn to absolute secrecy." He took a breath. "But you're right. Those generations are gone and Bellingwood no longer has anything to worry about from that. It was just such a frightening thing for a young man."

"What?" Simon asked. "This sounds ominous."

"It's really not. I just always associated it with something that scared Granddad."

"What's going on, Ken?"

"Each of these men also had that symbol tattooed on them. It was right here." With his right hand, he reached across his chest and tapped the space just under the arm pit on his left side. "When Granddad needed help as an old man, I went over with my dad. We got Granddad into the shower and I saw it. I asked what it was. Granddad got this look of horror on his face. Mostly that I'd seen it at all. He covered it up right away and told me I could never ask about it or talk about it. I asked Dad later what it was about and he told me that Granddad had been through some bad stuff when he was younger and this was a reminder of it.

Then he reiterated that I couldn't ask any more questions, that too many people might be hurt."

"At that point?" Polly asked. "Surely the fed was long gone. There wasn't any more whiskey being brewed. The men were safe."

"They really weren't sure if they were safe," Lucy said. "They had no idea what had happened to the files that federal officer had on them." She looked at Greg again.

He tapped the journal from his mother. "He warned of contingencies should they ever talk or try to expose him. The files could be released to local authorities at any time and they'd be taken away and put in a federal penitentiary until they died. Their families would know what they'd done and exposed to potential retribution from the mob in Chicago as well as from the police."

"So one man scared all of these men that badly?" Polly asked.

"One man and mobsters with guns," Greg said.

She realized that she'd become used to the mechanical voice speaking for him.

Lucy spoke up. "One woman told Greg's mother that years after everything settled down, Franklin Bell was long since dead, the hotel was closed and Prohibition was over, her father received a letter in the mail. When he opened it, he literally fainted to the floor. She brought him around and picked up the letter. The letter was from someone in Chicago threatening him again if he ever talked about what had happened in Bellingwood. He snatched it out of her hands and burned it in the flame on the stove. Then he warned her to never talk about it."

"I think they all got those letters," Ken said. "I wonder who could have been cruel enough to remind them fifteen or twenty years later that they were still owned by the mob?"

Simon grinned across the table at Polly. "How do you feel about your lovely home now?"

"I'll admit this is a little creepy," she said. "I keep wondering how many other weird twists this house is going to give us."

"What about those gold coins?" Paul asked.

Greg looked at his wife.

"I forgot to tell you, honey," Lucy said. "Polly found gold coins in a mantle in an upstairs room."

He frowned. "What were those from?"

Polly shrugged. "I don't know for sure. I assumed it was from this group of men. And as you talked, I assumed it might be part of a payoff or maybe income from whiskey."

Greg didn't look like he quite bought that idea.

"Maybe it has something to do with the serial killer," she said and picked up another folder from the box. "Margie Deacon thought that these deaths were connected. Her uncle Deke Deacon was looking into them. His girlfriend was the first death in the list. She died in nineteen-thirteen."

"Do you know anything about this, Greg?" Ken asked.

He shook his head. "This is new. May I keep this?"

"Sure," Polly said. "You should talk to Andy Specek. She's going through all of Margie Deacon's boxes trying to categorize things."

His eyes lit up and Lucy smiled. "He wants to write a book on the hidden history of Bellingwood."

"You have a good start, buddy," Ken said, stretching. He draped his arm over the back of Paul Bradford's chair. "After all these years, it might be good to finally have it out in the open."

"Most people don't even realize it existed," Simon said.

Paul Bradford took his phone out of his pocket again and groaned. "He didn't call this time, he sent a text. I need to get back to the shop. They can't live without me."

Simon scooted his chair back. "The boy is my ride."

"I'm sorry," Paul said. "We aren't planning to solve the serial killer mystery right now, are we?" He smiled across the table at Greg. "Are you?"

"Might take more time than that," Greg said.

"Don't get up," Paul said to Lucy. "Thank you for helping us. It's disappointing to know that my grandfather was held hostage like that, but it explains why he was so hell-bent on building a successful business and getting Dad in there as soon as possible. He wanted to make sure his family was taken care of if something ever happened to him. It also explains why some of those families that you're discovering were such a big part of my childhood. I'd forgotten about all of that. They weren't Dad's friends, but they were my grandfather's friends. Anyway, thank you for an interesting afternoon and for your hospitality, Lucy." He put his hand on Polly's shoulder. "I suppose I should thank you for clearing up part of my family's history, even if it is ..." He paused and grinned. "... creepy."

Ken stood as well and gathered napkins and cups. "Let me help you clean up."

"No," Lucy said. "Don't worry about that. It's nothing. Are you okay?"

"I am," he replied. "It's strange that those few moments out of my youth had such a big impact on me. I need to be more considerate of what I say to my girls. I'd hate them to get to be my age and remember something I said out of fear or anger. It's a good lesson." He reached across the table and patted the top of Greg's hand. "Buddy, it's so good to spend time again with you. I've missed you."

"Come over any time," Greg said.

"Really?"

Greg nodded and gave him a hint of a smile.

"You can count on it, then. Thanks for everything, Lucy. And Polly, I'm sure I'll see you soon. Just stay out of trouble, okay?"

"Whatever."

Polly lifted the box she'd carried home from the library to the table. "Greg, do you want to keep this here? I'd love to tell you that I will go through it all, but things get crazy at my house."

"Yes. Please," he said.

She opened the metal box and drew out the ledgers. "I barely got into these. They all have that symbol in the back of them and lots of names and numbers. Are you interested in them as well?"

Lucy laughed. "He would be ecstatic to have all of this information."

"I hate to land it all on you," Polly said. "But if you want more, I can bring other boxes from Margie Deacon's house to you any time you're ready for them. Do you have enough room?" She laughed as she said the last words.

"We'll make room until he's gone through it all," Lucy said. "It's exciting to have something like this to learn and discuss. It spices up our evening conversations, that's for sure."

"Thank you, Polly," Greg said. His eyes had grown misty. "This has been fun for me."

CHAPTER TWENTY-SEVEN

Once she was back on the street, Polly made a left turn and drove north a few blocks. She didn't spend much time in this part of town. There were quite a few nice homes. Henry was working on somebody's house up here this week. She wondered if she'd find his truck. Her phone buzzed with a text and she slowed to a stop at an intersection. There were no stop signs, but there was also very little traffic. Checking to make sure no one was going to be upset if she lingered, Polly looked at her phone.

"I'm nervous. I'm at the coffee shop. I'm really early."

"Oh Tab, I love you. There is nothing to be nervous about. I've invited another person to dinner too. There will be plenty of distractions tonight."

"What are you doing right now? Can I just come over?"

"I'm actually riding around town. Just finished a meeting and I'm not ready to be a parent again."

"I guess I'll have more coffee then."

"I can grow up," Polly texted back. *"I'll come down and meet you."*

"Don't hurry. I'll eat brownies and muffins, too."

Polly laughed out loud. *"I'll be there soon."* She made another left turn and peered at a truck parked in a driveway. Not Henry's, but it was the same blue color as the truck that those two characters had jumped in when she chased them away from Sycamore House. She drove slowly down the street and peered inside the home, but couldn't see anything. Rather than drive off, Polly quickly went around the block and stopped two houses away from the truck, pulling in behind a small car parked on the street.

She took her phone out and rubbed her fingers across the face of it before finally opening the phone app. She called Lydia.

"Hello, dear," Lydia said. "What are you doing today?"

"Probably getting myself into trouble. Can you help me?"

"What kind of trouble?"

"I'm not sure yet. You know everyone in town. Do you happen to know who lives at two-twenty-one Tyler Street?"

"Is something happening there?"

"I hope not. I'm just curious."

"Tyler Street," Lydia said out loud. "Who lives over there? Is it on the north or south side? "Then she giggled. "Sorry. I know better. Odd numbers are on the north side. Is it the cute little white house with green shutters?"

"Yeah."

Beside the yellow monstrosity?"

"Yes. That's the one," Polly replied with a laugh.

"I thought so. That's your friend, Adele."

"Adele Mansfield? Does she live alone?"

"Of course, dear. Is something wrong with Adele?"

Polly really didn't want to worry Lydia if this was nothing. She also knew that what she was about to do would make her friend go ballistic. "No," Polly said. "I was just driving around and thought it seemed familiar."

"What in the world are you doing in that neighborhood?"

"Honestly, Henry's working on a house back here somewhere. I had a few extra minutes and thought I'd look for him." There, she hadn't completely lied to Lydia.

"You be careful," Lydia said. "Call me later."

"Okay." Polly grimaced at her phone. The woman knew something was up. "Talk to you later."

She took a deep breath, pulled back out onto the street and drove ahead and into Adele's driveway, effectively blocking the blue truck. Now was as good a time as any to say hello. Adele's older sister had been friends with Polly's caregiver, Mary Shore. They'd never really gotten a chance to talk about memories that Adele had of Mary. It was one of those things Polly wanted to find time to do, but days and weeks passed and here she was. She got out of the truck and strode up to the front door, her left hand on the phone inside her jacket pocket.

Polly paused to question whether she really should do this, then rang the doorbell before she could question it any further. She waited and waited. When Adele didn't come to the door, Polly leaned to the side to look inside the front window. A shadow moved from the living room into another room, but she couldn't be sure what it was. This was stupid.

She rang the doorbell again. "Adele," she called out. "I have those things from this morning's meeting at church." Polly hoped that didn't sound too ridiculous. Adele and Lydia were in the same women's group that met at the church on Tuesdays.

There was still no answer so Polly walked back along the sidewalk to the garage. She tried the door handle into the garage and it opened right up. Sure enough, Adele's car was there. She was home unless she'd gone out with friends. But then why would there be a strange pickup truck in her driveway?

Polly got into her own truck and took her phone out again to place another phone call.

"Are you here?" Tab asked.

"No. But I need you to come to me."

"Your house?"

"No. I should probably call Chief Wallers, but I'm not sure that we've really got a problem. I'm sitting in the driveway of an older woman I know. She's not answering her phone and there's a strange pickup truck here. I'm pretty sure it's the same one I chased off the Sycamore House property."

"What do you mean?"

"Ken didn't talk to you guys? That surprises me."

"I haven't been in the office since Sunday. What's going on?"

"Your thieves who beat up little old ladies might be here in Bellingwood."

"What? You need to call the ..." Tab took a breath. "You're calling me. Do you really think it's them?"

"I really do. I should call Ken."

A car door slammed and the sound of the ignition firing echoed through the phone. "Tell me where I'm going," Tab said. "I'll call the office."

"It's two-two-one Tyler. Just come up north to Tyler and go left two blocks. You'll see my truck parked behind theirs."

"You really get yourself into this stuff, don't you, Polly. I'm hanging up. You go ahead and call Ken."

Polly called Ken's cell phone. Every time she did this, it struck her how absolutely crazy it was that she had so many law enforcement officers in her contacts list.

"Well, hello there, Polly. You didn't get enough of me today?"

"I'm at Adele Mansfield's house, parked behind a truck."

"What truck?" As soon as the words were out of his mouth, she heard him catch on. "That truck. What are you doing?"

"I've called Tab Hudson. She's on her way and she's calling the sheriff's office. But this is yours too."

"Oh the tangled webs we weave," he said. "I'm on my way. Please be careful."

"I'm worried about Adele. I just rang her doorbell. She didn't answer."

"You didn't," he sighed. "But of course you did."

"Tab's here. I'm safe now."

"No you're not. I'm four blocks away. Tell her to wait for me."

That made Polly laugh. Tab was as bull-headed as Polly when it came to wading into trouble. That was probably one of the reasons Polly liked her so much.

Tab Hudson parked in front of the house and got out of her car. She looked incredible with her hair down. Polly was so glad she got to know the young woman outside of her job. Her jacket was open and Polly smiled at the girl's outfit. She was wearing jeans and a bright blouse with a short, dark-blue crocheted vest.

Polly rolled her window down. "Ken's a couple of blocks away. You don't look like you're about to kick some ass."

"I certainly wasn't planning on it," Tab said. "You should go home."

Polly laughed out loud until she snorted. "Like that's going to happen. I'm only here for Adele. She's a friend. I hope she's okay."

"Me too. These men aren't very nice."

A sharp rap on Polly's passenger door got both of their attention. Polly rolled that window down, too.

"I'll slip around the back if you want to knock on the front door, Deputy," Ken said. "Do you have a weapon?"

Tab shook her head. "I'm in town for a blind date."

He blinked and smiled at Polly. "Your work?"

"Shut up. What do you want *me* to do?"

"I want you to go home, but at the very least stay in your truck. Bert's on his way."

"So are Aaron and Stu," Tab said.

"These guys aren't going to know what hit them." Polly smiled as the two met at the front of her truck and Ken handed something to Tab.

When Tab arrived at the front door, Polly realized she now held a gun. Tab knocked on the door and announced herself as a sheriff's deputy, then reached down to try the handle. Polly hadn't thought of that.

The door was unlocked and Tab pushed it open, placing her foot across the threshold. The young woman was pretty impressive. Polly could no longer hear what that she said, but in moments, Tab was inside the house. Polly slunk down in her seat. She shouldn't be here.

All of a sudden, the door beside the garage burst open and one of the men rushed outside. He glanced up to see her truck blocking his own, looked back at the house, and took off at a run toward the street. In a move that she'd seen several times on television, but had no idea if it would work, Polly slammed her truck door open as he passed by, sending him to the ground in a heap. She jumped down out of the truck and landed on top of him, straddling the poor guy with her legs. Without another thought, she dropped, pressing one knee to his chest.

He looked up at her and started to struggle. Polly reacted, jamming the base of her palm into his nose. Tears spurted from his eyes as blood flowed from his nose.

"Don't move," she said. "I'll hit you again."

He went limp under her and Polly didn't know what to do next. Adrenaline was pumping through her body and she flexed her leg muscles, causing him to cringe.

"Damn it," Polly said. "You really are just a coward. You go after little old ladies who won't fight back."

He put his hand on his face, pulled it away and groaned at the blood.

That wasn't doing much for Polly either. It occurred to her that she was thankful for the adrenaline. It was the only thing keeping her from vomiting all over him. That started her laughing. How embarrassing to have your captor puke all over the top of you.

"Polly?"

She looked up as Aaron exited his car and came toward her.

"What in the hell did you do?"

"He tried to run. I hit him with my truck's door." Polly pointed at the man's nose. "That was when I hit him with my hand."

"I think you have him subdued," Aaron said. He put his hand under her arm and helped her to stand upright. "Are you okay? Why are you laughing?"

"Because there's so much blood and I thought it would be unseemly to puke on him. That would be embarrassing for a poor, cowardly thief who beats old ladies."

Bert Bradford had arrived at Aaron's side.

Aaron pointed to the house. "The chief and Deputy Hudson are inside. Make sure they have everything locked down. I think Polly took care of this one."

The young man on the ground watched Aaron and Polly, his eyes darting back and forth.

"Do you have one of your dog's towels in there?" Aaron asked, nodding at the truck.

Polly was thankful to step away from the bloody nose and walked around the truck to retrieve one of the towels she always kept handy. It was clean, just well-worn and no longer useful in the house. She took it back to Aaron, who knelt down and put it gently on the man's face.

"Go ahead and hold that there," Aaron said. "We'll get someone to look at you."

The front door of the house opened to Bert escorting the second young man out, his hands cuffed behind him.

Tab and Ken followed.

"How's Adele?" Polly asked, walking toward them.

"They hurt her," Tab said. "She's going to be okay, but her face is bruised. She'll have a nasty black eye. We've called the squad. I want to make sure they didn't hurt her anywhere else."

"Can I go in?"

Tab looked at the man lying in the driveway. "Did you do that?"

Polly looked down. "Kinda."

Ken laughed out loud. "She's a menace to anyone who crosses her, that's for sure. What did you do to his nose?"

"Just hit him." Polly pointed at the base of her palm. "In the nose."

"Ohhh," he groaned. "That's nasty. Nice job, girl. How did you get him to the ground?"

"Her truck door," Tab said. "I can see it happening."

Polly shook her head and rushed inside, wincing as she saw Adele propped up on the sofa. "Oh, Adele. I'm sorry. I wish I'd gotten here earlier."

The woman opened her eyes. "You came back. I heard your voice and they wouldn't let me go to the door. I hoped you wouldn't leave."

"Of course I wouldn't," Polly said.

Adele tried to wink, but cringed instead. "I'm still alive. Not dead."

"Maybe you're the one to break my streak."

"That would be nice. You're such a sweet girl. Thank you for stopping by today. I didn't even realize you knew where I lived."

"I didn't," Polly admitted. "I saw their truck and called Lydia to find out who lived here. When she told me it was you, I knew I had to make sure you were okay."

Adele leaned back and whimpered in pain.

"It's more than just your face, isn't it?" Polly asked.

Adele touched her side.

"Make sure the EMTs know about that," Polly said. "You might have a bruised rib. Or maybe it's just going to be a nasty bruise." Polly sat on the coffee table and took Adele's hand in hers. She was thankful that this had turned out well.

Sirens rang through the neighborhood and wound down.

"I never imagined they would come for me," Adele said. "This is embarrassing."

"Not embarrassing. You were hurt by some terrible people."

"I thought they were those missionaries," Adele said. "They were in the house before I realized that they really weren't. Those nice boys come through and are so polite. These two weren't polite at all."

"You're okay. And Adele, we caught them today. They've hurt a lot of people these last few weeks. It's over now. Not only are you safe, but so are a lot of other people."

"Good. Make sure Chief Wallers makes 'em pay."

"I'll do that." Polly stood as the two emergency workers came in. She pulled the coffee table away and stepped back. "I'm going to let Lydia know what's going on," she said to Adele. "And I'll check on you later."

"Thank you, Polly," the woman said. "I love you."

Polly nearly wept. All of the emotion of the encounter rolled over her and she took a deep breath before leaving. When she got outside, she started to laugh. "What are you doing here?" she asked Henry.

"I was on Madison when all hell broke loose over here," he said. "Something in the pit of my stomach told me you'd be close by. I drove to the corner there and saw your truck. What in the world?"

"This is Adele Mansfield's house," Polly said as if that should explain everything.

"I know who lives here. But why are you here?"

"Because that pickup truck didn't belong and I was worried about her." Polly bit her lower lip. He didn't know about Verna Olson yet either. Damn, she was going to be in trouble. "We're having another guest at dinner tonight, too."

"Who's that?"

"Verna Olson. I rescued her from these two this morning."

Aaron put his hand on Henry's shoulder. "It might be a good idea for you to take a deep breath. You're gasping for air."

The young man who had been lying on the ground was now in the back seat of Bert's police car, his head leaning back, still holding Polly's towel against his nose.

Henry pointed at him. "Aaron says you did that."

"Yeah."

"And you positioned your truck behind theirs so they couldn't escape?"

"I guess."

"And you made Tab come here in her dressy clothes to help you take out a couple of bad guys?"

"You're making this sound really bad," Polly said.

"Why were you here in the first place?"

"I was wandering around looking for you."

He let out a harsh laugh. "Next time, just call. I'll tell you exactly where I am so you don't do any more of this wandering around crap."

"Hey," she said. "At least I didn't find any dead bodies. This has been a good week. I find them alive and they go to the hospital and get all better."

"And you punch out thieves. What happened with Verna Olson this morning?"

Polly linked her arm through his. "Maybe we should talk about that later. I also had a really good time at Greg Parker's this afternoon. We've figured out part of the mystery of the Bell House. There were some bad, bad people involved in its construction."

"Oh fabulous," he said. "That's just what I need to hear."

"They held a lot of people in town hostage."

"Who did?"

"Mobsters out of Chicago."

"I can't believe I don't know about this."

"Nobody but those involved knew about it," Polly said. "It had to be that way or their family's lives were on the line."

"People we know?"

She pointed at Ken, who was talking to Bert and Tab. "His grandfather. Paul Bradford's grandfather. Verna Olson's father. We identified a couple more names and families from the tally boards. Those people were all part of it. They were brewing whiskey for Franklin Bell and got caught up in this whole mess. Easy money is just never easy."

"You've had quite the day."

"Let's hope the evening isn't quite as exciting."

He unhooked his arm and wrapped it around her waist. "Do you think there's any possibility of JJ and Tab liking each other enough to begin a relationship?"

Polly looked up at him. "I'm pretty good at this. If I didn't think so, I wouldn't have organized a meeting."

"And Verna Olson?"

"Hmmm," Polly said. "I should probably tell her that these two have been caught. She could go home tonight rather than stay at the hotel."

"She's staying at the hotel? You do have a lot to tell me."

"I invited her to dinner since she doesn't have a car there and has no way of getting supper."

"You're quite the rescuer, aren't you?"

"Hush." Polly stepped forward to meet Tab. "Do you have to go to the office?"

"No. Chief Wallers and the sheriff said they'll take care of paperwork for this one. I don't even know which one is taking those two in. But it isn't mine to worry about now."

"Thanks for coming when I called," Polly said.

Tab chuckled. "Would you have gone in without me?"

"We'll never know," Henry interrupted. "I don't want to know. Don't make her say it out loud."

The EMTs came out of the house with Adele on a gurney, her neck in a brace.

"Is she going to be okay?" Polly asked.

"Yes ma'am. We just want to make sure. They'll do some x-rays and maybe a CT scan."

"I'll call Lydia," Polly said to Adele.

"Thank you again, Polly." Adele reached out and took Polly's hand, then let go as they moved her to the ambulance.

"You go on, too," Aaron said to Polly. "We'll make sure everything is closed up here. Enjoy your evening."

"I'll meet you at home," Henry said. "Go straight home. Do not pass any more crime scenes and stop. Are you following her, Tab?"

"I'd probably better. Just to make sure she's safe."

He chuckled. "Can I hire you full-time?"

"Stop it," Polly said. She opened the door to her truck. "I'll see you at the house."

CHAPTER TWENTY-EIGHT

When Polly and Tab arrived at the Bell House, Polly was surprised to see Kayla with Noah and Elijah working on homework at the kitchen table. "Where are Andrew and Rebecca?"

"Still at school," Elijah said, jumping up. He ran across the room to give Polly a hug and stared at Tab. "You're pretty."

She smiled down at him. "Thank you."

"What do you mean, still at school?" Polly asked.

"They had their first play practice. I don't have to be there for a couple of weeks, so I told her that I'd stay with the boys. We walked the dogs and everything. They're nearly done with their homework." Kayla sighed. "I have to ask Stephanie for help tonight. Hopefully, she'll know what I'm working on."

Polly swiped her phone open to see if she'd gotten any messages from Rebecca. There was nothing. "You boys finish up and put your things away." She shook her head. "I'm sorry. Thank you, Kayla. I appreciate you. You're a good friend."

Kayla shrugged. "I come here every afternoon." Then she looked at Polly. "Unless you don't want me to. I can go to

Sycamore House to wait for Stephanie."

"Of course I want you to come here," Polly said. "And today, I'm thankful you did." She took off her coat and put it on a hook in the mudroom, then waited for Tab to take hers off. She processed on what needed to happen for dinner tonight and realized that if Rebecca hadn't come home, the rolls weren't going to be finished. She'd also forgotten to stop at the coffee shop for cupcakes. The day had been insane and she desperately needed to take a breath.

"Can I help with something?" Tab asked.

Polly gritted her teeth and said softly. "I expected Rebecca to be home after school and she's not. I'm annoyed that she didn't tell me and now I need to figure out how to get some things taken care of."

"Like what?"

"I was going to make rolls for tonight and I need to pick up the cupcakes." Polly nodded. "Henry can do that. Let me call him."

"Would you let me make biscuits instead of rolls?" Tab asked. "They won't take any time at all." She grinned. "How about those cheddar biscuits. Do you have cheese?"

Polly gestured to the refrigerator. "Look in the lower drawer. I bet we do." She swiped open her phone app and placed a call to Henry.

"I'm almost there, sweetie-pie," he said.

"Can you turn around?"

"And go where?"

"I forgot to pick up the cupcakes at Sweet Beans."

He laughed. "After your day, I'm not surprised. I'll pick them up. Anything else?"

Tab had found a package of shredded cheddar cheese. It would be a little different than the flavors Polly had planned, but at this point, whatever happened would be fine. "No," she said. "I think we're good."

"Then your wish is my command."

"I love you, too," Polly responded. After she ended the call, she sent a quick text to Rebecca asking where she was.

Noah closed his school book and scooted back. "I'm all done."

"Good for you," Polly said. "Pack up your backpack and put it where it belongs. Since Rebecca isn't here, could you make sure that the cats all have their food and plenty of water?"

His eyes lit up at being asked to do something and he jumped down from his chair.

"I'm done, too," Elijah said. "Can I help?"

"You sure can. After you've packed your backpack and put it away, take everything off the table except for what Kayla's working on." Polly opened the cupboard to take out the plates and remembered that they were still in the dishwasher. At least they were clean and dry. She opened the door and cursed under her breath. No they weren't. "I don't have time for this," she muttered. It would take too long to run it at this point, so she filled the sink.

"Everything okay?" Tab asked. She'd finally found a mixing bowl. Polly had been too distracted to even attempt to help her. Not that she had any better idea where things were hiding in this kitchen yet.

"Dishwasher didn't run. My fault."

Kayla closed her books. "I can wash dishes."

"Oh honey, you've already helped so much. I can do this." As soon as Polly said the words, she realized she'd better check the crock pot and make sure it had turned on. She took the lid off and breathed in the warm smell of the beef tips. At least one thing had worked out.

"It's okay. I like washing dishes." Kayla ran her hands under the warm water. "What do you need out of the dishwasher?"

Polly stepped around the open door and hugged Kayla, then kissed her forehead. "You are a lifesaver. Thank you. Eight plates, silverware and glasses. Let's start there."

Kayla lifted the silverware caddy out and set it down in the sink. "That will soak while I wash the plates."

"You're so smart." Polly went to the pantry and pulled opened the bag of onions she'd purchased the other day, then grabbed a bulb of garlic. She needed to work faster than this. Mushrooms from the fridge, then green beans and noodles from the freezer. "Do you need anything, Tab?" she asked and chuckled at the flour on Tab's blouse.

The girl had taken off her vest and looked down. "Rats," she said. "I was trying so hard."

"There are aprons in the pantry. Protect yourself."

Elijah held up a stack of mail that Polly had been going through earlier this morning. "Where should I put this?"

"On my bed," Polly replied.

He ran out of the room as Noah came back in. "The cats have food and water. What now?"

"How are you at drying dishes?" Polly asked.

"I'm very careful. I won't drop one. I promise."

"Good deal. You help Kayla, then."

Elijah ran back in. "What about me?"

"When the plates are dry, you take them one by one to the table and put them in front of a chair. Can you do that?"

He nodded enthusiastically. Polly was thankful they still wanted to help.

The dogs ran to the back door and Rebecca and Andrew came in, chattering excitedly.

"Henry picked us up," she said. "It was cold." She looked around at the little factory line that was going on and then saw Polly's face. "Shi.." She stopped herself from saying anything more. "I'm sorry. I totally forgot. Mrs. Edison had play practice tonight and I had to be there."

"Put your things away," Polly said evenly.

Henry came in the back door with a box from Sweet Beans and took in the chaos of the room. He set the box on the counter beside the door and turned Rebecca and Andrew back into the mudroom. "Hang up your things. Make sure it's neat in here." He sidled up to Polly. "What happened to the dishwasher?"

"My fault. I forgot to turn it on last night. Kayla's been a big help."

He gestured with his head to the mudroom. "You didn't know she wasn't coming home?"

"Nope. Probably my fault there, too. I should have asked."

Henry kissed her cheek. "What can I do?"

Polly put her hand on her forehead. "I need to call Mrs. Olson. Can you fill the stock pot with water and bring it to a boil for the noodles?"

The man went right for the correct cupboard. This was going to drive her crazy. Polly walked into the foyer and took a deep breath. Even with the mess, this was quieter. She placed the call.

"Hello?" Mrs. Olson said.

"Hi Verna, this is Polly. I wanted to let you know that we caught the thieves today. You're perfectly safe now."

"That's wonderful news." Verna laughed. "But I'm going to enjoy spending tonight in a hotel. All of these amenities and I don't have to make my bed in the morning. Trixie and I will enjoy it very much."

"I might send Henry over to pick you up for supper, if that's okay."

"Dear, you don't need to feed me tonight. I have everything I need right here. In fact, I rather think I will enjoy a nice quiet evening with television, snack food from the machines and an ice-cold cola. I never have those things, you know. It's an adventure."

"Are you certain?" Polly asked. "I would love for you to come over."

"Thank you, but enjoy your family this evening."

Polly took a breath. "I discovered everything about those years you didn't want to talk about. How the mob had held everyone's family hostage. That had to have been very frightening for the families involved."

Verna's breath caught. "I was young, but when the letter came and my mother opened it, I remember her screaming for my father. She was terrified that they would come to hurt us. Daddy wanted to leave Bellingwood, but then he discovered that everyone involved had gotten a letter. They couldn't all run, and by that time, he had a good job and a family."

"I'm glad it's over."

"I am too, dear. Thank you for the care you gave to me today. I spoke with your Mr. Greyson and he will take me back to my home in the morning. But not too early, because I'm going to sleep in." The smile in her voice was apparent.

"Have a wonderful evening," Polly said. "Maybe we can have you visit for dinner another time."

"I would like that. Good night."

Polly went back into the kitchen. "Mrs. Olson won't be joining us. She has decided to enjoy the indulgence of a night in a hotel room."

Tab turned away from the oven. "I hope this is a normal oven. I set the timer."

"It should be fine," Polly said.

Elijah had set seven of the places and she did a quick count in her head again. Hayden wouldn't be here, so it was Tab and J. J., plus four kids, her and Henry. "Just one more, Elijah," she said.

Kayla was drying her hands on a towel. "I'm sorry. Stephanie should be outside in a minute. Rebecca is going to finish washing the silverware."

"Honey, you are amazing. You have taken really good care of me tonight." Polly walked out to the mud room with her. She reached into her back pocket as Kayla put on her coat. "I know that you love coming here, but you babysat the boys and helped me a lot. Take this." Polly pushed ten dollars into Kayla's hand.

"I don't need to be paid," Kayla protested. "I always come after school."

"But you had more responsibility today and it means the world to me that you were here for my boys. Thank you."

"Thanks." Kayla slid the money into a pocket of her backpack and jumped at the car horn honking outside. "That's Stephanie. I'll see you tomorrow."

Polly gave her another hug. "You were awesome today."

Kayla opened the back door and then yelled, "Andrew. Your mom is here." She giggled. "Sorry. See ya."

Polly moved out of the way as Andrew rushed into the room, grabbed up his backpack and coat. "See ya tomorrow, Rebecca. Bye, Polly."

She took a breath as he ran down the steps. Two gone. This was better.

Rebecca and Henry had made quick work of the silverware and glasses, so Polly went back to work on her green beans dish.

"What next?" Henry asked.

"A big glass of wine."

"Seriously?"

"No. Just a wish."

"You know JJ will probably bring wine tonight."

"Then you'd better get glasses down. I don't even know where they are."

"Do you need serving dishes, Polly?" Rebecca asked, pointing at the dishwasher.

What Polly wanted was to grab her hair and run screaming from the room. What she did was nod. "Three bowls."

"Anything else?" Elijah asked, pointing at the table. Tab had helped him set the silverware around the plates and showed him how to fold napkins in half and put them under the fork.

"Salt and pepper, plus the butter dish," Polly said. She smiled as the words came out of her mouth. Those were the three things that Mary always insisted be on the table at every meal. It had become habit as Polly grew older.

While the minced garlic and diced onions sautéed, she went back to the pantry for an open bottle of red wine. She'd stumbled on this recipe one night and couldn't believe how wonderful it tasted. Next, in went the chopped mushrooms and green beans. She tossed them around in the oil, dropped a dash of salt and pepper in, then stirred it a few more times. Finally, she poured in some red wine, let it come to a boil, turned the heat to simmer and put a lid on the pan. That was one dish that would be ready on time. Henry had already dropped the noodles into the boiling water and set a timer. When the first ding happened, Polly looked around.

"The biscuits," Tab said, leaving Elijah and Noah at the table.

"I can't believe you made her work for her dinner," Henry said.

Rebecca spun around, horrified. "I didn't turn on the rolls. I'm so sorry, Polly."

"We'll talk later."

"I have to clean bathrooms, don't I."

Polly chuckled. "Not this time. We just need to talk about schedules."

The dogs ran for the back door again and Heath came in. "Smells good ..." He stopped when he saw Tab. "Uh. Hi."

"How are you, Heath?"

"I'm good."

Noah and Elijah tore across the room to him. "We helped set the table for dinner," Elijah said. "I didn't drop a plate or anything."

"Good for you guys." He stepped into the kitchen and held out a few papers to Henry. "That's something about the college meeting next week. Are you still okay with going with me?"

"I wouldn't miss it," Henry said. "You want Polly too?"

Heath shrugged. "It's okay either way."

They'd talk about that later, too. If he didn't want her, she'd stay home. But otherwise, she was as excited as anyone about what was coming up for him.

~~~

Polly sat back in her chair and took another drink of wine. Sure enough, JJ brought two bottles. He and Tab were talking about the years he'd lived in San Francisco. Heath had already taken Noah and Elijah back to their room to start getting ready for bed and Rebecca was in her room working on homework.

Even after the chaos at the beginning of the evening, dinner had come off flawlessly. Polly wasn't sure who she'd been trying to impress. JJ wouldn't have cared whether they ate hot dogs and hamburgers and Tab had experienced it all without batting an eye.

Henry got up from the table and brought back the opened bottle. "Polly?" He sat down in the chair beside her.

She put her glass up and he filled it, then handed the bottle to JJ. "Heard any more from Ryan and Patrick?"

"They're moving back to California," JJ said. "I don't want to get back into games right now, so I'm staying put. They promised to be here when things are busy in the summer and fall. Don't know how long that will last, though. I think Patrick misses the life. Bellingwood was too quiet for him."

"I thought it would be too quiet for you," Polly said. "You're kind of a wild man."

"Yes ma'am," he replied with a smile. "But ..." JJ shrugged. "I thought about it and I didn't really have any friends out there except those two. I don't have a lot here, but I like the people who come in to Secret Woods and I feel like I'm just starting to get to know a few more people. It will take time, but I'm in no hurry."

"Do you like making wine?" Tab asked.

He shrugged again. "I don't really make it. I just run the business. But I like that. And maybe once they're gone, I'll get more involved in the actual behind-the-scenes work. I'm going to have to come up with money to buy them out. They've given me a lot of time, but if they're not going to be part of it, I might as well just own it outright." He pursed his lips, sighed and looked at Henry. "What do you think?"

"I think it sounds like a good idea," Henry said. "If you can afford it."

"That's why I say I'm going to have to learn stuff. A lot of stuff. We hired people to do what we didn't want to do, but without their money, I can't afford that. The booking software and then accounting. It's not like I can't learn it. I was a business major." He huffed a laugh. "Just barely made it through, but I did. It would be nice not to be part of the Terrible Threesome, too."

Tab chuckled.

"People around town knew us as pranksters."

"That's a good word for it," Henry said. "You were good kids with too many smarts, too much money and too much time on your hands."

"I didn't have any money."

"You had Patrick's money."

"We did," JJ agreed. "The nice thing is, that there are new people in the area who don't know me from those days. The older people might forgive me someday."

"Left a mark, did ya?" Tab asked with a smile.

He chuckled. "Let's just say that Bellingwood didn't miss me when I was gone."

"I can't believe you came back, then," she said.

"The money coming in from Sword Lords was huge," he said. "I kept feeling smaller and smaller out there. Like the place was going to swallow me up. Then we had a chance to sell the company and make tons more money. After that, what were we supposed to do? I think all of us were lost and this was the only place we'd ever felt safe. I guess Patrick and Ryan got their second wind, though. Why'd you come back, Polly?"

"Iowa is Iowa," she said. "When the world tried to overwhelm me, this was the only place I wanted to be, too."

"Do you regret not being in the big city?"

She blew out a breath. "Not in the least." Polly took Henry's hand. "I found myself when I moved into Bellingwood. I loved my life in Boston, but now it feels like that Polly was a completely different person. I didn't really start living until I got here."

Rebecca came into the kitchen. "Can I talk to you for a minute, Polly?"

Polly smiled and put her hand on Henry's thigh as she stood up. "Sure, what's up?"

The two walked toward Rebecca's room.

"I'm sorry about screwing up today. I totally didn't think about dinner tonight." She handed Polly a piece of paper. "I wrote out all of my play rehearsals. And here is my flute contest day. I tried to remember everything that's going on. Are you still mad at me?"

Polly gave her a quick hug. "This is what I wanted to talk to you about. Thank you. I think I have a better idea, though. Would you use a calendar on your phone? We can share it. When you know what's going on, you just enter the information and then I can look at it and know."

"Yeah?"

"Absolutely. If businesses can do it with their sales people, why can't families do the same thing?"

"That's so cool. You're really not mad?"

"I was annoyed, but I was also overwhelmed."

"I knew that the little boys needed someone here and you were busy. That's why I asked Kayla to stay with them."

"You did the right thing, but you probably should have called or at least sent me a text."

Rebecca's shoulders drooped. "I was going to. I was almost there and Julie Fincher took me into the office to look at some poster she was working on for Spanish club. Then I had to go to practice and I forgot."

"No more forgetting, okay? We'll both be better about talking through your day. Do you have play practice tomorrow, too?"

"Yeah, but not Thursday or Friday."

"Okay. I'll be sure that I'm home for the boys tomorrow."

"Kayla can babysit."

"She shouldn't be expected to do that at the last minute. We can schedule the nights she babysits."

"Can you believe I made it into the play?" Rebecca asked.

"I'm so proud of you. You're very talented." Polly swallowed. "What I can't believe is that you'll be in high school next year. I'm not ready for you to be gone every night."

"I won't be."

Polly laughed. "Yes you will. I didn't do half the things that you're going to want to do and I was gone a lot. It will be awesome."

"I'm going to take a shower. Can I use your bathroom since they're still here?"

"Of course you can." Polly pulled Rebecca close. "I'm awfully glad you're in my life."

"I'm still sorry about messing up your dinner."

"It all worked out." Polly left the room and headed down to Noah and Elijah's room. She heard Heath reading out loud and stopped just outside the door, then realized the dogs had already announced her arrival, so she stepped in. "I didn't mean to interrupt."

"It's okay," Heath said. "They begged."

"You boys need to go to sleep so Heath can work on his own homework," Polly said.

"Just one more page," Elijah begged.

Polly walked around to his side of the bed and kissed his forehead. "When Heath says he's finished, you have to close your eyes and sleep. Deal?"

Elijah smiled at her.

She walked back to Noah's side and sat down on the bed, then leaned over and kissed his cheek. "You were great helpers tonight. Thank you."

"I like helping," he said.

Polly rubbed his back and stood up, then surprised Heath by kissing his forehead. "Thank you." She patted the bed and Obiwan jumped up, settling between the two boys. Han followed her back down the hall and around to the kitchen.

"We should be going," Tab said.

JJ looked at her in surprise and stood. "Yeah. Tomorrow's another day."

"It's okay," Polly said. "I just tucked the kids in. You don't have to hurry off."

Tab gave her a quick hug. "I have to work in the morning." She chuckled. "At least I know where you are tonight, so there won't be any deaths to investigate. And you caught the thieves who were giving us so much trouble. Tomorrow should be an easy day."

"You just jinxed it, you know," Polly said, walking with them to the back door.

"As soon as it was out of my mouth, I knew that." Tab pointed at her coat and JJ grabbed it, then helped her into it. "Thank you so much for dinner tonight. You have a wonderful home here."

"Thank you, guys," JJ said. "This was nice. I love your kids."

Polly and Henry stood at the side door as the two left.

JJ opened Tab's car door for her and stood to talk with her for a few moments after she climbed in. Then he got in his own car, backed out, and drove away.

Tab waved, backed out and followed him.

"You did it again," Henry said.

"We'll see, but I think they both had a nice time."

"Kids all settled?"

She smiled at him. "Heath was reading to the boys. It was the sweetest thing."

"You were talking about how your time in Boston seemed like it belonged to a different person."

"And my childhood and youth in Story City is a completely different person," Polly said. "I'd like to stay this person for the rest of my life, though. How about you?"

"Every day with you is like I'm with a different person," Henry said with a laugh. "I never know what to expect."

"It's a good thing you love me."

"More than I can even say."

THANK YOU FOR READING!

I'm so glad you enjoy these stories about Polly Giller and her friends. There are many ways to stay in touch with Diane and the Bellingwood community.

You can find more details about Sycamore House and Bellingwood at the website: http://nammynools.com/

Join the Bellingwood Facebook page:
https://www.facebook.com/pollygiller
for news about upcoming books, conversations while I'm writing and you're reading, and a continued look at life in a small town.

Diane Greenwood Muir's Amazon Author Page is a great place to watch for new releases.

Follow Diane on Twitter at twitter.com/nammynools for regular updates and notifications.

Recipes and decorating ideas found in the books can often be found on Pinterest at: http://pinterest.com/nammynools/

And if you are looking for Sycamore House swag, check out Polly's CafePress store: http://www.cafepress.com/sycamorehouse

Made in United States
Orlando, FL
12 September 2022

22333057R00173